Praise for the novels of
New York Times bestselling author Heather Graham

"Heather Graham delivers a harrowing journey as she always does: perfectly.... Intelligent, fast-paced and frightening at all times, and the team of characters still keep the reader's attention to the very end."
—*Suspense Magazine* on *The Final Deception*

"Immediately entertaining and engrossing... Graham provides plenty of face time and intimate connection, all lightened with humor, to reassure and satisfy romance readers. Though part of a series, this installment stands well alone."
—*Publishers Weekly* on *A Dangerous Game*

"Taut, complex; and leavened with humor, this riveting thriller has...a shade more suspense than romance, [and] it will appeal to fans of both genres."
—*Library Journal* on *A Dangerous Game*

"Intense... A wild, mindboggling thriller from start to finish."
—*The Reading Cafe* on *The Forbidden*

"An enthralling read with a totally unexpected twist at the end."
—*Fresh Fiction* on *Deadly Touch*

"Graham strikes a fine balance between romantic suspense and a gothic ghost story in her latest Krewe of Hunters tale."
—*Booklist* on *The Summoning*

Also by *New York Times* bestselling author Heather Graham

Look for Heather Graham's next novel
THE MURDER MACHINE
available soon from MIRA.

For additional books by Heather Graham,
visit theoriginalheathergraham.com.

HEATHER GRAHAM

LEGACY OF
BLOOD

/|| MIRA

/ll MIRA™

ISBN-13: 978-0-7783-1025-9

Legacy of Blood

Recycling programs
for this product may
not exist in your area.

Mira
22 Adelaide St. West, 41st Floor
Toronto, Ontario M5H 4E3, Canada
www.Harlequin.com

Printed in U.S.A.

For Susan and Kevin Cella with lots of love—amazing friends who do so very much in the world of mystery novels!

CAST OF CHARACTERS

The Krewe of Hunters—
a specialized FBI unit that uses its members' "unique abilities"
to bring justice to strange or unorthodox cases

The Euro Special Assistance Team, or "Blackbird"—
a newly formed group created to extend the Krewe's reach
into Europe to assist with crimes abroad

Jeannette LaFarge—
deep auburn hair, a police officer before entering the academy,
Blackbird agent who is often extremely professional
in both dress and appearance

Daniel Murray—
handsome and young, cut out for undercover work,
with the National Crime Agency and just off solving a case
with Blackbird in Scotland

Gervais LaBlanc—
an old friend of Jackson Crow's, determined to find justice for all,
an inspector with Parisian law enforcement

Mason Carter—
six-five, dark hair, blue eyes, head of the Blackbird division

Della Hamilton, Luke Kendrick, Carly MacDonald—
fellow Blackbird agents assisting with the case in France

Lorraine Devante—
a gray-haired woman of about forty, runs a bed-and-breakfast

Delphine Matisse—
CEO of her family's wine business and owner
of her own bed-and-breakfast in Reims

Jules Bastien—
charming magician in his early thirties

Marnette "Marnie" Magnon—
Jules's lovely assistant

Tomas and Giselle Deauville—
owners of a small local vineyard near Reims

George and Leticia Montague—
owners of a small local vineyard near Reims

Alphonse "Luc" Monte—
a handsome waiter at La Maison de Riviere

Henriette Beaumont—
a long-ago resident of the region, anxious to help, died 1794,
one of seven thousand people executed during the Reign of Terror
(September 1793–July 1794)

Jake Clayton—
tall ghost in uniform, Ninety-Second Airborne Division,
died 1944 during the Normandy invasion

Prologue

Once upon a time...

And not so long ago, Gervais LaBlanc thought ruefully, he would not have been alone staring at the body of the deceased.

"Inspector?"

He was not going to be so alone now in the autopsy room.

The one-word question was voiced in English, and he turned, ready to greet the young woman he was expecting, Jeannette LaFarge. *Special Agent* Jeannette LaFarge, he reminded himself, here with him because Gervais had called on his good friend, Jackson Crow.

Jackson managed a special unit in the United States that had recently created a European division to work with the inspectors and detectives of other countries when asked. Gervais couldn't recall the official title of Jackson's unit—he just knew that Jackson Crow and his people could often get answers when cases were...bizarre, perpetuated by those intent on recreating horrific events from history or adding their own terrifying spin to them.

They were known as the Krewe of Hunters.

This woman, the first to arrive of the team he'd been promised, barely seemed old enough to have entered the FBI, much less the mysterious and successful Krewe of Hunters. She was an attractive young woman with richly colored reddish-brown hair swept into a braided ponytail at her nape, large eyes and impressive cheekbones. For all her youth and beauty, she was an experienced professional; Gervais had read up on her. She had graduated with a degree in criminology at the age of twenty-one, spent three years as a police officer before gaining entrance to the FBI Academy, and been recruited by Jackson Crow three years later. And since he knew Jackson so well, he knew that his old friend would not have sent anyone who couldn't keep up with an investigation—and perhaps even lead the way.

"Special Agent LaFarge, welcome, and thank you for coming so quickly," he said.

She smiled at him. "Thank you. And I'm grateful you're so well-versed in English. I can say *please*, *thank you*, and buy croissants and coffee with my French. Maybe it's a little bit better than that, but not much, I'm afraid," she told him.

"You're the first of your team to arrive. And again, I am grateful." He pointed to the glass window; he had the right to be inside during the autopsy, but he had opted to remain here, watching and waiting for Agent LaFarge. There were no deep, grave secrets that would be fathomed from the work that had been done on the corpse.

The woman had died from exsanguination.

He managed a smile for his American counterpart. "Two years studying with the FBI, which is where I met your field director, Jackson Crow," he told her. "But LaFarge—a French name?"

She smiled. "Indeed, but from many years ago. Apparently, and to my dad's great pride, his great-great-great whatever came to the States with the Marquis de Lafayette during the American Revolution and stayed on. I'm afraid our gift with the language faded through the years."

"Linguistics is not the talent we seek from your team," Gervais murmured, turning back to the corpse. He let out a long breath and told her, "I'm afraid that the newspapers will sensationalize these killings. One reporter has already created a headline reading, *Vampire at work in Paris*!" He inhaled and let out a deep sigh. "I am a reader, and I pay attention to events happening in Europe. So I'm well-versed on the investigation that started the Blackbird international twist on your unit, or whatever it might be, when a so-called vampire struck, bringing your specialized unit first to Norway."

The woman nodded. "But apparently, no one is pretending to be a vampire in these cases—no *fang* marks in the neck or elsewhere."

Gervais shook his head.

"And still," he said, "people—the world over—sensationalize what is tragic." He grimaced, remembering his previous thoughts. "Once upon a time, years ago but then again not all that many in the great scheme of things, the morgue was one of the biggest attractions in the city. In 1864, the morgue was rebuilt right behind Notre Dame, with the police and officials hoping it would help speed up the identification of bodies found in the Seine and other surrounding areas. Even guidebooks for Paris included the morgue—the famed Thomas Cook guidebooks among them. People came by the tens of thousands to view the latest bodies through the glass. Parents lifted their children high to look over the crowds so that they might understand the dangers in the world. Before electricity and any kind of cooling abilities, the bodies would bloat and become horrible and still people came as if the dead were a major attraction. The morgue was open from dawn to dusk, and it was free. Nothing like a free attraction. Thousands upon thousands of people came…" He gave himself a mental shake. He was an inspector; he needed to find the truth behind the recent homicides, not wax on about a history that seemed as disturbing as the murders he was seeking to solve. "My pardon, Special Agent. It's just—"

She nodded in understanding, and then continued with, "They closed the morgue to the viewing public in 1907, when a great majority of people along with those in the government determined that gawking at the dead was not a good thing."

He smiled, nodded and gave himself another mental shake. "You know our history," he told her.

"I love history," she assured him. "American and world history. We are all, in essence as human beings, subject to the same desires, fears, failures and triumphs. And we all have our share of heroes and beasts. Not vampires— human beasts. There are those who call themselves vampires these days, those who have meetings in which they share their own blood with one another, and those who consider themselves to be *spiritual* vampires who indulge in sucking energy from others rather than blood."

"Well, this…"

He pointed toward the glass and the young woman lying on the slab right behind it.

"She has been drained of blood—completely. But as you said, there are no bite marks on her, she was not attacked by anything with fangs. Our medical examiner believes whoever has been doing this has medical knowledge. Perhaps it's not a doctor, but a phlebotomist maybe, or someone with nursing training, or..."

"A butcher?" Jeannette murmured.

"Possibly, but...butchers are better at dismembering corpses, taking organs. These bodies haven't been molested in any way. None of the victims were raped. They were simply—and completely—drained of their blood. And so...we have the media crying *vampire*. And that is the last thing we need in such an investigation."

The woman behind the glass had been young, lovely, and Gervais assumed that until her death, she had been filled with vitality and a longing for adventure and all that life had to offer.

Now...her blond hair appeared to be an eerie halo around the whiteness of her face.

Just like the other two.

Virginia Bond of Chicago and Patricia Gutterman of Berlin. Visitors to Paris, young women who had come to see the glory of Notre Dame, the Eiffel Tower, the Louvre, the Champs-Élysées and so much more that this city, his beautiful city, had to offer.

And now...

They were waiting for an identity for this third girl discovered just outside the city in another incredibly popular destination, the vineyards of Reims. Because of the severity of the crimes, he was handling the investigation with a base in Paris.

After all...

It was where the victims had been staying, where they had last been seen alive…

"Not a vampire," Jeannette LaFarge murmured at his side. "But…"

"Pardon?"

"Perhaps something out of legend, but a vastly different legend. One that might well have been an incredible conspiracy to seize hold of property and power and one which may have held some truth. At this stage of history, it's doubtful we'll ever know the truth."

"S'il vous plaît," Gervais murmured, frowning.

"Once upon a time," she said, turning to meet his gaze, "there lived a woman named Elizabeth Báthory, born into one of the most noble families of Hungary and its environs—country lines were different in her day."

"Mais oui, I know this story, yes!" Gervais said. "She married into another family that held great lands, titles and positions. Her husband died in battle, and she was left to manage great estates, but…she had very powerful relations trying to wrest them from her."

Jeannette smiled grimly and nodded. "We both know our history. But history is, as we all know, told by the victors. In this case, the legend may be far different from the truth, but the legend created around her calls her the Blood Countess. She was tried for killing over six hundred young women, bathing in their blood to restore her youth. She was locked away in a castle for her crimes while those considered to be her associates were burned at the stake. Whether she was set up or truly responsible or evil, it's possible that someone is taking a page from the book of her legend."

One

Jeannette stared at the charming house near *Le Trocadéro et son esplanade* in central Paris, thinking that it was delightful. She could imagine being just out of college, thrilled to be taking a dreamed-of trip to the amazing city, seeing such sights as the Louvre, Versailles, the Arc de Triomphe, Notre Dame…

And winding up dead, bloodless, in the trampled fields of a vineyard.

She let out a soft breath and glanced at her watch. Gervais should be meeting her there any minute; she stood at the entrance to Lorraine Dupont's Inn, basically a bed-and-breakfast.

It was where Virginia Bond, the first of the victims discovered drained of their blood in the fields just outside Paris, had been staying for her dream graduation trip to the city.

Gervais had been back at his office, going through every piece of information he had on the first two women who had been killed and identified. He was awaiting word on the autopsy results, and he was also waiting for anything that might be discovered about the latest still-unnamed young woman who had been killed. The one they had viewed earlier that morning.

Gervais had told her Lorraine Dupont spoke English perfectly, and she was welcome to begin speaking to the woman without him present. But Jeannette didn't want to appear to be an intruder when the French might well want their own people dealing with the situation and resent any interference by an American.

She felt someone standing by her side and turned quickly, thinking Gervais had arrived or some other members of Blackbird might have made it to Paris from their vacation in Italy—but she doubted that. This had all happened extremely quickly, and she knew it hadn't even been a full twenty-four hours since Gervais had called on Jackson Crow for help.

No…

Not Gervais. Not members of her team. There was a young man standing next to her. He was wearing blue jeans and a denim jacket over a polo shirt. His hair was somewhat long, a bit shaggy, dark and fell over his forehead in what she assumed he thought to be a rakish angle. He couldn't have been more than twenty-five, twenty-eight, tops. He was tall, with a way of standing that seemed to hint at hard muscles and wiry strength. He looked her way and arched a brow. His eyes were almost indigo, blue, but as dark as blue could possibly be, and the way he looked at her was strange, as if he might be deadly serious and straight as an arrow—or a jerk who had just paused to give her a hard time.

"I think we should go in," he said.

English. But he wasn't American. There was a soft burr in his voice.

"Look, sir, I don't know what your game is—"

"Game?" He frowned and shook his head in a way that wasn't complimentary. "Didn't you speak with Jackson? My name is Daniel. Daniel Murray. Recently given the title of special agent when the powers that be from the US, the UK, Interpol…added me into the ranks of Blackbird. Gervais told me you'd be here. I thought Gervais might have told you I'd be joining you. The rest of our *krewe* is due to arrive tonight. They were caught a little off guard."

"Sorry, sorry!" Jeannette murmured quickly. So, this was Daniel Murray? Jackson had told her Daniel had worked with their group in Scotland and proved himself invaluable; and he'd specifically asked that since it was a group that was working internationally, he might apply to join as an international. Jackson had also said he was young and possessed a "boyish" charm that often served them well.

So far, she wasn't seeing the charm.

She also knew Jackson had spoken with him via a video interview, and that Mason, Della, Luke and Carly had all sworn by him.

Then again, she'd met Mason briefly on one of her first cases in the US and wasn't sure she'd ever met the others. She'd just expected…

Someone older. With extreme maturity and dignity and…

Then again, maybe he'd expected her *to be older!*

"I'm sorry! I thought—"

"That I was some jerky bloke on the street trying to pick you up?" he asked.

She winced. "No, no—"

He laughed. "Let's not start off with lies. Anyway, I speak decent grew-up-in-the-UK French, but the owner here was born in Britain and moved here when she was married. I believe we'll be fine speaking with her in English."

Jeannette nodded, feeling uncomfortably as if she was the one making the mistakes; she had not known Madame Dupont was originally British.

"So, shall we?" he asked.

She nodded. "Yes, of course."

He led the way up to the doorway of the charming home, glanced at her and knocked on the door.

It was quickly answered by an older, gray-haired woman of about forty. She was petite with bright blue eyes and an anxious expression.

"Police?" she asked them.

"More or less," Daniel said. "Special Agents LaFarge and Murray, ma'am. And we are so sorry to bother you—I know how upsetting this must be—"

"No, no, you don't!" the woman told them, switching to English. She shook her head. "She was... She was so lovely! So excited to be here. She had a grandmother from France, a woman who wasn't in good health but filled her mind with dreams of Paris. So, so sweet!"

"I'm so sorry," Jeannette murmured.

"No, I'm sorry, please! Come in. *Café au lait?* Tea? I haven't had the heart to allow any boarders since I heard about Virginia! But I'm so accustomed to being a bed-and-breakfast establishment that I start the day with croissants on the table, tea and coffee, and—"

"I would love a *café au lait*!" Jeannette said, looking at Daniel, who quickly smiled in agreement. In truth, it wasn't "breakfast" at all anymore as they were now moving toward noon, but it was both sad and strangely nice to see that someone who had barely known the young woman was so deeply disturbed by her death. That meant she would share all the help she could give them.

They entered the house. It was as appealing inside as it was out, with the parlor large and inviting with upholstered chairs and a sofa, an open ceiling overhead, and a nook where someone might set up to work on business or personal papers or on a computer.

"Come through, please!" she told them, heading off to the left.

The dining room was very large, offering several small tables that could seat two to four guests along with buffet tables on the side.

Mrs. Dupont quickly moved to one with an espresso machine, starting on their *café au laits*.

"Please! Have a seat," she told them.

They did so, choosing a table close to where she was creating their drinks.

She talked nervously as she worked. "Well, as I assume you can tell, I am an Englishwoman, but I've lived here for over twenty-five years. My dear husband was a Frenchman, a professor, a wonderful man. And when he passed, of course, he left me the home. We had no children, and my parents are long gone... I thought that opening the house as an inn would allow me...company. And it has been wonderful. I welcome so many charming young people, and I do tend to get young men and women as guests. I offer great rates and many of those who are more mature—"

"Older?" Daniel offered.

"Aye, indeed!" she said. "Those folks prefer the finer hotels on the Champs-Élysées, but the young ones just want to get here and see the amazing sights of Paris. And Virginia… Ah! I felt that I'd found a true friend, a godchild, a—"

She broke off, shaking her head, trying not to cry.

Jeannette glanced at Daniel and thought he was experiencing the same feelings. The worst part of this job was having to deal with the pain of the survivors. They always had to remember that the best part was stopping monsters and saving others from the pain.

Daniel spoke up. "Mrs. Dupont, we are so very sorry for the pain you're feeling, and yet we're hoping you can help us catch whoever did this to her. Did she tell you what she was doing each day? Did she ask for your help? Did you give her suggestions?"

The coffees were finished and the woman brought them to the table, taking a seat between the two of them.

"She wanted to see and do everything!" the woman told them. "Her first day, she went to the Louvre. She spent the entire day there. And she spent the evening with me, joking that she loved it so much she should find a French husband, too."

"Did she find anyone while she was here?" Jeannette asked. "Someone with whom to enjoy the sights?"

Mrs. Dupont shook her head. "Not a man, and I think she was joking about that. She was anxious to begin her life, too, since she graduated from college. Poor girl lost her parents her first year at university and managed to graduate, anyway. She majored in fine arts and had already been offered a teaching position that would have started as soon as she returned home. She loved the theater and children, older and younger, but she would have been teaching high school drama."

"So, who came for her things? Her parents were gone, but—" Daniel began.

"Oh, she had many friends, but no family. And no one seemed to know what to do, so I packed up her belongings that were here and they're at the station right now and... Well, I believe an American man who is the head of whatever law enforcement it is that brings Americans—"

"I'm a Scot," Daniel reminded her.

"Sorry! Brings international law enforcement here is planning to see to her funeral," Mrs. Dupont finished.

"Jackson Crow?" Jeannette asked.

"Yes, he's making arrangements with an Adam Harrison," Mrs. Dupont said.

No surprise there, Jeannette thought. Adam had created the Krewe to hunt the strangest human monsters on earth—he was also an incredible humanitarian.

"Did she connect with anyone here?" Jeannette asked.

"Ah, yes, that she did!" Mrs. Dupont said, nodding. "Oh, Virginia! She wanted to do everything, and she had a special student/teacher discount card. She took me to the Moulin Rouge—with champagne included. But, of course... Let's see, she made friends with a girl who was visiting from Canada, Shelley Milton. They went to a few offshoot places together. A dinner theater, a magic show...and I believe Shelley also went with her to Versailles. Oh, and the wine region."

"The wine region—when she disappeared?" Daniel asked.

"Oh, um…"

The woman paused, wincing, letting out a long sigh.

"I don't—I don't clean rooms nightly. People know that. I didn't… Oh, dear God! I didn't even know she didn't return right away. And I hadn't known she was going to the wine region the day I'm presuming she disappeared—"

"You were such good friends, but you didn't even know she was missing?" Jeannette asked.

Lorraine Dupont started to sob softly.

Daniel glared at her, arching a brow.

She stared back at him. *It had been a valid question!*

But Jeannette leaned forward, placing a hand gently on Lorraine Dupont's. "I'm so sorry—I didn't mean to cause you further pain. I just want, very badly, for us to catch whoever did this to her. So, forgive me, please—"

"I should have! I should have. But she was so eager— she didn't always bother with breakfast so I didn't think anything of it when she wasn't up in the morning. She would go out early, come back late… But when she did see me, she'd be so excited to tell me about her day!" She paused, wincing, shaking her head. "I think I told all this to Gervais LaBlanc, I'm sure you know, yes, of course, Gervais called me to tell me you'd be coming by. I just… I called the police when I realized she hadn't been here in more than a night but…they didn't find her body for about a week. And then after that… The papers! The papers are saying a vampire is loose in the city of Paris! But, of course, no one believes in vampires. Some people do. But there are people… I read about the vampire or the man who thought he was a vampire, that monster Dante, but—"

"We don't believe this is the same kind of killer—" Jeannette began, but Lorraine Dupont interrupted her immediately.

"Of course! This monster is taking all the blood from his victims! What else could it be?" she demanded.

Jeannette glanced at Daniel, who took over with his own reply. "Madame Dupont, the vampire legend speaks of blood being a necessity. But there are others out there who are just sick. Maybe they feel it will cure leukemia or another form of cancer. Maybe the killer—he or she—just enjoys taking blood to…cook with it. Maybe it's more than one killer."

"If one consumes blood, one might be called a vampire! Oh, dear!" Lorraine looked horrified again. "A…ritual. The blood is a ritual. This is worse! This could be a cult of blood drinkers alive and well in Paris!"

"Madame," Daniel said gently, "please, you mustn't fret so much. We don't have answers yet—that's why we're talking to you, even though Gervais already had a conversation with you. We may each discover something—a little thing—that you remember that could send us in the right direction, to help us understand what Virginia and the other victims might have had in common."

"Wine," Jeannette said. "They were all found in wine country. And there are tours, so many of them! The distance from here to Reims—and many, many vineyards—isn't far at all. A few hours." She shook her head. "So many people take the wine tasting tours. Of course, the wines are quite incredible and you can learn subtle differences and…they were found in vineyards, right? In fields that were recently harvested—or whatever one does with grapes and vines. I mean, it's like they would be found, but…one never knows when, right? And there was another girl."

Jeannette glanced at Daniel.

"Two more girls," she said quietly. "That's why it's so important we retrace their footsteps. We need to find out where they went and what they did that was in common."

"Oh, no, oh—" Lorraine broke off, staring at the two of them. "Then it's true!" she whispered.

"What is true?" Daniel asked her.

"There really is a vampire on the loose!" she declared.

"No, there is a real human being behind this, madame," Jeannette assured her. "And we are so sorry for the loss of your young friend, and equally grateful for whatever help you give us."

There was a knock at the door. Lorraine Dupont gave herself a little shake, as if the physical movement could clear her mind. "Excuse me!" she told them.

She stood and hurried to the door. Instinctively, Jeannette stood and Daniel did the same.

"Shelley!" Lorraine Dupont said, sadness in her tone again. "Please, come in! I was just talking to the investigators about you and— Shelley?"

"She's running!" Jeannette said, surprised and glancing quickly at Daniel as she hurried to the door.

The young woman was already halfway down the block.

At her side, Daniel shrugged and murmured, "See, sometimes it's good that we're young!"

He was already in motion. Jeannette was quickly after Shelley, shouting as she ran, "Hey! She's not a suspect in this. We're hoping to have her as a witness!"

"If you're not worried about something you've done, why run?" he shouted back.

They were hitting a well-traversed tourist area with a beautiful fountain in the center of a square surrounded by boutiques and cafés.

"Going right!" Jeannette called, adding, "Don't run her down as if she were a quarterback holding the ball!"

"American football!" he shouted back. "I'll think of myself as a referee!"

She circled around the fountain carefully dodging citizens and tourists alike, glad that she did know the simple, *"Pardonnez-moi!"*

Parisians stopped, swirling around in confusion. There was little that Jeannette could do other than try to smile as she rushed by them, forgetting any concept of French and saying, "It's okay, it's okay!"

When she came around the base of the beautiful equestrian statue in the center of the fountain, she discovered the girl had stopped running. She was bent over, gasping for breath.

"Hey!" Jeannette said gently. "Please, please, please! Don't run. We're the good guys, I swear it. We just want your help."

The girl looked up at Jeannette. She looked to be about the same age as Virginia, young, a recent college graduate, living out her dream. She had a headful of rich chestnut hair, a slim, pretty face and enormous brown eyes. Her mouth opened. Nothing came out.

Daniel came speeding around the other side of the fountain, stopping short when he saw Jeannette with the young woman.

She looked up at him as if she would panic.

Apparently, Daniel had dealt with victims or witnesses before; he immediately sank to his knees before the frightened woman so that he was looking up at her.

"Shelley, please, we just need your help!" he told her.

She suddenly stood; Daniel did the same, the two of them blocking her.

But she wasn't attempting to run.

She was looking desperately through the crowd—many of them still frowning and staring at her. Daniel assured them, she assumed, in quick and easy French that everything was all right.

"Shelley, Shelley, who are you looking for?" Jeannette asked.

"I—I—I don't know. But...they're out there!" Shelley said.

"They? Who are they?" Daniel asked quietly. He very gently took the young woman by her upper arms to look into her eyes as he spoke. "Shelley, please, you're scared. We want to help you. We want to stop whoever took your friend. But we need help!"

"I just know they're out there!" she whispered.

Daniel glanced at Jeannette.

"I just saw the news!" she whispered. "Now there are three! They took Virginia. And they took Patricia! Now... Oh, my God, I don't even know who, but they've taken a third girl and...they'll get me, too! I must get out of here, I... I don't have the money. I need to go home. I need to get out of Paris. No, no, no—I can't even get on an airplane alone!"

"Shelley, you knew Patricia? She was a young German woman, right?" Jeannette said softly.

Shelley blinked and managed to nod. "Patricia...

Never called her Pat or Patty. She was Patricia. I told her it was a German thing." Shelley started to laugh, but it was the kind of laugh that indicated she might have been about to cry. "She said that quite a few German things were better than American things—like most Americans only knowing how to speak one language. Patricia…she spoke German, French, Spanish and English—fluently. She was smart, she was funny…"

Tears streamed down her face.

"Shelley, please. We're not going to let anything happen to you," Daniel promised her. "Please! You can help us get justice for them. And you can help us protect you. Knowing that the two of them—two young women from different countries—became friends in Paris and did many things together can help us trace what might have happened. Shelley—"

The young woman was shaking her head.

"They fly by night. There is no protection."

"They fly by night?" Daniel repeated. "Shelley."

"It…it sounds ridiculous, but… I read the papers! They sell English language papers here, and you can go online and everything is translated. It goes all over the world! A year or so ago, maybe two years ago…there was a vampire in Norway—"

Daniel interrupted her.

"There was no vampire in Norway—it was a man. And trust me, he just killed, pretending to be a vampire and trying to get other people to pretend to be vampires. And he is gone, gone, gone. Shelley, please, we need your help—"

In turn, Shelley interrupted him.

"How can you protect me? Are you going to sleep with me at night?" Shelley asked.

"We can arrange for a French policewoman to be by your side," Jeannette assured her.

Shelley winced and fell back to sit down at the base of the statue. She shook her head. "They're everywhere. They're watching. I know it!"

"Then we'll find a way to watch them back," Daniel promised her. "But I need you to come with us—I need you to help us."

She looked up at him, shaking her head.

"There was a third woman," she said.

Jeannette nodded. "It has been in the media that a third woman was found, and I'm afraid the media survives by sensationalizing everything. They need to be warning people, not creating stories about vampires."

"The third woman…" Shelley murmured again.

"She hasn't been identified yet," Daniel told her.

Shelley gave them a pained grimace.

"I think I know who she is," she told them gravely before bursting into sobs again.

Daniel Murray stood silently by Shelley as she looked through the glass at the body of the latest victim to be discovered in the vineyards.

The medical examiner moved the sheet, displaying the woman's face.

Shelley let out a strangled sob, turned and threw herself into his arms. He looked over her shoulders at Jeannette, arching a brow as he patted Shelley's back, trying to reassure her.

Jeannette gave him a nod, indicating she'd lead them

out. Naturally, they were both feeling tremendous empathy for the young woman. First, she had to feel the pain of losing people she had quickly come to call friends and then, just as naturally, she had to be terrified for her own life.

As they exited the viewing room, they found Gervais LaBlanc waiting for them.

LaBlanc was great. Daniel hadn't had the opportunity to work with him long yet, but he was methodical and quick to share—and just as quick to welcome any help he could get. And for Daniel, it was his first time working outside of Scotland. Thankfully, LaBlanc was making that easy.

He just wished he'd met Jeannette first, so he could have gotten a feel for what working with her was going to be like. Of course, the rest of their Blackbird division of the Krewe of Hunters would be here soon enough. And he had come to work well with them.

Even as they were about to greet Gervais, Shelley clung harder to his shoulder, still sobbing.

"Shelley, Shelley, please, we are so, so sorry, but we need her name now, and everything you know about these young women—" Daniel began.

"I'll be next! I'll be next!" Shelley cried.

"We're not going to let that happen," Daniel assured her.

"No, we will not!" Jeannette promised, pulling Shelley gently from Daniel so she could introduce her to Gervais LaBlanc. Daniel saw she stared determinedly at LaBlanc as she introduced him to Shelley, adding words that couldn't be a lie.

"This young lady must have twenty-four-hour protection until we catch whoever is responsible for this."

"I will have officers with her twenty-four seven," LaBlanc promised. "Now, Miss—"

"Officers! Cops are crooked, we all know that. How can I possibly—ohhh, I should have never said anything!" Shelley cried. "Don't you watch TV?"

Daniel inhaled for patience and told her, "Every once in a while, you get a bad cop, just like you get someone bad in any profession. But most police officers put their lives on the line for others and are good people and—"

"I promise you. Only good officers," LaBlanc said.

"And how can you guarantee that?" Shelley whispered.

"Well," LaBlanc said dryly, "one of them will be one of my sons. He will be with you constantly. We have a house—he will sleep in the parlor when he needs to do so. The home is wired, next to one of our stations. Whoever is doing this, however, is not breaking into places. This killer is finding victims through places they go. You were all at different rooming houses, correct?"

Shelley nodded.

"What we need to know now," Jeannette said gently, "is who this young woman might be?"

"And then, please, we need to know how you met and everything you did while you were together in Paris," Daniel finished.

Shelley nodded. "Catherine Blakely. She was here from Australia." She winced. "She, uh, just graduated, too, and worked much of the summer to get the money to come here. Paris was a dream for so many of us!"

"If you have any contact information for her friends or family, we need it, please," LaBlanc said.

"She's an orphan. Grew up in a group home. Some

of her fellows there were her friends, but…no one close that I know about," Shelley said, shaking her head. "Oh, my God! I'm terrified! I can't believe it. Three victims. And I knew them all!"

"Where did you meet?" Daniel asked. "And where did you go together?"

"Many places… Um, the Louvre, Versailles, Notre Dame, other churches, dinner at several cafés, cheap ones, shows, music, performers, magicians… Oh, we loved shows. Saw three of them, and I can list the places where we went together and the things that we did, I just need—"

"You need a minute, time to calm down, mourn your friend," Jeannette said very gently. "Of course. Let's get you out of here."

LaBlanc was on the phone, arranging housing and guards for Shelley.

Daniel looked at his new partner. Capable, so it seemed. Well, she wouldn't have been chosen for this assignment if she didn't have the stomach, stamina, determination and experience for it.

And yet…

She looked as if she could easily have been friends herself with these girls. She could pass for a recent college graduate, someone sweet and innocent…

He was horrified to realize he was thinking of her as bait for a killer.

But that was part of the job.

Jeannette gazed at Daniel over the young woman's head.

And he knew she was thinking the same thing. Retracing the victims' movements might not avail them of much, and yet it was something they needed to do. The Louvre was often the main stop for tourists in the city. Hundreds of people visited it daily along with Notre Dame and Versailles...

"Where did you first meet?" Daniel asked, looking at Shelley.

"Oh, wine country! We were all on a tour out in Reims to do wine tastings. The region is famous for its champagne and... Oh! That's where the bodies were found, right?"

That was true. And, of course...

It had to be on their list. They needed to see where the bodies had been left. And they needed to retrace every movement the girls had made together.

"Mademoiselle," LaBlanc said, "please. We will take you to safety. And we'll have you sit, relax, have some water—"

"Coffee. Coffee, please. Since it shouldn't be a giant glass of wine right now!" Shelley said.

"That can come. But while you make those lists for us," Jeannette said gently, "we'll start with a tour of the wine country."

She looked at Daniel.

He turned to Shelley again.

"We need the name of the company you used, please," he said.

"It's called City of Light Tours," Shelley told them. She started to sob again. "So much for light! We all came seeking that light, and all they found was...darkness!"

Two

Shelley knew they had taken the City of Light tour; she knew they had met early on in their trips to the city and they'd gone to Notre Dame together and to the Louvre and Versailles. But she needed to think…to remember…to write down every little place they had gone, the shows, the cafés…the little places where they had gone where they might have been seen.

They tried to calm her down. As they did so, Jeannette had to admit to herself that Daniel Murray was good when speaking with someone bereaved. One thing was important: there was no doubt these girls had met on their first tour—one often taken from Paris. A tour of the nearby wine country.

Eventually, they left Shelley with Gervais so he could bring her to headquarters, set her up in a safe house and introduce her to her personal bodyguards. They needed to set themselves up at the headquarters that had been arranged for Blackbird, a place where they could work and where Gervais LaBlanc could also join them to keep the Paris inspectors and officers abreast of everything that was happening and where they could in turn learn from the Paris police.

"They met heading out to the wine country," Jeannette said as the two of them arrived at the house on Île de la Cité, or "City Island," that would be their home and workplace for the duration of the case. "The bodies were found in the wine country."

"It stands to reason that we should head to the wine country," Daniel said.

The house was accessed through a code, which Daniel keyed in. Opening the door, he surveyed their new domain.

"It's very similar to where we stayed in Edinburgh," he murmured.

"It's, uh, great. I think," Jeannette told him. She smiled. "I wasn't in Edinburgh, so I don't know. It's the first time I've worked outside the United States."

He smiled at her in turn. "It's the first time I've worked out of Great Britain," he told her. "Trust me, I'm just as lost."

"I didn't say I was lost," she protested. But *his* laughter made her laugh. "Okay, it's new—but the same. We work the same."

"Of course," he told her. "But having this house with such easy access to the station, tech help and all that works well."

The headquarters they had been given was a house at the southern end of Île de la Cité with easy access to water and land routes; across the water from it was the Institut médico-légal de Paris just off the Seine, and also near the Viaduc d'Austerlitz. The house had been built in the late 1700s, but it had been updated and offered a sparkling new kitchen and baths in each of the five bedrooms. An entry led to a grand hall or large living room, off from which was a dining room that could be reached through a domed arch. The house gave them a place to live and work throughout the day—and night.

For Jeannette, it was wonderfully different. Her last assignment had been an equally heartrending one. She'd gone undercover to infiltrate a cult and discovered the reason three young people had died. She'd lived in a dorm with four other women; food had been rationed.

After that, this was…

"Nice," she murmured aloud.

"Right. So, we plan from here. We discuss here, we share here. The dining table becomes the great work center," Daniel said. "And right now—"

"I'm not sure what to do. The first tour we can make is tomorrow morning beginning at ten o'clock. And that would mean leaving here bright and early or—"

"Or, we could leave tonight and check out Reims before taking the tour."

"Well, there is a bus that leaves from here," Jeannette said.

"Did Shelley and her friends take the bus from here or pick up the tour once they were already in Reims?" Daniel asked her.

"City of Light Tours…" Jeannette murmured, looking at the site on her phone. "There are tours that encompass leaving from Paris and returning to Paris, but…there are also tours that leave from Reims."

Daniel had his phone out, too. She heard him speaking to Gervais, asking him to find out from Shelley which tour they did.

He ended the call and looked at her. "They left from Reims. Shelley said she went out there first because she wanted to see some of the things that Reims was famous for—along with the wine country." He hesitated, shaking his head. "That poor girl," he murmured.

"All right, so…do we know where she was staying in Reims?" Jeannette asked.

He nodded. "Aye. A bed-and-breakfast that is owned by a member of one of the local wine houses, a Mademoiselle Delphine Matisse. Shelley booked through an online site. We can do the same if you want to head out and see where she started."

"We could spend the late afternoon at the Louvre," Jeannette murmured.

Daniel nodded. "Aye, there is that!" he told her. "But I would like to get out there. Get a feel for the great houses, and of course, get in the city itself to find out what kind of reputation the champagne and wine houses have. Right. We have the massive houses, those responsible for the hundred-dollar bottles that are known around the world. But there are smaller houses, or smaller vineyards, I should say. I just think—"

"That you want to drive out to Reims now?" Jeannette asked him.

"Start from the start," he said.

She nodded, looking at him. In truth, the man resembled a young rock star more than a dedicated law enforcement official. He was striking with the thatch of hair over his forehead and the structure of his cheekbones and jaw, but his smile allowed for him to appear as if he hadn't a care in the world.

"What?" he asked her.

She shook her head. "Sorry. Just curious. Do you play the guitar?" she asked him.

"Yeah. I play and I have a guitar. I play for fun. Love music. Don't you?" he asked.

"Sure. Who doesn't? Sorry, I was digressing. Just curious. Did you always want to be in law enforcement?"

He arched a brow. "I probably wanted to be something else at some time. But my father was murdered when I was thirteen. I knew then and there that I wanted to be the one to... Well, you can't fix murder. But you can give a family a sense of peace. Anyway, back to now. Gervais has let us have the use of a little economy car. We can get online now and make our reservation."

She frowned. How were they going to play it? As a couple, as...

He grinned as if reading her mind. "We shouldn't be a couple. Just good friends, maybe even a brother and sister. Or cousins—that would work better. Use our own names, and oh, yeah, that will allow for the difference in accents. I grew up in Scotland, you grew up in the US, but we always agreed that when we graduated college, I'd show you the sights in France!"

"Okay. Good story." She pulled out her phone. "I'll get our reservation."

"Good. I'll report in and give Jackson and Mason and all a heads-up—since Mason and that group are supposed to reach Paris tonight, they might want to head out to join us. Or first meet with Shelley, too. See if they can learn something we didn't, and that Gervais hasn't managed to discover."

"It's a plan," Jeannette agreed.

"Hey. It's a good thing we didn't unpack, eh?"

She smiled and went online to make their reservations. As she did so, she heard Daniel speaking with the head of Blackbird, Mason Carter.

Her mission accomplished, Jeannette waited for him to finish the conversation. She felt a bit like the odd one out. She knew Daniel had worked with Luke Kendrick and Carly MacDonald in Scotland; he might be the only one of their number now who wasn't American, but he did have a rapport with the rest of a team she had yet to meet.

"All is good—they'll be here in a few hours. They'll set up here and meet with Gervais. I didn't know he had a son who was with the *préfecture de police*—did you?"

"I did not. But I suppose it's not surprising. Many children of police officers become police officers."

"Right. 'Tis true. Anyway, are we set?"

"We are," she said. "Two rooms at the bed-and-breakfast owned by Delphine Matisse in the city of Reims near the pickup point for City of Light Tours." He laughed. They had just brought their travel bags in. Daniel pointed to them and grinned.

"On the road again!"

"On the road again," she agreed.

As they headed out, he asked, "You want to drive?"

"You afraid?" she teased. "I mean, it's the wrong side of the road down here for you, isn't it?"

He smiled easily, taking the teasing well.

"I just didn't want to assume I would do the driving."

"Hmm."

"Hmm?" he queried.

"Should I be afraid?" she asked.

"I'll drive!" he said, groaning.

They headed out to the car, throwing their bags back into the trunk. "Eighty miles, they say," Jeannette murmured, looking at her phone. A message popped up as she did so. She glanced over at Daniel. "Gervais sent a list of places Shelley visited with the other girls in Reims."

"Champagne region, here we come," he murmured. He slid behind the wheel and said, "Along with the champagne and wine, the area offers spectacular architecture."

"You've been there before?"

"From the UK, France is right across the water," he said.

"Of course. So…"

Jeannette used her phone to begin to look up the area where they were traveling. Reims did offer so much more than just wine. "Founded by the Gauls, a major city in the Roman Empire," she murmured aloud.

"Hey, Londinium, or London. Those Romans got around," Daniel responded. "But around 451 AD, Attila the Hun torched the city."

"Ouch," Jeannette said, smiling as she read about the city on her phone. "I see that here! Ooh, we need to see the Reims Cathedral for French Gothic architecture and the Palace of Tao! I—"

"The things Shelley and friends would have wanted to see," he murmured. He quickly glanced her way, shaking his head. "Were these girls specifically marked, do you think? Or were they victims of happenstance, in the wrong place at the wrong time?"

Jeannette shook her head. "Well, three girls who met each other here are the victims—but did they go somewhere they might have been seen? Did they look like easy prey? The bodies weren't hidden—but they weren't left in obvious places as if they were on display, either. But! It does seem like a bit too much of a coincidence that they had become friends."

"Or appeared vulnerable and happened to be in the same places," Daniel said. "And all drained of blood. No sexual assault, not tortured, just drained of blood."

"Don't start with the vampire thing!" she groaned.

"There are sick people out there who want to think they're vampires. Blackbird began when they were seeking a would-be vampire. And—" He broke off.

"And you think that might mean there are really vampires out there?" she asked.

"Nope. I've read enough history. The legends don't just date back to Bram Stoker and *Dracula*. They had lamia in Greece and *Varney the Vampire*—or *The Feast of Blood*—came out serialized in 1845, before Bram Stoker took the creature to new heights. Most ancient peoples had gods and demons—and bloodsuckers. The last woman accused of witchcraft and legally burned in Scotland was Janet Horne, back in 1727, so think of it this way—human beings have always been superstitious, believing what they want to believe. Werewolves can be attributed to the disease of lycanthropy. Oh! The American *vampire*, Mercy Brown, 1892! Her grave was exhumed because it was suspected she was practicing evil deeds, now attributed to tuberculosis making its way through her family. But still, her heart and liver were extracted and burned before she could be put back to rest again."

"Do you think someone believes that kind of legend now?" Jeannette asked him, frowning. "Because..."

"Some say Bram Stoker took inspiration for Dracula from Vlad Dracul. And maybe he borrowed from *Varney the Vampire*. Others say he studied the history of Elizabeth Báthory," Daniel said. "Who knows? The point I'm making is that—"

"Daniel," Jeannette interrupted softly, "we do speak with the dead."

He smiled, nodding. "I know. But we've discovered the truth behind other legendary creatures and—"

She laughed, interrupting him. "Oh, seriously, come on! There are always programs on in which scientists are looking for Bigfoot!"

He grinned, nodding. "Right. Ape-man. Aye, but... we are looking for a killer—or killers here—the point being, I don't think this is just for fun. That came out wrong. I mean, I think we're looking for a killer who believes in the power of human blood."

Jeannette nodded. "I agree. Except... Okay, when I was with Gervais LaBlanc, after the autopsy on the last victim, I was thinking about Elizabeth Báthory."

"Really?" he asked, glancing her way.

She nodded. "Okay, there are two lines of thought on her in scholarly circles. One theory revolves around the fact that so many in her household were involved. There were so many witnesses, and so many young women really disappeared that she had to have been guilty. Then again, some say the family dynamics were such that relatives and even the Hapsburg Empire might have been setting her up. Of course, here's what is sad— those in her household, three servants I believe, were executed while she was walled up in her castle. To begin with," Jeannette continued, wincing, "her mother was a Báthory, her father was a Báthory, she was related to rulers across the area, including the king of Poland. She was married, and some say she didn't start her killing spree until her husband died while others claimed it was something she'd been doing forever. And some claimed her husband—deceased at the time of her arrest—enjoyed torturing victims with her. But—"

"But?"

"She was known for horrendous torture, covering victims in honey and watching as the bugs chewed them to pieces, stripping them and slicing them…all kinds of horrific things."

"I see where you're going," Daniel said. "These victims have just been drained of blood."

"Not tortured," Jeannette said.

"Here's something I find interesting as well on the other side," Daniel said. "I do know a little about history. All right, from what legend and history say, she might have tortured and killed anywhere from a dozen to over six hundred young women. Quite a difference there. But supposedly, at first, she was killing the poor—those without families to worry if they were missing, those barely existing. Then again, according to history and/or legend, she started on the daughters of lower gentry who came to be part of her noble household and they started disappearing. It was only when the more upper-class women began disappearing that she came under scrutiny. Of course, we need to remember that what was part of Hungary at the time is now part of Slovakia. Transylvania was separately ruled but not part of the country of Romania, but it was ruled by her relatives. And after her husband's death, she was in control of a multitude of castles, villages and land. Put her away—and you get control of that property. As you said, some historians believe that members of the Hapsburg Empire were part of it," he said thoughtfully. Then he shrugged. "And we're kind of back to where we started. The victims we've discovered have not been cut or tortured, no honey, no bugs consuming bodies…"

He paused, shrugged and shook his head. "Different world today."

"Yes, but money and power still talk," Jeannette reminded him.

"And we're not in any part of the Hungarian Empire—we're in France." Daniel shook his head.

"True. So, a purist vampire?" Jeannette asked, growing frustrated.

Their phones started ringing at the same time. "Has to be a group call—Mason or one of those guys," he said. "Want to get it on yours since it's in your hand?" he asked, grinning.

It was Mason, and Jeannette put her phone on speaker.

"You there yet?" Mason asked.

"Almost," Daniel told him. "I figure we'll check in, walk the streets, see if anyone else is hanging around."

"What time is your tour in the morning?" Mason asked.

"There's one at ten," Jeannette said. "I was thinking—"

"Anything later?" Mason asked over the phone.

"Sure. They have one that starts at two and lasts into the evening. I had just thought—"

"Gervais has decided to meet you out there in the morning—he wants you to see where the bodies were found, and it's going to take a few hours. If you're closing in on Reims, you'll see why—there are fields after fields after fields out there, owned by different houses, in different stages of growth, along with some land that's just wild. All three of our victims were found out there, but in different fields, all three of them belonging to different wine houses and near some stretches that are just fallow and overgrown. It's beautiful country, but...you don't want to be out there alone at night. There can be times when a car doesn't pass on certain roads for hours, and the darkness can hide just about anything."

"That's fine, Mason. We'll meet Gervais wherever he wants."

"He knows where you're staying. He'll meet you there."

"Fine, thanks. You guys are in Paris?"

"Yes, we're with Shelley, seeing where they're keeping her safe and meeting her guards. Nothing will be random—she'll have the same three people all the way through. All three are dedicated. Two awake, one sleeping... Nothing, no one, will get to her."

"Do you think she's an intended victim?" Jeannette asked.

"We don't know. But we're not going to take any chances. Della is talking to her now about all the things they did together. We'll start... But... Well, as I guess we all figured out, every tourist in Paris goes to the Louvre and Notre Dame. We'll see where else," Mason said. "Anyway, you're going to get there too late for much tonight, although you should take the time to have a great dinner and sample some champagne," Mason told them.

"Thanks. Will do," Jeannette told him.

Mason ended the call and Jeannette looked over at Daniel. "I think he just told us to go drink champagne."

"Want to hear something sad?" he asked her.

"What's that?"

"I don't like champagne. The supposedly better a champagne is, the worse it usually tastes to me."

"Ah! A Scot. A whiskey man!"

"Sometimes," he said with a shrug. "But I will sample champagne. The one good thing is this—you will never need to worry that I will over imbibe on the stuff!"

Jeannette grinned and looked out the window. She knew they were nearing Reims, which was a major city; but along the way, there were fields. Fields and fields and fields. Planted in different ways, perhaps in different stages. She knew that wine usually came from grapes, and that it could be made from other fruits, but she knew very little about the growing process.

"Fields and fields and fields for miles!" she murmured.

"And how many people have you seen?" Daniel asked dryly.

She grinned. "Well, it's getting later in the day."

"Thankfully, we were told to have some dinner. And look ahead! We're getting closer to civilization."

She understood why the city of Reims was a popular tourist destination, along with the fact that it was the capital of the champagne and wine world here. The buildings were impressive, spanning hundreds of years of architecture. Many structures appeared to be gothic, some dated back to the baroque period, and mixed in were buildings from various centuries along with more modern housing and office buildings.

They passed the cathedral at a distance, and Jeannette was glad she wasn't driving; the soaring arches and pinnacles were stunning. She winced suddenly, thinking of what a joy the trip must have been to the young women whose dreams had ended so tragically.

And then she wondered as well…

In a city so old, who might they find?

Daniel was watching the GPS and turned off to the left.

"Down this street and…nice!"

The bed-and-breakfast they had come to was small, but Jeannette thought the house must have been built and altered through the years, much like the cathedral. The front door had an archway that appeared gothic, smaller than the grand doorway at the cathedral, but similar in appearance. There were four towers that extended over the four corners of the place. A stone wall surrounded it, but the gates to the driveway were open. Daniel pulled in, guiding the car into what appeared to be spaces for parking to the side of the semicircular drive.

They got out of the car, and both of them stared at the house.

The front door opened and a woman came out. She wore an attractive teal business suit, and her light brown hair was swept back into a chignon. She smiled and called out to them, and appeared to be in her late forties.

"*Bienvenue! Pardonnez-moi*, welcome!" she called out to them.

They didn't go for their bags but walked to her as she came toward them with her hand extended in greeting. "I'm Delphine Matisse, and welcome to Reims. You are Jeannette and Daniel? You came together. I have reservations for two rooms. I did not know you were a couple."

"Cousins, not romantically involved, yuck!" Daniel said, giving her a great grin and turning on the charm he seemed so capable of drawing up at a moment's notice. He took the woman's extended hand. "We even grew up in different countries!" he told her. "But Jeannette just graduated from college, and I always promised I'd bring her here once she got her degree."

"Oh, how nice! Well, welcome back, monsieur," she told Daniel. She turned to Jeannette and said, "This is your first trip to Reims?"

"It is. And I'm fascinated and bowled over by the beauty of the place already!" Jeannette assured her.

"*Très bien!*" Delphine said. "I am sorry! English—"

"Madame Matisse, I am in your country, and I don't expect people to speak my language. I know bits and pieces of French, enough to say, *merci*!"

The woman smiled and nodded. "I do hope you enjoy your stay. Now, keys for you both, the old-fashioned kind I'm afraid. One opens the front door, and the other opens your bedrooms. There are only three bedrooms, and the other is not occupied at this moment. If you need anything, my number is on the refrigerator. I'm often busy but my secretary will help you. Please! Enjoy."

"You don't stay here? It is your home, right?" Daniel asked.

"I am CEO of our family company at this time," she said. "We aren't far. We are on the wine tasting tours, so you will see our main home," Delphine explained. "Ah, this house! I do love it. So many special memories were made in this place. Well, it is amazing to have such a heritage, and hard work, also. Now, I will leave you. And I hope you will enjoy yourselves."

"Oh, we will!" Jeannette said enthusiastically. "We heard this was wonderful. And we're about to head out to find some food—"

"The restaurants are outstanding. Oh, of course, you will see La Maison Familiale d'Henri Matisse on your tour, but…most carry a delightful bubbly that you must try. We are very proud of our products. So I must go, but I hope to see you tomorrow!"

"Of course! We look forward to it."

She gave Daniel a special smile and asked again, "You are not together…really?"

"No, no!" Jeannette assured her. "Cousins. Like Daniel said—yuck!"

She handed each of them a little key ring with two keys each, not looking at Jeannette as she did so, but apparently appreciating Daniel's smile and the light in his eyes.

Then Delphine waved as she headed toward her car.

"I will hope to see you tomorrow!" she called. "Definitely, before you leave. I'll give you a very special tour!"

Jeannette lowered her head smiling; that was for Daniel.

She wasn't that up on sports cars, but she had a feeling the car parked next to their little economy number was something special.

"Maserati, top of the line," Daniel murmured, smiling as he waved goodbye.

"I think she likes you," Jeannette said, laughing as Delphine drove away at last.

He shrugged, studying the keys she had handed him. "Interesting," he said.

"What's that?"

"These keys. Who knows how many copies of these may be out there?"

Jeannette shook her head. "Nothing happened to anyone here," she reminded him. "The other girls didn't stay here—just Shelley."

"I know. I've been in law enforcement too long," he said. "I'm suspicious of everything."

"Great. Now you have me thinking," Jeannette said.

"Let's take a look and then eat!" Daniel said.

"That will work for me," she agreed. "Of course, we must try the Matisse bubbly."

He groaned, turning the key in the lock of the front door. They entered the bed-and-breakfast. Delphine Matisse had seen to it that while the facade might be historical, the house was up to date. The interior featured both a modern kitchen and baths. And it appeared that the living room and bedrooms had all been furnished by the most trendy manufacturers.

They surveyed the place, discovering quickly that the towers were basically for show. Stairs led them up to a window that allowed for a fantastic view of fields beyond the city toward the rear, as well as great views of the city itself from the front. Once, they might have been used to make a defensive stand, except Jeannette wasn't sure what a place that was so small might have defended.

The bedrooms were on the ground floor, but they didn't bring their bags in yet, rather heading out quickly.

In the car, Daniel asked, "And Shelley suggested...?"

"La Maison de Rivière," Jeannette told him. "Shelley dined there with the other girls. Who knows what we might discover there?"

Daniel shook his head.

"What?"

"The bodies were discovered out here. Aye, the lasses met on the tour out here that we're taking tomorrow, but..."

"But?"

"There's a Paris connection. I don't know what it is, I just..."

Studying him, Jeannette nodded. "They met out here. Maybe they were seen out here, then seen again in Paris...or..."

"I keep reminding myself we're just beginning to investigate," Daniel said. "There are six members of Blackbird now working this. I just feel an...urgency."

Studying his eyes, Jeannette felt she understood.

"We need to do everything we can as quickly as possible," she agreed. "Lest..."

"Lest we find another victim. Because whoever is doing this for whatever reason, well, they're not going to stop until—"

"Someone stops them," Jeannette said. "I understand. But we follow in the footsteps of the victims, and we study every clue. The others are in Paris—we do have a team."

Daniel nodded. "I know. So. Let's eat…and see just what we might discover, nourish our bodies, and expand our—"

"Minds!" Jeannette said.

"I was going to say *our list of clues*, but whatever!" Daniel told her.

She smiled in turn.

She had been worried about meeting him, skeptical of a new partner who knew members of Blackbird already and might not appreciate her presence, but…

Maybe he wasn't going to be half bad, after all.

Three

The restaurant was just two blocks from the bed-and-breakfast owned by Delphine Matisse and naturally, it did indeed carry Matisse wines along with French specialties, something they discovered as soon as they were seated.

Matisse wines were advertised on a placard on the table.

The hostess had given them menus, and Daniel was already perusing the food.

"Were you thinking about the snails?" Daniel asked Jeannette as he studied the menu.

"No, and I'm not having duck legs, either!" she told him. She winced. "Not at all sure about some of these, and I'm feeling a little... Well, the French are known for their cuisine!"

"And the snails are probably excellent," Daniel said, grinning.

"Good. You feel free to enjoy them. I'll watch."

"Hey. Lots of people eat snails."

"And they are welcome to enjoy. To me...a snail is a creepy critter from the lawn."

"But you'll eat a cow?"

She shook her head, laughing. "You might have just turned me into a vegetarian. But, hmm, I think I will try a Matisse sparkling wine. This one looks good!"

Fortunately, the menu was in French and English so Jeannette didn't need to rely on her schoolgirl knowledge of the language. Then again, she had the feeling Daniel did have a real comprehension of French; she didn't think they'd wind up in too much trouble.

She pointed at the separate wine menu. "'Light and lightly sweet, one of our fan favorites!'" she read.

Their waiter came to their table, greeting them in French. Jeannette was glad she could at least return, *"Bonsoir!"*

"Lovely, mademoiselle!" he told her. "I do speak English fluently. And I'm happy to help you in any way."

He was young. A good-looking man in his late twenties or early thirties, Jeannette thought. She smiled at him and asked, "I was thinking about this sparkling wine, light and sweet? Any thoughts?"

"Yes, very nice and light," he told her. "And from one of our small but prestigious houses. Have you toured the vineyards yet?"

"No, but we met Madame Matisse this morning," Daniel said. "My cousin and I are staying there."

"Oh, your cousin!" the waiter said, beaming at Jeannette. "A special trip?"

"Graduation," Daniel said. "She's visited my part of the family in Scotland and saw London, but Paris and a tour of the vineyards was a special graduation trip."

"Wonderful. I'm Alphonse, and if you need anything, just call my name. Two of the Matisse?" he asked them.

"I would love a beer," Daniel said, shrugging as he looked at Jeannette.

"Perfect. The House of Matisse also brews a great dark beer, a stout," Alphonse told them.

"Wonderful," Jeannette said. "We're staying at her house, and the accommodations are great and reasonable. She's so nice that I want to support her business."

Alphonse nodded. "She always appears to be lovely," he murmured.

"Oh! Is it all a facade?" Daniel asked him.

Alphonse shook his head. "No, no, she took over when her husband died. And I know she wants to groom her son to take over after her, but..." He shrugged. "He doesn't want to live that life anymore. Oh, she had a husband. He was big in politics, and together, they were... What do you call it? Quite the power couple. Anyway, she works very hard, hires locals and tries to make tourists have a great time. She's great. Not like—" he broke off, looking pained and embarrassed.

"Not like who?" Daniel asked.

"I'm sorry, I shouldn't have—"

"No, no, please!" Jeannette said sweetly. "Please, please, warn us about where we should be putting our tourist dollars and where we shouldn't, and where...well, you know, frankly, we can hang out and imbibe and..."

He still looked uncomfortable, but Jeannette hoped her honest smile was swaying him.

"There are a few other smaller family-owned vineyards. Head of one is Tomas Deauville, and he...he and his wife think that the world should bow to them."

"Extremely entitled?" Daniel asked. He shook his head.

Alphonse nodded grimly. "They come in here sometimes like they own the world, treat us all as if we were their personal slaves, and while we're different from America, with certain gratuities built in, most people throw down a few euros when they've had good service. Not the Deauville couple."

"I don't think we'll even stop at their winery!" Jeannette said.

Alphonse shrugged. "If you're on a tour, you'll probably go by. But..."

"We certainly will not buy anything there!" Jeannette murmured. "I've waitressed and I know the kind of people you're talking about!"

Alphonse nodded grimly. "Then there is Leticia Montague and her husband, George. Inherited money, and again... I guess when you grow up with everything in the world, you keep expecting it." He leaned closer to the table and murmured, "And their wine stinks! Literally. And to drink. But... I'm afraid that if you're taking the local tour—the long one—you'll see their *welcome* bistro."

"Do you actually see any of these people?" Daniel asked Alphonse. "I mean, don't they have tons of employees working for them?"

"Oh, of course, but sometimes they stop in. I heard a woman here complaining the other day that Leticia was the rudest human being she'd ever seen. She was screaming at her people in front of a tour that had just come in, treating them as if they were the dirt her grapes were grown in! Then, of course, she turns it on for the guests, all Miss Smiles and welcome." He paused. "I guess that's why we all like Delphine Matisse. She behaves as if we're all part of humanity and are all due respect."

"That's really great to hear!" Jeannette assured him.

Alphonse suddenly grew serious and frowned. "You are visitors, new here. But I believe people have heard about the recent murders with the bodies discovered out here—on the news in about every language known to man. I don't remind you of this to scare you, but just to… Well, we believe this area is just the disposal place for the bodies. The girls were murdered elsewhere. But I remind you just so that you are very careful." He sighed. "Some were worried no one would come here. But…we are busier than ever. Maybe people hope to find more than grapevines." He winced. "Like the morgue years ago…the bodies of the deceased were free entertainment. Oh, of course, so the police could discover their identities. I don't believe we carried wallets or cell phones around at the time, so…" He broke off, shaking his head. "So, murder and horror—and we are more popular than ever. Still, be careful, be careful." He grinned suddenly. "Cousins. Mademoiselle is your cousin, but, monsieur, you must protect the mademoiselle, as you are family."

"Of course. Aye, we've heard, and thank you! We will be careful," Daniel promised.

"Pardonnez-moi!" Alphonse said suddenly. "The boss is looking at me. I'd best move on to work a bit harder! As soon as you have ordered."

An older man was watching their table, a brow arched as he stared at Alphonse.

Alphonse smiled and asked quickly, "Have you decided on food?"

"I think I'll take the *dos de cabillaud*," Jeannette told him. "It's just fish filets, right?"

He laughed. "*Oui*, mademoiselle. Cod, as you call it."

"So, I turned you into a pescatarian," Daniel teased. "Fine. I'll be polite and go with the same!"

Looking at Jeannette and giving her an appreciative smile, Alphonse told them, "It is very good here. A specialty. Be right back with your drinks!"

He left their table, stopped at another, then hurried to the bar to get their drinks before disappearing into the kitchen with their food order.

"I think this one really likes *you*!" Daniel said, grinning.

"And he warned us both."

Daniel laughed. "And I guess he doesn't realize you carry your own big gun. Maybe that's best."

"I make good bait."

"It's believable that you might have just graduated from college. I don't like the idea of bait—"

"Sometimes it's necessary and it works."

Daniel didn't argue, but he didn't look happy. "Such strange murders are world news, and I'm assuming the killer or killers had to expect that, maybe even to want it. They must be a little on edge out here—all the bodies discovered here. Though, as Alphonse said, they weren't killed where their bodies were discovered."

"So, they were killed in Paris or another nearby city or even here—good-sized city, plenty of places where they may have a setup for draining the blood of their victims. They might have been killed just about anywhere. But—"

"Close. Somewhere close," Daniel said. "Anyway,

there's that boss of Alphonse's. I think I'll have a little chat with him."

"Tell the boss how helpful and wonderful Alphonse was, and how we'll be coming back here and recommending the place and giving it five stars because of him!" Jeannette said.

"Exactly. We just got a great deal of information from him. And—"

"You think a vineyard owner could be involved in these murders?" Jeannette asked.

"It's possible. Still, of course, we need to follow any Paris connections, all the places the girls went together. And…well, we're here. We need to take that tour tomorrow after we head out with Gervais LaBlanc and see what we can see."

"Forewarned and forearmed now?" Jeannette asked.

"It will be interesting if we see any of these people from today. And here's the thing—just because you're a terribly nasty and entitled asshole, it doesn't make you a murderer," Daniel said.

"True."

"Let me go speak to Alphonse's boss and sing his praises."

He left the table. While he was gone and speaking to the man Alphonse had indicated to be his boss, the waiter returned to the table with their drinks.

"If you have free time and you want a guide, remember where to find me!" he told her. "I work evenings, off during the morning, and my days of total freedom are Sunday and Monday!"

She smiled and thanked him.

Daniel returned to the table. "I think I did good

things for our informative friend," he told her. "And I overheard a bit of the last. You have made a conquest."

Jeannette groaned.

"Hey, we may need that conquest at some time!"

"Ah, well, I think your conquest may be the more important one," she told him. "Madame Matisse is the good one—socially, she must come across the others at times. Hmm. Again, not that being an ass makes one a murderer, but then again, being nice doesn't make one innocent of all evil, either!"

"Well, we've got to get back. Let's appreciate Alphonse's friendship. One never knows what one might need when," Daniel said.

The sparkling wine was good, light and easy, just as it was described. Daniel shrugged and said his beer was fine; it was beer.

The food came and the fish was excellent.

"This is really good," Daniel said. "I guess I'm glad I turned you into a pescatarian. Wonderful choice."

Jeannette grinned. "See? There you go."

He leaned a little closer as he said, "Now the boss is watching us."

"Maybe he watches all tourists. Or, did you offend him?"

"I don't think so. I told him how charming it was and how we'd get on all the online sites and give them five stars."

"Maybe he's just curious."

"Maybe. Anyway, in case I need help with my mental notes, his name is Damon Barnier."

"Your mental notes? I can hardly reside within your head!" Jeannette told him.

"No, I write things down at night. Helps me."

She nodded, taking another bite of her fish. "I have no idea why..." she murmured.

"Why what?"

"I keep going back to Elizabeth Báthory. But again, these victims have been found pristine other than being dead and completely drained of their blood. Whether true or not, the court case against the woman listed horrible tortures done to her servants, mostly young women. And according to modern reports, it didn't matter when poor servant girls went missing, no one noticed until girls who came to her court to be ladies-in-waiting, more or less girls from good families gaining prestige from the Báthory name, began to disappear. Oh! And while some said the torture and killing didn't begin until her husband died, others said he was involved! That they enjoyed the torture together, and she just continued after he passed away. And they put their victims in freezing water until they died. They cut them with knives and scissors. They did the thing where they covered them in honey and watched them become eaten alive by insects. So..."

"This isn't Hungary, you know."

Jeannette shrugged. "And her castle is now in Slovakia and her family ruled Transylvania, which was part of Hungary then and is part of Romania now. But the thing isn't the place—"

"I know," he told her quietly. "What is truth may not matter. Place may not matter. What someone admires or believes—some very sick someone—is what matters. But we don't need to jump to the concept of a vampire or a Countess Báthory. We're looking for a vicious serial killer in the here and now."

"I know that and I don't mean to harp—"

"That said, knowing history is a good thing here! Our last case involved a twist on history, intentional or not, so..."

"Right. Sorry."

"No, no! Don't be sorry. Theories are great. We just follow the evidence and see if it fits the theory rather than making the evidence fit the theory."

Jeannette nodded and was startled to suddenly yawn. "Excuse me!" she apologized.

He laughed. "Don't apologize. I'm feeling the same. I'm going to go talk to Monsieur Barnier once again, and tell him the food was great, too. Lots of sucking up never hurts."

"Sucking up is good," she assured him.

Daniel excused himself and headed over to the man.

Alphonse returned to their table, frowning slightly, the bill in his hand.

"No dessert?" he asked. "We French, you know, we are famous for delicious desserts!"

"No, thank you. I'm tired, and tomorrow we are taking the tour," Jeannette told him.

He set the bill down and she reached for her bag.

"I didn't mean that *you* must pay—" Alphonse said.

She laughed. "Cousins, remember? We're not dating!" she told him. "Family credit card."

Not really a lie; it was a Blackbird card. And the way they worked, Blackbird was family.

"Oh, that's right. Cousins. You can call on me anytime!"

He collected the card and set his own on the table, grimacing. "Yes, even waiters have cards. You never know who you're going to meet, or if you'll need to be available for future work! Call me if you need suggestions, if you need help with anything!" he told her.

She smiled. "Will do."

Daniel returned to the table but didn't sit. "We've paid?"

"Need the credit card back," she told him.

He laughed softly. "And Alphonse was insulted that you paid and not me?"

"I told him it was a family credit card."

He grinned. "Good. I'll sign and we'll give him a gratuity even if there's already a gratuity. Although… hmm, I'm not sure if he cares if he gets a gratuity from you!"

"Ah, but it will be from you!"

Alphonse returned and Daniel signed the bill— adding on a nice-sized tip despite it already being in the bill.

Accepting the signed check, Alphonse beamed, staring at Daniel. "Seriously, you call me if you need anything. Anything at all." He turned to Jeannette, smiling. "You have my card!"

"I do," she assured him.

They left the restaurant and began the walk back to Delphine Matisse's bed-and-breakfast.

"Now we know all about nasty, elitist people," Daniel murmured. "And still…"

"The girls met on the tour but did a dozen things in the city of Paris. And there are good, nice people in Paris. Considering the size of the city, there are surely nasty, elitist people there, too. Right now—"

"We know nothing. So, let's get some sleep," he

suggested. "A nice atmospheric house all to ourselves. Sleep with your gun close, and so will I."

"I always do," she murmured. "I wonder…"

"What?"

"I'm just curious. I mean, it sounds as if Delphine Matisse is almost a saint, but what if she happens to be around tomorrow? Would she know who Gervais LaBlanc is and why he might be coming to pick us up? Does that matter?"

"He won't come in—we'll know when he's on the way and we'll just go out and meet him. I know he handles—or supervises—most of the major cases in Paris, but there are police out here, too. And we're here through the new international division in agreement with the UK, so I doubt if anyone but local law enforcement would have any idea of the real purpose for our visit."

"Everyone knows what has gone on," Jeannette said. "And as Alphonse just said, it apparently isn't keeping people away. Rather, it's drawing them out here."

"While the killing may still take place elsewhere," Daniel murmured.

"I guess we're kind of a weird species," Jeannette murmured. "Strange, LaBlanc was talking about the old Paris morgue today, and now Alphonse has mentioned it. That was then, but this is now."

"Home sweet home—for the night, at least," Daniel murmured.

They had reached their bed-and-breakfast. Daniel unlocked the door and told her, "I'll get our bags out of the car."

"Thanks."

She walked in and thought about the girls. Shelley had stayed here, and she could only imagine how she had felt heading out to see the wine country, then so excited to find friends her age who were also going to be staying in Paris, friends with whom she could enjoy the sights of the renowned city.

Daniel came in with the bags. "You want to check out the rooms and pick one?"

"A bed is a bed," she said with a shrug. "I'm not buying the place. Any room is fine."

He grinned. "Okay, I'll go back."

He left her bag in front of her, grabbed his own, and headed through the entry and parlor toward the rear.

He paused. "Again. I made sure the main door was locked, but…sleep with your bedroom door locked and your gun—"

"Near me and ready. Always," she assured him. "Thanks, Daniel."

"Sure! Hey, first up starts the coffee," he said.

"You're a Brit! No tea?"

He laughed. "Aye, I'm a Brit, a Scot first and… maybe part American! Coffee!"

He disappeared. She dragged her bag to the first room, smiling slightly as she realized it had been a day—just a day. She had arrived early that morning via the private jet Adam Harrison had provided the Blackbird team, met Gervais LaBlanc at the morgue, gone to the bed-and-breakfast, met Shelley, headed to wine country…

A long, long day. She was exhausted and tomorrow would be a long day, too.

She entered the first bedroom and opened her carry-on suitcase; she was extremely proud of the fact she'd learned to carry clothing for a week in the one bag. She smiled, thinking she had done so because of commercial flying. So much easier to just have one carry-on that went with her everywhere than waiting for luggage. Now, of course…

She could bring whatever she wanted on the private jet.

She showered quickly, and remembering Daniel's concerns, kept her gun within reach on the back of the commode right next to the shower as she did so.

Bathing was uneventful. She dressed in a long flannel gown and curled into bed.

Her mind continued to race. They had three bodies drained of blood; a serial killer was at work. But what were they dealing with?

Her new partner wasn't half bad, despite having just met that morning.

And they seemed to be working out well enough. She had to admit she was glad he was fluent—or close to fluent—in French. And they could both pass for being very young. Maybe even vulnerable.

If needed, she could be bait. And Daniel…

He could slide into just about any group with his easy, friendly manner, his charming brogue, his…charisma?

He was fine. She was still looking forward to the arrival of the rest of the Krewe. They were here, she reminded herself, here—or not far, anyway! They were working at the Paris house, and she had worked once with Mason, so…

Strange. They were all Krewe for a reason, their unique abilities. She knew Daniel's father had been murdered, which had made him want to be in law enforcement.

And yet, she and Daniel hadn't really had a chance to talk about that all day. And tomorrow...

They'd surely be thrown out of the country and not just out of the case if they started talking about their need to seek out a dead man or woman who might have seen something that the living hadn't. And still...

She closed her eyes and willed sleep to come. It was elusive.

It was critical they be at their best come the morning! And somewhere, sometime, during the day...

She smiled. She would get to know Daniel better and...

It hurt. It always hurt, still, after so many years...

But if she and Daniel were going to be partners...

Maybe she'd need to tell him her own story.

Coffee!

Stepping out, dressed as a tourist and ready for the day, Daniel smelled the coffee the minute he opened his door. Jeannette was an early riser; most importantly, she was someone who made a point of pushing the button on the coffeepot immediately.

She was in the kitchen sipping a cup when he entered.

"Wow, thank you, fantastic!" he said, heading for the pot.

"What?" Jeannette asked.

"You brewed the coffee!"

"I thought that you did. I'll bet it's on a timer. I'm sorry. Darn," Jeannette said, grinning. "I should have taken credit. I thought you woke up and came out here and started it."

He laughed. "I'll still give you the credit. I walked out here—and there was coffee. Well, okay, realistically, Delphine Matisse must have been here to check out the condition of her property before we came in and set it up for her arriving guests," Daniel said. He shrugged. "I've heard that our spirit friends can gain the power to do little things…like push a brew button, but I've not heard of them managing to take a bag of coffee out of a cupboard and get it going into a pot."

"Ah! That's right, Madame Matisse was here," Jeannette murmured.

"Nice hostess," Daniel agreed, taking out his phone. "Giving Mason a call, see if they checked anything out last night." He shook his head. "They probably divided up and tried a few places, but…"

"You don't see how staking out the Louvre or Notre Dame is going to get us anywhere?"

He shrugged. "Always good to follow the steps of those you're researching," he murmured.

"Daniel." He heard Mason's voice at the other end of the call.

"Aye, Mason, putting the phone on speaker. In the kitchen here with Jeannette, ready for Gervais's arrival."

"He should be any minute," Mason told him. "Anything—"

"We had a great waiter last night, one who told us how great Madame Matisse is as a person, good to locals, the owner of a family vineyard and owner of this B&B. He also gave us names of a few people he considered to be monsters—"

"As in monsters who are known to kill?" Mason asked.

"No, monsters who are known to be elitist jerks, rude and cruel to their employees—and who demand everything in the world and don't add a single euro for an extra tip."

"Get all the names to Angela in New York and—"

"My people in Scotland?" Daniel suggested. "They're good, too."

"I never meant to imply anything but," Mason assured him. "Well, hopefully, you'll discover something else today with Gervais or on the tour."

"What about you?"

"We tried out a couple of the shows the girls went to," Mason told him. "We're checking on all the cast members, crew, et cetera, on them. But…"

"Nothing that screams blood-thieving vampiric monsters?" Daniel asked dryly.

"No. But according to Shelley, they went to many venues together while they were in Paris. They were excited, they tried to cram everything into the days that they had. But again, we're also getting lists of attendees for the nights the girls were there. All sales were credit card, so…"

"You will have a hell of a lot of people to sift through," Daniel said.

"Exactly."

"Hey!" Jeannette said suddenly. "I heard a car— Gervais is out there."

"All right, go," Mason said. "Keep communication lines open. We are going to split today, get to the Louvre and Notre Dame and watch to see if anyone has an eye out scanning the crowds for victims. I'm not hopeful, but we're covering all bases, and we'll head to a few more shows tonight."

"Right. I'll call back later."

Daniel ended the call and followed Jeannette out to the car where Gervais was waiting for them in the driver's seat.

"I'll take the back seat. I'll text those names we got last night to Angela—"

"I'll do it because I can double it to our people with the National Crime Agency," Daniel told her.

"Oh, okay," Jeannette said. She slid in next to Gervais while he chose the seat behind the driver.

"Bonjour," Gervais told them.

"Bonjour!" Jeannette returned, smiling at Gervais. "I know that one!" she assured him.

Gervais laughed softly.

"Alors, here we go!" Gervais told them.

Daniel doubled a message to Krewe headquarters in the States and to his people in Scotland, letting them know they didn't know anything about the vineyard owners except that they were disliked, which, of course, didn't mean anything.

Tomas Deauville…they hadn't gotten his wife's name, but that would be an easy find for their tech teams. Leticia and George Montague. The elitists. And, of course, he added the name of Delphine Matisse. He also thought that he would add the names of those at the restaurant—the manager, Monsieur Damon Barnier, and their informative waiter, Alphonse…

"Jeannette, what is Alphonse's surname? It must be on that card he gave you," Daniel said.

"You made friends here already?" Gervais asked.

"A waiter—one quick to tell us about a few of the smaller family vineyard owners," Jeannette explained to him. "He said that Delphine was great—"

"Indeed," Gervais said, nodding. "Her land borders that on which we found one of the bodies. She gave our forensic team access to her offices and all workspaces when she heard what was going on."

"So, sounds like she is the real deal," Jeannette murmured to him. She turned to look at Daniel. "Alphonse's last name is Monte. I'll shoot a pic of the card and get it to you."

"And to me," Gervais said.

"Of course!"

"Maybe we'll dine at his place again."

But then again...

Whoever was doing this did feel entitled. Maybe that meant they were entitled to end the lives of those they thought to be lesser human beings.

His message sent, he looked out the window. They had left the city of Reims behind and were traveling through countryside that was incredibly picturesque. Fields stretched out endlessly, some flat, some gently rolling. Some appeared to be freshly planted while others were rich with greenery. Now and then, they passed an area that seemed too wild, but just as beautiful with low brush and occasional wildflowers.

Jeannette was watching their drive as well. She murmured, "How beautiful it is out here."

"Yes, the landscape is beautiful," Gervais said. "And then you'll have the tour this afternoon, and you'll see more of the wine country. But also, I do hope you can see some of the wonders of Reims while you're here. It's truly a rich city in its architecture and so much more, Notre-Dame Saint-Jacques, Basilique Saint-Remi, the Palace of Tau... The artwork and history in all are amazing. Rather sad that you have come here and... Well, we all know. We signed up for this, and there are those good days when we save a life. All right...well, the first site is just ahead."

He pulled off the road, explaining, "This little stretch of land belonged to a small family vineyard, but the family died out about five years ago. The distant relatives are in Australia and have never been to France, and they don't want to run a vineyard. The land is up for sale. It's overgrown...but the owners have been negotiating with a few of the neighboring vineyards, and they can't be responsible—as I said, they've never been to France."

Daniel stepped out of the car, looking across the expanse of the field. Those fields that were planted were pristine in their order, no matter what their stage of growth.

This field...

The grass was long, and here and there were large clumps of small trees and bushes. The plants here, far from being any kind of grape or other wine fruit, were bushes, some thicker than others, some low to the ground, some rising higher.

"How long has this been vacant?" Daniel asked Gervais.

"Five, six years," Gervais said, shrugging. "Here, follow me."

A trail had been created of flattened grass and shrubbery, probably from forensic workers searching through the area. He and Jeannette followed Gervais through the recently created path until they came to an area by a small bush.

There were still markers on the ground, perhaps forgotten by the team or perhaps left until the case was closed—one way or another.

"This is where we found Patricia Gutterman, the young lady from Germany," Gervais said. "She was here, lying as if she slept, except…she was pale as snow, her eyes were closed… They called me immediately. The first young lady had already been found, another field just a ways up." He shook his head, looking over at Jeannette. "Then, of course, there was the young lady we saw yesterday morning, just after her completed autopsy."

"And she was found out here," Jeannette murmured. "I can't imagine poor Shelley, how shocked she must have been when a second body was found and identified as one of her new friends as well, and now the third…"

"The girls were all about the same age, and all rather on their own, from what I understand," Daniel said. "I'm wondering if…"

"What?" Jeannette asked.

"It doesn't sound as if they have the kind of families who would immediately demand results, as if they were more or less… Not friendless! I don't mean that at all, but…"

"Murders are often solved more quickly when parents or siblings hound the police day after day?" Gervais asked.

"Sad, but sometimes true. Maybe not even here, but possibly in someone's mind…"

"That implies they are getting to know these girls, that they're not just attacked after leaving a crowd," Gervais said.

"Aye," Daniel murmured. "Whoever did this met Shelley, Patricia and the others and talked with them. The killer is going to be someone Shelley would recognize."

"Quite possibly true," Gervais murmured, and then he frowned. Daniel noted he was watching Jeannette, who had started walking farther back into the wildness of the field.

"Jeannette?" Daniel called. She had walked deep into the field, far from the road.

She paused. But she didn't turn.

She bent down and then stood, looking back at them.

"What is it?" Gervais shouted.

She shook her head sadly. "These murders didn't just start. Please…not sleeping, not pristine. This victim has been here a while."

Daniel ran quickly to Jeannette's position and looked down.

Decayed, rotting material remained.

It covered bones and bits and pieces of dried flesh, long since rotted, long since ravaged by animals and insects.

Daniel closed his eyes for a minute.

Just how many corpses were there to be found in these vineyards, renowned around the world?

Four

Jeannette stood in the field by Gervais LaBlanc and Daniel and listened as one of LaBlanc's forensic experts spoke to him—in French. He was agitated and angry with himself, and she was only able to catch so many words. But the gist of his conversation had to do with the way they had created grids on the field after the body had been discovered here, and they had followed protocol going back into the field as far as had seemed reasonable and even possible when seeking evidence.

But they'd missed the remains of someone who had died long enough ago for creatures and the elements to have set in. And he was disgusted with himself.

Jeannette looked at Daniel, wishing she knew how to reassure the man. Gervais was giving him his full attention, ready to explain that no one could have possibly known beyond a reasonable distance there might be more.

"Daniel, tell him I believe I had to move a large branch, and I was way back from the road—they did what they could!"

"Monsieur, *s'il vous plaît!*" he murmured.

Daniel spoke for her as she had asked.

Finally, the man nodded, still looking pained and shaking his head. He went on to join a member of his team who was creating a larger grid to be explored.

"You found those remains no more than one hundred feet farther back from the grid they had created," Gervais told her. He frowned, looking at Daniel. "Only one hundred feet, I think. In kil—"

"Yes, one hundred feet nails it," Daniel assured him. "And Jeannette, hmm. Good find. No, terrible find, but it suggests this has been going on much longer than we suspected."

"Of course," Gervais said, "this may not be related—"

"I'm not a medical examiner," Jeannette said, "and the head is almost down to nothing but skull, and still... those remains belonged to a woman, probably a young one. But, of course," she murmured, indicating the doctor who was kneeling down by the remains, her two young assistants standing back, ready to transfer the remains from the ground to a gurney when she was ready, "I believe we'll know soon enough."

"We'll know age and sex, yes. I spoke with Dr. Allard, and she has suggested that the remains are so degraded she may not be able to tell us the cause of death. But..." Gervais let the word roll as he frowned, prompting Daniel to step in.

"If I understood correctly, I heard her say she believes there are cuts in a few of the bones, which she believes were antemortem," he told Jeannette.

Jeannette frowned in turn. "Then she was tortured or killed by being cut?"

"Possibly," Gervais said.

"Well, we were hoping to find something out here," Daniel said. "We wanted to make a discovery. And we did make a discovery," he added dryly. "Just not what we thought."

"Not what I'd hoped to find at all," Jeannette said.

Daniel set a hand on her shoulder and looked into her eyes. "Jeannette, she's been dead for a while. You having found her might at the very least help get justice for her and for all of them. Whether she was found or not doesn't change the fact that someone apparently killed her," he said softly.

She nodded, closing her eyes for a minute as she thought her first fears about his easy charm and almost boyish good looks meant nothing. He had what was often needed: a way with people. He had an empathy in his soul that was real. And...

She realized bizarrely at that moment she was attracted to him. Even as slight as their single day together had been, she felt closer to him than she did to many people she had known for years.

She gave herself a mental shake. They were standing in a field for the dead. This was not a time to worry about anything personal at all.

The remains of the woman were being transferred to the gurney.

Gervais turned to them. "Well, there are two more sites."

"Right. And we can't do anything more for that poor lass," Daniel murmured. "Should we move on? Of course, now we know this body has been here—"

"Don't worry. I have alerted both the national and

local police. This area will be combed now from front to back," Gervais assured them.

"Then we should move on," Daniel said. He looked at Jeannette. "I'll take the back seat again and give our new information to Mason and the rest of the team in Paris. Gervais, I believe Mason or Della will arrive in time for the autopsy. Is that all right?"

"Of course. Our doctors are as eager as anyone else to see this solved," Gervais said.

They headed toward the car with Gervais pausing just to confer briefly with the head of the forensic team working in the area.

As they walked on to the car, Gervais shook his head. "There is so little we can get out here. Time, nature and the elements—all play havoc with evidence."

"They do," Jeannette agreed.

When they reached the car, Daniel took the back seat as he had suggested. Jeannette slid into the front with Gervais again.

"As we drive, we will pass the road that leads to the Matisse estate," Gervais said. "I am sorry for Delphine. She will be distraught to learn we've found yet another body."

Will she be? Jeannette wondered. *Is her being nice a facade? The bodies are being found so very close to her property.*

"That will be to our left," Gervais continued. "Now to our right, the land belongs to one of the most popular and renowned houses. And then we will pass land that belongs to one of the *elitist* couples you heard about the other night from the young waiter, and the second estate is just past that, property that belongs to Tomas

Deauville and his wife, Giselle, and after that, the winery and castle owned by Leticia Montague and her husband, George."

"Castle?" Jeannette asked him.

"Small castle, built in the late 1700s by the Montague family. But I suppose having inherited a castle might have added to her belief that she is above others. Some seem to have forgotten all about the French Revolution," Gervais said, shrugging.

"I just keep thinking back to Madame Báthory," Jeannette told him. "Of course, she lived in a castle." She winced. "I've read a great deal about her. Some believe she was truly one of the most brutal and demented serial killers to ever exist. Others believe she was set up by family members who wanted her property. Some accused her of twelve murders, others suggest up to six hundred."

"If I remember my history, she tortured her victims—"

"And some suggest the killing started after her husband's death, and others say they started the torture and murder as a couple."

"But there you have it—torture," Gervais told her, frowning.

"And so far, the doctor has told us she sees cuts on the bones here," Jeannette said. "Perhaps the girl we just discovered was tortured."

"Why change their method of killing?" Gervais asked. "Go from torture to fairy-tale beauty?"

Jeannette shrugged, shaking her head. "I don't know and I may be entirely off. Frankly, I'm here because my last assignment had to do with victims discovered who were drained of blood. My Krewe teammates and

I were able to infiltrate a cult. They weren't torturing people—they were sacrificing them. At this moment, we don't know the motive behind these killings—other than someone is taking blood."

"And we are here at the second site, where the young American was found. We are in disputed land between a major house and the house of Deauville. And we're on land bordering their estate. Again, the body was discovered just off the road. One of the tour bus drivers—sitting high in his seat as he drove—thought he was seeing someone who had imbibed a bit too much wine and fallen asleep in the field. He called the police. The local police were the ones to discover her."

He pulled the car off the road. Daniel got out quickly. Jeannette joined him as he stood by the road and stared out at the field.

"Mason and Della are on their way to the autopsy," he told Jeannette and Gervais. "Maybe something will be discovered."

"And maybe not," Gervais said dully. "But…"

"I suggest we walk a bit of a distance in different directions and see if… Well, let's hope we don't see any more victims, but we'll go back farther into the field, at least."

Gervais nodded. "The body was discovered right there," he told them.

The body hadn't been left far off the road at all, Jeannette noted. She nodded. "We are getting the feel for the sites—both old and new," she told Gervais.

"Let's walk it," Daniel said.

They did. Moving in different directions, they walked. They spent at least thirty minutes at the task.

When they returned to the road, Gervais noted, "I think you're going to be too late for the tour. Because of the discovery of the body this morning..."

Jeannette glanced at her watch. They'd started out early, about eight in the morning, but it was true. They'd then spent hours at the last site once they'd discovered the body, and she hadn't once thought about the tour.

"We can take it tomorrow," Daniel said. "We have one more site. Gervais, is there a way to drop by and meet with Madame Matisse or with Tomas and Giselle Deauville—or Leticia Montague? We have our rooms at the B&B another night, but..."

"Admitting who you are may not matter?" Gervais asked him.

"Jeannette?" Daniel asked.

"Maybe we need to get everything we can from the *nice* one," Jeannette said. "I don't suppose it matters if she knows who we are at this point."

"Fine, last site, and then we head to see Delphine," Gervais said.

They never made it to see Delphine Matisse.

This time, Jeannette was not the one to discover the remains. Daniel had taken off with long strides as he walked deep into the overgrown field.

This time...the body was still in a middling stage of decay.

And while it couldn't possibly be...

Jeannette couldn't help but think that somehow she could still smell a hint of honey on the air as insects buzzed and buzzed around.

* * *

By the time they finished at the third site, the day was beginning to wane. But as he reported via phone to Mason, Daniel was surprised their leader suggested they return to Paris—if just for a few hours.

"Autopsy results on the latest victim won't be available until tomorrow morning, but I intend to be present for that. And I'm still meeting with the MEs tonight," Mason told him. "I know you want to take the tour, but I have Della, Luke and Carly heading to a stage show by a small local company. I would like to get to a lot of these smaller venues and see what's going on with them. There's a magic show you can just make if you come back."

"Magic show. All right. And then—"

"When it's over, you can go back to the bed-and-breakfast in Reims. Yeah, I know, it's a lot of driving."

"I never minded driving," Daniel said.

"Even on the wrong side of the road for you?" Mason inquired lightly.

"Aye, even on the wrong side of the road! We'll head in. I'll let the others know. I do want to get back here tomorrow. Not just because of the tour. I want Gervais to bring us to see our small local vineyard owners—houses of Matisse, Deauville and Montague."

"All right. Do you really think a vineyard owner could be involved in this?" Mason asked. "I believe the only way someone could have picked on the victims we know is by seeing them somewhere in Paris where they were able to get a conversation going. If we can get any kind of a suspect, Shelley might be able to tell us if they talked to him—or her—at any of the venues they attended."

"We can start by showing Shelley pictures of the vineyard owners," Daniel told him.

"Already done. She doesn't recognize any of them. But..."

"But people with money can hire others."

"Even for murder," Mason agreed. "All right. We're all on for tonight. I'll send you both the information you'll need."

"Right."

They ended the call and he walked over to Gervais and Jeannette to tell them the plan. Gervais nodded. "I believe, too, that the girls were targeted in Paris." He shook his head. "You will see tomorrow. When you're on the tour... Well, you're with others. So many would need to be involved, bus drivers—who do a head count—waiters, guides... It would be hard to make someone disappear in the middle of a tour."

"And each was last seen alive in Paris," Jeannette murmured. She looked at them both and smiled grimly. "So..."

"Back to your car," Gervais assured him.

In the back seat, Daniel looked at his messages.

"Gervais, are you going to the magic show with us?" he asked.

"No, I am meeting with Mason and our medical and forensic teams. Though again, this last autopsy will take place in the morning."

"So," Jeannette murmured, and she glanced to the back seat to meet Daniel's gaze. "We get to go to a magic show. Well, hmm, I always did love magicians!"

"A night out on the town in Paris," Daniel murmured. "What's not to like?"

Gervais dropped them back at the bed-and-breakfast so Daniel could pick up his car. He looked at the house.

"What?" Jeannette asked.

"I'm wondering again just how many people might have keys to this house."

"You think someone might come here? But Shelley is the one who stayed here—and she's the one who wasn't killed," Jeannette reminded him.

"There's nothing in your luggage but clothing?" Daniel asked her.

"Nothing. Everything is on me or in my bag. You?" She grimaced at him. "You're not carrying a purse or bag or anything. Not even a backpack."

He laughed. "Deep pockets. My gun is beneath my jacket, and my ID and wallet are in a pocket."

"So, we just leave clothing, maybe in a certain way, and find out if anyone else does have keys?"

"Let's do it. Quickly. We need to get to Paris if we're going to make the show."

After quickly setting up their clothing and luggage, they were on their way.

"Traffic," Daniel muttered. "Good thing our tickets are at the box office. We're going to just make it to the show." He winced. "We'll get food after."

"It's amazing, but after the bodies…" Jeannette murmured.

"Well, that can make you lose your appetite," Daniel agreed. "But like a car starts to sputter when it's almost empty, our bodies will start to complain to us. Let's see the show first. Maybe they sell popcorn."

"I'm ever hopeful, but it's a magic show not a cinema!" Jeannette reminded him.

She leaned back against the passenger seat and closed her eyes.

"Tired?"

She shrugged but did not open her eyes. "I was just thinking that two days ago I didn't even know you."

He laughed. "Do you wish you could go back?"

She shook her head, still not opening her eyes. "You're all right."

"Great. I was thinking the same thing about you. I mean you look like a college student, but—"

"College student?" she protested. "Oh! And you think you look mature and dignified? Mr. Rock Star!"

He laughed. "I meant it in the best way. You're a stunning woman, truly beautiful."

"Oh! Ah, thanks. And you're…"

"Not a stunning woman."

She laughed. "Nope, classically—*coolly*—handsome, like a rock star."

"I'll take it!" He gave her a quick smile before turning his eyes to the road. He grew serious then and asked her, "When…when did you find out that you were Krewe material?" This was his chance to get to know her a bit; they were in the car. They had been partnered up—and he had to admit, he was naturally curious about her backstory. Reims was considered easy access from Paris, but it was still a long drive. Maybe that meant it was time to share a bit about one another.

She shrugged. "My story isn't different from most. My favorite great-uncle passed away when I was about nine. I adored him. He was the guy who was up for anything—he'd take me to those restaurants themed toward kids where they have pizza and video games. I won the fourth-grade spelling bee and, to celebrate, he took me to Disney World. He passed away unexpectedly from a sudden heart attack. When my family and I were at the funeral and I was crying my eyes out, he came and sat by me. Of course, I was a kid, so I told my parents. My dad warned me not to say anything or else children's services might come and take me away. Almost everyone I know in the Krewe had similar things happen to them. We always had to keep the secret, because other people would think we were crazy and thought we needed to be put away in a juvenile mental facility. But…"

She paused, looking at him, smiling. "The great thing is this. I still get to see him. And he gets to tell me how proud of me he is. He doesn't like to hang around at the cemetery—even though our ancestor who fought in the Revolutionary War is also buried there in the family plot—but I know where he hangs out. He likes a local sports bar. I take my phone—or a friend from the Krewe—with me and get a table there and talk with him to tell him about my cases… I never felt cursed. I just knew to be careful. And you—I'll bet that your story is similar."

Daniel smiled, shaking his head. "I'm afraid to tell you. I'm a bit of a late bloomer—when it comes to the *talents* needed by the Krewe. You may not think I'm worthy once I do."

She frowned. "You mean that you can't—"

"No, I can. But it's recent. I always knew there was something. I could feel it. I'd know when there was a presence there. But it was only recently, our last case, when we met an extremely helpful ghost and…I could suddenly see clearly and hear clearly and… Well, it's all new to me. I'm not an old pro like you and the rest of the team."

He was surprised when she smiled at him. "But it's different for everyone and sometimes comes in late—as it did for you—for many. That doesn't make it any less valid."

"Thanks," he said lightly. "Of course, that's why I put in to join Blackbird and why I'm so very grateful that Blackbird exists—and that we could figure out a way to get a Scot on the team!"

"The point of Blackbird is to be international," Jeannette told him. She frowned suddenly. "Paris. We're on Île de la Cité—the oldest part of the city! Historians believe the area—an island in the middle of the Seine—had a Gallic settlement as early as 300 BC. The Lutetia and another Gallic tribe, the Parisii, were nearby, all establishing trade routes and more using the island. Then the Romans came in and then Germanic tribes. Then there were the Huns and the Franks and…"

Daniel laughed. "The point being there are surely millions of dead souls running around on Île de la Cité alone. But remember, we can only speak with them when they want to speak with us."

Jeannette nodded. "We could sure use some help on this."

"And until we do have help, we need to help ourselves," Daniel said. "Remember, that's why our respective countries and their law enforcement agencies teach us about evidence, motive, profiling, investigation techniques…"

She smiled and nodded, not looking his way. "Right. Of course. I just wish…"

"What?"

"I would like to know more about what the medical and forensic teams have to say," she told him.

"Mason will give us everything he learns, you know that. We must watch a magician. We get to see a fun show. Gee, just like punishment!" he teased.

"All right, all right. It's just we get on these things, and it feels like we need to keep moving until we get somewhere."

"Abracadabra," he said. "Who knows. Maybe we'll magically come up with a clue!"

Jeannette smiled. "I guess today was disturbing. We thought we were looking at one thing, and it turns out we were looking at another. Though I would assume with today's tech, we'll get identification on the bodies we discovered today. Someone must have reported them as missing."

"Maybe."

"What do you mean? Everyone knows someone!"

"That's true, but…whoever is doing this deliberately left the bodies to be discovered. Right by the side of the road. Well, the most recent bodies. Maybe—assuming the same killer or killers—they were disappointed that their handiwork took so long to be found. But according to Shelley, the girls we have identified were here because they earned the trips themselves, because they were more or less on their own. As we were talking about before—there was no one incensed and deter-

mined to hound a police station daily about their missing friend or relative."

"No one cared at first," Jeannette murmured.

"Pardon?"

Jeannette turned to look at him. "I am sorry. Back to
the Madame Báthory case. Supposedly, the first girls
who were tortured and killed were just poor girls from
the surrounding area who were lucky to be servants,
even to a cruel mistress. It didn't matter back then if
poor girls disappeared. I like to think that we've changed
in that respect, but...sometimes, you know, a politician's
kids or the child of a rich man goes missing and all the
powers that be lose their minds. But as Krewe," she
said firmly, "we won't let that happen. Anyway, this
part is fairly shared by all historians and scholars—
Madame Báthory was known to fly into rages; and
according to historians, she possibly had fits or sei-
zures. But that's not the point. The point is that no one
cared when those girls disappeared. The case against
her never made it into court until daughters of the lesser
nobility—who were there to gain prestige, to learn
courtly manners, whatever—began to disappear. And
back to the point, back then—or even now—when
you're *someone*, it seems people pay attention."

"All right, we have two people murdered in the past
who were discovered today. We have no idea who they
are as of yet. They were possibly tortured. Now we
have three new victims. They were not tortured. The
first victims were more or less hidden in the back of the
fields, but the new victims were left just off the road.
Theories are great, but again, we don't twist evidence
to fit our theories," he reminded her.

"I know that," Jeannette assured him. "And I don't intend to fit anything into anything. And as you've said, we're not in Hungary, Slovakia, Transylvania or Romania. We're in France! Oh, and we're almost back to Paris! To see a magic show. Wow!" She glanced his way. "If only I were five!"

Daniel laughed. "Well, come on! We'll pretend we're five. Besides, this guy may be good."

"Who is this guy?"

"Monsieur Illusion Incroyable."

"Half French, half English?"

Daniel laughed. "Illusion—same in both languages. *Incroyable*—incredible."

"Ah, so Mister Incredible Illusion," Jeannette said.

"Exactly as they advertise in Paris for the English-speaking tourists. And you'll be glad to know we're almost there. Oh, by the way, Shelley told Gervais's son the magic show was one of the favorite things they did—agreed on by all."

"Did they meet the illusionist?"

"They did."

"Then we must, too."

"Way ahead of you. Mason signed us up for backstage passes after the show. And…Paris! We've returned—we're in the city, and once I fight traffic…"

"Don't fight traffic, just go with it!"

Daniel laughed again. "Don't worry. I'm driving like a Continental, I promise."

They reached the small theater where the marquee announced the amazing magician was having a three-month run. At the box office, he picked up their tickets.

"Nice. We're right up front," he told Jeannette.

"Where we can study his sleight of hand!" she said.

They found their seats, where they had a tremendous view of the stage. French rock songs began to play and the group playing was very good, the music making it immaterial as to what language the songs were being sung in.

Then the monsieur of incredible illusion made his entrance. He just suddenly appeared in a burst of silver-gray fog.

Trap door beneath him, easy enough!

He went on to introduce himself and his lovely assistant, a pretty brunette in a skimpy outfit consisting of a feathered bra-top and split skirt that glittered with her every movement.

Daniel studied the magician himself. He was in his late twenties or early thirties, old enough to appear experienced and capable, young enough to be charming and handsome. The stage was set with a glass-enclosed box, a trunk and several stands. And with sleight of hand, all eyes were on the magician as he spoke.

A man who could easily charm others.

He performed much of what might customarily be seen at such a show, but he called upon audience members frequently, pulling a rabbit from one woman's bag, a bird from the baseball cap of a young man and then introducing his special disappearing box—and calling on an audience volunteer.

Hands went up throughout the theater.

But the man stared straight at Jeannette, which was easy enough as they were seated in the second row.

"Mademoiselle? Will you be so kind?"

Daniel knew the magician had taken Jeannette by

surprise; she was silent, just staring at him for several seconds.

Then she shrugged, gave the magician a brilliant smile and rose. She walked toward the stage as the audience gave her a round of applause.

He wasn't sure why he felt such a sudden grip of unease. They were at a magic show—in the company of perhaps five hundred audience members along with those working the show. And he knew it was ridiculous.

But they were investigating heinous murders.

And the master of illusion meant to make her disappear.

He gritted his teeth, well aware he would be an idiot to object.

And still…

Jeannette was charming on stage as she apologized for her poor use of the French language, but she managed *pardonnez-moi* and *merci* and her name just fine. She went on to explain she was there with him—her cousin—and she loved magic.

Then she was ushered into the box.

His assistant didn't appear to help with drapes to cover the box.

Rather, the same fog suddenly arose—and just as suddenly disappeared.

And the box was empty.

"Voilà!" the master illusionist declared and received tremendous applause from the audience.

"Où est la dame?" he demanded of his audience.

Where, indeed, part of him wondered with great anxiety.

And the agent within him knew it was an extra bonus

in their work that Jeannette would understand the working methods in the magician's theater.

He clapped his hands, announcing in French that she would reappear.

The fog rose...

And fell.

There was no sign of Jeannette.

Daniel almost jumped out of his seat, logic reminding him the show was just one of many, many venues the girls had attended; a man wasn't going to take a chance of kidnapping, committing murder or even bloodletting in the front of such a crowd.

Except even the magician appeared to be frowning and seemed concerned as he repeated, *"Où est la dame, où est la dame?"*

Daniel jerked out of his seat. No help for it, he was growing more and more concerned.

Exactly! Where the hell is she?

Five

Jeannette was surprised by the smoothness with which the magician's "magic" worked. She was standing in the box, and then she was down and rising again, but in something that was moving lower and lower…

She ducked and smiled at herself as she realized she was back on stage already—just in the trunk instead of in the box.

She heard a cry of dismay from the audience.

Then the sound of footsteps and the magician talking.

Of course, it was all fine…

She heard him as he walked over to his trunk and tapped on it, and she popped up and accepted his hand to rise and stepped over the edges.

She was sincerely thanked and soundly applauded before she was able to leave the stage and make her way back to her seat. Daniel was standing, as were others in the audience, allowing her to pass and take her seat. He didn't appear to be enjoying the show. She frowned, looking at him before sitting down. He shrugged and gave his head a little shake, indicating he'd tell her later.

The magician ended his show, and the band played again as the audience exited.

They showed their special tickets and a man in a suit allowed them in the line to see the magician. There were several others who had backstage passes as well; Daniel indicated that they should let the others go first.

They did. And she smiled, showing Daniel, who seemed distracted, when the magician pulled a euro from a little boy's ear. The child was delighted, and to his credit the magician appeared equally happy.

He seemed to be a man who truly enjoyed others and wanted to make them happy. She realized she didn't even know his name.

That was easily solved. Daniel stepped forward, offering the magician his hand, and introducing himself as Daniel Murray and bringing her forward to introduce herself as his cousin, Jeannette LaFarge.

The magician, striking in his white shirt and black tux, greeted them effusively.

"My lovely new assistant!" he said to Jeannette. "Your cousin was wonderful on stage," he told Daniel. "Yes, I speak English," he quickly added, laughing. "I had an American grandmother. My name is Jules Bastien. And magic as well as entertaining kids and those who want to be kids is the joy of my life!"

"Well, you are incredibly good at what you do, Mr. Bastien," Daniel told him.

"Jules, and, like it or not," he said cheerfully, "I will call you Daniel and your cousin Jeannette!"

"We like it fine," Jeannette told him.

"I need to ask you about something not quite so happy," Daniel told the man, pulling out his phone. "We have a friend here, Shelley. She came to see your show with a few of her friends—girls she met here who were all on their dream trips to Paris—and three of them wound up dead. And I'm wondering if you saw them and saw if they went anywhere with anyone."

He had his phone out; the pictures of the dead girls as they were in life were on his phone.

Jules stared at the phone and then at Daniel. His face appeared to register true horror. Then he went off in French, speaking so quickly Jeannette doubted even Daniel understood a word he said.

Jules sank into his chair. Tears filled his eyes. Then he gave himself a shake, physically and mentally, Jeannette imagined.

"These…these are the girls on the news? Drained of blood… *Oh, mon dieu!* They…they were lovely, they were in the show, they came backstage. *Mais oui*, yes, yes, I knew them, I talked with them!"

"We are so sorry," Daniel said. "But as you can imagine, our friend Shelley is devastated. We were hoping that maybe you saw something…"

His face scrunched. "My mother was even here that night. She chatted with them back here, so very nice, she said they proved good manners and kindness could be found in every country in the world. Was someone watching them…? Did they meet up with someone after the show? *Mais, oui!* They met up with me at a café!"

Daniel and Jeannette stared at one another, surprised. And naturally…

"No, no. No, no! I would never hurt these lovely ladies. They made the night for me. I had no idea, I… There are cameras! Not backstage, not below where…

where magic is done," he said dryly. "But there are cameras. You can see who came to the show. In fact…there was a man. A man who came to see the show. And he was at the same café later."

"Did you know him?"

"No, but all our ticket sales are by credit card only." He lifted his hands in a lost manner. "I am not an accountant but I have one. For me… I employ him and my assistant and that is all. Each act here manages their own box office. My accountant says that the way to stay clean is by credit cards, all reported. So, if you think someone was here…"

His voice trailed and he looked both confused and suspicious.

"You are not Shelley's friends. You are police. But you are American."

Daniel nodded. "Special Agent LaFarge is not my cousin—she is my partner. We are with a special international force, which has been invited in."

"Of course, of course. *Mon dieu.* But…it will help, right? The tapes from the entry? I can show you the man who came to the performance and seemed to have followed us to the café. I thought that I had a fan. But… perhaps he followed them!" Jules said.

"That is more than possible. And we appreciate getting your security tapes. And if we may, we'll send in a sketch artist and you can describe this man for us as well, if you will."

"I will do anything. Anything," he said, shaking his head sadly again. "This is… It is so, so horrible. I can't… I didn't know… You know, you hear on the news about horrible things but you never think that they will touch you. So much worse for their families, but... I knew them! I wondered why Patricia did not respond to my calls!"

"They all gave you their phone numbers?" Jeannette asked.

"Just as I gave them mine."

"You really befriended them," Jeannette said. "Thank you for your help. We'll have someone come here—discreetly, of course—for that sketch and to collect the security tapes. Thank you. They'll come right away."

He nodded dully.

"I'm sorry if you intended to leave now—" Jeannette began.

"No, no. I want to help... I... Shelley! Shelley, she is all right?" he asked hopefully.

Daniel nodded. "She is fine."

"But—if the other girls were taken—" Jules began.

"Excuse me," Daniel said, stepping back.

As Daniel pulled out his phone to call Mason and tell him about Jules and the girls at the magic show, Jeannette continued to speak gently to the magician.

Unless Jules was truly a superb actor as well as magician, he was devastated by what he had learned.

Then again, Daniel had come across those who could lie incredibly well, cry on cue and fake emotion to a tee during his days working law enforcement.

Mason knew, of course, that Daniel and Jeannette were driving back to Reims for the night. However, he did suggest they stay until he was able to get someone else out there.

When he finished the call, Jeannette was talking to Jules about the boxes on stage.

"Patricia played your part when the girls came to the show," he said. He managed to give her a sad smile. "And she was like you, going along with the fall in the glass box and rise into the trunk. My assistant is usually there, below in the staging basement, explaining what happened."

He frowned in sudden panic. "But...*mon dieu!*" He went on in French, speaking quickly. Daniel caught the gist of it.

Jules didn't know where his assistant was.

"Marni is usually here, talking to people in line... Did she speak to you when the box fell?" Jules asked Jeannette.

"No one spoke to me," Jeannette told him.

Jules shook his head, heading to the double doors that led from his greeting room. "I don't know where Marni is... Now that you've shown me those pictures..."

"Let's check the show security team and the video. Maybe she had to leave suddenly, a family matter," Jeannette suggested, gently setting a hand on his arm.

"Security, yes. I must ask Nils, he might know... It's so chaotic when the show ends, maybe she told him where she was going. I don't..."

He stopped speaking. And Daniel could quickly see why. His "lovely assistant" was in street clothing, a maxi dress and jacket, and she was limping her way to him, speaking in French, her words hurried and upset.

Jules let out a sigh, shaking his head. Daniel turned to Jeannette and started to tell her what he had understood.

"She tripped when she was heading down to make sure that the box and trunk worked smoothly and the volunteer didn't panic," Daniel said.

"And a guest using the restroom heard her cry out

and got her to her dressing room—it was lucky the guest was a nurse and found a wrap for her ankle in their emergency medical kit," he explained.

Jeannette nodded. "And she's so sorry!" she said softly.

He nodded.

Marni and Jules began a rapid dialogue with the magician assuring his assistant he wasn't angry in the least, he was just so relieved to see her.

As they talked, they heard a bit of a commotion at the end of the hallway.

Daniel saw that Luke Kendrick had arrived with another man, the sketch artist or tech with the French police.

He and Jeannette could leave for the trip back to Reims. But he realized Jeannette had never met Luke, so he introduced the two. Then Luke explained that Carly and Della were still working other angles, but the communication there seemed to be great; he'd had a man meet him almost immediately who was ready to go work with Jules on a sketch.

Luke Kendrick was a tall man, an inch over Daniel's six-three, with a lean face, striking green eyes and a reassuring manner. Jeannette greeted him warmly as Luke told her he'd heard all about her from Mason. They were delighted to have her on the team.

Jules and Marni watched them, frowning.

Daniel realized Marni knew nothing about the murders of the women Jules had met during the show. Tears stung Jules's eyes again as he explained; Marni was horrified as she held his hands and shook her head.

"Only Shelley… Only Shelley is still…alive!" Jules said.

Marni closed her eyes and hung her head in horror. She spoke English fluently as well, it seemed, because she looked up at them all and said softly, "We've all seen the news, of course! One would need to be deaf and blind to have missed it! But that we had met the young women, that they were here..."

She shuddered in fear herself.

"Nils and I will see you home safely!" Jules told her.

"Great idea," Jeannette said. "Everyone must be very, very careful."

"Shelley..." Jules murmured.

"Don't worry. Shelley will not be taken," Daniel said firmly. He handed the man one of their cards. "Please, help my colleague Luke now. The man you're talking about may be guilty of nothing except watching pretty women. But...all our numbers are on this card. So please, call if you see anything—or anyone. If you see this man again or anyone behaving suspiciously in any manner whatsoever, please."

"Oh, I do so swear!" Jules said passionately.

"I've got this," Luke told him. Daniel smiled.

He and Jeannette turned to leave at last.

"And you thought we'd be useless at the magic show," he murmured.

"Well, the fact that Jules saw this man may mean nothing," she murmured. "Then again..."

"Then again?"

"He is a hell of a magician," Jeannette said, looking at him. "Maybe he's a hell of a killer, too—one able to make a performance out of a pack of lies. Though maybe..."

"Maybe?"

"There's Marni. The disappearing assistant," Jeannette stated.

"What do you think might have really caused her to disappear? Not a magician's wand, that's for sure!"

"No," Jeannette agreed, "not a magician's wand. But we will have something…"

"Video. It may help us. And credit card receipts."

"Here's hoping," Jeannette said as they reached the car. "And still…"

"Still?"

"It's a long drive!" She shrugged and grimaced, looking his way. "Maybe I'll take a bit of a nap."

"Yes, sleep away," he told her.

"If only. I will be going over everything we saw and heard in my mind the entire way. Isn't it too bad we don't have switches for our minds? Like it's time to rest, so let's turn off?"

He grinned back at her. "That's why you're good at what you do," he told her. "The car is just ahead."

He pointed to the car. But Jeannette paused. Looking down the road, she saw a small medieval church. It wasn't one of the grand cathedrals, but it was a beautiful period building and it was surrounded by a churchyard.

"Do you think that…"

"That there might be dead people in the cemetery?" Daniel asked dryly.

"Daniel!"

"Sorry, I guess…we'll take a quick walk. But do you really think some random soul is going to be able to help us?"

"Only if they saw something," Jeannette said.

She paused at the front of the church where she

could read that it had been founded and built in 1785. Gothic pillars rose to beautiful arches; cherubs or angels seemed to dance above them.

The graveyard surrounding the church was equally atmospheric. It was beautiful and charming with aging marble and stone and funereal statues, crosses and more.

"Interesting architecture. It was built just four years before the start of the French Revolution," she murmured.

"A ten-year war, in essence, with Napoleon rising at the end to compromise the ideals he supposedly believed in when he declared himself emperor," Daniel said. "He was probably one of the greatest military commanders the world has ever seen. But…"

"Absolute power corrupts absolutely?" Jeannette asked.

"I'm not a student of the French Revolution," he said with a shrug. "But… Well, the man went into exile, made it back to power and then went into exile a second time. Oh, I understand he allowed slavery again in French colonies—not so nice by my book."

"And the United States fought the Civil War to end slavery," Jeannette said. "And we still haven't stamped it out across the world! But—"

"My point is just that people are…people. You know." He gave a little shudder. "The guillotine was supposed to be a humane way to execute someone. Except…"

"Except!" a quiet voice broke in. "Can you imagine the emotional agony as one is led to the guillotine, set into the structure, awaiting the fall of the blade?"

They were walking alongside a low stone wall. Beyond it were numerous graves. Fine angels stood guard over many sites, family tombs rose high above the ground and handsome aging memorials dotted the place. But the voice didn't come from the graveyard.

It came from behind Jeannette and she turned quickly, startled—even though she'd hoped to find a remaining soul to help them.

The woman standing behind them had been about forty at her death. She had a serene smile, and she seemed amused, perhaps because she had drawn a re-action from Jeannette. Her apparel seemed to be pre-Victorian. She wore a corset, a corset cover, a petticoat, or a pannier, all in shades of blue. Her hair was secured at her nape and a blue ribbon was threaded through it.

"Except?" Jeannette said. "You speak English?"

The woman seemed startled. "You hear me clearly," she said.

Jeannette and Daniel both nodded.

"Two…two who see and hear me, oh, one can go years and years! Well, then, hello! *Bonjour!* Dear young sir!" she told Daniel. "You will forgive me. My English is American English, and you are a Brit, are you not?"

"Scottish," Daniel told her.

She nodded safely. "And you, dear mademoiselle, are American!"

"I am," Jeannette told her. "Jeannette LaFarge and this gentleman is Daniel Murray."

"The pleasure is mine," she told him. "Mademoi-selle Henriette Beaumont. I was in awe of the Ameri-cans when they gained their independence, and so my English is theirs! Oh! And I fear I may promise you that the guillotine was quick—but you are right. Knowing you are about to meet the blade… Terrifying! And yet, it was so important to me to meet that blade showing no fear. So much was so very wrong with our feudal society and the king's refusal to see to our freedoms… but! I'm sorry, I fathom now you were seeking help from someone…physically departed from this world?"

"What happened to you?" Jeannette asked, forgetting her own quest. She couldn't imagine the horror of knowing she was going to be executed.

Their new friend sighed softly. "I spoke out," she said. "But…but now, I have been able to see the world change. Sometimes I wish I could shake people and remind them we must respect one another, that we are all human, but…but I have seen good things, too! So, how may I help you?"

"There is someone here in Paris or in Reims who is murdering women, killing them, draining them of blood," he said.

"I have seen the news," she told them sadly, shaking her head. "I fear I cannot tell you who is doing this."

"Have you seen anything unusual?" Daniel asked her. "Three of the women most recently killed were at the magic show just a block over. Then they were at a café, which I believe is right around the corner. Did you see anything of interest?"

Henriette was quiet and thoughtful.

"Will you come back to see me?" she asked. "I have a few friends, a few who have also lingered, who—" she paused, smiling "—*haunt* that café for the rich smell of the coffee and the large-screen television there."

"We must travel back out to Reims tonight," Jeannette told her. "But we can come back. We would so appreciate anything you might tell us!"

"Are you looking for a loved one?" she asked, her brows furrowing with the pain she was feeling for them.

"We are law enforcement," Daniel explained. "Part of an international force. We were asked here by the French police."

"Because they know you speak with the dead?"

Jeannette looked at Daniel and then shook her head. "No, they don't. But we are part of an agency in the United States that recognizes others with our gifts and…we have a good solve rate," she told Henriette. "So…"

"That is so wonderful. I will do all that I can to help you," Henriette promised. "But you must understand that…well, even being dead, we only see what we see."

"We understand that," Daniel assured her. "And we are eternally grateful for anything that you tell us—any little clue can make a difference."

"But you are going to Reims," Henriette said.

"We will do a tour and some investigation but return tomorrow night," Jeannette told her.

"Then find me here. I will wait by the large statue of St. Michael there, beyond the stone wall and beneath the archway of trees. Midnight?"

"Midnight!" Jeannette promised.

Daniel was smiling at the woman as he shook his head. "I am so grateful we found you—or that you found us."

Henriette smiled. "I like to think that I remain to help. I was able to see the French Revolution through to fruition. Now…well, I have not left this plane of existence, and so I feel that I remain to help. I am grateful to do so."

"I wish I could hug you," Daniel said.

She laughed. "I will hug you!"

She enveloped him, and he looked over her shoulder at Jeannette, grimacing from the cold.

Then she stepped back and said, "Get going! It is a bit of a drive to Reims."

"Yes, it is. And thank you!" Jeannette said.

Not really thinking, she grabbed Daniel's hand and they started down the street together. She realized, as they neared the car, what they were doing.

And she released him. He didn't seem to notice one way or the other.

"That was a great idea! You are incredible!" he told her.

She smiled. "Uh—thanks! It was just an idea. And she didn't know anything—"

"But she may find out something. And…this is why I wanted so desperately to be part of the Krewe—part of Blackbird!" he told her. "And I didn't think of such a thing, but…Jeannette, you are the most amazing partner!"

"Well, thank you. You're not so bad yourself," she told him.

"Feel free to nap," he told her as they got into the car.

"I just might do that. No, never mind. I won't turn off. I'll keep you company. Let's move onward and hope…"

"Hey. A tour tomorrow. How bad can it be?" he asked.

"Never, never, ask that question! Because sometimes," she warned him, "you get to find out!"

Six

"That's Gervais's car," Daniel said, frowning as they reached Delphine Matisse's bed-and-breakfast in Reims.

"That's his car, so where's Gervais?" Jeannette murmured.

"Inside?" Daniel suggested, looking at her and arching a brow.

"Quite possibly. As you noted, there could be dozens of keys out there. But…"

"Yep, a tourist leaves with a key, you just charge them for it and get a few more old-fashioned keys cut. But as far as Gervais having one… Let's assume he's seen Delphine Matisse in our absence, and she gave him a key. Which means, of course, that while it may be confusing to her as it is to other people in France, she now knows that we're law enforcement," Daniel said. He hesitated and turned to her. "Thank you. Seriously. I knew forever that there was something I couldn't quite touch. Then with the Krewe… But thank you for thinking we could find help today. I guess I'm not really there yet."

She smiled. "As far as a partner goes," she assured him, "you're there."

"Thanks," he said softly. He wanted to linger longer. To say more and he wasn't sure what. But they couldn't. In fact, if Gervais was in the house, they needed to move.

They headed on in with Daniel using his key to open the door. As they suspected, Gervais was sitting on the sofa in the parlor.

"You're here," Gervais said, "at last."

"And you're here. I thought you were meeting with the medical and forensic teams and Mason Carter and—"

"I did. Then I quickly drove back out here," Gervais told them, shaking his head. "We did our best to keep the new discoveries from hitting the media, and I'm not sure we did it well at all. And once this goes on the air, with the things that were done…"

"Autopsy results aren't until tomorrow, right?" Daniel said.

Gervais nodded dully. "But one of our people took a long look at the bones and…remains from the first field. It's impossible to tell time of death but…there are cuts on the bones. Many, many cuts. And—" he paused, shaking his head "—I spoke with Dr. Domini, one of our head people. He said he suspects that the cuts were done while the woman was alive, and death would have been slow and miserable. No fingerprints, obviously, but they were able to get a dental impression. And while I just started going through files here, it looks like three months ago, a young woman named Michelle Andre went missing. She was an orphan and grew up in a home. She left when she was eighteen and lived on the streets. Yes, Paris has many homeless, tens of thousands, I fear. She was finally reported missing by friends when they hadn't seen her in any of her usual haunts for a week. Naturally, her disappearance wasn't considered red-letter—such young women easily move on to other places. And when one such person disappears, well it's legal for an adult to move on to another city. But now…"

"You think the remains we discovered belong to Michelle Andre?" Daniel asked.

"I can't help but wonder," Gervais said. "After the meeting I heard about your discussions with the magician and drove out here to catch up with you."

"Did you rent a room from Madame Matisse?" Jeannette asked him, confused.

Gervais smiled. "No. I thought you might have gotten here before me." His smile faded and he frowned. "The door was open."

"Open?"

"Yes."

Daniel looked at Jeannette, arching a brow.

"Gervais, give us a minute, will you?" he asked. "We left a locked door. We'll just check our things."

He and Jeannette looked at one another and split from the parlor, walking to their separate rooms. He had left shirts and pants folded in different ways in his bag.

And it was obvious. Someone had been through his luggage.

He met Jeannette back in the hall. She looked at him and nodded. They returned to the parlor where Gervais was standing, frowning as he looked at the two of them.

"Someone has been in here in our absence," Daniel told him. "They must suspect something—they went through our luggage."

"Then this isn't safe!" Gervais said. "I have a room in a hotel in Reims. You must—"

"Stay here," Jeannette said firmly.

"But we do not want to lose the lives of American and Scottish investigators while searching for this killer," Gervais said.

"We're fine," Daniel told him. "We will tag team."

"Tag team?" Gervais said.

"Sleep in shifts, watch. We have already been very careful," Jeannette assured him.

"We suspected someone might come in, that there were many keys out in the world somewhere. Madame Matisse is not a hotelier—there is no security. And while Shelley is the only one of the four friends who met on the tour that day who is still with us, she was staying at this bed-and-breakfast. There may be an answer here. And if someone does come in the night, we'll be ready," Daniel said.

"I will get patrol out here!" Gervais said.

"No, no, Gervais. We need any chance we might get to find out what is going on," Jeannette said. "Please, we have weapons. We know how to use them. And we know how to work as a team."

Gervais shook his head. "As you wish. And the plan—"

"Tomorrow, we will take the early tour and see if anything whatsoever pops out from it," Daniel told him.

"I think that you call them *throwaway people*," Gervais said, shaking his head and staring blankly ahead. "The lost…homeless, those…"

"You're upset that the disappearance of Michelle Andre didn't bring about a bigger investigation?" Jeannette asked him quietly.

Gervais nodded. "It's just that...I had people working the case. And what they learned was tragic, heartbreaking. Her parents died when she was five. She was shuffled from household to household, and there were allegations of abuse at the last home where she lived. Her friends admitted she was surviving as a prostitute and that she dabbled in drugs. She'd talked about going to America, Canada or Australia. We questioned dozens of people. And in the end..."

"Gervais, that is not on you," Jeannette told him. "No one could have known they needed to go through every field in France to try to find her. And..."

She glanced at Daniel.

"You're afraid there are more. You believe that this murder spree began a long time ago, but the killers started with the homeless and the down and out?" he asked Gervais.

"Two bodies. Today, we discovered two more bodies. As you said, these fields are endless, yes. Most of the fields are worked for the product that makes this region so famous. But as you saw...not every stretch of earth is used for growing at all times. And just as in all major cities—" Gervais paused, looking frustrated "—we have people who become lost in the fringes of society and they become vulnerable, easy prey for those with cruel intentions!"

"You said you have teams out searching the fields," Daniel reminded him. "If there are more bodies out there, your people will find them now."

He nodded. "I don't suppose there is a country in the free world where such people do not exist. And in other countries, sometimes, the lost and hopeless are openly considered fair game!"

Jeannette walked over to the man. Gervais LaBlanc had a flawless reputation. Daniel knew that Jeannette had been given the man's résumé just as he had. LaBlanc had a faultless service record through the years. He had entered law enforcement because he cared and he had risen through the ranks. That this was happening and had happened on his watch was appalling to him.

"Gervais," Jeannette reminded him gently. "There is a truism that we hear in my country which I believe embraces the world. We cannot control the actions of others—we can control our reactions to them. And you, monsieur, respond and react in the best way possible. When you know something, you react. That is what we do now. We can't change the past. We can't bring the dead back to life. But we can find justice for them. You have a small army behind you, and you have us. We have a motto in the Krewe—we don't stop until a case is solved."

Gervais LaBlanc looked at Jeannette and grimaced, nodding slowly. "It just appalls me that this has been going on beneath our noses!"

"But we know now," Daniel reminded him.

Gervais stood suddenly. "I am off to my hotel room. Take your tour in the morning. Then, I believe, it will be time to speak with the small vineyard owners near the fields where the dead have been found. Someone knows something!"

"And we'll have a sketch and video surveillance," Daniel reminded him.

"I can, at the least, see that a patrol car drives by through the night. Cars do patrol Reims, you know," Gervais reminded him.

"That will be fine. And we have your number on speed dial," Jeannette said.

"Of course," Gervais said. "Then, you must get to sleep. In shifts!"

"In shifts," Daniel said.

They walked Gervais to the door. When he was out, Daniel looked around the room. There was a heavy armchair in the circle of furniture central to the parlor.

He pulled it over to the front door; someone would have to create a great deal of noise to get the door open and push the chair back far enough to enter.

"Good. Back door?" Jeannette asked.

"Let's find something."

They did. They rigged the back door with a cord that stretched to the refrigerator.

"We'll need to undo all this in the morning," Jeannette murmured. "And the windows. There are windows everywhere."

He nodded. "I'll take first shift."

"All right. But first," Jeannette murmured.

"First?"

"We have towers. Let's see what we can see."

"All right," he agreed.

She headed back out to the parlor and the stairs that led to the home's observation tower toward the west.

The night was quiet. The view of the lights and the

city with its amazing architecture and skyline was beautiful, even in the night.

The yard below them was clear.

"We need sleep," Daniel reminded her.

"We do. You're sure—"

"Go to sleep. I'll be right in the parlor. You'll keep the door open."

She nodded, looking at him for a moment, and then telling him, "Make sure you wake me to give yourself at least four hours!"

"I promise," he told her.

She nodded and started to head into her bedroom. But she paused and looked back at him. "Actually, wouldn't it be too easy if someone tried to break in, knowing who and what we really are, to kill us in our sleep? Easy solve since, of course, they'd never get past the chair!"

He grinned. "Easy solve. Go to sleep."

She walked on in, and he looked around the room as he wondered what he could do to stay awake. He flicked on the television and was surprised to discover it was set on a British channel that was giving the news in English.

Of course, the strange murders in the Paris environs were taking precedence. He listened; it was suspected there were more dead than the three young women so recently discovered, but the anchor did not have verification of that fact. There were a few shots of Gervais, speaking with reporters, begging people to love Paris— but to do so carefully. To enjoy the wine region and all the environs—but to be careful. Then, as reporters began to surge at him, voicing questions in many languages, he put his hand up. Surrounded by officers, he moved on into the offices and labs where he was meeting with Mason and the forensic and medical teams.

The footage had been taken just before dark.

"Gervais, we will not let this rest!" he murmured aloud.

He thought about gun laws in France, something he had, of course, studied as soon as he'd become a Blackbird agent and known about the assignment. Not that any of the victims appeared to have been shot, but as UK law enforcement, he had learned you didn't need a gun to kill.

France was a combination between the "Wild, Wild West" laws of the United States and handguns not being available to the average citizen in some other countries. Special indications that a person needed to protect one's self were needed for the possibility of that kind of carry. But hunters were allowed to have shotguns and rifles. They had to be licensed, and the person could not be guilty of a felony and had to be mentally stable.

The victims had not been shot—not as indicated so far. But that didn't mean a gun hadn't been used to force them into the situations in which they had been killed. It was strange, enough to make him wonder if they were after different killers. It appeared the first bodies had been ravaged with cuts, tortured. And the last three...

He shook his head.

He heard something; he wasn't sure what it was, just something that wasn't the TV. He didn't know if it had come from inside or outside.

He got up, standing dead still, listening. He heard his own heartbeat.

But Jeannette came hurrying out of the bedroom, looking at him with a frown.

"You heard it?" she said.

"I heard—something. No clue what!" he told her.

She nodded. She had changed into a long flannel nightgown—but she was carrying her Glock and was ever ready.

"I'm going to move the chair," he said quietly.

He did so, moving it as quietly as he could. And then they waited, both ready for whoever might have arrived.

The door opened. While there was a light at the entry, it didn't help much. They saw a figure in black, masked, stunned, and dead still as he stared at the two of them, waiting for him at the entry.

But then he ran.

Daniel took off after him, aware that Jeannette was running at his side. He was fast and he knew it—but so was the black-masked figure running down the street, who veered into another yard and disappeared around a house.

"Left!" he shouted to Jeannette.

"Right!" she called back, veering around. If they were lucky, if there was a fence or a wall in back, the person would be caught between.

They were out of luck.

No wall, no fence. Daniel gritted his teeth as he ran, dismayed to see the rear of the house led back into darkness—and an overgrown field—right into the city.

But he tore into the darkness, certain he saw the black-clad figure just ahead.

And he wasn't mistaken.

Plowing through the foliage, he was able to take a single leap and bring the intruder down.

Jeannette was right behind him, her Glock out and aimed.

Daniel stood, dragging the person up, warning, "Don't! Don't fight!"

He went still. Daniel reached over, pulling the mask off the man's face. It was dark, but he knew he'd never seen the man before. He was late twenties or early thirties, dark-haired, light-eyed, clad in a black long-sleeved knit shirt and black trousers—and he was now minus the mask Daniel had removed. *"Qui êtes-vous?"* he demanded.

The man started to laugh. "Bad French!" he said.

"Fine, who are you and why were you breaking into the house?" he demanded.

The man started to move, and Jeannette warned him, "Don't—I'm permitted to carry this Glock and my aim is damned good. Since you understand English so well, I'm sure you're understanding me."

"I'm not... Fine. You're Americans... Well, she is. I don't know what the hell you are," the man said.

"Scottish," Daniel told him.

"Oh, now that's even funnier!"

"Jeannette, cover him, please."

She was in her flannel nightgown. He had his phone in his pocket. He called Gervais and told him, "Caught a guy trying to break in," he said.

"Really? They're going to believe a foreigner over me? I was minding my own business when you suddenly attacked me!"

"No, I don't think it's going to go that way," Daniel told him with a shrug.

Almost instantly, they heard sirens.

The man didn't look so cocky. Officers came out into the field; they'd obviously spoken with Gervais and immediately cuffed the man despite his furious protests in raging French.

"Monsieur, mademoiselle, Chief Inspector LaBlanc will meet you at the station at your convenience," one of the officers told them.

"Thank you," Jeannette said. "We'll be right there. I'll just, um, get dressed!"

The officer nodded, then he and the others left with the intruder. Daniel realized he was still holding the man's black ski mask—if that's what it was. It had covered his head and his face with just the openings for his eyes, nose and mouth.

Daniel looked at Jeannette.

"This is not really professional attire," she said dryly.

He laughed, and then his laughter faded. Not professional, but sweetly stunning. Her hair was free, waving around her shoulders. She wore a long flannel gown well. She was the perfect…partner. He knew that more with every minute spent with her. But strangely, at that minute, he also wanted to draw her closer. Physically. And he had to shake the thought. He wanted to be the best possible agent, the best possible man, but he was human. It was impossible not to be drawn to her, more so as they worked so closely together, as they learned to instinctively take cues from one another…

"Daniel?"

"Right. Let's get back to the house and then onward to the station."

"So much for spotting one another," she murmured. "This sleep thing seems to be fairly elusive."

"I think we'll spend tonight with our team," he told her. "We will need sleep."

"I would like to think I could go forever—but I'm afraid you're right. We will have to sleep!"

They returned to the house. Jeannette was fast; she wasn't in her room a full five minutes before she was dressed and ready to meet him in the parlor.

He spoke with Gervais. The masked man they'd arrested was being held at the station, and he was waiting alone in an interrogation room. So far, he'd spent his time cursing, swearing he'd been minding his own business when Daniel had started chasing him and his "girlfriend" had pulled a gun.

When they arrived at the station, or *commissariat*, they were led down a hall to where Gervais stood in an observation room, watching the man from behind a two-way mirror. He nodded in acknowledgment when they arrived and indicated their would-be intruder. "I've never seen him before. He was carrying identification. His name is Claude Chirac and he's from Paris. No criminal record—I have people researching him now. I walked in and assured him that he was being held by the French police, that he is in police custody. And even though you were foreigners, you were authorized by our government to detain him. The officers read him his rights and offered him legal counsel—so far, he doesn't want representation. He went off on me. He speaks English. I'm not sure what we might get from him, but we can hold him for twenty-four hours. We can then ask for an extension, but max is forty-eight hours. Then a judge determines the next steps. Our legal system is a good one, but—"

"We understand there are laws everywhere—and the French legal system, like most in the free world, allows only so much. We all need to be grateful we can't be held forever without proper legal procedure," Jeannette assured him.

"Of course, he is under what we call *garde à vue*, but especially since he can claim he was minding his own business and you hunted him down..." Gervais said glumly.

"Once he's out, he can be followed?" Daniel asked.

Gervais nodded. "Precisely."

"And we do have something more," Daniel said.

"What's that?" Gervais asked.

Daniel produced the black mask he had taken from the man.

"Yes, strange way to dress to mind your own business!" Gervais said.

"I'll pay him a visit," Jeannette said. Daniel nodded at her, and she turned to head into the interrogation room where Chirac was waiting.

Places might have different names, actions might have different names, and yet it was true: laws were similar in the "free" world. Daniel wouldn't have wanted it to be different—except that sometimes it did make the truth something incredibly difficult to find.

Especially when the bodies of the innocent continued to stack up.

Seven

"I understand that you speak English fluently," Jeannette said, entering the room and taking a seat across from Claude Chirac.

He glared at her, groaned and waved a hand in dismissal of her. "Of course. Only Americans are oblivious to others. This is Europe."

"Oh, I didn't say I don't speak other languages. Though I'm afraid I'm still in the learning arena when it comes to French. I'm hoping to learn more daily. I love the country. It is beautiful and historic and most of the people here are as nice as can be."

The man leaned toward her. "I'm as nice as can be— unless I'm being hunted down like a dog and attacked viciously!"

"Interesting." Jeannette nodded her head as if she were weighing his words. "You do realize we have the black mask you were wearing to hide your identity. Of course," she lied, "they've already taken your fingerprints from the door where you attempted to break into Madame Matisse's bed-and-breakfast."

That took him a minute but he shook his head. "I reached the wrong house."

"What house were you trying to reach?"

"That of my friend!"

"And what is your friend's name?"

"That is none of your concern!" he informed her furiously. "What do you think you have on me? I opened the wrong door. And your boyfriend came after me like a savage dog! You pulled a gun on me. I will appear before a judge, and it is you who will pay for your actions."

"I really don't think so," Jeannette said sweetly. She decided to try another lie. "You see, we know you were already in the house. I mean, your argument is a good one—who doesn't show up at the wrong house now and then? But the door was locked—and you opened it." She smiled and leaned closer. "Just as you opened it before—when you came into the house in our absence to go through our belongings. Just what were you looking for?"

"I don't know what you're talking about!"

"Ah, you're forgetting the world that we live in! DNA, monsieur. DNA and fingerprints!"

"I wore gloves!" he exploded.

She sat back. She hadn't expected her lies to work so well.

"Then save yourself," she said softly. "Tell us what you were doing, what you were looking for. Whoever you were doing this for…they will not come to save you and you know it."

"I'm just a thief!" he exclaimed. "I am just a thief who was hoping to find something worth stealing."

"Then why come back?" Jeannette asked him. "If

you went through our things and found nothing, why did you come back?"

He smiled and leaned forward. "You were back. Perhaps you carried your valuables with you, wallets, money... I didn't intend to hurt anyone. But you had a look about you...as if you might have money or rings or jewelry."

"Why are you lying?"

He sat back. "I am not lying. You have me. I was trying to rob you. That is all. I will not say another word. They may charge me with anything they like—they may lock me up from here to forever. I will not say another word."

"Okay."

Jeannette stood up to leave the room.

"I will not say another word!" he shouted.

"You just did. Whatever. I don't care. Bye. Enjoy."

She left Chirac and walked around to join Daniel and Gervais in the observation room.

"So?" she murmured.

"So, he's lying," Daniel said. "Hey, good lies on your part. Good thing he didn't know it would have been impossible for us to get forensic teams in there so quickly and have lab reports back. And he's admitted, on tape, that he was trying to break in and rob us."

"At the least," Gervais said, "a judge will now hold him."

"We need to find out everything about this man that we possibly can," Daniel said. "Gervais, he didn't pull a gun on me, but—"

"He was carrying a box cutter. The officers took it off him when they brought him in," Gervais told them.

Jeannette shook her head. "I don't think he's the

one doing this. I think he's a pawn—and maybe Daniel should go at him now."

Daniel looked through the two-way glass. "I'll take a go at it, but I don't think this man is going to give in. I agree with Jeannette. I don't think he committed murder himself—he may not even know that he was working for a murderer. There are two possibilities. One, he was trying to find out more about the relationship between Jeannette and I because she could easily fit into the current victimology, or two, someone suspects who and what we are and just wants to know for sure."

Gervais nodded. "Obviously, with the new victims, this has been going on for some time. And I believe whoever is doing it does see themselves as being above the law, and perhaps above all other humanity."

Daniel nodded. "And while I'm no psychologist, this guy isn't it. He probably is a thief—just a guy looking to make a little money somewhere, somehow."

"But he does know something," Gervais said.

"Okay. I'll take a stab at him."

"We can try again later, too," Gervais said. "With what he's said, we will have forty-eight hours. Our holding capacities are not known for their elegance. Hours can weigh heavily. Try now—we will try again after he's worked with a toilet that's not the cleanest and a few other distractions."

Daniel nodded.

Jeannette stood with Gervais as Daniel headed on into the interrogation room. They watched and listened as Daniel took his turn with Claude Chirac.

Daniel sat and shrugged. "Last chance," he said.

"I said I'm not saying another word," Chirac told him.

"That's fine. I believe the judge may well decide to bring you up on murder charges," Daniel said with a shrug.

"Murder!" Chirac protested. "What? No, no, no! You are just a Scandinavian bully—"

"Scottish. Scottish bully," Daniel said. "And you're a murderer. A home-grown murderer if you like that better."

"I didn't murder anyone!" the man protested.

Daniel shrugged again. "Maybe the person who hired you—"

"I told you I'm just a thief!"

"And you are so obviously lying," Daniel said. "You see, you breaking into that house…well, you did it for a reason. You did it for the person committing the murders. That makes you guilty of conspiring to commit murder."

"I… No. You'll never make a charge like that stick to me!" Chirac protested.

"I guess you're a gambling man," Daniel said. He leaned closer to him. "And now you're wondering which way to hedge your bet. Do you tell us the truth, and hope we can make a murder charge stick on the person you did this for—someone who terrifies you because you know they are capable of murder because they have committed murder? You see, I think you're torn right now, because what lies before you is terrifying one way or another. Stick with your lie, walk out of this place and they just might kill you immediately, wondering what you've said—or what you might say. Or you could let us lock you up, and who knows how far it all extends. Can they reach you in police custody?"

He stood up and walked out, leaving Chirac sitting in silence.

He entered the observation room, and Jeannette smiled at him as she nodded. "I think he just might tell us something more after he's sat around for a bit!"

"Maybe. Maybe not," Daniel said. "But upping the possible charges gives him something to think about. He's still too stunned to realize we wouldn't have much on him, so..."

"All right," Gervais said. "You two go. Go back. You'll get at least four hours of sleep. And the gig is up. I can guarantee you the involved parties will know by now that you are law enforcement. Even if they don't respect the fact that you have jurisdiction here. But I am not sending you home alone after this—there will be a patrol car parked right in front of the house. No. There will be a patrol car parked in front *and* an officer with you inside. I will see you after your tour, as planned."

"And Claude may break by the afternoon," Daniel murmured.

Jeannette nodded grimly. She wasn't sure she liked the idea of that much security for two people who were law enforcement themselves, but she did feel the need to sleep.

They drove ahead of the officers Gervais was sending for their protection. When they headed into the house, a big man accompanied them, who grinned and assured them his real prowess was the ability to sense danger. He was a nice guy and made Jeannette laugh.

Yet, despite this reassurance, in the house, in her room, Jeannette lay awake. She was tempted to rise and walk into Daniel's room, a place where she might sleep in greater security. Maybe it wasn't so wrong to want to be closer to him.

Eventually, she did sleep, and woke to a tap on the door. It was Daniel, telling her the coffee was on, and they needed to move to make the early tour.

She leaped out of bed and was ready in about five minutes. She was grateful that either Daniel or the officer had already brewed coffee.

The brew had seldom tasted quite so good.

"We'll pack up quickly," Daniel said. "And—" he turned to their massive French guard "—thank you!" he told the man.

"Merci, merci beaucoup!" Jeannette added. Okay, so she wasn't fluent. She had made sure she knew *please* and *thank you*.

"Je t'en prie!" the fellow said. He nodded, waved and left them.

They packed up quickly and hurried on to the meeting point in front of the train station by the tourist office.

The bus was comfortable, and both their driver and guide were friendly and personable. The tour they were taking was given in English. Jeannette was impressed by the fact their bus was filled with people from all over—many from the States and Canada, but others from Spain, Norway, Finland and she assumed more, since she didn't get a chance to chat with everyone on the bus.

The region was famous for its champagne. It was fascinating and enjoyable to explore the House of Mumm and a few of the larger historic wineries. But she and Daniel were really waiting the whole time for their visits to a few of the smaller houses—those of Matisse, Deauville and Montague.

Montague was first. It was where they were scheduled to have their *déjeuner*, or lunch. And Jeannette quickly saw that Alphonse's assessment of Leticia Montague had been spot on. She and Daniel were first to get off the bus, and as they approached the welcome point, they could hear someone's angry voice chastising someone for something. The woman was speaking fast in French, and Jeannette looked at Daniel. The words being said were way too quick for Jeannette to begin to understand with her lack of fluency.

"Apparently, her people did not clean the room to her liking," Daniel told her.

But as they headed on in, the staff was standing respectfully by the side of the room where there were plates, glasses and carafes filled with the winery's offerings.

"Welcome, welcome, *bienvenue* to Chez Montague!"

It was the same woman speaking. Leticia Montague. She was in the center of the room, beautifully dressed in a medieval gown, thick brunette hair swept into a curling cascade. She was an attractive and poised woman in her early forties, Jeannette thought, all smiles for the tour.

Didn't she know that she could be heard when she screamed like a virago?

Apparently not. She went on to explain that the House of Montague had been producing some of the finest wines to be had anywhere since the late 1500s and thus her attire as she greeted them. She talked about the fact the house also created some of the finest Chardonnay, Pinot Noir and Pinot Meunier to be tasted anywhere. Their *déjeuner*, specially prepared by the House of Montague, was *jambon de Reims* and, if she did say so herself, the best *biscuits roses*, or famous pink biscuits, to be found in the whole of the country.

Jeannette and Daniel were seated with a couple from Portugal and three college students from Canada. They laughed and chatted about the tour while the wines and food were served. The couple were older, pleasant, but quiet. The girls were not.

"They told us that if you're touring the wine country, you should not be driving!" one of the young women, a blonde with bright blue eyes who had introduced herself as Clara Miller, told them.

"No, not a good idea at all!" Jeannette agreed. She glanced at Daniel, thinking the girls should be on high alert.

They had to be just about the same age as those who had met such horrible fates in the region.

"You need to be careful all the way around," Daniel said quietly.

The girl grew somber. "We've heard," she told them. "But we don't intend to be apart from one another for a single second."

"Excellent plan," Daniel said. "Stick with it."

"Well, it would be really cool if we were hanging around with you all the time!" one of her friends said, grinning. "Whoops, sorry!" she blurted, looking at Jeannette.

"That's cool," Jeannette assured her. "He's just my cousin."

Servers came by, explaining the champagne and wine selections as they poured for them.

One young woman seemed new at the job and nervous. As she was pouring, a bit of the bubbly spilled on the table in front of Jeannette.

"S'il vous plaît, pardonnez-moi!" she begged instantly, far more distressed by a bit of a spill than she needed to be.

But Jeannette quickly saw why. Leticia Montague—in all her splendor—was rushing to the table. She was more careful now, simply telling the girl to get to the kitchen while she apologized to Jeannette.

"It is nothing," Jeannette assured her. "Nothing at all. Your waitress is simply charming and sweet and excellent. A little spill is nothing."

The woman offered her a smile, but Jeannette thought that beneath the curve of her lips, she was about to growl.

"We strive for perfection! A spill is not perfection," she said, sweeping on by the table.

"It's a good thing you ate already. She might have been ready to spit in your food!" Clara Miller said softly.

So the girl had seen something beneath the smile, too.

Jeannette looked at Daniel and arched a brow.

He spoke softly just for her. "Okay, we know the woman is a bitch. We were told, forewarned. That doesn't mean—"

"That she's a killer," Jeannette whispered in return. "And it doesn't mean she isn't!"

He nodded. "So, where is home for you?" he asked the girls.

"Clara is from Toronto. We grew up together, and, oh, sorry, I'm Emily Grant, and this is Red—sorry, Veronica Oglesby. We went to school over in Alberta, but now we're forming our own company in Toronto!"

"That's wonderful," Jeannette said. "A company that…?"

The girl introduced as Emily told her, "Tech! We're going to be the new social media giant. I mean, we grew up in an age when kids tried them all, saw what was bad about social media, what was good. We're all great with computers. We're going to give it a try, anyway."

"That sounds wonderful!" Jeannette assured her. "We'll be waiting to see. What do you think you're going to call it?"

"We haven't decided yet. We just know it won't be a letter from the alphabet!" Clara told them.

Madame Leticia Montague appeared again in the center of the room, thanking them all for their visit. She spoke so sweetly that Clara murmured to Jeannette, "It's like honey dripping from her lips!"

Jeannette smiled and nodded. It was time to move on.

Their next stop was the House of Deauville, where they were greeted by both Tomas and his wife, Giselle. Like Leticia Montague, Giselle Deauville was dressed in period clothing. She was an attractive woman of about fifty with dark eyes and dark hair swept up in a chignon. She explained that while the family had been working the vineyards for hundreds of years, it wasn't until the late 1700s that they were able to buy their land and become the best of the best, unique, catering only to the finest palates.

"Wow. A little full of herself, huh?" Clara murmured.

Jeannette grinned and continued to study the woman and her husband. Tomas Deauville was a man of medium height and build with a thatch of almost snow-white hair and blue eyes. He smiled as she spoke, saying only one word when she finished. *"Bienvenue!"*

The wine tasting was different here. There was no lunch, but each table offered a charcuterie board so that there was something to snack on as the wines were sampled.

Jeannette glanced at Daniel. He grinned.

They had both been careful to avoid "tasting" too much.

She grinned in return and studied their host and hostess once again. They were going from table to table, welcoming guests.

When they reached the table Jeannette and Daniel had chosen with their new friends, it was Giselle Deauville who did the talking again. Her English held a British rather than an American accent, but she was beyond fluent in the language.

"We so hope you enjoy yourselves and all that you have experienced in the House of Deauville!" she told them.

"Everything is lovely," the third of the girls, the pretty redhead so aptly named Veronica "Red" Oglesby, assured her. "I think this is my favorite!"

She indicated her glass of champagne.

Giselle Deauville looked at her husband. Jeannette thought he gave her a barely perceptible nod.

"That is wonderful! Of course, you and your friends are welcome back at any time! Tomas, darling, give her a card, please. Call. Perhaps we can arrange a more private tour!" she said sweetly.

She moved on.

Daniel quickly leaned toward the girls. "Don't," he

said quietly. "Don't do anything that takes you away from the company of others!"

Clara looked bewildered. "The three of us will stay together. But these people... I mean, we're at the House of Deauville! They are surely just fine!"

"It doesn't matter where you are," Daniel said. "Please! Think of the murders that have taken place in the area. Don't trust anyone. Well, that would include us, and even then...just, watch out for one another."

"Don't take any chances!" Jeannette warned softly. "And...they're saying thank you now. Time to move on to our last stop!"

In the bus, Jeannette whispered to Daniel, "You got the same...vibe?"

"Something seemed off. She needed his approval. But...when we're with Gervais, we can find out if anything has jumped out of the woodwork from all the research the techs in three different countries have been doing. They may just be nice people—"

"Who are full of themselves."

He smiled. "The world is full of all kinds. You can be rich and renowned and nice and kind and decent as can be. And you can be rich and renowned and an ass. Just like you can be a regular Joe and as nice as can be—"

"And a regular Joe and an ass," Jeannette agreed. "But...you can be rich or regular or poor, innocent— or guilty as all hell."

"We're heading toward the end of the tour," Daniel noted.

"Madame Matisse. The nice one," Jeannette murmured.

"And more charcuterie, probably," Daniel said. "The trays have been great. But…"

"After today you don't want to see another one for a while?" she teased.

He made a face. "Or wine. Beer bloke here. Or—"

"Or a good Scotch?"

He shrugged and Jeannette grinned, leaning her head back and closing her eyes for a minute. She was tired.

"Do we talk to her now?" Jeannette asked. "Madame Matisse, I mean. Or when we go back with Gervais?"

"Let's see what she has to say to us."

Jeannette nodded. "Good plan."

They arrived at the Matisse winery. As they got out of the bus and headed into the tour, Clara came up to Jeannette and asked, "Hey, can we hang with you guys again at the tasting?"

"Well, of course," Jeannette said.

They saw how the winery functioned and headed on into the room reserved for the tasting.

Madame Matisse was there, ready to greet the arrivals. She went through the usual, welcoming everyone, explaining the family vineyards and admitting she married into the winery. She missed her dear husband, but she was proud to carry on in his name. "We hope that the Matisse brand of rare and exceptional quality will continue through the next centuries and beyond!"

Clara, Emily and Red, at the table with them as they'd requested, applauded loudly, as did the rest of the room.

"She's lovely!" Red announced.

"I'll bet she's the nicest," Emily agreed. She made a face. "That other lady was just pretending to be nice."

"But!" Clara told them, leaning forward, though it was unlikely she would be heard around the room as people at every table were chattering away with the servers who arrived at the tables, giving descriptions of each wine. "I have found most people to be very nice! I mean, sometimes, you know, the French get a reputation for being a bit..."

"Snotty!" Emily said. "But it's not true. Everyone here and in Paris has been kind to us and our French is really bad."

"In general, I believe in the best in people—around the world. But that's the thing—no matter what country we're in, we're all human beings. So, it's great to find out that people are nice—just remember bad eggs come in every ethnicity known to man," Daniel said.

"Most of the world over just want to live our lives, love our families—and travel and see the world!" Clara announced.

Emily nudged her. "Hush, now! The wine is coming!"

A server arrived to describe a very special champagne to them, and the pouring went around the table. Jeannette glanced at Daniel.

This was the last stop. And while the food was supplied and the "tastings" were small, several people on the tour were showing signs of the amount of alcohol they had managed to consume.

Their three new young friends were growing even more chatty, having a good time.

Maybe too good a time.

They're young, they're bright—they deserve to let loose a little! Jeannette thought.

But she couldn't help worrying about them. They

fit in far too well with the victimology they had witnessed so far.

Just as the other vineyard owners had done, Madame Delphine Matisse made her way around the tables. She was charming with the girls, telling them how delighted she was to see them and asking them if they were staying in Paris or Reims or even elsewhere.

The girls were staying in Paris. They had taken an early train to get the bus that morning.

Madame Matisse nodded and said they must come back to Reims.

"We are famous for our vineyards, of course. But Reims itself…you must see the grandeur of the Palais du Tau, and, oh! The Basilique Saint-Remi, Église Saint-Jacques de Reims! And not just the architectural splendor of our churches, we have an amazing planetarium, so many gardens… Ah, *oui*! You must come back, and, always, you are invited for a sip of wine!" she told them.

Then her gaze fell on Jeannette and Daniel. She just gave them a nod, then turned back to the girls. "Call me, anytime. I also own a home that is listed on the tour sites that is quite comfortable, three bedrooms for privacy, kitchen…dining room, all nice and convenient. Ask this lovely couple—" she began, indicating Jeannette and Daniel.

"Not a couple! Cousins!" Clara interrupted.

"Ah, so that is why they needed two rooms," Delphine Matisse said dryly, staring at Jeannette and Daniel again with a little secret smile. "But—"

"It's a wonderful place to stay," Jeannette offered. "Comfortable home. You make your own coffee in the morning, and you're in the thick of the action—it's so easy to get to so many places."

"Oh, wonderful! We will come back!" Red promised. "And we will make sure we can stay in your home in the city and come back for delicious wine!"

Madame Matisse left them to deliver a sweeping thank-you speech to all those who had come and remind them that it was a beautiful region, they must come and stay and enjoy Reims and the great champagne as often as they could. "Of course, do not forget Paris," she added at the end, a little twinkle in her eyes that brought laughter to the crowd.

Then they filed back out to the bus. Once they were seated, Jeannette whispered to Daniel, "This may sound absurd, but I'm worried for this trio of young ladies."

"I know. We'll talk to Gervais and see if we can get him to post a protective detail on them."

"That would make me feel much better," Jeannette assured him.

They had spoken with many people on the tour, including the sweet but quiet Portuguese couple; as they returned to the bus's position by the train station, they said many goodbyes. But the three girls who had somewhat latched onto them remained to give them a special farewell.

They hugged Jeannette first—but saved their best hugs for Daniel. He looked at Jeannette over Clara's head, wincing. She grinned and mouthed, *Can't help you, cousin!*

But she did help him. She didn't want to hand out a business card so she walked over and told Clara, "Hey, let me get your phone number—you're all set for calls here, right? I'll call you and my number will be in your phone, and then you can call us if you think you need us for anything or if you find something incredible to do or…whatever! We can keep in touch."

"Yes, yes, of course, great!" Clara said. She rattled off numbers and Jeannette quickly put them into her phone and dialed.

"Got it!" Clara said.

"Oh, that's super!" Emily said.

"Yes, we can do something else together, great fun!" Red agreed. "Clara," she added, "back off! Our turn!"

They both hugged Daniel, too, leaving Jeannette to grin at his discomfort.

"Oh!" Clara said. "Are you going to be in Paris? I realize how close we are here, but still, getting here and back…we're talking about more than a few hours. Though I would love to come back. We've been invited to return! And the city is beautiful, the architecture, the churches! We didn't get to see anything—"

"Except a lot of wine!" Red said. She made a face. "It was delicious and fun—and I'm ready for bed now!"

"There is no way to do everything in Paris and Reims unless we all had weeks and weeks," Daniel said. "But we'll see some amazing sights!"

"Right! Together!" Clara said.

Almost as an afterthought, Clara hugged her again then Emily and Red did the same. And with their train back to Paris about to leave, they were finally off.

But even as the girls headed for the train, Jeannette pulled her phone out. They were due to meet with Gervais any minute, but she couldn't help getting the feeling the girls might well be in trouble. Gervais answered her call on the first ring, reminding her he was waiting for them at the house.

"Yes, I know, Gervais, but we need some help," she told him. She went on to quickly explain their conversations with the three girls—and how they had been especially noticed at one of the wine houses. It had made them uneasy and worried. She gave him their names and descriptions, and he promised he'd have them guarded.

"There were just a few comments made about them returning to visit... The trips on the tour were interesting. I'm glad we made them before officially meeting these people. They may just be friendly...though, to be honest, our waiter, Alphonse, rather had them pegged. Delphine Matisse did come off as being more down to earth, and I did hear some screaming at another winery. Which, of course, may mean nothing. But the girls we came to spend time with on the tour fit the victimology, so..."

"I understand. I will see to it. And you must come to meet me quickly. We need to move now," Gervais told her. "I'm going to want to get back to Paris. We have Claude Chirac in custody and can still hope for something from him. Our tech people have surveillance for us to see, and any information from the medical examiners may help us."

"On our way!" Jeannette promised.

"Are you expecting someone?" he asked suddenly.

"No, we've already gotten all our things out of the rooms."

"Hmm. Maybe the car is moving on. No matter. Get here."

"Right away."

She ended the call and looked at Daniel.

"You know, it is different," he reminded her.

"What do you mean?" she asked.

"That threesome is staying together—they won't be alone. I could be wrong, but whoever selected the victims we discovered preyed upon them when they were alone."

She nodded. "I can't help but feel we need to get back to Paris. And it may be a streak of paranoia, but I'm worried about those girls."

"Paranoia in this situation may be a good thing. But if Gervais said he'll discreetly guard them, he will see that it's done. You know that."

"Of course."

"And they will call."

"And we will. As soon as we've revisited the wineries with Gervais."

He had already turned to head back to Madame Matisse's bed-and-breakfast. But as they arrived, they saw another car.

"I don't suppose we need to head to our hostess's winery anymore. It appears she's beat us here," Daniel said dryly.

"To help?" Jeannette murmured.

"Or to protest her innocence as quickly as possible— and find out just exactly what we do know already?" Daniel asked.

"I guess we are about to find out."

Eight

Madame Matisse was, indeed, in the house with Gervais.

Since they weren't guests anymore, Daniel decided they should knock at the door.

He glanced at Jeannette, who nodded and gave a few raps on the wood. Madame Matisse was there within seconds, throwing the door open.

"My guests!" she said, arching a brow but smiling as well. "I should have known that my dear friend Gervais would be watching all around. Come in, come in. We were just talking in the parlor. In spite of all else, I do hope you enjoyed your stay here?"

"It's a lovely place," Daniel told her.

"But…" Jeannette began, wincing and hesitating, "you might want to think about your method of cutting keys."

"Oh!" she said, shaking her head. "Sometimes…I'm so busy I forget to make sure I've gotten them back. But from now on, I'll tack on a massive fine in euros—that will, I believe, assure that all my keys will be returned."

"Maybe change the locks, too," Daniel suggested.

"Yes, yes, Gervais told me that someone was in here while you were out. And that you have a man in custody! I am horrified. And he told me you were coming to see me as well as a few others whose lands border the fields where the bodies were found. I wanted to assure him once again that anything of mine is open to him for anything that is needed! This is horrifying, horrifying! Someone using the beauty of our land to dispose of their brutal…psychotic intentions! I'm sorry. I am standing at a door, talking, when you must come back in. I brewed coffee… *S'il vous plaît*… I'm not sure what else Gervais needed from me—he did say you would have come to me had I not come here. Of course, he had to tell me about you, but I remain confused. You're an American, Jeannette—though great French name—and you, Monsieur Murray, are a Scot? And you are seeking a French killer?"

"Long story," Daniel murmured.

"Not so long, really. It's a bit like Interpol. We're an offshoot of an American unit, but we're the team that works in Europe, especially when an American might have been a victim—or when an American might be a murderer," Jeannette said.

"And a Scot?"

"We're all international!" Jeannette said pleasantly. "And I would love coffee."

Madame Matisse turned to head back into the house. Gervais was standing by one of the large sofas in the parlor, waiting for them.

"So. We do not need to go to the House of Matisse," he said. "The House of Matisse came to us."

Delphine had headed straight into the kitchen. She had expected them, obviously; but of course, Gervais would have told her he was waiting there for the two of them—and why.

She quickly returned from the kitchen carrying a tray with coffee and all that might be wanted to go with it. She set it on the little table in front of the sofa and busied herself preparing cups that Jeannette handed around until finally they all sat.

"I was hoping Delphine might know if any of her employees had been behaving strangely lately, if any were new…"

Delphine was shaking her head.

"I swear to you! No one from the House of Matisse is doing this! I have no new employees. My people have been with me for years. Of course, I have seen to it that Gervais has received every one of their names along with copies of their IDs. When my husband was alive, he wasn't against helping someone who had gotten into minor trouble—if they were honest and really on the mend. He was such a good man and wanted to help people," Delphine assured them, smiling sadly. "But! He was no fool He wanted every piece of information on them. As it stands, we have only one employee currently who has any kind of record regarding an arrest. That is Sonia Garcia, from Spain, and she was caught at the age of twenty-one with drugs, did her stint in rehab and has been a model employee ever since—she was born in Madrid but is a French citizen now. My people have been with me forever—even those who come to clean and watch out for this place. Two maids rotate, and they've both been with me for over twenty years," she finished. Her shoulders lifted and fell as she shook her head. "Again, you're welcome to tear apart anything near my winery—or at my winery—if it will help."

"Thank you, Delphine," Gervais said sincerely. "And thank you for driving over here! Isn't there an afternoon tour today? I know how you love to be the one to welcome people to the winery, giving it all a wonderful, personal touch!"

She laughed softly. "Well, I managed to snag my son for one afternoon. I keep thinking he'll come around. Oh, I don't believe he'll sell it after I'm gone. However, he has no interest in running it, but I do keep hoping! He has his own work and he loves it, so…"

"We'd love to meet him," Daniel told her.

A son. Another person of interest?

"Well, we will arrange it!" Delphine said, rising. She smiled at Daniel and Jeannette as they rose as well.

"You should be seeing us out," Gervais told her. "These two are sleeping in Paris tonight."

"Oh, yes, your keys, and I should lock you out. No, in this instance, you keep the keys. The rooms do lock, you know. Because sometimes they are rented to two different parties. But… I don't know. After this…maybe I'll just stop renting it out. But…it's a great location and I don't want to get rid of it. When it just sits there… Sorry! That's a whole different decision!"

"The coffee service—" Jeannette began, but Delphine quickly interrupted her.

"Not to worry. I pay well—it will be picked up in the morning. I know you have a few other destinations, and I don't know why you must drive back tonight—" She broke off abruptly. "Of course, I do. These horrible things that are happening. I'm sorry. Do find me anytime you need me, anytime. I can try to help with anything at all!"

"Thank you, most sincerely," Gervais said.

Jeannette smiled at her, taking her hand. *"Merci. Merci beaucoup,"* she told her.

Delphine nodded and smiled. Daniel echoed the words.

Then they exited the house with Delphine locking up behind them all.

They let her drive out first.

"Well, we've got two cars, but I'll drive," Gervais told them. "I know this terrain best. Two quick stops. Places you now know. The House of Deauville and the House of Montague."

"Have you told them we're coming?" Jeannette asked him.

"Yes. We will first go out to the Deauville winery," Gervais told them.

"Charming," Jeannette murmured.

Daniel looked at her. She made a face before arching a brow at him, giving him his choice of the seats in the car. He nodded, grinning in return and indicating she should take the front seat next to Gervais.

They were quickly on the road.

"So, you met Monsieur and Madame Deauville this morning?" he queried.

"Oh, yes, charming!" Jeannette said. "She was charming—too charming. She and her husband both noted our trio of young single women and made a point of asking them to return."

"Madame does have a reputation for being quite

the...virago with her servants and just the opposite with guests when she feels as if she's performing on stage," Gervais said. "I believe you have that in the States as well—and even Scotland—very rich people with old money who have one face when publicity is concerned and quite another when it comes to those they see as beneath them, people who consider themselves..."

"A wee bit above all others?" Daniel asked. "They are everywhere. Just as people almost as good as Mother Teresa might exist anywhere. We are the human family, for all the good and bad."

"But bad aspects can become part of a norm," Jeannette murmured.

There was something about the way she said the words. He wondered about her past assignments. Of course, she was too young to have accrued too many, but...

One case could play havoc with the soul and psyche.

"They are expecting us and they know why we're coming," Gervais warned them. "They don't have much respect for law enforcement."

That was proven when they arrived. Giselle and Tomas Deauville must have been waiting for them. When Gervais drove up to the house, the door opened and the two stepped out.

"I guess we're not being invited in," Daniel murmured.

"We're not young and cute," Jeannette said.

"Yeah we are!" Daniel teased in return.

"You are both just adorable," Gervais muttered, shaking his head. "But..."

"But we're not vulnerable-looking girls who might fit the bill," Daniel said.

"Ah, well, Jeannette might look perfect under the right circumstances," Gervais said. "But in this case…"

"At least you are punctual!" Tomas Deauville snapped as they walked from the car to where he stood with Giselle before the house. He stared hard at Daniel and Jeannette. "Who are these people, and why are they back here with you?" he demanded.

"Monsieur Deauville, Madame, these people are Special Agents LaFarge and Murray. They are with an international team of law enforcement and are experts at cases such as the one we are facing now."

"If they're such experts, why are there so many bodies?" Giselle demanded.

Daniel started to answer, but Gervais had been prepared for the question.

"I asked them in after the bodies were discovered. And we're here—"

"Yes, yes, and I will keep speaking English for these two!" Tomas snapped. "You found a body or bodies on land that borders mine. But you cannot be such a fool as to believe—"

"Oh, sir, we are not here to accuse you of anything!" Jeannette said sweetly. "We know that you're the most knowledgeable person regarding the area, regarding anyone who might work out here! Perhaps there is someone who has given you trouble, who has behaved suspiciously, who has a bone to pick with any of the wineries in the area, especially those, like you, who own the small family estates who still produce the finest quality!"

Jeannette knew how to play it—how to speak to people like Tomas and Giselle Deauville. She was charming and more, putting the right reverence into her voice to address such fine and amazing people.

Giselle almost smiled at her before turning to her husband. *"Je pense..."*

"English, my love," Tomas said, nodding in Jeannette's direction. "But I know what you're about to say." He looked at Daniel, Jeannette and Gervais. "There was a man working for us. The rest of our employees have been with us forever, most from back in my father's day. But this man came to us from the House of Montague. He is a big man, very strong, able to move heavy casks easily. He worked with precision. He came every day, and then he was gone."

"What is his name?" Gervais asked.

"Aristide Broussard," Giselle told them. "He was happy here, we believed. Though, of course, I understand that..."

"He was fired from the House of Montague," Tomas said. "I was in need when he came here and he said that he was sorry—he'd snapped when Leticia had yelled at him. I have seen Leticia in action, so... I thought I should give him a chance."

"But we believe he must have gone on somewhere else. He just didn't show up for work one day," Giselle told them. Then she turned to study Daniel and Jeannette again. "So, you came on the tour. You were, as they say in American gangster movies, *casing the joint*?"

Jeannette laughed softly and Daniel smiled.

"We truly wanted to take the tour. It is touted as the

best," he assured her. "But beyond that, we picked the tour purposely this morning, yes, because we would see the smaller houses and those bordering fields where the dead have been found."

"Honesty," Giselle said. "That is appreciated."

"I don't know," Tomas murmured. "This man... Aristide. He was needy—he had no money. But he seemed to be a very decent man."

"We expect the best out of our people," Giselle said. "That is the only way to create the very best product. But..."

"We aren't as..." Tomas started to say.

"You don't run around screaming like Leticia?" Gervais asked flatly.

"We aren't screamers," Tomas said. "Our people know. Too many marks against you—and you're gone. But as I said, our people have been here with us forever. Now, if that is all, we have welcomed two tours here today and we'd like some time alone."

"Of course, thank you. And you know how to reach me should you think of anything, anything at all," Gervais said.

The Deauville couple gave them all a curt and serious nod and turned to enter their home.

Daniel, Jeannette and Gervais returned to the car.

"One to go," Gervais muttered. "I saved the best for last."

"The best, the worst, however one chooses to see it!" Jeannette said. "What do you think about this man they're talking about—Aristide Broussard?"

"I think we need to find him," Gervais said.

"I'm calling our people to see if they can find any

kind of a trail on the internet," Daniel murmured. He started to call his old station and then smiled to himself. He was Blackbird now, part of the Krewe of Hunters.

He dialed the Krewe number.

As usual, he was answered on the first ring, which surprised him when he realized that it was early evening here, and therefore it was late in the States.

It was Angela Hawkins who answered him. He had yet to meet her other than via video calls, but he was a bit in awe. She was Jackson Crow's wife and second-in-command. She was something of a magician, so it seemed, as she was balancing a job that often encompassed all hours along with a family—and pets!

"I'm sorry, I just realized the time for you—"

"Not to worry. I would have let the night team take it if I weren't ready to help."

He explained the situation and apologized again. Gervais surely had people, too. They were good at their jobs. In fact, Gervais's people had done the research on the victims and were still seeking IDs on those they didn't know.

But Angela cheerfully assured him that they'd get right on researching the name—and she would be back with him that night. She also told him they were sharing across the Atlantic.

"You never know when a discovery in one place might trigger another across the pond," she told him. "I'll get back with you."

"All right, we have great people on tech in general," he murmured, ending the call. "But I do believe Angela is the best of the best."

"She is," Jeannette agreed.

"My people—" Gervais began.

"Are talented and wonderful, too, and thank God for that!" Daniel said quickly. "We need everyone on this."

"And so we do," Gervais said. "And here we are, just ahead…the House of Montague."

Gervais drove safely but fast, and they were indeed approaching the Montague estate.

Leticia Montague and her husband were not standing outside waiting for them. In fact, when they knocked at the door, they were ignored. At last, a maid came to the door and said she had informed monsieur and madame that LaBlanc had arrived. They had told her that LaBlanc would just have to wait.

Gervais smiled for the maid.

"That is fine. We are at their convenience."

They stood outside and waited. Daniel found himself watching Jeannette as she studied both the house and the endless fields that seemed to stretch from it.

The land was also dotted with outbuildings, work buildings, and there was even an old barn attached to the property.

Finally, Leticia and George Montague appeared at the door.

They were not invited in.

And Leticia let them have it immediately, starting her tirade in French and switching to English as she stared at Jeannette with narrowed eyes.

"This is the greatest offense! You have dead bodies— so you come here? How dare you accuse us of having anything to do with the death of these girls. We are law-abiding citizens, we pay the taxes that allow for your salary, and this is ridiculous among other things that you dare to come here making it appear to others that there is a reason! Talk quickly! Tell him, George, that we are offended to the ends of the earth!" she snapped.

"I'm so sorry," Jeannette said sweetly. "So very sorry you are so easily offended! The police have come to you for help, not to make accusations!" she said.

For a moment, it seemed the woman was confused by Jeannette's words, not at all sure whether to be further offended or simply to go with the words that suggested she could help.

"I don't know why you're here," she said simply. "Because bodies are found in fields that border ours? That's ridiculous. How could we know anything? You didn't even know anything. I understand that a body might have been there for months!"

"Because the bodies have been left out here, we were hoping you might know of someone who has visited or someone who has been an employee who might have been involved," Gervais told her, his tone level and easy. "This is extremely sad, and it is bad for the wine region, bad for Paris and exceptionally bad for the young ladies who have been murdered. We are seeking any little iota of help we might get."

"Leticia," George said, determined then to do the speaking. "Monsieur, what is it that you would like to ask us? You mean, do we have any strange employees, have we had visitors… Well, on visitors, I cannot tell you. We have so many! Two tours are given several days during the week, depending on the season. But I don't believe I've seen anything that would suggest someone was a murderer."

"I understand you had one employee you fired a few months ago," Daniel said.

"Just what are you doing here? You're not French!" she snapped at him.

"They are with an international law enforcement agency," Gervais said simply. "Special Agents Murray and LaFarge."

"Sneaks! Slimy snakes, coming on the tour—then accusing us of murder!" Leticia snapped.

"We are not accusing you of anything. We are asking for help," Jeannette reminded her. "And we did hear you fired a man. Aristide Broussard. Can you tell us why?"

"Because he was a horrible employee!" Leticia said. "I would give him an order, and he would refuse to carry it out. Lazy wretch!" She shook her head. "I hear that fool, Deauville, gave him a job. And then he walked out on Deauville. I told you—he was a horrid employee!"

"Was he violent in any way? I understand he was a big man," Gervais said.

Leticia and George looked at one another and shook their heads. "No. He was just… He was like a big lump. He didn't work," George said. "But…he has disappeared, from what I understand. Perhaps you should be looking for him."

"Is there anything or anyone else—"

"You should see Delphine Matisse!" Leticia snapped. "*Madame Smile*—you mark my words, her smile is a lie! Talk to her. I wouldn't doubt that she was dragging people out into the fields for their blood. The woman is obsessed with herself. She's too old. She wants another child. Someone who will want to take over the vineyard and love it the way she does. Maybe killing young women makes her think she can steal their youth. Don't accuse us—"

"You do have quite a temper, snapping at your help," Jeannette said thoughtfully.

Leticia frowned fiercely. "No. I mean, things must be proper and people must learn. And we just like everyone to enjoy our hospitality."

"We are happy to host those who love the vineyard!" George said, annoyed. "It is excellent publicity for us when someone especially appreciates our vineyard. And speaking of young women…they are on social media. Tons and tons of it. They do so much for us."

"I would so hate to see anything happen to them!" Jeannette said, her tone still just as sweet.

Daniel lowered his head as he tried not to smile. There was still a warning in her words, no matter how pleasantly they were spoken.

Leticia looked as if she wanted to snap back at Jeannette. If Jeannette had been an employee, she'd have been fired.

But she wasn't an employee.

Still, in Leticia's world, Jeannette was beneath her.

She waved a hand in the air. "Don't come back here!" she warned.

"Hmm. I'm rather fond of social media, too," Jeannette told her, still maintaining her pleasant tone and a sweet smile.

George stepped in. "Honestly, monsieur," he said, making a point of addressing Gervais and pretending Daniel and Jeannette weren't even there, "there is only the one employee. And while I saw no violence in the man, I don't suppose such a murderer displays his intentions when he is out and about in the world. If I were you, monsieur, I would find him."

"We will make every effort to do that," Gervais assured him.

"Thank you so much for your time!" Jeannette said.

The two turned and headed back into their house, slamming the door with finality.

"That was fun," Daniel noted.

"Then again, the woman is practically a demon," Gervais said. "But it doesn't mean she finds young women to murder."

"No, and if I remember clearly, it was at the Deauville winery where the couple really showed an interest in the girls, but I suppose I am suspicious of everyone, including Delphine Matisse. She told the girls when they came back that they must stay at her bed-and-breakfast," Jeannette said.

"Let's hope we get more when we get back to Paris," Gervais said wearily. "I will get you to your car and see you—" he paused, shrugging and grinning "—back at the ranch! That is an American expression, is it not?"

"It is," Jeannette assured him, smiling.

They were quiet as Gervais drove, all deep in thought. Daniel noted his phone pinging, and he quickly looked at the message that was coming in.

It was from Angela.

She had found what information there was to be had on Aristide Broussard. Born in Paris, orphaned at the age of five, he'd grown up in a group home. He had been an average student, had not been able to afford to go on to a university or college, and had worked in restaurants before finding his job in the vineyards. He had no record.

He didn't even have parking tickets, and he did own a vehicle—a ten-year-old economy car. There was nothing to suggest he had been violent at any stage in his life. He'd been an able soccer player in school until a knee injury had sidelined any future in that respect.

He read aloud so Jeannette and Gervais could hear him. The ending of the message was worrisome.

"He hasn't used his phone in the last several days, and it goes straight to voice mail when called," Daniel said. "His credit cards haven't been used in a week."

"Perpetrator? Or victim?" Jeannette asked softly.

"None of the victims have been male," Gervais reminded her.

"Thus far," Jeannette said quietly.

They had reached the Matisse bed-and-breakfast. "Back at the ranch," Gervais repeated, smiling as he let them out.

"We'll be going straight there," Daniel promised.

They headed to their car and followed Gervais out.

It was a long drive back, and Daniel didn't intend to follow Gervais all the way. There was traffic through Reims and he knew it would get busier as they neared Paris.

He glanced at Jeannette as he drove, noting once again how she could easily pass for a beautiful young woman just out of college and happily off on a dream trip. But maybe she wasn't going to need to play that part. He knew if she did...

They had only known one another for days. Being attracted to her made lots of sense—she was stunning—but his past typically made emotional attachment difficult. Her face might have been sculpted by Michelangelo, her eyes so quickly flashed humor and empathy, and her smile was purely seductive and engaging.

He winced inwardly. He wasn't good at relationships, and it was his own fault. He had recently enjoyed the company of a young woman he met on their last case in Edinburgh.

He had been the one to step back. It was his own... weirdness.

His "talent" or his "curse."

But Jeannette is an old hand at the spirit business; she doesn't think I'm crazy. She sees the dead, too. She's carried on conversations and...

"What are you thinking?" he asked her.

She shook her head. "We are nowhere. We've met nice people and nasty people, and we've seen them in action. But the fact that a few of these people are elitists doesn't mean they're capable of murder, though..."

"What?"

"I get the feeling that to people like the Deauville and Montague couples, the death of someone not in their financial or social strata might be as meaningless as the squashing of a bug. And that brings me back to..."

He smiled, looking ahead. "You keep thinking about the crimes—or the setup—of Elizabeth Báthory."

She nodded. "On the one hand, she had incredible power. And back then, anyone suspected of witchcraft was burned alive, theft might result in a hand being chopped off—minor infractions were legally handled on a local level. There are a number of reports regarding her merciless beating of a servant who pulled her hair while brushing it… And the woman had a lot going for *and against* her from birth. I mean the inbreeding in that family—a line of Báthory for her mother, another line of Báthory for her father. Oh, and medical experts now believe she suffered from epilepsy, a disease not understood, which might indicate to some back then that she was in league with the devil when she had her fits. Then there's her husband—Ferenc Nádasdy. He was a heroic warrior, but there are rumors that when she was very young, Elizabeth had an affair with someone not of the gentry. Supposedly, Nádasdy kept his promise of marriage, but he had the man cut to ribbons, castrated and fed to hungry dogs while still alive. And on the battlefield…he tortured his enemies before putting them to death. He was a sadist when it came to any prisoner of war. Rumors regarding Elizabeth's murders rose after his death, but those who believe in her guilt also believe that the torture and murder of young women began while he was alive. Violence was a fact of life. There were constantly wars going on between the Calvinists, Catholics and Turks, and they were horrible from the get-go, but…"

"So, she was guilty," Daniel said.

Jeannette shrugged. "I don't know. There's another school of thought. After her husband's death, Elizabeth was extremely rich and powerful. Matthias, then king of Hungary, owed a tremendous debt to the family. He called upon Elizabeth's cousin, György Thurzó, then count palatine of Hungary, to investigate. There was a trial and her *accomplices*, those servants who supposedly aided her in her regime of torture and murder, were brought in. They stood trial and there were depositions from those on Báthory estates and the surrounding areas that declared Elizabeth and her servants guilty of six hundred murders. Elizabeth wasn't allowed at the trial, and she was not allowed to defend herself. Three of her servants were executed. The family was allowed to manage her incarceration in exchange for a cancellation of the debt that Matthias owed. She was kept prisoner in Čachtice Castle—Hungary at the time, Slovakia now—until her death. So…even then!" She paused, looking over at Daniel. "Was she an inbred elitist who could be cruel but was set up by others, or a horrendous murderer of six hundred or more young women?"

"You think one of our vineyard couples—George and Leticia Montague or Giselle and Tomas Deauville—might be thinking they're Nádasdy and Elizabeth?"

She shook her head. "Is that ridiculous? Especially with all the speculation these days among scholars that Elizabeth might have been set up?"

"It doesn't matter what happened—it matters what people think happened," Daniel told her. "I'm truly impressed with your knowledge of history. Many people know about the woman, the *Blood Countess*, but you have your facts and figures."

"I majored in criminology. I had a great professor in my senior year. He believes that no matter how much technology comes into the world, human beings are human beings. And while we supposedly progress, we are still ruled by human factors, both mentally and physically. We can improve our biology by doing the right things, but we will still be born with mental defects and/or factors in our lives—abuse, poverty, et cetera—which will continue to haunt the mind. He believed that studying the past was incredibly important in understanding the present and the future."

"Sounds like a great class."

"It was," Jeannette assured him. "So, I can't get that strange history out of my mind—and we're in France, not Hungary, Slovakia or Transylvania. But I can't stop the feeling that someone here is pulling the strings and has accomplices or *servants* helping them. And who has that kind of money and influence? Vineyard owners."

"I understand that. Still, there could just be a sick cult around here somewhere using blood for rituals. We need to keep an open mind."

"I know that," she told him. She glanced in his direction again, wincing. "That was my last assignment—I went undercover to take down a cult."

"And you took it down?"

She nodded.

"That's impressive!"

"I admit, it was a situation that was in some ways like what we're looking at here. Except they were taking blood from anyone. Corpses were found in the Blue Ridge Mountains. No blood. Police first spoke with a minister who pretended to be horrified. They discovered he became a minister online—not to infer in any way that there aren't very good people who do that. Anyway, statistics proved his church—a cabin on his private property—was dead center of where the corpses were discovered. I was sent in as the daughter of a fellow who had been the owner of property nearby and had just passed away. And…" She looked at him again, giving him something between a smile and a grimace. "And I got lucky. Mr. Nathaniel Murphy was hanging around, horrified by what had been going on. With him, I was able to bring more Krewe members in before they were about to have another sacrifice. Their thing was that they were saving their victims' immortal souls with their ritual. But…"

"This doesn't strike you as the same thing."

"No. Of course, I could be wrong—"

"We're on our way back to Paris, lass. We'll be meeting with the troops. We'll have more to go on and we'll have more to give them," Daniel told her. "I didn't get to work in the United States with the Krewe of Hunters the way that you did," he told her. "But there is something I learned working with Blackbird in Scotland—we don't stop. We go on until we find the truth."

She smiled, nodding, looking down.

"And," he reminded her, "thanks to you, we have some of that help you were referring to before."

She looked over at him again but he didn't turn to her. They were closing in on Paris, and the traffic was growing heavy, even though it was long after any kind of rush hour.

"Henriette Beaumont, our spirit who is seeking friends and watching to see what she can see," Daniel said. "Remember? The lovely lady we met because you thought we should check out the cemetery near the magic show."

"Right. And okay! Yes, we're just getting back to Paris, and there's a lot we need to do here, but I want to get out to those fields again—alone. Just us, just us and our team and see if… Well, many of those vineyards have been there for hundreds of years. There may be someone hanging around who could help?" she said hopefully.

"We'll get back out there. And see what else might be found in the fields. And maybe when this thing is solved—"

"We could visit a few of the wonders of Reims?" she asked.

"Architecture, history, churches!" he agreed. "Just no more wine!"

She laughed at that. "No more wine."

Their phones were chiming. He gave a little nod; whatever was coming through was coming through to them both.

He waited and Jeannette quickly pulled out her phone and looked at the message they were receiving.

"Gervais," she told him. She was smiling as she looked down at the phone. "He wants to make sure we remember where the house is located, and we need to head there. And he's had his people add supplies. He wants us to be aware the house is complete with a standing bulletin board, computers, police access, kitchen— lots of coffee—and more. If you don't remember where, I'll program in the address."

Daniel laughed softly. "I remember where. It's great having a place where we can both work and sleep. We're ready to talk at any time, share information, brainstorm. With coffee."

Jeannette laughed. "It is nice. Yes, Gervais has done well for us. Numeric entry, security cameras every- where, alarms everywhere. We key in at the gate, bring the car through and park in front, different key-in code for the front door."

"Gervais is a damned good bloke. He's competent—and I think he asked Blackbird in because, for one, he's already worked with the others!" Daniel said. "And I think he's smart enough to realize that at times, he may be too close to people and even to these cities to have the open mind others might have when investigating here."

"He is a good guy. But as you said, he asked us to come. That's another important lesson that not everyone wants to heed—learn to ask for help if it's out there and you need it."

"Agreed on that! And there's nothing like a great team."

"Absolutely nothing like a Blackbird team," she told him quietly. "We all went through half of our lives believing we were…weird. We were warned never to say anything to anybody lest we wind up in mental facilities. We had parents who cared about us, some not knowing, some knowing full well because a few of our scientific minds believe one day they'll discover this ability is a rare thing that is carried genetically and… Well, anyway! We're lucky. And you're luckier than most! You came into full bloom with your talent with Blackbird!"

"Oh, so true. So true!" he agreed. "And now…"

"Now?"

He grinned at her. "Now I may find myself visiting a lot of cemeteries so I can find some ancestors. Aye, I know it doesn't work on command, and maybe it works for us when it's necessary, but…I am grateful!"

"Speaking of cemeteries—we are supposed to go back to the cemetery tonight and find Henriette by the statue of St. Michael."

"And we will. We'll get to headquarters first, find out anything else that might have been discovered and then we'll go to the cemetery. And, hopefully…"

He was stopped at a light when he felt his phone buzzing again.

"I've got it!" Jeannette assured him. She glanced over at Daniel. "This time it's Mason."

"And?"

"We almost had a break in the case!" she told him.

"Almost?"

"Video surveillance picked up Claude Chirac escorting one of the girls to a van."

"So, how is that almost? He's obviously guilty—"

"Of escorting her to a van. But here's the *almost*," Jeannette said. "Chirac managed to commit suicide in holding. He might have been guilty, but the man was more afraid of someone out there than he was of a sentence in a French prison."

Nine

Jeannette was glad they were meeting at their house-headquarters—and not at the facility where Claude Chirac had been held. She didn't think their presence would be welcome now.

Things happened despite the best intentions. And she didn't want any member of their team to become reproachful to the Paris police—which she didn't think would happen—but she didn't want the Paris police to believe their foreign guests were blaming them.

Someone was most probably already taking the blame, and the interference of others would not be welcome. Even their being there could give officers the appearance they were casting blame, and that would not help them in any way.

Chirac was dead. It was obvious now he had been involved. Whether he was the killer still seemed unlikely to Jeannette.

She believed he had been a procurer, and he brought the victims they desired to someone else.

No, the man would field no more questions. It was

impossible to bring Claude Chirac back to life, and she sincerely doubted his soul would remain—he had made his choice. Their best move now was to discover where he had been in the past days—and just whom he might have been working with and for.

They arrived more quickly than Jeannette had expected.

Daniel was a good driver. He mentally and easily switched to the right—or correct—side of the road to drive on.

The house *was* great. It was just an average house, really, but on the busy Île de la Cité. It had a yard, a horseshoe-shaped drive behind the gate, parking for several cars and offered five bedrooms.

Mason, Della, Luke and Carly had already settled in when they arrived; they learned Gervais LaBlanc would be arriving soon.

He would be stopping to receive more details on the death of Claude Chirac.

The foursome greeted them as good friends, and Jeannette had to admit to being just a little jealous. The four of them had all worked together before. She did know Mason, though. He'd been on the Krewe investigation team on one of her first cases, which had involved a murder at a haunted house.

The haunted New England house was, indeed, haunted by a ghost killed during the War of 1812—but the ghost had done no evil. The ghost had, in fact, been instrumental in the investigation that proved a greedy wife had managed to murder her husband.

Jeannette had wondered if the murdered husband might have stayed on as well, but he had not. Nor, she had learned, had the killer wife who had passed away from a burst appendix just months later in prison.

Captain Nathaniel Winters, the spirit remaining in the house he had built, assured her that evil souls seldom stayed. He'd seen it once—just once. Evil souls were collected not by fire or pure darkness, but by a strange gray fog, or so it had been in his experience. He wondered if perhaps the man hadn't gone to a different plane, perhaps a place where the soul might be cleansed. But ghosts, he assured her, were almost never evil in any way. They were memories of the past, and the past was the roadway to the future. It was so important to be recalled.

"Jeannette!" Mason said, making a point of addressing her personally as if he knew she was feeling just a little on the outside. "Head on up. This place is big. You have your choice of bedrooms that are left. Since you took off for Reims right away, you haven't stayed here yet so you haven't seen the layout. But Gervais was amazing about procuring this for us. It's often used for anti-terrorist teams. Anyway, all the bedrooms have bathrooms, so settle in and we'll get working."

"We were here," she reminded him. "We just didn't stay long enough to settle in."

"Right. Sorry. But it is livable—and workable!"

Jeannette gave him a nod and a smile; then she hesitated, shaking her head with dismay. "So, Chirac really committed suicide?" she asked.

"Gervais doesn't believe anyone could have gotten to him, so, yes, we think so," Mason told her.

"That's so…strange. He just didn't seem like a man who would do such a thing," Jeannette said.

"I know Gervais implicitly trusts all the officers involved with holding the man. And none of us thought the man would kill himself," Mason said. "And in that interrogation room, it was no easy task for him. And to do what he did..."

Della joined Mason, adding, "We tried with the man, tried to get him to talk, to give us anything. Mason and I went in, Luke went in, Carly went in. And we believed that if we could have kept hammering at him, we would have eventually gotten something. And we were keeping him up, keeping him in the interrogation room. There was a guard on duty, but he was told to watch the door, make certain the man didn't attempt to escape. Nothing about the man suggested suicide—a man with an ego like his is not considered a danger to himself. But we should have all known that there are no guarantees on human behavior. Chirac used the sleeves from his shirt to strangle himself. Of course, we discovered him when we were finally able to go through hours and hours of video footage and found him on it with one of our victims. But whoever he was getting girls for...that person is far more terrifying to him than death itself."

"What else have we learned from the magician? Maybe he saw someone else? We received video from the box office, right?" Daniel asked her.

"The sketch hasn't given us much yet. And we researched his assistant, the disappearing Marni. Her full name is Marnette Magnon, no record, originally from Nice, moved to Paris when she was twelve. She has a degree in the performing arts, and only one parking ticket."

"On paper, she's a little angel," Mason said dryly.

"Anything else at all?" Daniel asked.

Della nodded. "We've worked with the magician, investigated Marni, worked with the sketch the magician did with the artist and police, and gathered information on all employees in the region at the various wineries. Also, this is what we're starting on now. We've got more video in. When everyone is settled in, we'll get into it. We have computers at the dining room table. We're connected with French tech, British tech and American tech. But here's one thing. The cause of this may be coming from the wine region, but it's likely that all the victims were taken from Paris. And since Chirac was seen at the venue where the magician has been launching his show, it's likely we may find something else."

Jeannette nodded. She turned. Daniel had grabbed her bag as well as his own and was looking at Della.

"Up the stairs?" he asked her.

"If you like. We've taken two of the rooms up there. There's one more up there and through that hallway, there are two more bedrooms down here," Della told him.

"Hmm. Maybe I'll opt for the downstairs," Daniel said. He laughed. "Easier to get to the dining room table, and the coffeepot! Oh, sorry. Jeannette, I can pop this up there for you if that's your preference."

"You had me at *coffeepot*," she told him. She smiled as he nodded.

"I'll give you the closest!" he promised.

Carly and Luke joined Jeannette, Mason and Della where they stood, nodding to her and smiling, as if to make sure she knew that she was welcome in their company, that she was part of it. She had to admit, it gave her a good feeling.

"I was telling Daniel I knew it was important we get back here and have all the facts, but I want to go back to those fields again," Jeannette told them. "Strange feeling, I can't help but feel—fear, really—that there are more bodies and maybe..."

"Maybe someone most cops don't see to ask for any help they might give?" Luke suggested.

She smiled and shrugged. "Yeah. And that brings up something we need to do. Daniel and I met a revolutionary ghost—referring to the French Revolution, of course—and she was going to see if she could find out anything else."

Daniel had reappeared already and said, "Jeannette thought to see if we could find anyone, anyone at all, who might help us. She thought to walk by the church and cemetery near the theater where the magician is performing. We said we'd be back out there tonight, because she was going to see if she could discover anything else that might help us."

"Hmm, the gift or curse thing. It's continuing, huh?" Luke asked Daniel. "Are we talking about a lingering spirit?"

Jeannette knew, of course, because Daniel had told her his story. Luke was teasing him lightly. Good. A little levity helped sometimes.

Daniel nodded, indicating Jeannette with a smile. "She's still the expert, but..."

Jeannette laughed softly. "I'm not sure we can be experts. We can just seek to use what makes us different when it may work."

"Jeannette also has a theory on all this that we should explore," Daniel said.

"As in you think a vineyard owner may be involved?" Mason asked. "The major houses have CEOs, heads of different departments—"

"Not a major house," Jeannette told him. "There are three of the small family-owned businesses we're looking at." She glanced over at Daniel.

And he supported her theory. "Gervais took us out after our tour, and we met the owners of the three smaller vineyards near the fields where the bodies were found," he said. "Two of the couples apparently believe they are just about royalty. They like putting on a show when people are around them, but they behaved as if the mere thought that they might have so much as walked by someone who would do this was the most offensive thing in the world."

"Well," Carly said, speaking up. "Most people—unless they are killers—are offended when someone suggests they're bloodsuckers."

Daniel grinned at that. "Okay. These are not *most* people. Certainly not if you were to ask them! They are, I believe, in their own minds at least, akin to gods. They have horrible reputations for being rude and above all others, thinking the rest of the world is not on their social level and is unworthy of living so, and killing lesser human beings wouldn't be such a big thing."

"Gotcha," Carly assured him. "So, nasty enough to just be nasty, or nasty enough to be serial killers."

The door opened and closed; Gervais had arrived. It was growing late, close to ten o'clock, but he looked at them all and asked, "Food anywhere? Of course, there's food in the kitchen, but…"

"I'll see what we have. It will be fun to explore a good French restaurant! I want to grab a bottle of water if we have it for the ride," Daniel told Jeannette.

"Good idea."

"I'll get you one."

He walked on into the kitchen. Jeannette determined to follow him. But she made a face first and murmured, "As long as the food and drink are not…"

"Human in any way?" Mason asked dryly. "Sorry. When we're in this long enough, we deal with just about everything."

"Too true!" she agreed.

She winced and hurried after Daniel.

"Hey!" he called out. "Gervais! How about a microwavable sandwich or—"

"Delicious!" Gervais called to him.

Daniel grinned at Jeannette. "You know, I'm a capable lad, Jeannette. I do know how to use a microwave."

"I didn't come in here to help you, just to thank you," she told him.

"For?"

"Supporting my theory."

"Well, we haven't brought up your Elizabeth Báthory correlation yet—"

"We don't really need to."

"Maybe we do," he said quietly. "Because maybe, it has merit."

He popped the sandwich he was preparing for Gervais in the microwave. As he did so, Gervais came into the kitchen. "Food! Aren't you two hungry?" he asked.

Jeannette laughed. "Don't forget, we spent half the day eating. A major lunch, then wine, more wine and charcuterie trays!"

"Ah, true. I forgot to tell you," Gervais told them, nodding his head toward the dining room. "No one has stopped in any direction of this investigation. Your people here…they are already in there, busy studying traffic, bank and other camera footage. Everything has been made available to all your emails."

"Let's hope we're not hacked," Jeannette murmured.

"Won't matter if we are. None of our information is up there—just a lot of video footage. If someone wants to study it, well…" He shrugged, reaching for the sandwich Daniel handed him.

"Nice! Cold water in the refrigerator!" Daniel said, grabbing two bottles. "We're heading out again—we're going to watch for the man in the sketch outside the theater. Maybe we'll get lucky." He spoke to Gervais and turned to Jeannette.

"Let's take a quick look at the computers and some of the footage—just a quick look—and get going!" Daniel told Jeannette. He set his hand on her shoulder and lowered his voice so that Gervais wouldn't hear. "I don't know that much yet, but I don't think ghosts have bedtimes. Still, I don't want her to think we're not coming."

"Eat up, Gervais! Nothing like a microwavable sandwich," she teased.

"When you're as hungry as I am…it is pure ambrosia!" he assured them.

"Yep—been there!" she assured him, and they headed out to the dining room, greeting the others again, who were already busy at work. Seats across from one another were available.

"We'll take a quick look," Jeannette murmured, looking at Daniel and nodding to Mason.

Mason nodded in return.

"Get the lay of the computers and the footage the teams have put together?" Daniel asked Jeannette.

She nodded and they sat across from one another, turning on their computers to find the footage and start watching for just a minute.

The others, she knew, might be at it all night. She was suddenly somewhat relieved her most important duty for the night was to meet a ghost in the cemetery.

The traffic cams were good, darned good, she thought. They were set up to catch cars speeding and running lights, but the cameras by the magic show had caught most of the street as well. The bad thing was that they seemed endless. The good thing was that there were several of them to do the work.

She frowned, seeing a man leave the magic show. She thought she might have seen him that day at one of the vineyards. She wasn't sure which one. The servers had moved about swiftly. Most of the men she had seen dealing with the wine and tour guests had been brown-haired and around forty. But she thought that maybe she was looking at one of the men who had poured wine for them...

"Daniel," she said, hitting the pause button on her computer. "Sorry!" she murmured, looking around the table. "Daniel and I were on the wine tour today, and I think I'm seeing a man leaving the show who was working at one of the vineyards."

Daniel was already up and coming around the table. He stared at the image on her computer. The footage was of the crowd leaving the theater. People were close together, but there was a split second in the video in which the man's face was clear.

He had been leaning behind her to study the screen. Daniel stood straight and looked around the table, addressing them all. "This may mean nothing at all, but we did see this man today. We saw him at the House of Deauville."

Thankfully, Daniel remembers which house we were at when we saw the man!

The others were all up and behind Jeannette, looking over her shoulder at the man who had been captured so briefly on the video—including Gervais, who was just swallowing the last of his sandwich.

"Keep the pause on that—I'll get the image to the police departments in Paris and out to Reims and environs. We can also compare it to the lists of employees we've received from the various houses," Gervais said. "Of course, all our tech people in all countries are researching and looking for the man we learned about, Aristide Broussard," he added.

"Great," Jeannette murmured. She looked up at Daniel. He hadn't taken his seat again.

"We keep that appointment," he told her. He must have remembered Gervais LaBlanc did not know why the Krewe was called on in unusual and special circumstances.

They didn't want to make their French host worried he had brought in a "krewe" of crazies.

"Right, of course." The others backed away and she stood.

"House of Deauville, you said?" Mason asked.

"Aye," Daniel told him.

Mason looked at Gervais. "We also need to ask the owners about this man. And see their reactions. The man from the sketch."

"Interesting. Quickly, did you want to break down the rest of your theory, Jeannette?" Della asked.

She glanced quickly at Daniel and lifted her shoulders and shrugged. "I couldn't help thinking about what the truth might be—since what has been passed down might well have been a setup and a lie, or even a rumor enhanced by legendary status that has become accepted truth—regarding Madame Báthory. Historical record clearly indicates that as a warrior in battle, her husband was a fierce and brutal man when it came to his enemies, not just executing them but torturing them first. He died in battle before she was accused of murder, and that was only when girls sent to learn their manners and probably their places in life at Elizabeth's gynaeceum, or the area of the home exclusively for women. When the poor, untitled and unlanded disappeared, no one said anything, but—" she paused, shrugging, looking at Daniel "—we've talked about the fact that what was real may not matter. What people believe to be real is what is important. I was wondering if…if one of our elite vineyard owners considers themselves not to *be* Elizabeth Báthory, but perhaps thinks in the same vein—of that which she was accused of. There is documentation that she was harsh with her servants, quick to hand out physical punishments. In her defense, most people of her social strata were hard on their servants. But this killer… really thinks that they're above all else and that they are due the entertainment of watching others suffer. Back then and perhaps now—there are people not among a high social sphere who just don't matter, who are just not worthy of anything—including life. We all know that to some, watching another human being tortured is pure entertainment. Think back to the days when executions were a public spectacle. Let's face it, we've all seen some sick stuff!"

"Aye, agreed!" Daniel murmured.

Mason was nodding. "Gervais," he said, "Jeannette and Daniel wanted to get back out to the wine region, anyway. Perhaps we should do all the work we can do here discovering the identity of this person while they head—with you—out to see the vineyard owners in person. It's late now and by the time you got there tonight, it wouldn't be great. Oh, and the two of you wanted to go, um, watch the theater exit at the magician's show," he finished.

Gervais nodded. "It's too late now, and we can't go banging on their doors without due cause at this time. I think you're right—that we need to see their reactions in person. We'll start with the House of Deauville. Whether this man is a full-time employee or not, the two of you saw him there today. There is a connection."

"Decided," Della murmured, already back at her computer. "Enhancing image!" she said.

"Go!" Gervais told Daniel and Jeannette.

As the door closed behind them, Daniel murmured, "Seems like we just got here."

"We did," she said dryly. "But I do hope Henriette

is still there. We should have hurried. We had told her that we'd find her—"

"She's been hanging around more than two hundred years. I think she'll wait for us," Daniel said. "I think it's going to prove to be important that we did look at those little bits of video—and that you caught that man's image. We don't have Chirac anymore—"

"Daniel, you don't think there's any way the Paris police are involved, do you?" Jeannette asked.

"I doubt it. Let's face it. We all know a few bad eggs slip in with the fresh ones now and then. It's far more likely that a weary man was seated by a door, maybe even drifting off, but not neglecting his duty to make sure a door didn't open or close. They were worried about him trying to walk out somehow—not leave in the way that he did."

"You don't think that—"

"That the guard—instead of guarding him—tied the knots himself? No, I really don't. For one, it would have been far too risky. And a superior officer might have walked by at any time—it's a busy place. You don't think—"

"No, I don't. But one must look at every possibility."

"And we'll keep that one on the back burner!"

"Agreed."

It was late, but Paris nightlife was alive and well. And still, they had no difficulty finding parking by the cemetery.

But as they walked toward the statue of St. Michael, Jeannette paused. Down the street, she could see the theater where the magician was performing.

The street was quiet. But the show wouldn't let out for another twenty minutes or so.

"We'll go back to the show as soon as possible, maybe tomorrow night," Daniel said. "Watch it again, have another lovely chat with our magician."

"He seemed so real to me," Jeannette murmured. "I believe he cared about the girls. And Shelley. I think he was truly concerned about her."

"He did give that appearance."

"But you don't believe he's innocent in all this?" Jeannette asked.

"No, I didn't say that. I'm just saying anyone can give a certain appearance—and not what they appear to be at all."

"He gave his information to everyone and promised to contact us if he saw anything weird at all," Jeannette murmured. "Ah, but! We still have the disappearing magician's assistant."

"Disappearing," Daniel said, "part of the game."

"But just what game?" Jeannette murmured.

"She has a clean record," Daniel murmured. "Gervais is no fool, not to mention he's working with our people in the States. And I believe he's even including my old British agency. France is just a hop, skip and a jump—"

"Or ferry or *Chunnel*," Jeannette offered.

"Close enough that the British authorities would like this killer stopped before they decide to hop across a bit of water and seize hold like ye olde William the Conqueror," Daniel said dryly.

"And that still doesn't mean—"

"Right. Anyone connected in any way remains a suspect," Daniel agreed.

"Okay, so the show isn't out yet. After we meet with Henriette, we could hang around a while longer and watch when the show empties out. Oh! Maybe we could even pretend that we had those backstage tickets that we had last time—"

"Give me a second to call Gervais. He can set it up."

"You're not going to say we'd like to go in again right after we talk to our ghost, are you?" she asked him.

"I'll say we wanted to watch who came and went ourselves...and then I'll tell him you had the brilliant idea we should talk to the magician again!"

"You think Gervais can manage to get us passes now? The show is almost over."

"I think Gervais can do just about anything."

He pulled out his cell phone and Jeannette listened, grinning, as he spoke with Gervais. He had barely hung up, so it seemed, when he looked at his phone again.

"We're in," he told her politely.

"Now, that's great. Although—"

"You think he's everything he seems to be."

"He is a magician, so it's hard to say," Jeannette told him. "Then again, we do need to find this other man."

"Other man?"

"The man in the sketch."

"Right."

"And it makes me curious and worries me. Claude Chirac tried to break in on us, apparently knowing why we are here. But there is another man, a different man in the sketch. Maybe he's the man who has disappeared from two wineries."

"So...whoever is calling the shots has people working for them. People who are so afraid of their power that they'd rather kill themselves than face the idea of this person getting to them," Daniel said.

Jeannette shook her head sadly. "Well, this happens in the States and around the world. People do wind up shanked or otherwise killed while serving prison sentences. But worse is trying—and succeeding—at suicide by strangling yourself with your shirtsleeves."

"The bones," Daniel said. "Medical examiners are still studying the decomposed bodies that were there before the newest victims were found. It's quite possible those victims were tortured."

"But can you torture a man if you're trying to shank him and get away with it when you're in prison?" Jeannette wondered dryly.

"No. You can't torture him. But you can torture and kill his wife, his children...someone he loves," Daniel said. "We need to see if we can find Henriette and quickly. The show is going to let out soon."

"You're right! The statue!" Jeannette said.

She hurried ahead of him.

Like many things in Paris—yards, streets, houses—the cemetery was beautiful with fine funerary art.

The statue stood near a corner and was clearly visible. St. Michael stood high over the dragon, ready to do battle for good. He was larger than life and on a pedestal.

Leaning against the foundation, Henriette waited for them.

"My friends!" she called softly. "Just step over the brick wall, it is so small. The police will not be angry, many people slip in at night. So long as you don't seek to vandalize what we see as sacred, you will be fine."

Jeannette smiled as they slipped over the wall and joined her. "No vandalism, I promise," Jeannette told her.

"Je promets!" Daniel said, speaking French very seriously.

Henriette smiled in return. "I have spoken with friends. They told me about people, women, young, they saw on the streets, so sad and homeless. Then, suddenly, they would be gone. And the police... Well, most of the time, there was no outcry. People come and go. But my friend, Piers, he said that too many seemed to come and go in the last months."

"Maybe victims we haven't discovered yet, and possibly a few that we have," Jeannette murmured.

"And they were not among the elite," Daniel murmured, and she knew he was referring to her theory regarding a would-be Elizabeth Báthory.

"The elite?" Henriette said curiously. "But we are not that society anymore. Oh! You mean the world hasn't changed as far as people existing who *think* they are elite."

Daniel smiled sadly and nodded.

"Ah! That I could carry a sword! Whoever does this thing—"

"Deserves to rot in prison for the rest of their life," Daniel told her. "Remember, they abolished the death penalty in France in 1981."

"Ah, yes, lest an innocent man—or woman—die. And that is good. Still, for some...a guillotine blade would be too merciful! But! None of my friends saw anyone young and lovely taken from the theater by a suspicious person. So... I have watched since you came and last night, I saw the magician himself. Leaving with a woman."

Jeannette glanced quickly at Daniel.

Dear lord, is there to be another victim already?

Henriette didn't notice her expression and kept talking. "No young girls, none alone, no one taking a young woman anywhere. But! I did see the magician, Jules Bastien, leaving with a woman, an older woman. She had a very nice car. Silver. I'm not familiar with makes or models, but it was an expensive car, I know that."

"Who was the woman?" Jeannette asked. "He was dating an older woman?"

"No, no, I don't think so," Henriette told her. She appeared to be perplexed. "It was quite strange. I thought I knew who the woman might be. I have seen her picture on flyers in the city, on a billboard. And the magician, he called her *Maman*."

"The magician's mother is rich, then," Jeannette murmured. "But do you know who she is? You said you saw her face on billboards, flyers, advertisements? Do you know who she is?"

"*Mais oui!* She is known all through the region!" Henriette said.

"But why, and what is her name?" Daniel asked.

"Oh, of course! She is Madame Delphine, the great lady of the House of Matisse!"

Ten

"What the hell!" Jeannette exploded.

Daniel gave her a quick glance. He almost smiled. She had just managed to scare the hell out of a ghost. Henriette jumped back as if she'd been touched by a branding iron.

"I'm sorry, I'm so sorry… I just… I'm so stunned, and not even because of what you've told us but by the fact that we didn't know!" Jeannette apologized quickly.

Henriette still seemed a bit confused but she nodded solemnly and said, "*De rien*. It's nothing. It's all right."

"Thank you, thank you, and again, I'm so sorry," Jeannette said.

"You're sure about what you heard?" Daniel asked Henriette.

"*Mais oui!* I was right there, I heard clearly," Henriette said. "But…perhaps she is not really his *maman*, perhaps it was a word of affection for an older woman."

"We'll find out," Daniel told her.

Jeannette moved closer, as if she'd take Henriette's hand if it were possible. "And we do mean thank you, and if you will—"

"Oh, I will continue to watch! It is my extreme pleasure to help you in any way. I longed, always, to be a voice of the people. I was in life perhaps a bit ahead of my time. But now here with you, if I can help save the life of one woman, it will be my greatest joy."

"You arc amazing," Daniel told her. "And we are grateful to have you on our team." He turned to Jeannette and said, "I think his show has run long tonight—but if he's already seeing his people with backstage passes, we'd best get over there."

"Go. I will be here each night—if you are not able to make it, I will wait for the next night," Henriette told them.

They repeated their thanks and started back out to the sidewalk and then down to the theater.

"How is this possible? How could he be her son? She is a Matisse—known and respected in this region. He said nothing to us—while giving us information that he'd known the girls and all—about having any relationship with the wineries whatsoever. Jules Bastien. Why an assumed name? And worse than that, how did our tech departments *not* find the connection—and even worse, why didn't Gervais tell us?" Jeannette asked, shaking her head.

"Maybe Gervais didn't know," Daniel suggested.

"How could he not know? He's worked in Paris and the environs for years. He knew all our suspects in the vineyards, at least casually. He has been privy to the murders from the beginning. Oh! When we were speaking to Madame Matisse at her bed-and-breakfast, her *son* was giving the tour for her. How did we not see any of this?"

"All right, as Henriette suggested, maybe he was just calling her *Maman* with affection for a rich supporter. And Paris and its environs are the largest metropolitan area in Europe—over eleven million people and that doesn't include Reims. So that adds in another couple of hundred thousand people. Gervais LaBlanc's expertise is Paris, where—as in most major cities—he has enough crime to deal with. Now, I do think that other vineyard owners might know if he is or isn't her son, but we asked about employees, not family. I don't know. I just don't know. Let's talk to this bloke and then when we return to the house—"

"You think anyone will be awake by the time we get back?" she asked.

He smiled at her. "Someone will be."

"Oh. I get it. Someone is always awake and on guard?" she asked him.

He smiled and nodded. "I think we're doing three-hour shifts. Gervais isn't staying at the house, so that means there are six of us, giving each person a night on and a night off for however long it takes. I think I heard Mason talking about doing something like that with Della and Luke."

"Good plan," Jeannette murmured. "And here we are."

They moved through people leaving the theater, and reached the hallway where those with backstage passes were in a line to speak with the magician.

They walked quietly to the end of the line and waited. They could hear children laughing with pleasure, and Daniel realized he was hoping against hope that Jules Bastien, the young and charming magician, was not involved in what was happening.

And yet...

The bodies of the dead had been found in fields surrounded by the working vineyards. And he hadn't seen fit to mention the fact that despite the name he went by, he was the son of one of those small family-owned vineyards where the dead had been found.

Jeannette glanced at him while they waited and then gave him a nudge.

Marni was sweeping by them, carrying a bag that appeared to be filled with little boxes of children's "magic" toys. She saw them and stopped dead. One of the little "Disappearing Coin!" boxes fell to the floor, and Daniel quickly bent to retrieve it.

When he stood, she was staring at him and Jeannette in surprise.

"You're back?" she asked, frowning. "I didn't see you in the audience!"

"We need to speak with Jules," Jeannette told her.

"Oh. Oh... I thought he had told you everything he could. He is so upset by all this and since you spoke with him, he's been so worried about Shelley," Marni said.

"Shelley is fine. She's being guarded by the best," Daniel told her. He smiled. "We'll make sure to let Jules know she really is okay."

And would Jules want to speak with her? Find out where she was? Perhaps...?

There would be no way he would be told where Shelley was being guarded. No way in hell.

"Oh, that would be great. I didn't get to know that group the way he did. I didn't go to the coffee shop with them, but it is heartbreaking that girls were killed, and that Shelley remains in danger," Marni said. "I'm sorry.

Death, I guess, is what you deal with all the time. But to Jules, I'm afraid, this is all personal."

"Of course. And it's heartbreaking to us as well," Jeannette assured her. "It doesn't matter how long you're in law enforcement, it's never easy to deal with. The death of innocents with their lives stretching before them remains tragic and heartbreaking. And that's why we try to stop it," she finished softly.

"Of course, of course!" she murmured.

The woman in front of Jeannette with a small boy at her side spoke quickly to Marni in French, and Marni gave them a nod to reply to the woman.

"That lady is not patient," Daniel explained softly to Jeannette. "She wants Marni to hurry the people in front of her."

"Good thing we're patient, right?" she asked him, smiling sweetly.

"We're just a pair of saints," he told her. "So, while we're being patient," he told her, "why don't you tell me a story?"

"Ah…you want *Goldilocks* or *Rumpelstiltskin*?" she asked.

He grinned at her. "No. You worked with Mason Carter before?"

"I worked with Mason on one of my first cases. And it was… Well, it was the best. No, I mean, it was horrible. There was a murder, but a very patriotic ghost stepped in and helped. There were some longtime Krewe agents working with us. Of course, Angela and Jackson were on the computer with us all the time, but we were also with Jake Mallory and another agent Whitney Tremont, both of whom had been with the Krewe for years and years. They're great agents. Anyway, the case ended with a good resolution, but…I never met Luke, Carly or Della before they arrived here."

"They are why I'm here," he told her. "I don't think I'd have ever been comfortable in my own skin if it hadn't been for them. I got to learn I wasn't imagining things, creating phantoms in my mind, and I knew…"

"You knew?"

He shrugged. "I love Scotland. I loved working with the National Crime Agency. But once I had worked with the Krewe—or with our Blackbird unit—I knew that being with such a group was what I needed for my sanity."

"See, you should have just played the guitar and become a rock star. Then you could be unstable and no one would care!"

He laughed and she whispered, "Shh! The impatient lady is going in at last!"

The woman went in just ahead of them, leaving them standing in the open doorway.

Jules Bastien looked up, frowned curiously, gave them a wave, and turned his attention to the woman and her little boy.

It seemed she was determined to take her time with the magician—she had waited, after all.

But eventually, Marni, now at Jules's side, explained to her that others were still waiting, and the show had gone on very late that night.

She left, pushing past Daniel and Jeannette.

Jules had been seated, but he rose to greet them as they came in.

"Bonsoir!" he told them, right before growing anx-

ious. "Did something else happen? Shelley! Oh, no. Has someone else been found, is everything all right? I can't help it; I am so worried about Shelley!"

"Shelley is fine. And trust me, she'll remain fine," Daniel assured him.

"Then—" Jules began, but he shook his head and murmured, "I'm sorry, I'm sorry. Let me grab you a couple of chairs. Oh! Marni is here—is that all right?"

"It's fine," Jeannette assured him. "And we can grab a few chairs!"

But Jeannette didn't have to get a chair; Daniel dragged one over as did Jules as Marni grabbed the chair she'd been using to sit at his side and pushed it in a bit closer.

"I've given LaBlanc every bit of surveillance video, and I've thought and I've thought—" Jules began.

"Except you didn't think to tell us that Delphine Matisse is your mother," Daniel said.

The man looked truly confused. He was a magician. A performer.

And an excellent actor.

Daniel wondered if he was going to disavow the relationship. And if he did, maybe referring to Delphine as *Maman* had been just a term of respectful affection.

But he didn't disavow the relationship.

"I'm sorry. I don't see the relevance. Yes, Delphine is my mother," Jules stated.

"But you don't go by the name Matisse. Which, I think, might be a gold mine for you here," Jeannette said.

Jules shook his head. "I wanted to be a magician since I was a little kid. I saw a few movies and a few documentaries on the great Harry Houdini. I was fascinated, and I watched everything I could on David Copperfield, Criss Angel and more. At first, when I was a child in the single digits, my mom was happy to humor me. She thought I would grow up and fall in love with the vineyard and the excellence of our wines—especially our champagne. Magic is my passion. I love what I do. I love it when the children are so excited and amazed. I'm only here—at this theater—for another two weeks. Then I have a run in London and after that, on to New York City!"

"Didn't you give the welcome speech for your mother the other day?"

He sighed deeply. "She told me she had to see Gervais LaBlanc, and she was desperate. She said I had plenty of time to speak and get back here to Paris. I told her that I would do what she needed, but she really needed to understand I didn't want to manage the vineyards. I was grateful—she and my father have been wonderful parents—but I love magic."

"All right," Daniel told him. "I think your loving magic is fine. It's great to have that kind of passion for your work. But…you know the dead were found out by the vineyards and…you never mentioned your relationship to us? And what's with your name? Our techs didn't even make the association."

"My name?" he asked. He looked away and then back to them. "I changed it legally."

"How did you do that, leaving no record?" Daniel persisted.

He looked away again, shaking his head. "Paris is one thing, but…the Matisse name is renowned—for champagne and wine. And I wanted to make it on talent and the art of my craft. I meant to work hard. I didn't want favors—or an audience—because of my family name."

"That's understandable," Jeannette said, "and applaudable. But I still don't understand why you didn't tell us."

He shook his head. "I don't ever use my family connection. Ever."

Daniel leaned forward. "Monsieur Bastien, it's time you start thinking about that family connection. Don't you realize how serious this is for you? You knew the girls. We have on video that one of the murdered women was taken from just in front of your show. The bodies have been discovered near your family estates. Think about it. If you were an investigator, wouldn't that raise a few flags for you?"

Jules Bastien stared back at him, shaking his head in bewilderment. "But... I know you've met my mother. She's amazing. I didn't turn away from the vineyard because of her. I'm out here with my name changed to pursue the dream I've nurtured since I was a small child. My mother would never hurt anyone. She goes out of her way for people. I have never seen her be anything but friendly and nice to everyone," he said.

"Maybe your mother is the nicest human being in the world," Jeannette said gently. "But here you are. Victims were seen at your shows—"

Marni broke in angrily. "They were here, but they were all over Paris as well! Those girls might have been taken from anywhere—"

"But we know one was taken from here," Jeannette said quietly.

"But—but—" Marni began.

"Do you know anything about all this?" Jeannette asked her.

"No!"

"Wait, wait, wait!" Jules protested. "I have tried. I have been helpful. I'm the one who gave LaBlanc most of the video surveillance he has—"

"Along with traffic cams and bank cams and more," Daniel reminded him.

Jules just shook his head. "I will do anything you want. I'll provide DNA, fingerprints—blood samples, if you want. I will help in any way. But I promise you, neither I and my mother nor the House of Matisse could possibly have had anything to do with any of this!" He winced, shaking his head suddenly. "Why here? Leticia Montague is a horrible human being. At any moment, she is in the middle of a tirade. Her husband, George, isn't much better. He's quieter, but he's meaner. When I was a kid and my mother took me to their place, they were talking about trials with the weather. I was just playing and strayed into the wrong place on what I thought was the lawn. He practically ripped my arm off, dragging me back to where I was supposed to be and he told my mother I needed a good thrashing. And that Deauville place! Giselle has been known to kill stray cats that dare wander onto her property, and Tomas is known to have throttled a dog once. I don't understand why you're... asking *me* about my mother and about...me!"

"Really! How dare you!" Marni muttered.

"We aren't accusing anyone of anything. We're investigating, trying to get all the facts," Daniel said. "And we couldn't begin to understand how you never mentioned to us that Delphine Matisse was your mother. And, Jules, it's because you knew the girls, and because bodies were found near your family property. But we have had the pleasure of meeting George and Leticia Montague, as well as Tomas and Giselle Deauville. And we can agree they are not the nicest people."

"No matter what facade they put on for guests!" Marni announced.

Daniel inclined his head and rose, waiting for Jeannette to do the same.

"Thank you," she told Jules. "We do sincerely appreciate all the help you have given us. But any little detail could be extremely important. We just wish that you had thought to tell us about your name change. Oh, by the way! Why is there no record of your birth as Jules Matisse?"

He looked back at them and shrugged. "I don't know. I swear to you, it's not anything I did. I went through the courts. Bastien is also an old family name. The records should have shown my birth and my name change. I never asked that anything be hidden—not where it would be illegal. Then again…" he murmured.

"Then again?" Daniel asked.

"Money can buy just about any kind of corruption, despite the very good and decent people who are usually working in such areas. Not me—or my mother—I swear it. I have no idea why you couldn't find the association through legal searches," he said.

"Well, to be honest, we weren't doing the searches. Our brilliant tech and computer people did them," Daniel said.

That made Jules smile. He nodded. "I swear to you, I

know nothing about records, how one pulls up records, what can be proved and what can't be proved."

"By the way, was your mother angry?" Jeannette asked.

"About me changing my name?" Jules asked.

"Yes—and becoming a magician," Jeannette added.

He smiled and shook his head. "She still thinks I'm going to wake up one day and want to become a master of the vineyards. She isn't angry. Maybe disappointed? I don't think she'd care at all if the Deauville and Montague couples didn't express how sad it was that I had no interest. That's why I was glad that, although it put me in a bit of a rush, I could get out there and help. Don't get me wrong! I love my home, love where I grew up... The endless fields are beautiful. But I love magic."

"And you're very good at it," Jeannette assured him. "Not just the magic itself, but you're excellent with a crowd."

"And your love for what you do comes through," Daniel told him.

"Thank you," Jules said.

"He is the best!" Marni announced. "You need to get back out there and attack the right people!" she said.

"We aren't attacking anyone," Daniel said patiently. "We're trying to get to the truth, trying to save the lives of other young women. Oh—and we do plan on getting out there."

"If and when you want or need me, I'm more than happy to go back out with you and my mother. I will help you tear apart anything you want on any piece of property that is owned by the House of Matisse," Jules said determinedly.

"We'll get out of your hair," Jeannette said. "Thank you again for the time you've given us. And," she added pleasantly, "Marni, thank you, too."

Marni nodded. She didn't stand with Jules to say goodbye.

Daniel set a hand on Jeannette's shoulder and they headed out.

When they reached the street, well out of earshot, she turned to him. "Well?"

"Marni was angry."

"And Jules was not," she murmured. "But…"

"Yeah. There is the connection between the girls, his magic show and the Reims wine region. No matter how mean and nasty the other vineyard owners might be, they weren't in Paris that we know of. And we now know Madame Matisse was here, and Jules had a connection… I don't know," Daniel said.

"He wasn't angry. He wasn't angry with us at all over what might be construed as an accusation," Jeannette reminded him.

"No. He acted like an innocent man."

"Well, hmm. Are we on guard duty tonight, do you think?" she asked.

He laughed. "No, we're already past the division of time. Way past. But let's get back. I almost said something to him about tomorrow, but I thought you wanted to get back out to the fields without any suspects involved. I wonder if anyone saw anything else on the video. I'm sure they've arranged to get a few stills. But maybe, if you want to spend the day in the fields, Gervais or someone else could go to the estates—"

"Well, that would be good. But since we're the ones

who saw the man at the Deauville estates, perhaps we need to get there first. Of course, they're going to be using every possible means to find this man—Aristide Broussard—who seems to have disappeared from France. I'm just curious if…" Daniel let his voice trail with his thought.

But Jeannette picked it right up.

"You're curious if this happened to be an upright and decent man who didn't like something about the people he was working for. Maybe he didn't like getting yelled at as if he were a child or an indentured servant and didn't like to see it happening to others, either," she said.

"Well, obviously, the techs will be doing all the usual steps. Getting information on his cell phone, following up on his credit cards—everything should be on record," he said.

"Should be," she agreed.

They reached the car and drove back to the house and keyed in the codes to the gate and the door.

The house was just about dead silent, but Daniel knew someone was still awake. He walked through to the dining room and, as he had expected, he found Mason seated at a computer.

He looked up at Daniel. "Anything?"

"Yeah. We had quite a talk with Jules Bastien—after learning he'd been born Jules Matisse. Our very friendly revolutionary ghost overheard a conversation between Jules and Delphine, a conversation in which he referred to her as *Maman*. She said it might not have meant anything, but as it turned out, it did."

Mason nodded, thoughtful, and then asked them, "Why would someone with a name like that, seeking a career where the name could buy him some instant fame, change it?"

"Well, if he's honest, he wanted to make it on his own," Daniel said.

"I believed him," Jeannette said as she came around from his side. "And still… Jules admitted the first night to knowing the girls. He liked them, and they went to a coffee shop with him. We saw the footage of Claude Chirac escorting one of the dead women into a van. I don't know what my passion is with getting back out to the vineyards, but—"

"It's all figured out," Mason assured her. "Luke and Carly will be in Paris following up on any new leads. Gervais, Della and I will head out to the wineries. We thought about it both ways. One would be with the two of you telling the Deauville couple very flatly you saw the man there. Or Gervais, Della and I could go out to say we'd heard the man worked for them and we'd like to discover who he is so we can ask him if he can help us in any way. If we're all out there, then if we get no response whatsoever from Giselle or Tomas, you'll be close enough to take a second stab at it. By the way, Della slipped in to see Shelley for a bit tonight, and she's doing as well as can be expected. She hasn't wanted to wander out—she wants us to catch the killers. She is so scared."

"I don't blame her," Jeannette said softly.

"Neither do I. I'm praying we solve this thing sooner rather than later," Mason told them. He sat back. "So, for now—go to sleep!" He grinned. "Tomorrow night, you get your hours!"

Daniel laughed. "I'm out."

"Me, too."

They went through the parlor area and down the hallway that led to the downstairs bedrooms.

"Thank you," Jeannette said to him.

"For?"

She smiled. "Humoring me. Police have been over those fields. People who know them. And I want to go walk through them. Some instinct is calling me—"

"And when instinct calls, we should listen," he assured her.

She smiled and headed into her room, the first door on the right.

"Good night."

"Good night."

His room was the last. He went on in and closed his door, flicked on the light, and noted there were two other doors in the room. One was open and led to the bathroom. The other was at the back of the room. He walked toward it, curious. He hadn't noticed it earlier when he'd dropped their bags off.

At the door, with his hand on the knob, he smiled and hesitated, shaking his head.

He was sure it was a connecting door to Jeannette's room. Turning around, he went in the bathroom to shower. He set his gun on the commode, shed his clothing and stepped into the shower, grateful for the spray of hot water that streamed over him. He wished he could turn off his thoughts. Or that human beings were capable of being ruled only by logic.

He couldn't help thinking about Jules Bastien.

It seemed the man was truly honest, truly telling the truth. And his mother was the only one of the five small vineyard owners who seemed to be liked by just about everyone.

At length, he turned the shower off, dismayed as he dried off to realize his thoughts were shifting. He'd wanted to turn off the events of the day, to clear his head...

And instead, he found himself thinking about the connecting door. About Jeannette.

He toweled dry and had the towel wrapped around his waist when the door at the back of the room began to open.

Any unexpected noise awakened the cop in him; he'd taken his gun from the top of the commode to the dresser where he'd been drawing a comb through his hair.

Gun swept up, he turned to face the door.

It shouldn't have been a surprise; it was Jeannette standing there. Obviously, she'd been curious—as he had been—and, maybe just as obviously, she was checking it out.

She, too, was wearing a towel.

"Hey," he said.

"Uh, hey, sorry."

"Why are you sorry?" he asked, amused.

"Well, I should have knocked—"

"That's okay. Come in. What's up?" he asked her.

She grinned. "You are."

"What?"

He was surprised when she took several steps closer to him and began to speak awkwardly. "I, um, wow, um, I was just thinking I was so keyed up and I... Well, everyone seems to be paired up, and I couldn't help but wonder if some of this isn't done very carefully, I mean not just for our special talents or the fact that we are all good, decent, hardworking agents, but..."

He couldn't help it. He was a fool. He should just walk across the room and sweep her into his arms. But he couldn't help but smile and say, "But..."

"Oh, wow, I'm so sorry. I shouldn't have interrupted you. I was..."

She took a step backward. Enough levity, he was being a fool. From the moment he'd met her, he'd known she was a beautiful, intelligent, serious agent, a person with a serious work ethic and a sense of humor, lovely...

Sensual. Worthy of every basic human admiration and...

And desire.

He believed he'd never been a wanker, a man who played upon feelings, emotions and sexuality. He'd never taken anyone for granted, but when he'd tried to draw close...

His fear of what he was had taken over. The knowledge that he was different, that he could never be completely honest. But here, now...

She was stunning, bright, funny, dedicated, everything he could ever desire and want. And she was here; she had come to him.

He hurried across the room and arched his brows in question as he lifted his arms to set around her. She gave him a slight querying glance, as if she'd never been sure of herself, either.

Then she smiled and slipped into his arms.

"So, I'm not interrupting, am I?" she inquired.

"Just a few hours of staring at the ceiling while mentally torturing myself, because I don't have the answers," he assured her.

"That was…well, what I thought I'd do tonight, too. Then I thought we might do it together. Then I wondered if you'd been thinking we were very good partners and…hmm. I think we like one another, and… Oh!"

She stepped back suddenly. "I'm sorry. Are you involved at home? I mean I wouldn't want—"

"I'll be honest. Recently, there was someone I was interested in, but I knew that wasn't going to happen. It was over before I joined Blackbird."

"I…uh, it's okay if I'm breakup sex," she said.

He shook his head. "Not breakup sex. I chose to end it for very good reasons. But let me ask the same, and again, it's okay—"

She grinned suddenly, shaking her head. "No involvement here in forever so…"

She pressed closer to him, lowering her voice, though there was no way they could be heard from the dining room or any other part of the house. "I believe that maybe…we are who and what we are. And maybe, in the great design of the world, we're meant to be together?"

He grinned at that. "Or in the great design of Adam Harrison and Jackson Crow. Which is okay with me," he whispered, stepping forward again, just holding her close, looking into her eyes and running his fingers down her cheek. "You're stunning!" he told her. "And bright and empathetic and dedicated and all the right things and…"

"You're pretty professional, too," she said, laughing.

"I started out with stunning," he reminded her.

"You're okay!" she teased. "And…hmm. I am bright. I mean…making it so easy and all! Oops, I didn't bring my Glock, but I'm sure yours is—"

"Close. Of course."

"But other than that, how smart, huh, to try to pick up an okay guy when you're both wearing nothing but towels?" she teased.

"Towels! Ah, well, lass, so easily remedied!"

He stripped his away. And when he pulled her close, the heat of their bodies melding was as intense as a jolt of electricity.

He let his lips cover hers at last, kissing deeply, tongues plunging, their embrace both sloppy and beautiful until they broke for air, looking at one another again.

He swept her up into his arms, startling her and causing her to grin as she wrapped her own arms around him.

"Sorry, trying to surpass that *okay* verdict!" he said.

"Your marks are going up," she teased.

Then they were on the bed.

They'd met just days ago, intense days, in which he felt he'd come to know her far better than those he might have known for years. And now…

He knew her with great and incredible intimacy, all the better for the brief but close and concentrated time they'd been together…

The feel of her skin was like flower petals. The warmth of her body a lava that flowed into him. Her eyes were crystal with both laughter and longing, and she moved as if the most natural act of human beings was an incredibly sensual and exotic dance.

Touching, kissing, fingertips, lips…

Coming together. Reaching the proverbial stars…

And then something almost as good, or on a different level, even better.

Just lying together, her head on his chest, his fingers lightly touching her hair. He was there, staring up at the ceiling, but he wasn't mentally flogging himself over the day.

He was feeling a sense of wonder.

"Um," she murmured, after a minute, "are you glad you let me in?"

"Glad and grateful." He laughed. "I'm glad you had the balls to take a chance."

She laughed in return.

"You told me something interesting tonight that I went on," she said.

"Oh? And what is that, lass?" he queried, rising on his elbow to look down at her.

"You said, *and when instinct calls, we should listen*," she told him, smiling up into his eyes.

He curled down at her side to pull her into his arms again. "Sometimes," he assured her, "I say very wise things!"

Eleven

"Ach! Morning!" Jeannette realized and jumped out of Daniel's bed, still somewhat amazed at herself that she'd acted without really thinking it out, that she followed through...

On my instincts, she thought with a smile.

But it was morning, 7:00 a.m., and time for the day to start. The professional day.

"See you at the coffeepot!" she told Daniel.

He laughed softly, rising himself, grabbing his towel and heading for the shower.

She grabbed her towel from the floor and fled into her own room and en suite, happy to stand under the hot water. She wondered if she should feel ashamed. She had brazenly walked in on a man.

She didn't feel ashamed in the least. She felt good. But...

She didn't know what lay ahead. She did know that, as of this moment in the day, Blackbird was what mattered. Being on the case...

Keeping another girl from dying. That was what mattered. And since it was daytime, it was time to wonder again if Jules Bastien aka Matisse was as real as he seemed. And if the equally wondrous Delphine was a true wonder of the world or...

If the facade hid a sickness of the human spirit that was beyond horrendous and cruel.

Showered and dressed—today in good boots that would easily travel over the growth in a long-dormant field—she left her bedroom to make her way quickly along the hall and to the coffeepot.

Daniel was already there, along with Gervais, Della and Luke.

"Among the great computers and other fantastic working conditions that Gervais has arranged, he has managed the best coffeepot known to man!" Luke said. "Jeannette, how would you like yours?"

She laughed. "I'm willing to bet Gervais has also arranged for sugar, artificial sweeteners and creamer that doesn't go bad. But as a cop my first year out of college, I learned to drink it black due to nothing else being left for rookies, or soured stuff. So, black will be fine for me!"

"Hey, we can make espresso and cappuccino in this thing, and we are in France! *Café au lait!*" Della told her.

Jeannette grinned. "I'll bet it's good black stuff," she said.

Della handed her a cup. She looked at Gervais. "Mason and I were going to head straight out with the maps created by the Reims police, showing where the bodies were found. I know many of the fields have just about been trampled flat, but—"

"That's fine," Gervais said. "My plan is this. To be there when the morning tour group arrives at the Deauville estate for their wine tasting. Luke, Carly and I will leave here soon, stop in at the police station, and be there if you need us for anything at any part of your search. Luke and Carly will be trying to track down Aristide Broussard from this end, and we'll all be ready to research and find the man you saw in the surveillance who was working at the Deauville estate."

"That's a good plan. What about backup if this man is at the Deauville estate—and ready to get violent? Or if Giselle or Tomas Deauville decide the gig is up and do something rash?" Jeannette asked.

Mason made an appearance just as she spoke, interrupting her with his arrival and a, "Hey! No slouch here. We'll be ready for anything. Also, we'll be stopping by to have a chat with the local police. Don't forget, before our very brief vacation, Della and I were working on the last touches of one of the first cases, so we're becoming quite comfortable in France, and with French behavior."

Jeannette grinned. "Whoa! Sorry. Mason, I know you're quite capable, but one never knows how many people—"

"Seriously, French police are on notice," he assured her. "So is this group," he said, looking at Gervais. "Heading out?"

"Heading on out," Gervais said. "Remember, everyone, three directions. Speed dial hits up everyone, including the Blackbird home offices, Jackson, Angela, or managing Krewe director at any time of day or night."

"So…?"

Daniel was speaking, addressing her, and Jeannette responded with, "Coffee to go, I guess."

"We have big carry cups in the cupboard," Gervais assured her. "*Alors!* I bought those myself."

"Well, thank you!" Jeannette assured him.

There was bustle around the cupboards and the sink as they all chose carry cups and passed out coffee. "And while Carly and I will be in Paris, we'll be ready to go anywhere we're needed," Luke reminded them all.

With nods of acknowledgment and waves, they all began to move.

She and Daniel were soon out in the car. Gervais pulled out ahead of them, and then they were on their way.

Jeannette had been afraid at first that they might be awkward with each other now. But Daniel asked, "Before I go too far, you brought a tablet, right? With the maps?"

She smiled and told him, "Yes, of course, I have the tablet and the maps."

"Of course. Thank God!" he teased. "It's a good thing one of us is perfect, since I'm just okay!"

She laughed, taking a long sip of her coffee, putting the cup in the holder and digging out her tablet. She studied the maps on the screen. They showed where the victims had been found, the identified victims, Patricia Gutterman, Virginia Bond and Catherine Blakely, and those still unidentified. They showed as well where the foot-by-foot searches had been carried out, surrounding the bodies and in some of the empty fields.

She began to frown as Daniel made his way through

the Paris traffic and headed toward Reims and the vine-yards surrounding the city.

The map also showed the field owned by the major companies—and the three that they had concentrated on owned by the Houses of Matisse, Deauville and Montague.

"Daniel," she murmured. "There's one field here… it's not far from the position where Patricia Gutterman's body was found." She looked up at him. "I'm sorry to say it seems to border land owned by the Matisse family, but…to the other side, there is land owned by the Montague family."

"And the police didn't search it?"

"She was found right by the road. They searched the peripheral area, but not very deep in. I don't know. Maybe the local police were not willing to start something that might be trespassing on private property? Or she was found before we discovered the still unidentified remains. But…"

He glanced over at her. "You know, I do trust your instincts."

"Well, is it just me? Or do you think there might be others out there and that eventually we might get a break with fingerprints, DNA or something that would be definitive about a direction to go in, at least?"

He looked straight ahead at the road as he replied, "It's all a strange mix. The older remains showed signs of torture. The bodies of the girls Shelley knew—Patricia, Virginia and Catherine—were pristine other than being drained of blood. But I think this is something that has been going on for a long time. And it brings me back to your theory. Whether it was Eliza-

beth Báthory—with or without her husband—or someone else within her family who wanted her property
and thought that blaming the torture and death on her
would be a good idea, the deaths went on a long time
before they stopped. We haven't identified the decomposed corpses. Most probably, as we discussed before,
they were homeless. They were poor. I believe we're far
better today as human beings in society. The girls we
know about weren't rich or poor, and it wouldn't have
mattered. Gervais LaBlanc would have been right on
the case. But…"

"You think the homeless—or wanderers, perhaps,
hitchhiking through Europe—might have been killed
over several years?" Jeannette asked.

"Exactly."

"Daniel, I want to start in that field. And if we wander onto private property, we'll apologize profusely.
But if it was something someone wanted to pursue, I
don't think a court anywhere in the world would find
us guilty of anything when we were desperately trying
to find truth and stop more murders from occurring."

He laughed. "Better sometimes to ask forgiveness
rather than to ask for permission?"

"Something like that. Except most of the land I'm
looking at is in flux—absentee owners, property for
sale, property forgotten… I think we're all right."

"When we get to Reims, you tell me where you want
to go."

"Pull over when you can. I'll explain on the map."

"Let me get out of all this traffic and we'll figure out
the best place to pull off the road and stop."

"Right!"

Twenty minutes later, the congestion eased up. Cars still went by now and then, but with much less frequency.

Daniel pulled off the road, and Jeannette showed him her tablet with the map drawn up. He studied the terrain. "This is land that appears to be owned here—by the Matisse family—and here—by the Deauvilles. And then not far over there, you have a plot that belongs to the Montague dynasty. But you're right, the body was so close to the road, they probably figured they were wasting resources to go too far back."

"Maybe we're wasting time—"

He grinned and shook his head. "No, lass, honestly, I love your instincts!"

Daniel put the car back in gear and headed to their new destination.

When they arrived they left the car and started out, traveling over land already trampled by police. Then they began to push their way through bracken, twisted long grasses and the occasional small trees.

"You ready for this?" Daniel asked her.

He had planned well as he wore denim jeans, a denim jacket and boots.

She thought she'd done almost as well, though she had opted for jeans, a flannel shirt, a sweatshirt and boots.

"I'm good," she assured him. "I can face any snagging twig!" she promised him. But then she caught his arm and said, "This is a lot of territory. I'm going to head to the west and straight. You want to take things toward the east and straight?"

"Got it," he told her. "If anything—"

"Scream blue blazes. You do the same."

He nodded and reached into his pocket for a pair of gloves to be ready if he discovered anything. She did the same.

Jeannette did as she had said and headed in a westward direction. At one point, she stopped and frowned.

While everywhere she walked now was overgrown and wild, it looked as if sometime in the past there had been something of a footpath through some of the foliage.

Before she could go any farther, though, she heard Daniel calling to her. "I'll keep talking so you can make your way to me," he told her.

"Oh, no, another body?" she called, hurrying toward the sound of his voice.

"No, not exactly!" he said.

She burst around a tree and saw him standing in an area of tall grass.

He wasn't alone. She blinked and knew the tall man in uniform who stood before Daniel wasn't a body.

Neither was he alive. And yet...

She could have sworn the uniform was American. One of her grandfathers had been a paratrooper in World War II, and she was sure he was wearing the same uniform.

He must have realized the way she was looking at him, because he nodded with a smile and said, "Yes, ma'am, 92nd Airborne Division. Name is Jake Clayton."

"I am so pleased to meet you and so sorry. And thankful. Thank you, sir, for serving your country— and giving your life in that service. Did you arrive—" she began.

"June 6th, 1944, part of the Normandy invasion," he said. "And it's all right. I was career military and left no wife or little ones behind, and I was able to see the victory of the Allied forces. In fact, did you know that a schoolhouse in Reims was where the Germans came to sign their first surrender? On May 7th, 1945, General Alfred Jodl of the German High Command was there when the first surrender papers were signed. Jodl wanted special terms—a surrender of those fighting the Western Allied forces. But General Dwight Eisenhower would not have it, and the surrender was unconditional. And I was here to learn about it when Dwight Eisenhower became president of the great nation we fought for! So… Well, I was able to see the world somewhat straighten itself out—for a time, of course. We are war-like creatures I fear, but…history is not helpful to the two of you now."

"Sir, we are both deeply respectful of history," Jeannette assured him.

"So this Scotty here has said!" the spirit of Jake Clayton told her. "But you're here about the happenings here, dreadful happenings. For several years now. At first… I didn't realize what was happening. Men came carrying or dragging bags, going through the brush, avoiding the planted fields. And at first, I didn't pay much attention, and you realize I am not always here. I enjoy a café in town. I have learned to speak and understand French well. I enjoy the news…and sometimes, I like to travel to the Normandy American Cemetery and Memorial. It's where my earthly remains rest, but as you both must know, those of us who remain also grow adept at hitchhiking and sometimes, but oh, so rarely, we find those who are like you, who see and hear us!"

"But you have seen people coming out here for—for years?" Jeannette asked.

He nodded gravely. "A little over two years, perhaps close to three... I believe the first time I saw something—and to this day, I'm not sure that what I saw was one of the bodies being left—might have been about three years ago. And then it was months...after that, months... But now, I have seen the police, and I know that they know. And I have been furious but ineffectual. Naturally, I would have spoken. I would have done something, but...you are the first of your kind I have seen in several decades now. I wish I could have helped earlier!"

"But you're helping now, so very much!" Jeannette said.

"I told Jake your theory has been that this has gone on for a very long time," Daniel said. "And you were right from the beginning."

"And you think that if we look, we will find human remains in the fields near here," Jeannette said.

"And I will help you look," Jake promised.

"Oh!" Daniel said, pulling out his phone and showing Jake a picture captured of the man from the Deauville estate who had been leaving the magic show. "Have you seen him?"

Jake barely looked at the image.

"Yes. I saw him! He was one of the men who dropped the poor girl by the road. I saw that. I so desperately wanted to do something! But now... I am helping you.

I will look as you will look. And if I find something, it will be incredible—because I will be able to tell you!"

"Thank you," Daniel said, and Jeannette nodded her sincere appreciation.

"Oh!" she said, realizing she and Daniel were both impressed by their new friend, and they needed to think clearly despite him. "I saw grass that had been flattened at some point not too, too long ago," she said. "I'm going back that way."

"I'll keep heading my way. We all call out if we find something," Daniel said.

"I'll call out—and you'll hear me!" Jake said.

Jeannette quickly retraced her footsteps, finding the location where she had seen the almost-flattened grass and brush.

Nothing, nothing and nothing.

She was beginning to lose heart when she came to a dead stop and stared.

She had discovered something that she had not expected.

It was a corpse, but...

Not so badly decomposed, and it had not been here long. It had not been brought through the trail she had just followed!

And it was not that of a young and beautiful woman.

It was the corpse of a man. Not just any man. The man that Gervais, Mason and Della had gone to the Deauville estate to try to find.

There was no reason to panic or rush; Jeannette's voice was strong and loud as she shouted that Daniel needed to join her.

When he reached her position, he saw she was crouched over a dead man.

The man they had just seen at the wine tasting, serving at the House of Deauville.

"Did you call the troops yet?" Daniel asked Jeannette.

"No. I—I called you and I looked at him, and... they're cleaning house, Daniel. I think they're trying to make sure anyone who might have been caught on surveillance, or anyone who might fall under suspicion in any way—and who might talk and reveal what is happening—is no longer able to do so."

He pulled out his phone and quickly alerted the team regarding what they had discovered.

Gervais promised that teams would arrive as quickly as possible. Of course, he reminded them to preserve the body as it now lay.

Daniel ended the call and looked at Jeannette. She was staring off into the distance.

"What?" he asked her.

"He wasn't brought here through the field the way that I came, the way you followed me," she said.

"No, this grass hasn't been flattened in a while," he agreed. "So..."

He pointed around the lone tree in the area, and they walked around it. He pointed.

"That's the Matisse property in that direction," Jeannette murmured, "according to our map, and it was prepared by the local authorities, so..."

"And the Matisse estate is in that direction, too," Daniel said, shaking his head. "This is baseless, but I can't help feeling our friend Jules Bastien was honestly and sincerely broken up about the deaths of the girls. And he was sincerely worried about Shelley."

"I know. He comes off as real," Jeannette said. "Oh, my God!" she exclaimed suddenly.

"What?"

He looked at her. She was wearing a truly pained expression.

"Daniel."

"What is it?"

"I believe, I'm, um, standing on...another corpse!" she said. "I need to move. I'm afraid to move. I don't want to mess up..."

"All right, you must move, you know that. But stay still and let me get to you. You can..."

He broke off.

She was right. She was standing on a corpse. This one was in a more advanced state of decomposition than they had expected.

Disarticulated bones were held together in places by drum-tight remnants of skin and bits and pieces of what appeared to have been leather material.

Had he been tortured? Stabbed dozens of times?

Walking through the tangle of grass, Jeannette had managed to step right where the stomach had once met up with the rib cage.

He stopped before his own feet could fall upon any of the bones or remnants of body and reached out but then drew back, telling her.

"Wait! Stand dead still. I'm just going to pick you up and move you."

"Can you do that from there?"

"Can and will," he promised.

He bent and balanced carefully before picking her up just below the arms and swinging her over to his side.

"Good job," she murmured.

"I try."

"Hey!" they heard, as she steadied herself.

It was their newfound ghost, Jake Clayton.

"I believe I have found someone… Oh! And so have you," he said.

"A few. Long gone and recent," Daniel said. "Around the tree."

Clayton walked around the tree and returned, frowning.

"That's the man you were looking for!" he said. He shook his head. "Cleaning out the trash, I imagine. Killers don't kill themselves. And not like that! He has a million cuts on him."

"Tortured," Jeannette murmured.

"In the way that a conquering warrior might torture a despised enemy," Daniel murmured.

"Never! That would be against—"

"Today, it would be a war crime. Hundreds of years ago, people got away with atrocities. And even now…" He thought about some of the recent events in the world. "Well, none of us can control certain people in warfare, but there was a Hungarian nobleman years ago who was known for torturing the Turks when they fell to him."

"Ah, I know exactly who you are talking about," Jake said. "Ferenc II Nádasdy, husband of the Blood Countess, Elizabeth Báthory. Now, finding the truth of history there is…for another time!" Jake said. "The other body is just steps ahead of where we were, Daniel. You turned when Jeannette called out, and I went forward.

I found one similar to this, but I believe the victim was a woman, and she's been there months to a few years." He paused for a minute. "I'm sorry—I don't know how to judge. The dead I'm familiar with died because of bullets or bombs, and sometimes in my arms."

"I'm so sorry for that," Jeannette murmured.

"Of course, of course," he murmured.

They could hear sirens, the sound coming closer and closer.

"I'll get to the road and lead them back here," Daniel said.

"And when we need to get to the third corpse," Jake said, "just say you're going to lead them. I'll be here. No one else will notice."

"Ah, you explain to Jake!" he told Jeannette, because if Mason and Della were there with Gervais, they would see their new friend, Jake Clayton, as well.

Daniel hurried on out to the road. At first, he could hear Jeannette's voice, and he smiled, thinking Jake was going to be amazed when he met Mason and Della. They would be able to explain that there was a man like Adam Harrison, a man who had seen something special possessed by a limited amount of people—a man who had gained the prestige needed and had the necessary financial resources to create a special unit of those with the ability to ask the dead to help stop crime.

Jake Clayton would like it, he knew. The man must have been one hell of a soldier.

Of course, that was the problem with meeting ghosts. Too often, it was difficult to imagine the pain they must have endured.

But it was also good to meet a man like Jake Clayton. A soldier who had fought for his country and now wanted to fight for humanity. He was a man who created his personal war on monsters in defense of the innocent.

Police cars drove up first with Gervais, and Mason and Della were in his car, following behind. Gervais got out of the car and directed the officer to pay heed to Daniel.

"Are you sure that you've discovered the man—"

"Yes. We are sure. But we found more as well. Just around a tree and about ten feet from the body of the man is a rotting corpse. I think male as well. Then there's another body… Gervais, this has been going on for some time."

"We have two medical examiners on the way along with a forensic team," Gervais told him. "If you'll lead the way?"

Daniel nodded. Gervais, Mason, Della and an officer followed him. Jeannette waited a foot from the body that couldn't have been there more than fifteen hours or so.

Their World War II ghost was by Jeannette's side. Mason and Della looked at him, arching a brow, but giving no clue whatsoever to Gervais or his French officers that they were seeing the spirit of a man long gone in the last great conflict to tear apart the world.

The officer said something to Gervais, who nodded, and the officer headed back toward the road. "He'll bring the others out as soon as they arrive. So, there is a dead man here," he said. "And there is another right around the tree. I don't think even the most experienced medical examiner in the world could say exactly how long this one has been here. Ah—"

"The corpse is so decomposed we might not have

realized it was there in the tangle of roots and grass around it," Daniel told the new arrivals.

"He's being kind," Jeannette said. "I was literally standing in it before I looked down and realized I was looking at human remains."

"And there's another?" Della asked.

"Aye, there is," Daniel murmured, looking at the spirit of Jake Clayton.

Clayton nodded, intrigued, aware that at least a few—if not all—of the newcomers could see him as well.

He started to lead the way.

"I'll stay here for the medical examiners and forensic team," Jeannette told the group.

"Yes, good," Gervais said. "They'll need to know where not to step on the remains that have been left here."

Daniel followed Jake Clayton—as if he were the one leading the way himself.

They came upon the corpse Jake had discovered. Like the remains beneath the tree, these had been there some time. Jagged bone stuck out here and there. The eye sockets were empty. Creatures and critters had long since consumed the organs and the soft flesh of the deceased.

"This is…a nightmare," Gervais murmured.

"What happened with Giselle Deauville and her husband? Were you able to speak with them, ask them anything about the man we know now to be dead?" Daniel asked as they all stood, studying the corpse.

"We never had a chance to talk," Mason told him, staring down at the remains. "We arrived with the tour and slipped in. In her, oh, so sweet welcoming speech, Giselle noted Gervais and nodded, indicating she knew we'd come to talk. But we received your call and came out here immediately. The conversation will change now. We'll be wanting to know how their employee of yesterday wound up sliced to ribbons and dead in a field today."

"The conversation will change, indeed," Daniel agreed. "I'll go back to Jeannette if you three can see what you can find out here," he murmured, turning around.

Jeannette was still waiting for the medical and forensic people to arrive, but she was hunkered down, staring at a piece of paper in her gloved hand, when he reached her.

"What is it?" he asked.

"This is a card. It can't have been here too long, but…" She looked up at him.

"What is it?"

"It's an advertisement with a phone number and website," she said, frowning and evidently not happy at all. "A business card, Daniel. A business card for Monsieur Illusion Incroyable. Daniel, this card is from Jules Bastien, née Matisse. Could we have been so horribly fooled by the man? Is he part and parcel of all this? Did he kill this man, aware that we were after him?"

Daniel studied the card. And he just didn't know.

Twelve

Their work in the field went on for hours; but eventually the Blackbird agents could do no more, and the work was left to medical examiners, their assistants and forensic teams.

Preliminary reports suggested that the two unknown bodies had been in the field any time between three to six months, perhaps up to a year and a half for one of them. While they couldn't give cause of death, lacerations on several bones of both victims suggested the victims had been tortured before death.

Jeannette had managed to get Jake Clayton alone with Mason and Della so she could introduce them. That was the high point of the day. Jake was incredulous he had met not just one, then two, but four living beings who could see him. He was equally pleased that finally he had been able to help—and might just be able to aid in actually bringing a heinous criminal to justice. Mason and Della, of course, were grateful to him. That part was good.

The new bodies…

Still, Jeannette could be grateful that her "instincts" had been worth following.

Of course, she thought, somewhat amused with herself, it seemed they had been good in another direction, too. She glanced at Daniel. He gave her a curious look, but nodded, approving again her idea that they needed to investigate further in the fields.

Since Gervais had decided to remain with his French teams, it was just Mason, Della, Daniel and Jeannette who determined that the morning cups of coffee had only gone so far. It was time to stop for something to eat.

Naturally, she suggested the restaurant where their waiter Alphonse worked.

And she was glad to see Alphonse was working today. Daniel asked that they be seated at one of his tables.

By the time they arrived, the lunch crowd was over, and it was an hour or so before even an early dinnertime would arrive.

Alphonse first appeared very happy to see them and to meet Mason and Della.

But when their drink orders had been taken and he returned to their table, he wore a worried frown.

"You have heard, of course, that our situation grows worse out here. Customers at lunch were saying there's a stretch of road filled with vehicles from the police spilling out all kinds of personnel and investigators. More bodies—everyone knows it. I am happy to see so many of you. I believe there is safety in numbers!" he told them.

"Alphonse—" Jeannette began.

"I know. I know. I figured out you're law people. You're Americans and…" he began, pausing as he looked at Daniel.

"Scottish," Daniel said.

"Right! Anyway… I don't care who anyone is—they can fall prey to monsters!" Alphonse said.

"Hey, I want you to be careful, too," Jeannette told him. "The bodies are male and female."

Alphonse looked around as if trying to make sure he could not be overheard. "I am not a policeman or any such thing, but just listening, doesn't it sound as if maybe the men who were killed were killed because they failed a greater power, the monster in charge?"

"That's possible. So," Mason suggested, "do yourself a favor. Don't think out loud and stay far, far away from any discussion regarding what's going on."

Alphonse nodded and looked away. "So! Have you seen anything in Reims yet? You must go by the churches, we have beautiful cathedrals and—"

"We actually recently learned the Nazis surrendered in Reims," Jeannette murmured.

"It is still a school, Lycée Roosevelt, but you can see it. And we are about four and a half hours, by vehicle, to the American Cemetery and Memorial in Normandy. But kings were crowned at the Cathedral of Reims. Truly, it's beautiful and remarkable. And we're very fortunate, of course, that it wasn't destroyed through the horror of World War II."

"Well, of course, we will try to see it," Daniel assured him. "But, Alphonse, while it's quiet here—despite us telling you to keep a low profile—is there anything that you've seen or heard—"

"Ah, the fields, and this place!" Alphonse said. He shook his head. "I see many people in here. Sometimes, even the local great families come by. Ah! Do you know what is strange? In the big companies, the major companies, the heads, the big money men, they are decent, they are polite, they tip... It's just...not always. There are..."

"Jerks?" Mason suggested.

"Wankers!" Daniel said decisively.

Alphonse paused to laugh. "*Mais, oui!* And still, it is Madame Giselle and Madame Leticia who..." He paused again, taking a breath, perhaps seeking the right explanation in English. "They behave as if we are worms on the floor."

Jeannette didn't have to say it out loud.

Della did.

"Being wretched elitists does not make them killers," she said.

Alphonse nodded. He grimaced. "Well, if being nice does, then Delphine Matisse is who you seek! Oh, food, what shall you eat?"

They ordered their meals, and Alphonse moved away from the table.

"I truly hate to say this," Mason said, leaning toward Jeannette, "because I know that you two have believed in the magician, Jules Bastien. But he lied to you—"

"He didn't really lie. We never asked the right questions. It never occurred to us to ask him if he was related to anyone in the wine country," Daniel said.

"A lie of omission," Della said quietly.

"All right, he—and his mother—come off like saints.

But you did just find his card by a body," Mason pointed out to Jeannette.

She nodded. "Trust me. I am rethinking. All right, Mason, he said we were welcome to come out with him to the House of Matisse at any time—and go through anything."

"Maybe we should hold him to it," Della suggested.

Jeannette looked at Daniel, who nodded. "It's a logical step at this time," he said. "So, I guess we go to see a magic show again tonight."

"Maybe we'll all go," Mason said thoughtfully. "We've, uh, in a way, solved the mystery of the man you saw working at the House of Deauville. The plot is growing thicker—more and more bodies—but we're running up against dead ends at every turn."

"A group party at a magic show. Sounds fun," Daniel agreed.

"Then, we'll let everyone know," Mason said, pulling out his phone.

"And," Daniel added, "while we're doing that…" He paused, shrugging, lowering his voice. "Alphonse just said that people from both the big places and the small are in here all the time. We'll talk to Jules Bastien tonight and make arrangements with him to come back out here. And as he suggested, we'll talk to him and his mother, and gently tear things apart. If we do so, I think we should go ahead and see if it's still possible to book a few rooms at the Matisse bed-and-breakfast."

"That's a good plan. We shouldn't overwhelm Jules and his mommy," Jeannette said, "but we'll all be within an easy commute if anything at all were to get out of control. I just…"

"Aye, it's hard, I know, to believe they could be culpable, but..." Daniel said.

"But yes, I wasn't expecting that card—"

"Which could mean anything. Just that someone involved picked it up at the show or even spoke with him or even knows him," Della said.

"Or it could mean it fell out of one of Jules's pockets when he was dumping a dead man," Jeannette admitted. "But one way or another, you're right. It's a good logical step. I guess we run it by Gervais?"

"Of course," Mason said. "He won't object. I feel quite badly for Gervais. This is his country, his home, and he's the law here. And he's finding that this situation is worse than it even appeared to be at first. And he—" Mason broke off.

Jeannette looked toward the door.

"Speak of the devil!" Della murmured.

They all laughed. "Hardly the devil," Mason murmured. "But, yes, wow. And here he is!"

Mason lifted a hand so that Gervais could see where they were sitting and join them. The Frenchman nodded and walked over to them, thanking Alphonse as he quickly supplied another chair for the table.

"I shouldn't be in a restaurant. I should be bathing in disinfectant," he said, shaking his head as he joined them. "The teams are still searching in that field. I'm hoping we did discover the last of the bodies...but..."

"You're worried there may be more in other fields?" Daniel asked him.

He nodded. "This...this has been going on under our noses for God only knows how long. I feel as if..."

"You didn't fail anyone," Mason told him quickly and

with assurance. "None of us has the power to change the fact that the world is filled with those who are unfortunate as well as those who do extremely well. When someone who is transient disappears, no one knows it—and if they did, they wouldn't know where to start. This isn't your fault, Gervais. When you were alerted to what was happening, you acted immediately. And honestly, we're good at what we do and we still must go through all the hoops and investigate until we do get somewhere."

Gervais nodded. He shrugged. "*C'est vrai*, we all need to be scrubbed of…death. But! *Alors!* I did stop because I haven't eaten."

"Which is why we're here," Daniel told him. "And we have a plan."

He explained to Gervais that they wanted to go to the magic show again. Then they wanted to make arrangements to be out in Reims the following day with part of their team, taking Jules Bastien up on his offer to show them the Matisse winery. The other part of the team would lurk nearby in case there was trouble—or if a small army was needed to tear the place apart.

Gervais nodded. "Put it all into action," he told them. "I will get you tickets. Can we make it back in time for the show tonight?"

"If we eat and run," Della said.

"And here comes our food," Jeannette noted. "And my plate is huge, Gervais. We may split it in half—"

"Della and I can share, and Gervais can take one of our plates," Mason said.

"But I can't eat all this!" Jeannette protested.

"Then Gervais will have a lot of food!" Daniel announced. "We'll just ask for another plate, and we can all pile on a few bites of delicacies for him!"

There was plenty of food to go around the table, and Gervais thanked them all while pulling out his phone to make arrangements for the magic show. Jeannette pulled out her own phone, discovering quickly that she could make reservations for three rooms the next night at Madame Matisse's B&B.

"We're set to go?" she asked Gervais.

He nodded, smiled and returned, "And on your end, we're good to go?"

"Three rooms rented via the booking site," she told him.

He nodded. "Good. Blackbird will take those—I have an arrangement with a hotel. At least...at least when we keep moving, I feel we are getting somewhere even when our clues lead us to solid walls. We find suspects—and they wind up dead themselves."

"Maybe the walls aren't so solid," Daniel offered. "Time to get the check and head on back!"

"There is still someone out there who hasn't been discovered as yet," Jeannette noted as Mason offered Alphonse his company credit card.

"The mysterious Aristide Broussard," Daniel said.

"They've been searching through every known avenue," Gervais said. "The last known phone he had hasn't been used in days. His credit cards haven't been used. When he disappeared from the House of Deauville, he did so cleanly. I'm afraid..."

"That he's in a field somewhere, too?" Della said quietly.

Gervais nodded.

"Either that," Daniel said, "or he knows he's in danger, and he's managing to keep himself off the grid. It's frightening what resources the very rich might have. Let's hope he's out there somewhere."

"And Shelley is doing fine?" Jeannette murmured, looking at Mason.

"She's fine—happy that she's safely hidden away," Mason said.

"And she doesn't want to go home?" Jeannette asked.

Mason shook his head. "No. She's in a safe house and under twenty-four-hour guard here. She's afraid she'd be in danger again at home, and she might not get the same protection."

"And what about the girls we met?" Jeannette asked Gervais. "They are still—"

"I have officers watching them and following them wherever they go. Officers are keeping guard at their little hotel through the night," he said.

Jeannette smiled. "Thank you!"

"Finding old bodies is one thing," Gervais said, and then he winced. "At least the new body discovered today may have been that of someone guilty of conspiracy to commit murder himself. No more innocent young women! Or men. But…"

"Let's get going or we won't make that magic show," Daniel said. "If we leave now, we may have time to shower first!"

At last, they all headed out to their cars.

And when they were driving back through Reims and toward Paris, Jeannette looked at Daniel curiously. "Interesting."

"What?"

"Gervais said he'd stay at a hotel. But there are six of us. I mean, obviously, he knows the others are together, but…no one blinked. About us, I mean. We have three rooms—"

"There is a couch," Daniel offered.

"I'm not sleeping on a couch!"

He laughed. "I was taking the high road!" he told her.

"No one is sleeping on a couch. And after last time, someone is keeping guard through the night, just as in Paris!"

Daniel nodded, grinning as he looked ahead.

"We'll deal with it, whatever."

"We'll admit we slept together," Jeannette said. "But we're *not* showering together now. We are not going to be late for that show!"

"Not to worry. We won't be late for the show."

They weren't. As unlikely as it seemed by the time they were leaving Reims and the wine region, they made it back to the house in Paris in time to shower and change—and for their entire team to arrive at the magic show on time.

At the house, Jeannette and Daniel had hurried to their own rooms—and showered and dressed for the evening in them.

They met in the hallway, grinning. Maybe it was the glitter of a new relationship. But they'd both known they hadn't the time for anything else.

Despite their speed, Gervais, also showered—*disinfected*, as he told them—was waiting for them. Jeannette and Daniel rode with him while Mason brought Della, Luke and Carly.

They arrived to discover they had backstage tickets again.

Jeannette looked at Gervais and told him, "I think you're the magician!"

"No, one of the young women in the main precinct is a genius at the internet and finding what is needed. She is the one, I fear, who is the magician. But the show is about to begin!"

Lights dimmed. Jules Bastien arrived suddenly, appearing out of the softness of the fog. Tonight, he walked through the audience to the stage.

He stopped to draw a golden coin from the ear of an audience member, laughing and telling her first in French and then in English that he was heartily sorry, it should have been a real gold coin. But it was, instead, a gold-covered chocolate, and delicious nonetheless!

He went on to produce several things out of thin air, and then to introduce his assistant. Marni appeared, lovely in her skimpy magician's assistant outfit, smiling and bowing and gathering applause.

Jeannette wasn't sure how, but she was certain he had seen her and Daniel in the audience and the others as well.

And when he needed a volunteer, he turned to her again, grinning and winking as he brought her up on stage.

She went into the glass box. That night, as she went down, she could hear Marni talking to her from the works below the stage.

"You are returned! Well, then, you know what will happen, I needn't reassure you!"

"I am fine, thanks," Jeannette assured her.

And she was. The trick worked as it had before. As Jeannette popped her head up from the trunk, Jules Bastien came to help her step from the box. She smiled, thanked him and bowed with him for the applause. Then she returned to her seat in the audience.

That night, though, he had a trick they hadn't seen before. A guillotine. For this trick, the person would be closed into a box. The blade would fall.

And it was Daniel he chose for the trick.

For a moment, Jeannette felt a sensation of pure panic. The concept of the guillotine had come up a few times too many for her liking.

The box was explained, the parting of it was explained and then the trick went into action.

Jeannette hadn't realized she was gripping her seat until she felt a hand fall on hers. She turned to see Della was smiling at her.

"It's a trick. He'd not going to dispatch Daniel here in front of the audience. Come on. It's okay. You were on stage. And remember, you're the one who believes in the man," she reminded her.

She did believe in Jules Bastien.

But she could be wrong, as noted by the fact she'd found his card next to a dead body that very day.

Of course, the trick went off without a hitch. The box was parted, as a head might be parted from a body.

It was put back together.

And Daniel emerged, unharmed, unscratched.

The show went on. And when it was over, they headed out to position themselves at the end of the line to speak privately with the magician.

When the last of Bastien's fans had gone through the

door to speak with him and it was their turn, they entered en masse. Jules didn't seem surprised.

"So..." he began, looking from one person to the next in their small crowd.

"I am not sure who you know and who you don't," Daniel told him politely.

"I have met Monsieur LaBlanc," Jules said, nodding to Gervais. He didn't seem distressed to see the man whose name was synonymous with law enforcement in Paris. He nodded politely. Daniel went on to introduce him to Mason, Della, Luke and Carly.

And to explain what they were doing there.

"Well, I hope you enjoyed the show. Jeannette, I knew, of course, you would be a wonderful volunteer. But Monsieur Murray! You were excellent, too. If all fails with law enforcement, you should consider a position on stage!"

They all laughed easily and Gervais started to go on, but Jules spoke before he could get a word out.

"I have seen the news. It is ablaze with the fact that bodies now seem to be as prevalent in the fields as wine grapes. It is incredibly distressing," Jules told them.

"That's why we have come to you for help," Jeannette told him. "Your mother has been wonderfully kind. But we'd like to come out to the House of Matisse, head into the fields and seriously speak to some of her workers, find out if any of them have seen anything, look around and see if the House of Matisse isn't being used by someone else as a staging place."

She was afraid he would protest and demand to know if that wasn't their way of saying his mother was guilty.

But Jules didn't protest at all. He let out a sigh.

"I'm not sure how it would look if you all—"

"No, no. Not all of us. Oh, we are all going to Reims," Jeannette told him.

"But it's because we figured that perhaps we could finally see the cathedral while these two were doing the talking!" Della said.

"She's in love with French history," Mason explained dryly.

"Oh, yes! And Reims is the most beautiful city!" Della went on.

"I want to see the little schoolhouse," Carly said, shaking her head. "She loves older history, and I love newer history and to think of all that has gone on in Reims!"

"We have reservations at your mother's bed-and-breakfast," Luke put in. "It's so convenient and these two—" he paused to indicate Jeannette and Daniel "—loved it! It's close to everything. All right, I think we're getting carried away. We understand it would not look good, given the circumstances, if we were all to descend upon you. And Jeannette and Daniel have met your mother."

"I told you, I would be happy to take you out there. Just remember, it will be a tour day tomorrow, and she presents herself at the hospitality suite for the tastings—"

"Of course! We won't interfere!" Jeannette assured him. "We can wander then and talk to the workers."

"D'accord," Jules said, nodding seriously to Gervais. "I have said I would do whatever was needed to help. I know my mother feels the same way. Shall I meet you

at the bed-and-breakfast? I run a bit late in my mornings and must drive out, too, so at eleven?"

"That would be wonderful," Jeannette said quietly.

Jules nodded. "Then it is set. And," he said to the others, "I hope you will enjoy Reims. It is truly one of the most beautiful cities, amazingly spared by the bombs of World War II. And with any luck and God's help, it will survive whatever wars man is determined to fight throughout time. *Bonsoir*, and *merci*!" he told them.

It wasn't until they were on their way out that Jeannette turned to Daniel, realizing they hadn't seen Marni at his side as he had greeted his fans.

"No Marni!" she murmured.

"She is good at disappearing," Daniel said, turning to Gervais. "Have we learned anything about her?" he asked.

"Nothing that creates a red flag, as you say," Gervais told him. "She is twenty-seven, grew up in Paris, attended university here…"

"Right. Maybe we should see if we can't dig a little more deeply into her life," Mason suggested. "And," he added, "maybe it should be at least one more of us with you tomorrow."

"I think an addition of one would be okay. Not Gervais. Too many people know his position with the Paris police," Jeannette said.

"Luke or I will come," Mason said. "We'll figure that—"

"No," Della said, "Mason, I think it would be better if it was Carly or I. Whoever is doing this—men have been killed, but I think we all believe they were killed because they were in danger of being brought in—and they might have spilled the truth. Carly and I are not as imposing to anyone involved in this as you or Luke might be."

"Ah, those fools!" Mason said lightly. "But you're right."

"All right. Three of us will go with Jules to the House of Matisse. The others will be nearby, ready to come at a moment's notice," Carly said.

They were still standing outside the theater. Jeannette was looking toward the cemetery.

"What is it?" Gervais asked her.

"Ah, nothing," she said.

Daniel hopped in to save her. She couldn't tell Gervais she was thinking they might just check in with the poor and wonderful woman, Henriette, who had met the guillotine during the turbulent early years of the French Revolution—for speaking out for the people, if Jeannette had gotten their conversations right, and she was certain she had.

"Gervais, the card we now have with evidence— Jules's card—was not mentioned on purpose. Should we have told him what we discovered?" Daniel asked.

"I think you were right," Gervais said. "The world knows that bodies were found. They do not know the body of a man who had worked for the House of Deauville was among them. If by chance Jules Bastien or his mother or anyone with the House of Matisse is involved, it's best they do not know we found anything that implied they were. So, I will drive you home for the evening. Tomorrow, I will meet you at the house here in Paris early so we may start out—and the lot of us are checked in for our stays in Reims."

Jeannette glanced back at Mason. "All right, we'll see everyone back at the house!"

She smiled and he nodded.

She knew he would go to the statue of St. Michael to see if Henriette happened to be there.

She and Daniel hurried on with Gervais, and he drove them to their headquarters on Île de la Cité.

He dropped them off and was serious and quiet as he did so. Jeannette turned to him before getting out of the car and said, "Gervais. Please. We will find out what's going on. I promise you."

He managed to smile. "I cannot help but think of those people out there, so many homeless here in Paris alone. And it seems it might well be those unfortunate in life who have been taken as pawns in a cruel murderer's designs. And it has been going on for a while. And I missed it."

"No one can know everyone or know who has come and who has gone. Gervais, this is not on you, please, remember that!"

He nodded. *"Bonsoir!"* He lifted a hand, and she stepped back as he drove off.

Daniel keyed in the gate and then the door and Jeannette yawned and told him, "Long day! I cannot wait for bed."

"Hmm. That can be taken a few ways," he teased.

She laughed. "Well, I mean—"

"Whatever we mean," he said with a sigh, "I'm afraid we're up tonight. One of us for the first few hours with the next for another few hours and then we both get to sleep."

"Oh, right! Of course," Jeannette said.

"If you're tired, I'm happy to take first guard," he said.

"No, if you don't mind, if I fall asleep, I'm afraid you might have a hard time waking me up!" she told him.

As they spoke, Mason and the others arrived.

"Anything?" Jeannette asked them anxiously.

"No, we hung around talking in front of the theater for a bit, saw nothing except people leaving the show or heading for the night spots," Della told her. "And then we tried walking by the statue of St. Michael, but your friend wasn't there. I wonder…"

"What's that?" Daniel asked.

Della shrugged. "I wonder if, when this is all over, we might still spend some time with her! She was a voice for revolution before the hierarchy went down, and thus she was a victim of those who didn't want to hear her demands for the people. Then, of course, the time of the Terror began and it was others who met the guillotine's blade. Napoleon, fighting so valiantly for the French people, turned around, called himself *consul*, and then crowned himself emperor of France! They say it brought an era of stability for a bit. And Napoleon went the way of many such a man, dying in exile. Henriette was dead herself then, but…"

"She is fascinating," Jeannette agreed. "Now go to bed, everyone! I am first guard!"

"As you wish. People, we have a long day tomorrow," Mason said. "Guard duty tonight will be Jeannette, Daniel and then it's—"

"It's me," Della reminded him. "So! Good night, all!"

One by one, everyone disappeared up the stairs except for Daniel.

"Go! Get some sleep!" she told him.

"Are you sure—"

"I am. Please. I am waking you up in exactly three hours!"

"No need. I set an alarm. I'll be out here."

Jeannette headed to the table and the computers, thinking she'd keep herself awake by going over video footage again.

She did so. She watched the magic show.

The footage was updated every day. Now when she looked at the last video, she could see what Henriette had seen, Jules Bastien with Madame Delphine Matisse.

Time seemed to weigh on her hands, and the images in front of her blurred. She made herself a cup of coffee and watched the time crawl by. She was getting nowhere, trying to think, trying to reason. She reminded herself again that they could be entirely wrong, that all three of the smaller houses they'd been investigating might have nothing at all to do with the bodies in the fields.

But how can that be? How can no one who lives or works out by the fields have seen anything at all in all this time? How could they avoid people if they didn't know when others came and went, when they didn't know which fields might be traveled and which might not?

She realized she was getting nowhere and was just sitting, staring at the screen, when Daniel came out and grinned at her and assured her she could finally go to sleep and stay asleep until morning.

She smiled at him and murmured, "Maybe," before disappearing into her room.

But she didn't stay there. She stripped, changed and slipped through the connecting door to his room.

She did fall asleep immediately.

But she heard him come in. She was curled to the other side and couldn't see him, but she knew he paused, surprised.

And then he came in, stripping down, gun on the bedside table, before trying very quietly to lie down beside her.

She rolled into his arms.

"You're awake!" he said, surprised.

"Some things are worth being awake for!" she assured him, sliding into his arms. "Oh!" she said worriedly, looking down into his eyes. "But you must be exhausted."

"Not that exhausted!" he assured her. "We have about three and a half hours... Use a half hour, that leaves us three or...you know, however it works out!"

She smiled. Because there was something about his arms around her, his touch, that seemed to help everything make sense...

And when the morning came, it would be so much better because...

Humanity could be beautiful, too.

Thirteen

Morning came early. Daniel realized for the first time in his professional career he was loath to honor the alarm clock and hop out of bed.

But he did.

Jeannette was as quick to rise, heading for the connecting door and turning back to grin at him. "Um, at least…let's see, Humphrey Bogart, *Casablanca*, um, 1942, I think? 'We'll always have Paris'?"

"What? You're done with me already?" he queried. "I thought I was at least *okay*?"

She laughed softly. "Not at all, Special Agent Murray. After this, maybe we'll have Reims as well!" Grinning, she started to move again but paused and this time said seriously, "I do hope that we'll see Jake Clayton today."

"We will," he said. "Again, I wish I might have known that man in life. Life is strange, of course, because our physical being is one thing. But with him, you can see so clearly that truly having honor, believing in a fight for one's country against the extermination of a group of people…being a soldier, bravely determined to enter the battle for what is right…it's in the soul. He'll be there. And he'll keep helping us. Like Henriette."

"They couldn't find her last night," Jeanńette reminded him.

"She might have been busy elsewhere, but she seems determined to stop this, too."

"Right! Shower!" she said, leaving the room quickly at last.

Luke and Carly were in the kitchen pouring coffee when they emerged. Mason and Della were right behind them.

"Remember, if there's trouble, we'll be close," Luke said.

"On speed dial," Daniel assured him. "Team player here, no cowboy!" he assured him.

Luke laughed. "Cowboys in Scotland?"

Mason and Della smiled as they heard and were followed by Gervais.

They were taking individual cars out to Reims, ready to divide and move in any direction when necessary.

"So," Gervais announced. "I will go to Madame Matisse's bed-and-breakfast with the team, and I will be there to meet up with Jules Bastien and Delphine Matisse. Delphine, of course, knows me. We were honest about needing help, hoping that—with no insult intended—one of her workers might be able to help us. But we don't mean to be threatening. But, of course, Delphine will come to the house first. She must—to give you keys," he said.

"Keys that many people seem to have?" Mason asked dryly.

"That is why we keep a team member on guard through the night, right?" Daniel asked him.

"True," Mason agreed. "But…"

"She should have had the place rekeyed immediately. There is a legal problem in there," Gervais said. "But one I don't want to get into now when we're playing for bigger stakes."

"Obviously not. We must not appear to be threatening, but rather needy," Daniel said.

"Exactly," Gervais agreed.

"Let's move," Mason said.

They headed out. Jeannette studied the landscape as they traveled. Daniel looked at her curiously.

"What?"

She shook her head. "So much history here! From the arrival of the Parisii…years of monarchs and royalty ruling, old wars, new wars. A man like Napoleon being such a force in the revolution—then climbing high to crown himself emperor! But I guess because of Jake Clayton, I keep thinking about the city, the people and World War II. And that sometime, I would like to be here just as a tourist. I have been before, but it's been a while. Notre Dame is amazing, and so is the Louvre and so much more! And honestly, I haven't seen the amazing sights in Reims."

"Ah, but think of it this way!" Daniel told her. "Today, you will see what tourists don't usually get to see. Even on a wine tour, guests don't get into the true living quarters of the dynastic wineries."

"Yeah? How far do you think she'll let us in? Of course, Jules has spoken with her by now, so if there is something that she needs to hide herself…"

"It will be gone."

"I still wonder if she can possibly be guilty," Jeannette said. "We'll learn what we can learn. And… Oh!"

"What is it?"

She was studying her phone.

"I just got a message. It's from Clara—"

"From who?"

"Clara Miller, one of the young women on the tour with us. Daniel, stop! We've got to turn around."

"Why? What's happened?"

He did as she instructed him, quickly finding a place where he could get around a circle to head back into the heart of Paris.

"I'm letting everyone know," she murmured as she hit the speed dial on her phone that would connect her with the others and put it on speaker so Daniel could talk and hear as well.

"We've got a problem, Gervais. You had guards on those girls Daniel and I met on the wine tour, right?"

"Of course. If I said it, I did it," he assured her.

"Clara Miller texted she'd seen the same man— and she knew, though we didn't tell her, that we were here investigating something. She was grateful for the guard. But they're at a morning improv show in a little place near Notre Dame. She says he was with them, but now he's disappeared. We're going back. It may be unnecessary, but—"

"I'll make calls and turn around," Gervais said.

Daniel glanced at Jeannette and said, "We'll run a little late. We'll see if Gervais can contact the officer on guard duty, and if not—"

"No more victims!" Mason said. "Go ahead. Keep in

contact. We'll keep on moving and then call you back. If necessary, we'll put our 'rip apart the House of Matisse' as late as necessary."

"Making calls," Gervais said.

"Me, too," Jeannette said. She quickly dialed Clara. She was grateful the girl answered, but she sounded as if she was terrified.

"I—I—we figured you were cops," she said nervously. "And…we were grateful, happy that you made sure to get guards on us. But this man…he didn't want us frightened. And when we saw him too many times… well, he said he'd be on and off duty. He was with us today, behind us. I mean, with us behind us, watching us. But now…the show is over. They're going to kick us out, and he isn't here and he isn't in front—"

"Where are you exactly?"

Clara nervously rattled off an address.

"And I think there's another man here. Another man we've seen before, and it might have been when we were on the tour—"

"At which house?" Jeannette asked.

"I don't know. You weren't sampling as much wine as we were. I don't remember. Oh, God, we're all so frightened. This place…there's an alley behind it, and we're not in the best area…not far from the Porte de la Chapelle, an old place, a little theater, but…we shouldn't have come. There are little streets, narrow passages… and I may be panicking and ridiculous, but I'm scared, so scared!"

"Don't move—we're checking on your guard right now and—"

"We're not far. I can get us there in five minutes," Daniel told her.

"Stay on the line with me," Jeannette told her.

Her connection was holding strong, but she didn't want to lose contact with Clara. It was all right; Daniel nodded at her and answered the call from Gervais.

"We can't reach the officer," Gervais told him. "I've called local—"

"We're almost where they are—we'll be there first," Daniel told them. "We're going in silent. If someone did something to that officer…maybe we'll get them."

"On my way, close behind," Gervais said.

"Oh, no, oh, no…" Clara said over the line.

Then she was gone.

But Daniel hadn't lied. He pulled off the road, heedless as to whether or not parking was legal, and the two of them hurried out of the car. Daniel pointed out the theater sign on the building just fifty feet down. They hurried and reached the front, where people were still walking out into the street.

Jeannette noted the narrow alley on the side of the theater.

"Going around!" she said.

"Coming through to the rear," he replied.

Jeannette drew her Glock from the small holster at the rear waistline of her jeans, usually hidden by the fall of her jacket.

The alley wouldn't allow for more than two people to pass at any time. It was littered with cigarette butts and small trash, but there was no one in it. She moved carefully but swiftly along it, pausing when she reached the rear of the theater in an area that offered a larger expanse of space along with receptacles for larger trash.

There was no one there.

Maybe...

Maybe something had just happened to the line. Maybe the girls were still safely inside the theater with Daniel calming them down.

She saw that another alley led from behind the dumpster by the building on the other side of the block—and toward the street on the other side as well.

She hurried to the dumpster. And that's when she paused.

There was a man on the ground. Bleeding. She knelt by his side, quickly checking for a pulse.

He was still alive. His pulse was slow and thready, but it was there.

She hit the speed dial on her phone and gave the information to the others. Gervais promised medical help for his officer immediately. Daniel said he hadn't found the girls, and he was coming through. She let them know she was racing through the next alley.

"Jeannette, I'm almost there!" Daniel told her.

"Right. Catch up!" she told him.

She ran through the next narrow alley, and slowed just as she reached the larger service area for the next building. And that's when she heard them.

Crying...

One of them begging.

"No, no, please...please..."

And then she heard the threat.

"I am not going to hurt you, but if you do not listen to me, this knife I have against your friend's ribs will pierce right through them. Walk! Walk! Move, smile and shut the hell up, no more screaming, stop the damned crying!"

Jeannette thought whoever had the girls was an American! Or at the very least, someone who spoke English fluently and sounded as if they hailed from the Midwest.

Inching along the wall, she realized they were just ahead of her, making their way through the next alley to the street.

Three? Someone is taking three women at a time and that same someone knocked out a police officer?

She was worried that the man most certainly had a knife against someone's ribs. But they were also getting closer and closer to the street. And through the narrow alleyway, she could see there was a dirty dark van waiting just at the end of the passage.

She had to stop them before they got to the van—and before endangering their lives.

"Clara!" she called out, hurrying forward, hoping she was playing it out to the best of her ability. "Clara, hey, it's Jeannie, and I thought we were all going out to the Louvre today! Hey, wait up, wait up! Clara, Emily, Red! Wait up! Wait up!"

She'd shoved her gun back in its holster and ran forward eagerly with a big smile as if she had just missed her friends.

She kept chattering as she reached the trembling women and the large man who was holding Clara. She pretended not to notice the circumstances.

"I know, I know, I know… I missed the improv show and I'm so sorry. And I—oh! Um, sorry, I didn't realize you were with a new friend! Hi, I'm Jeannie! Oh, my God, is something wrong? You're all so upset! Can I help? Can I do something?" she asked, as if she'd suddenly realized they were distressed and as if she truly were a friend who wanted to help.

The man stared at her furiously. His one arm was around Clara, and Jeannette didn't doubt he was holding a knife, and he was holding it flat against her ribs.

He appeared to be about forty and he had a rough look about him. He hadn't bothered to shave in a few days but his hair, a dull brown, had been cut short. He was wearing a long jacket, T-shirt and jeans, and she thought the man might have been one of the many homeless who had found their beds on the street in Paris.

He stared at her, weighing his options, she thought, just as she had weighed hers.

"You can shut the hell up. I have a knife about to plunge into your friend's guts. Now, do you want that? Do you want to be responsible for her intestines trailing down the alley? You'll do… What are you, twenty-four, twenty-five? You want her to live, you join the others."

"Join them where?" she asked.

"Walk right ahead and slide into the van," he told her.

She stared at him. Time to weigh her options again. She could do as he said and perhaps…

Perhaps find out what was going on. Or…

Get them all killed. No. She still had her Glock.

She spoke loudly. "Knife?" she demanded.

And he did as she asked, adjusting his arm so that she could see that he, indeed, carried a knife, one about six inches long, so sharp that it seemed to glisten in the poor light.

"As you can see," he said. "She will die. And you will be able to do nothing. I will slide this blade into her without hesitation, and you will not get me."

He started to press the knife into Clara. Clara stared at her with her large blue eyes desperately pleading. Shaking, holding each other, Emily and Red let out little sounds of distress, eyes bright as well with the tears they'd been shedding.

"Of course. You want us in a van, we'll get in a van," Jeannette said. She just needed to get him walking ahead of her. And like it or not, draw her Glock and shoot him in the back of the head before he could cause Clara further harm.

"Get in front of me!" he told her, eyes narrowing. "One more pain in the ass thing from any of you, and she dies!"

He started to move his arm, pressing the knife slowly but more deeply into Clara's side.

Then, an explosion rent the air.

The man staggered back from Clara and fell to the ground.

Clara, Emily and Red screamed and jumped back.

Jeannette turned. Daniel was running down the last few feet of the narrow alley toward them. And as he did so, the waiting van suddenly burned rubber and took off down the street.

"You're all right, you're all right!" Jeannette assured the girls, catching the sobbing Clara as she threw herself into Jeannette's arms.

Daniel went straight to the man on the ground to

check for a pulse or for any sign of life. But it wasn't there, and she knew the man was dead.

Daniel had been listening to the exchange. He knew he had to shoot to kill lest the knife sink any farther into Clara's flesh and destroy her organs.

Jeannette heard him swearing softly, but she had to hold Clara to keep her from jumping on him as she said, "Oh, my God, thank you, I'm alive, I'm sorry, I'm so sorry. We were so stupid, it's just that… Oh, he's dead, he's dead. I'm sorry, but I didn't want to die, thank you, thank you—"

The last words were barely out of her mouth before Jeannette realized Gervais LaBlanc had come through as well, and he was followed by two officers. Daniel stood and began speaking with one of them. He handed his Glock to Gervais and continued to speak in French. Jeannette could follow some of it; he was telling Gervais he'd been listening. He hadn't wanted to shoot.

There hadn't been a choice once the man had forced Jeannette ahead of him.

"Young ladies, you are all right?" Gervais asked, turning to them.

"Clara is cut up!" Emily announced. "The two of us are fine. No, we may never be really fine after this, but…he pretended he needed help. He got next to Clara with that knife. He said if he didn't get us out, he didn't care if he died. So he'd be happy to kill Clara if he needed to!" Emily explained.

"When we didn't see our officer, we were scared, and Clara had Jeannette's number so we texted and…" Red continued.

"We listened to him! We couldn't let him kill Clara!" Emily told them.

"Of course, of course," Gervais assured her.

"And we're all alive, oh, my God, we're all alive!" Red exclaimed.

It seemed that chaos reigned then, and perhaps naturally the girls were hysterical but relieved. Gervais quickly took charge of the situation, and it was necessary that they all—Jeannette, Daniel, Clara, Emily and Red—come to headquarters to make statements. With the shooting and the dead man, it was necessary for Daniel to turn in his weapon; but Jeannette was certain that before they found themselves in any other situation, he'd be given a replacement.

Jeannette and the girls described the van that had been waiting for them on the street, but they hadn't been able to see any license plate, sticker or any other kind of identification on the vehicle. The angle had been bad, and besides, as Daniel pointed out, the dirt was on purpose to hide anything that might give them a clue as to finding the vehicle. Gervais sent what description they could give out to officers in Paris and throughout France in case it might be spotted. Gervais told Jeannette, however, that he suspected the van had already been abandoned.

At headquarters, the girls gave their statements, and Jeannette and Daniel also wrote up their reports.

Before ending it, Daniel called Mason and told him of the incident. As it happened, they had barely arrived when the call was made.

Jules and Delphine were just appearing; Mason said he'd get back to them as soon as possible.

The girls were terrified but in speaking with one another, they decided they did not want to go home. No one could tell them what was really going on.

No one could assure them their journey couldn't be sabotaged, nor could they guarantee the girls' safety.

But there was an acceptable answer. The girls would be escorted to the safe house and share it with Shelley.

It had felt like forever since they'd turned back to get to the girls. It made no sense for them to try to do too much more with the day.

But when they finished at the station and waited to speak with Gervais, Mason called. Daniel took it, moved them to a corner and put the call low on speaker.

"They still want to see you," he told them. "Sorry. Delphine and Jules still want to see you. They know what happened, of course. I think news agencies were out with almost the same speed of the medical examiner and the police. By the way, anything new on the dead man?" he asked.

"No identification of any kind on him—not even a credit card," Daniel said. "They're working on it."

"And the officer who was attacked?"

"He's out of surgery, hanging on, but still unconscious," Jeannette told him.

"And it's just two o'clock. You do seem to enjoy eventful mornings," Mason said dryly. "All right, get out here."

"You or Luke and Carly or Della didn't go out with them?" Daniel asked.

"Jules wants you," Mason told them. "Apparently, so does Delphine. They were so disappointed, but I think your attack was just after ten and they had just gotten there… Well, the attack had already happened, and Jules knew about it, and he was horrified."

"I was afraid he was going to say he didn't have another day to give up to help us at the House of Matisse," Jeannette said.

"No. He's there—and waiting for you."

"But he has a show tonight—" Jeannette said.

"No, it's his one dark night. His day off. So, when you finish with the paperwork—"

"Get out there now?" Daniel asked.

"What was your plan?" Mason said lightly. "Sitting around with *café au lait* and croissants?"

"No, we were headed in that direction—" Jeannette began.

"When you arrive at the bed-and-breakfast, Jules will be here," Mason told them.

"Okay…?"

"He's watching a movie with us. An old American movie he thought was great. Kevin Kline and Meg Ryan, something called *French Kiss*. He wants to point out Paris landmarks and other wonders of France that are shown in the movie. Anyway, he said he promised *you* that they'd take you around, and he doesn't want to disappoint you. While paperwork takes a long time, the girls were attacked so early he said he can wait."

"All right, then. I'll let Gervais know," Daniel said.

"Fine. Della and Carly and Luke are doing great at cementing a friendship with the fellow, so I think things will go well," Mason said. "When you've gotten here, we'll make a stop-by with Gervais, if he's here, at the House of Deauville and do what we can to find out about a dead man who was working for them ever so recently! Time doesn't matter with Delphine and Jules. They're waiting for you."

"I think they are planning our visit, and we're giving them even more time. By the time we get there, the stage will be set and we'll leave thinking they are more wonderful than ever," Jeannette said dryly. "I don't know, it seemed a good plan at first. Now, I'm not sure."

"Sure or not, it's happening. And one never knows," Mason said.

"Right," Jeannette told him.

"On the way."

They ended the call.

"I need to ask one of the desk officers if they can get Gervais for us," Daniel told her. "I don't want to leave without saying anything, and I don't want to distract him with a phone call—"

"No need, here he comes," Jeannette pointed out.

Gervais strode toward them, his expression serious. "You're finished here, you can go out to Reims. I don't know—"

"We'll still be having a meeting with them. Apparently, today is the magician's dark day, and he said he had offered us the run of the place and was willing to wait. He's at the bed-and-breakfast, just waiting and watching movies," Jeannette explained.

Gervais nodded. "Fine. Go. I should be close behind you. I will stop at the bed-and-breakfast first, if any of your team is there, or perhaps meet up with them at the House of Deauville."

"All right. We didn't want to leave without you knowing," Daniel told him.

Gervais nodded and then he managed to give them

a grim smile. "Thank you both for your competence and your speed. My officer is going to live. If he'd been left much longer, he might have bled out from the knife wounds. And they are already escorting the young women to get their belongings. I believe they'll be happy to meet Shelley, and they will all do well together."

"Thank you, Gervais," Jeannette said.

He nodded and turned away, speaking as he walked. "Paperwork. Every country, I believe, demands paperwork. It can be endless!"

They left and started the drive out to Reims.

As they did so, Daniel told her, "That was really brilliant of you," he said.

"What was?" she asked, frowning.

"Letting those young women have a way to contact you. With all the visitors—all the young and lovely visitors—they might not have been victims. But you suspected they might become victims as they fit the profile. You saved their lives."

"Teamwork," she told him. "Once that man forced me in front of him, I was calculating wildly on what I was going to do. I figured on the one hand that if I got in the van, I'd know where the women were being taken, but I was afraid that one of them—"

"Or you!" Daniel interrupted.

"One of us might have wound up dead. I still had my Glock, but the way he had that knife… If he wasn't taken down completely by surprise, the blade could have gone in."

Daniel nodded. "I hate it, of course."

"Hate killing?"

He nodded. "But we're also taught we're obligated to save the lives of victims, so…"

"I think most of the French police who have been involved in this—who have seen the bodies of the dead— might be applauding you. But I know. It's never a good feeling."

"Right. So here we go again. Out of Paris…and out to Reims and then out to the beautiful and world-famous French vineyards!"

Jeannette smiled and leaned back. She had known it was going to be a long day. She just hadn't expected it to be this long already.

They drove in silence for a while. A surprisingly comfortable silence.

Then Jeannette thought to ask him, "Wow. I'm sorry. I should have offered. Do you want me to drive for a while?"

He laughed. "I'm fine. Unless you want to drive."

"I've never cared who drives," she assured him. "Just, hmm. What do we do when we get there?"

He laughed. "We take the last room. I don't think anyone is going to notice, not even to blink. Okay? I mean, I'm okay if you're okay."

She smiled, leaning back, closing her eyes again.

And soon the beautiful architecture of the city of Reims appeared on the skyline, and they were driving up to Madame Matisse's bed-and-breakfast.

They were greeted warmly and with a zillion questions from the team—and from Jules Bastien. She saw Mason was listening carefully to what was said in front of Jules, but not much of it mattered.

There wasn't anything they needed to hide.

Everything they knew was already in the hands of the media.

"At least *you're* all right!" Jules told them. "And those lovely young women. This is so terrible! What is happening out here? But as I told you, we will help you. My mother and I will help you in any way we can. I am ready to drive out there whenever you like!"

"Um, I need just a second. I'd like to wash my face. It will just take me a second, I promise," Jeannette said. She looked at Della, starting to frown. "Where—"

"Oh, you and Daniel are that first room over there. I think it's the same room you were in when you stayed here before," Della told her.

"Great. I'll be right out."

She did want to wash her face and her hands, as if she could wash away the events of the morning. The kidnappers had been stopped.

But what it meant was that nothing had been stopped at all. There was someone pulling the strings, someone with wealth and power.

Just as it had been with Elizabeth Báthory, and perhaps her husband, Nádasdy, who had been so vicious to his enemies at war. Others had been arrested with Elizabeth, others had been executed, but not until many, many had died.

She ran very cold water over her face. As she did so, Daniel called out to her. "I just brought our overnight bags in. And I'm putting them in the closet and—"

He broke off suddenly.

Staring at her own reflection, she frowned, grabbed a hand towel and dried her face and hands, and hurried out.

Daniel was fine.

He was standing in front of the closet, something in his hands, staring.

"Daniel?"

He turned to her, and she saw he was holding a book.

"Some of the hangers fell when I opened the door to slide the bags in there. I bent down to get them and in the back there was a pile of books written in different languages, as if someone supplied a little library for those who stayed here."

"Many places keep books for guests or have libraries in the house. Even hotels have them sometimes," she said.

"Books like this?"

He showed her what he was holding, and she walked closer to take it.

The book had a long title.

Jeannette read it out loud.

"Elizabeth Báthory, Rumor, Truth and Legend."

"I'm beginning to think," Daniel told her, "that your instincts are very, very good."

Fourteen

"Now, of course," Jeannette said, "the fact that it's back there doesn't necessarily mean the book belongs to Delphine. At most places where they have this kind of thing where there's a little supply of books, people often leave what they've brought and take what they're in the middle of reading."

Daniel arched a brow. "This is going on, but at some point someone was reading this book and left it here?"

Jeannette was studying the book. "It's in English. I don't think that would be Delphine's choice—she speaks English well, but French is her first language. People usually buy books in their native language. It was written fifteen years ago," she said, studying the publication page. "By N. Q. Middleton, professor of European history. It's probably an interesting book." She looked at him. "Good reading material? Maybe I'll take it."

"I'm not sure this is your typical lending library because the books are in the back of the closet," Daniel reminded her.

"But just because a book is here…"

"Jeannette, let's face it. None of us wants Jules or his mother to be connected. We need to keep open minds and… Well, the chap has waited for us. Let's go see what we can see," Daniel said.

"Right," she murmured. She hesitated. "Our team has the whole place here, but still…" she said thoughtfully, holding the book. "We know that there are keys out there."

"You're worried about someone knowing we've found the book?" he asked.

She nodded.

"I will put it back exactly where I found it," Daniel told her. "And don't forget—"

"Not to worry—we haven't opened our bags yet. If anyone else were to open it, I've created a poor man's booby trap. A scrap of paper that will dislodge. Anyway…"

"Smile," he told her. "We're on!"

They headed out to the room where the movie had just ended and the credits were running.

Jules had been sitting on the sofa by Della; he rose, as did the others, when Jeannette and Daniel arrived.

"Great movie, great views of Paris in it. And I do so sincerely hope you get to enjoy some of the history and beauty of our country!" Jules said enthusiastically. Then he grew somber. "I'm so sorry, we need to get serious here. I'm ready whenever you are."

"We are ready," Jeannette assured him.

"Shall I drive?" Jules asked politely.

"Better take your car just in case we need you quickly," Mason advised.

"Gervais is still busy in Paris, I imagine?" Jules asked.

"He is, I'm afraid," Mason told them.

"But!" Della said, jumping up. "Jules, may I come, too? I've so enjoyed the time we've spent watching the movie. I love hearing about Paris and Reims. You may be a magician, but you're also just an incredible guy!"

"Mais, oui!" Jules told her. "Delightful."

He looked around to see if any of them would dispute the idea, but everyone just smiled at him. Of course, Jeannette knew the rest of them would be leaving as soon as they were out with Jules. The others would be headed to the House of Deauville.

"Let's do it. Will you ride with me, Della?" Jules asked.

Despite her belief in the magician, Jeannette felt every muscle in her body tense. She'd already had to determine how *not* to let a knife slide into a woman's body that day. But it would be ridiculous for Jules— even if he was a guilty man—to offer any harm to Della when they were following right behind.

"All right, then," Daniel said. "We will follow right behind you, Jules."

They were finally out the door.

Jules and Della headed for his car; Jeannette and Daniel headed for theirs.

"I know what you're thinking," Daniel told Jeannette. "You're worried—"

"About Della. And surely it occurred to you—"

"Della is armed and very capable, trust me. But do we instinctively worry? Yes, but then we have faith in one another while we back one another up. All right?" he asked.

"Just stay close," Jeannette told him.

"Will do!" he promised.

And he did. He stayed behind just far enough to avoid rear-ending Jules's car.

They reached the Matisse estate and turned onto an elaborate drive, which had not been part of the tour. It led them in a semicircle to the front of the house, an elaborate building that appeared to have been built sometime in the Gothic era. It had pointed arches, flying buttresses and ribbed vaults, rising two stories and higher with the elegance of the architecture. Stained glass occupied several of the front windows, and the place looked like something out of a fairy tale.

"Wow," Jeannette noted.

"This part of the estate was not on the tour."

"Where were we…" Jeannette murmured, looking around as she exited the car.

"Down that way. We didn't see the house on the tour because we passed it when they were showing us the fields, the winery and the guesthouse where they served us during the tasting," Daniel said.

"Right, yes, of course…getting my bearings!" she told him. "But—"

"I'm willing to bet they have something like golf carts to move around the property to take them to the fields, the winery and the guesthouse," Daniel said. "I don't see Delphine Matisse cheerfully taking long, long walks on a daily basis. They know we want to talk to her workers."

Ahead of them, Jules and Della were out of the car as well. Jules called out to them.

"Please, come in! Maman is waiting."

"Oh, we are coming!" Jeannette assured him. "Jules…just the outside! This place is magnificent. And you…"

"I know, I know," he told her. "No one can understand why I don't just embrace being born into this incredible place and business. I am grateful. I had a great time as a boy living out here. I am incredibly grateful for my education… I just love magic. And my mother is all right with it, no matter what others say."

Daniel and Della stood close by them, respectfully silent.

Jules glanced at them and shrugged before continuing, "The Deauville and Montague families just don't understand. They're horrified by me, and by the fact that my mother isn't angry with me and won't disown me. To them… Well, you know. To them, we are part of a noble heritage, and I should probably be fed to the dogs or the like."

"Do you see them, um, socially?" Della asked him.

He shrugged. "Fundraisers, holidays, events when we're expected to be part of the excitement of an occasion," he said. "We're polite. My mother and Leticia were good friends once, but…then my mother raised a magician. Anyway, please, come in."

"With pleasure," Daniel assured him.

They walked the stone path, surrounded by flowering plants, to the front door. It opened as they arrived. Delphine Matisse herself was standing there, smiling.

"*Bienvenue*, welcome!" she told them, opening the

door wider. "I was so afraid we wouldn't all get to be out here together. Though, Jules, if they are not able to accomplish all they hoped for today, you do have tomorrow morning, right? Oh, darling, tonight being your night off, you are staying at the house tonight?" she asked.

"*Oui*, Maman," he told her. "Shall we get our guests out of the hallway?"

"Of course. I have *café au lait* ready, and *oui*, croissants, but other little delicacies as well. Please. As we indulge, perhaps you can explain exactly what it is I can do for you," Delphine said.

"We'd like a chance to speak with your employees. And, of course," Daniel told her, "we'd like your permission to be on your property when we're working on searches."

"Searches for more bodies," she murmured, shaking her head. "Of course. But first, please come. I do like to think I brew some of the best *café au lait* you will ever taste. And do indulge. My cook, Bessie, is quite amazing. We French do pride ourselves on our cuisine. Starting out with filled bodies and strong senses will be but an aid to you."

"Of course, and thank you," Daniel said.

"You had me at *café au lait*," Jeannette assured her.

"And me at the word *croissant*!" Della added.

Delphine swept out an arm, indicating they must come in.

The house's parlor to the left of the entry was beyond elegant. The furniture was French provincial, elegant with polished wood and metal fixings. The sofa was large and upholstered with rich embroidered blues. Armchairs matched.

There was no sign of a television or entertainment system of any kind in the room. It was a showplace.

But they weren't being led to sit in the parlor. They moved instead to the right of the entry and entered an exceptionally large dining room where their refreshments had been set around a table that could easily sit fourteen to sixteen people.

But Delphine Matisse indicated the settings were at the center of the table, which allowed them to sit three on one side and two on the other so they might face one another as they enjoyed the delicacies.

Delphine indicated she and her son would head to the opposite side of the table. Jeannette chose a chair with Daniel beside her and Della to his right.

"At least we'll eat well," Daniel murmured.

"If we're not poisoned," she whispered back.

"Hardly likely since Gervais knows exactly where we are. So…drink and eat up!"

They didn't see Bessie the cook; Delphine herself took pleasure in fixing cups and plates for them, explaining she was delighted for their company because she seldom dared indulge herself. "I am moving up in years and must take care of what goes into my frame!" she told them.

"You look so young!" Jeannette told her. And she did, for being the mother of a man in his late twenties.

"And quite lovely," Daniel assured her.

"Merci, merci beaucoup!" she said. "But age will take a toll. I am not obsessive, just careful."

"It works!" Della assured her. "I hope I do as well."

"Maman, you will be beautiful at any age," Jules assured her.

"Ah, what well-behaved guests!" she said. "Now, if I understand correctly, you wish to speak with our workers?"

"That is true. Anyone involved with any of the small wineries. You see," Daniel explained to her, "we believe someone who knows the region and knows it well must be involved."

Delphine nodded but then shook her head. "I am so confused. You know the media is referring to the last murders as being committed by the *Vampire of Paris*? Aren't these young women staying in Paris and—"

"Staying in Paris, yes. But the young women we've identified all came out to this region and went on the wine tours. Again, for the bodies to have been left as they were..."

Delphine shook her head again. "It is so very difficult to believe! And now more bodies have been found in the unused fields. It is terrible. So terrible. Just as we French pride ourselves on our cuisine, we pride ourselves on these wines. You must understand. Product is all-important. Indeed, these fields are our livelihood, but there would be deep shame in producing anything but excellence, and...to have such shame as brutal murders brought to our steps... It is against everything we believe!"

"Of course, Madame Matisse," Jeannette said, "we understand your feelings! And we understand as well that many of your employees have been with you forever and that you would trust them with your own life. But someone out here does know something."

She let out a little sigh. "Well, I am afraid that while many, many French men and women speak English very well, not all do. But Jules—"

"I intend to go with them, Maman," Jules said.

"And Daniel speaks French fluently," Jeannette said sweetly.

She wondered if she should have given the woman that information. Things might have been said in French with the speaker believing he or she hadn't been understood. But Jules already knew Daniel spoke French so perhaps it didn't matter.

"Of course, of course!" Delphine said. "Jules will take the cart, and you may head to the work areas. Now we have many different areas, you know. We produce still wine and sparkling wine. We are known as vintners—the selection of fruit is critical and fermentation is critical. But some of the field workers are due in on the trucks just about now, and I believe you might want to start with them. There will be about twenty men working today. I don't see how you can possibly speak with everyone today, but I assume those men might be those you wish to speak with first?"

What I'd really like, Jeannette thought, *is to rip your house apart!*

"Oh, Delphine!" Della said. "These croissants...you are right! They are amazing!"

Jeannette managed to smile and add, "Madame, you do create the most wonderful *café au lait* known to man, I am quite certain!"

Delphine Matisse smiled and acknowledged their compliments. "I am so pleased you have enjoyed our offerings! Please, it will grow dark, so I do suggest you start out now."

"Aye—" Daniel began.

But Jeannette interrupted him. "I'm so sorry! And let me see if I have this right—*est-ce que je peux utiliser vos toilettes, s'il vous plaît?*"

Madame Delphine laughed. "Excellent, my dear! Excellent. Come, I shall direct you."

They both rose, and Jeannette promised she'd be quick.

She wasn't sure what she was doing. Seeing one bathroom in the house wasn't going to help a lot, especially since she'd be led to a guest bathroom. Then again...

As Delphine led her from the dining room and through a long hallway with doors on either side, she asked Jeannette, "So, the press is claiming that a vampire is roaming freely in Paris. Of course, you do not believe in such things, do you?"

"I don't believe in vampires such as those written up in books. I do believe in human beings who convince themselves they need human blood, or who simply love the sensation of creating such a panic in cities like Paris and Reims."

"Ah, of course. And yet...the latest bodies. Or the older bodies. Those decomposed. They showed signs of..."

"Extreme torture," Jeannette said. "That is what the papers and media are saying, yes."

"And it is true?"

"It is."

Delphine shook her head. "It makes no sense. Torture, simply taking blood…bodies missed forever, new murders. It is all too horrible."

"And must be stopped," Jeannette said.

"Of course. Again, anything I can do. And here, mademoiselle, *la toilette*!"

"Merci beaucoup!"

Jeannette entered the bathroom and closed the door and let out a sigh.

She wished so, so badly she could determine if the woman was just curious for information, being as charming and giving as possible because it was all real…

Or if it was a further form of entertainment for her as she planned her next murder.

She couldn't forget the book that had been in the closet at Delphine Matisse's bed-and-breakfast.

And the bathroom…

As elegant as the rest of the house. Gold fixtures, an embossed shower curtain, a large mirrored cabinet and a shiny wood towel chest.

She searched through them quickly and discovered nothing except what she had expected, a room that was elegant and…

Elite.

Towels, shampoo, soap, skin softeners…

And nothing more.

But when she hurried back to the table, she discovered there was an interesting conversation going on.

"You see, French nobility has no legal status these days, but that does not mean many don't cling to their titles and trace their ancestry back to noble and royal houses," Delphine was explaining.

"And, yuck!" Jules added. "To other European houses as well. There was so much inbreeding when nobility reigned in Europe," he said, shaking his head. "I am grateful to say we are not related to anyone royal!"

"Well, we don't know that," Delphine argued. "We have not done any of those DNA kits nor looked on ancestry sites. Well, we know, of course, that Jules's father comes from a long line of distinguished vintners, but—"

"Too many royal houses were inbred to keep everything in the family in order to cling to power," Jules said. "The Hapsburgs ruled half of Europe for hundreds of years, and they were so tragically inbred that Charles II of Spain could barely speak or eat, his jaw was so badly deformed."

"Well, our neighbors do think they're royal, you know," Delphine reminded him. "But…get going! It's getting dark and the workers will be angry and uncooperative if they can't get home!"

Jeannette was dying to follow up on Delphine's last words, but since she was certain Jules knew what his mother had been about to say, they could question him about the "royalty" claims of his neighbors.

"Come, come!" Jules said. "We'll go through the back!"

"Through the back" took them along the hall with the bathrooms and into a huge pantry and on to the kitchen itself—then outside via a door at the end of the massive kitchen.

"Interesting," Jeannette murmured.

"What's that?" Jules asked her.

"Well, many things, but this house…it's hundreds of years old, right? And to have a kitchen this size!"

Jules laughed. "I think it was originally turned into a kitchen in the early 1900s," Jules told her. "My mother had it updated about ten years ago. Come on, the cart is just this way."

"Thank you for this," Daniel told him as they headed out.

"Yes, this is above and beyond," Della agreed.

"I'd like to say it's my pleasure but considering the circumstances… Anyway, consider this—if nothing else, this will be an extra special wine country tour," Jules said. "We'll pass growing fields filled with vines, and you'll see more of the operation."

"Wonderful!" Jeannette said.

He indicated the cart that did resemble a golf cart—with no space for clubs. The cart was parked near several others at a building just beyond the house. The lawn here was manicured but led out to a field that stretched out with sparse trees and growth to what was one of the growing fields, Jeannette thought.

But it could also be interesting to investigate the field that lay between the house and grapevines.

"Hop in!" Jules said.

He slid behind the wheel, and Jeannette sat in the seat next to him, thinking she wanted to be able to talk above the hum of the motor; Della and Daniel took seats in the back.

As it turned out, there wasn't much of a hum. The cart rode as smoothly as a Mercedes.

"Jules," she said. "I am so curious. Who do your neighbors think they are?"

He glanced at her. "Do you mean the Deauville and Montague couples?"

She shrugged and laughed. "If those are the neighbors you meant!"

"Well, I must admit, none of them have that enormous jawline that went with so many of the Hapsburgs. And that was the least of their problems—their gene pools were pathetic due to cousins who had been marrying cousins for hundreds of years. Epilepsy, hemophilia…things that created sick and sad lives. Ferdinand I of Austria was born with hydrocephalus, or water on the brain. It was said that he liked to roll around in trash cans. He also had epilepsy and that horrible Hapsburg jaw."

"But who—"

"Deauville. He thinks he's a Hapsburg. He's related through his mother's line, so he claims. I would never begin to suggest such a thing—if it were true! Seriously, in today's day and age, who the hell cares about royalty?"

"Um, the Brits, I guess," Daniel said from the back, which caused them all to laugh.

"Pageantry, maybe?" Della asked. "I don't know. Jeannette and I are Americans. But we get a kick out of watching the Brits."

"And I guess, some people feel things like that are important," Jeannette said. "But as far as your neighbors go—"

He groaned. "Once again, you're talking about Leticia and George Montague and Tomas and Giselle Deauville?" he asked. "Obviously, you all mean them. You're here. And I'm sure you'd be there, too, doing this, if they weren't such nasty people and you didn't know that they'd make you go through legal hoops to talk to anyone."

"Of course, their houses are of interest, too," Daniel said, leaning forward.

"Their houses? Or their employees?" Jules asked. "I'm sorry. I don't like them. Any of them. George and Leticia or Tomas and Giselle. As far as I'm concerned, they've been brutal to me and my mother. If magic were real, I would abracadabra them to an island somewhere."

"I'm sorry they've been so judgmental," Jeannette said. "I guess..."

"They think money and an inherited position allows them to condemn other people. Anyway, most of the time I don't care. My mother accepts my love for what I do. And sure, she would like it if I suddenly said all that I wanted in life was to take over the winery, but she still admires my talent! And I am a good magician!"

"You're a wonderful magician," Della assured him.

Daniel and Jeannette echoed her words: "Wonderful!"

"Well, thank you for that," Jules said.

"It's just the truth," Daniel told him. "And we're fond of the truth!"

"Still... Well, here we are. The workers are coming in. They've been advised that you want to talk to them, so..."

"We'll divide and conquer," Daniel told them. "We'll form three lines, if you don't mind helping out."

"Of course," Jules said.

They left the cart and started forward.

Daniel was right next to Jeannette then, and though

Jules was speaking quickly—projecting with his stage voice—Daniel was following what he was saying. And it was good. He was assuring the workers that law enforcement had come for help. They desperately needed help and needed to know if any one of them had seen anything unusual at all.

"He also added that those who spoke English well should speak with you," Daniel told her.

"Hey! I'm sorry. My Spanish and Italian are actually decent!" she told him.

He grinned. "Della's French is so-so. I'm taking those who don't speak any English at all."

The workers, tired and hungry as they might have been at the end of the day, fell into lines as they were instructed by Jules.

Then Jules came to stand by her and introduced her to the men as they came forward. And very nicely for her, each of them spoke English well.

"We're seeking any help. Have you seen anyone here who shouldn't be here, anyone with a van who seemed to be stopping to let something off, anything you found suspicious in any way?" Jeannette asked.

Three men went by, puzzled and sorry, but unable to help.

But the fourth, a fellow who couldn't have been more than twenty or twenty-one, did have something to tell her.

"I saw the kind of vehicle you're talking about not long ago. It was a van. And it was strange because it didn't just stay on the road and drive by at the same speed as most vehicles. There is little reason to stop around here—these are fields where we work each day.

But this van… It kept slowing down, as if someone was studying each place in the field. Then it went ahead. And I saw it stop and pull off the side of the road, up ahead, maybe…at the end of the line where we have our vines planted, just before the overgrown field that borders it," he told Jeannette.

"Did you see anything else? People getting out, carrying anything?" Jeannette asked.

"I'm sorry. I was busy, I just thought a tourist was lost or perhaps wanted to view the fields from afar or even…"

The man stopped speaking, looking at Jules uncomfortably.

Jules laughed softly and said, "I think you're suggesting you thought the van might have pulled over because someone in it wanted to relieve themselves," Jules said.

Jeannette laughed. "Thank you for your consideration. You thought someone in the van might need to take a pee?" she asked.

"Exactly," he said, flushing and looking away.

"Can you describe the van?" she asked.

"*Oui*…it was dirty. Really dirty. And either dark blue or black," the man told her.

Dirty. Dark blue or black. The same van I saw on the road this morning, waiting for the man with the knife who is now dead to bring the girls—and me—to…

Their murderer.

"Thank you!" she told him. "That information is very valuable."

He looked pleased to have helped her and then turned to Jules to ask him something in French. Jeannette was beginning to pick up the language in bits and pieces.

He was asking if he could go home.

"Mais oui!" she replied, reaching to shake his hand and thank him again. Jules nodded, and since he was the boss's son, his word was accepted as gold.

"Thank you, seriously," Jeannette murmured as she waited for the next man in line to step forward.

"His words were seriously helpful, right?" Jules asked her.

"They were."

He started to speak with the next man, but even as he did so, she heard Daniel shout out angrily.

"A runner!"

Jeannette saw one of the workers toward the end of Daniel's line had suddenly bolted.

He tore past around the building behind them to race toward the overgrown field that bordered the Matisse lands.

And it was necessary for Jeannette and Della to race after the man as well.

"Left!" Daniel cried.

"Right!" she told him, and she took off running.

But around the fermenting building, she could see nothing. The building marked the end of the growing fields and beyond that...

Grass. Bushes. Trees.

Della was tearing forward to her far right. She saw Daniel's head as he raced through the bracken to her far left.

Ahead, just ahead, she heard thrashing. The man was right before her.

She kept running. She could see so little.

But she could hear him. He was just ahead, turning

this way and that, but he was still in front of her in a perfect trajectory.

And then she saw him. Like the one man who had been so determined and hopeful that he might be helpful, this one was young. He was medium in build, dark-haired and fit.

And he could run.

But she had trained long and hard to be where she was with the Bureau and with the Blackbird division of the Krewe of Hunters.

She forced herself into another spur of energy and surged forward. She didn't threaten him with her gun.

She flew at his back, her strength and impetus bringing him down hard to the ground.

He was flat on his stomach but trying to twist and turn.

"Stop fighting!" she yelled at him.

And then Daniel was at her side and Della was coming up by him. Daniel hunkered by her, plastic cuffs ready to put around the man's wrists. In seconds, he had the fellow restrained.

Jeannette stood, and Daniel dragged the man to his feet and spoke quickly to him in French.

To Jeannette's surprise, the man began to laugh.

"You've got me!" he said. "You've got me. But for what?"

"For what? Several counts of murder!" Daniel snapped.

"Oh, okay, then. I did it. I did it all. No, I didn't. I didn't do anything at all."

"Why did you run?" Jeannette demanded.

"Because I wanted to see you run!" he said and started laughing again.

"We all ran. And you're under arrest for murder."

"You aren't even French. You can't arrest me," the man said.

"No? I'm sorry. We're authorized to hold you, and Gervais LaBlanc will do the arresting," Daniel told him.

He looked at Jeannette and told her, "Hey, you can hold me, baby!"

She let out a sound of disgust and turned away. As she did so, she was grateful to see someone else coming through the field.

Gervais! Gervais had arrived.

"Hey, here's the man who can arrest you!"

"Wait!" the man cried suddenly. "I am innocent. Leave me be! I can help. I am innocent, but I can tell you who is guilty!"

Fifteen

Daniel was glad Gervais was there to officially take custody of the man. They headed into a station in Reims with the man and left him to stew in an interrogation room as they watched him from an attached observation room.

He sat at the table, hands cuffed and folded before him, looking pained and miserable. It hadn't been difficult getting information on him. What he hadn't spilled out himself, Jules had easily supplied.

His name was Gabriel Menendez and he was an immigrant from Madrid. The strangest thing to Daniel was that Menendez, in appearance and manner—other than having run like an idiot—seemed to be intelligent. He easily slipped from French to English and back again in his conversations, and Daniel assumed he was equally fluent in his native language.

He had been with the House of Matisse for six years, having come north when he'd learned they were seeking workers for the vineyards.

Despite having toppled the man, Jeannette seemed

to be fine and not even out of breath. Gabriel Menendez had landed in some dirt but was obviously unhurt.

After reaching the station, Daniel put through a call and alerted the others as to what was going on. Mason told him they were still waiting to speak with Giselle and Tomas Deauville.

"The man you're holding—he says he's innocent but he knows who did it?"

"Yeah, that's what he said when we pulled him up," Daniel told him. "Gervais arrived and we're about to question him. He clammed up right after he saw Gervais. He hasn't asked for legal assistance. He's just told us now that he has nothing to say. Gervais, of course, threatened to arrest him for multiple murders to which he replied there was no proof against him because he was innocent. We're about to go in and talk about conspiracy to commit murder."

"Who should go in first?" Jeannette asked thoughtfully as she studied their suspect through the mirror as he sat just staring straight ahead.

"Hey, your tackle. Be careful, the pros might want to take you away from us!" Della said lightly. "Seriously, you bested him. What do you think, Daniel?"

"I think we may be here a long, long time—but he will break," Daniel said. "We'll be here." He turned. He'd almost forgotten he wanted Gervais's approval for their moves. They were guests in the country.

"Gervais?" Daniel asked.

"I say send in Jeannette first. He will respect her. I believe he doubted any woman could run as fast as he could or have the strength to stop him," Gervais said. "He will respect you."

Jeannette nodded. "All right, I'll be first up."

"Come. There is a guard at the door. This time, I've warned the officers that they must keep an eye on our suspects. Of course, he will make sure—" Gervais began.

"He's not going to leap out and try to take Jeannette out," Daniel said. "But it's always best to have a guard on alert."

Daniel and Della stayed in the observation room as Jeannette left with Gervais.

"Do you think this man really knows something?" Della asked Daniel.

"I think he knows something, but how helpful… He knows someone or knows of someone who is involved," Daniel said. "But why did he run? He could have just played it all innocent with us."

"Some people are lousy when it comes to acting," Della said. "Maybe it was one of those split-second decisions. But… Wow. That was some tackle Jeannette made. She was like a soaring missile! She's impressive. I've never worked with her before, but Mason knew her. He said she knew how to play a con, had a lot of courage, but was smart as well, and most importantly, she was a team player. And with Blackbird…that's what we need. Mason told me she was great. She's proving to be so."

Daniel nodded. "She is great. I agree. And…"

Della smiled at him. "I'm glad to hear the partnership is working out."

"How the hell do Jackson and Adam know who will fit with whom?" he wondered.

"Jackson Crow is a man of many talents. And Adam

Harrison is just one of the most generous and giving men to ever hit the earth. They manage to find misfits like us who would still do our best but live in miserable silence regarding our ability to reach out to the dead for help." She grinned at him. "I know you've only met them all via video channels, but they are truly remarkable people. With, of course, Angela Hawkins, who has our strange talent and is also one of the most brilliant researchers I've ever come across. Oh, Jeannette is in. It's showtime!" she said.

Daniel turned his attention back to the interrogation room.

"This is a false arrest," Gabriel Menendez insisted to Jeannette. "I just… I didn't want to talk to you. Who are you? What are you doing in France? And why are you here, picking on the House of Matisse?"

"Picking on the House of Matisse?" Jeannette said, looking puzzled as she stared at the man. "We love the House of Matisse."

"So, you're questioning Matisse workers, making it sound as if we're all guilty of something!"

"No, we're looking for help. And all we were doing is asking if anyone could help in any way, and one of the people we were going to ask ran away like a rabbit. So that person looks to be guilty of something."

"I am not guilty of anything!" Menendez insisted.

"You just said you are innocent, but you know who has been doing this, killing people, brutalizing them," Jeannette said flatly.

"I am innocent. I don't know what you people are doing, harassing us."

She shrugged. "Trying to keep people alive?"

He was silent for a minute. "Have you seen just how many people wind up dead?"

Jeannette frowned at the man. "You believe that if you speak with us, you'll wind up dead?"

"Again, I ask, have you seen how many people wind up dead?"

Jeannette seemed to carefully weigh the man's question. "I believe you're suggesting that if you talk to us, you'll be killed for doing so."

"Of course—and I'm not suggesting, I'm saying it outright!" Menendez told her.

Jeannette looked at him, shaking her head. "All right, then. We can let you walk out of here. But if we do that…well, we can't protect you. And everyone saw us bring you in here, so they're going to assume we got something out of you. And…" She lifted her hands as if she were sorry.

And if he was right—the minute he was out, he was in deadly danger.

The man looked down.

"Lock me up," he said. "Lock me up and they'll know I didn't talk!"

It was Jeannette's turn to be silent for a few seconds. "And more people will die. How many people do you want to die?"

"I don't want anyone to die—but especially not me. And…"

"And?"

He shook his head. "I—I don't know who is giving the orders."

"Okay, let me understand this. You know of someone who is involved in all this—perhaps someone who is kidnapping the victims and bringing them to someone else?"

He didn't answer.

"I'm right on that. But please, Mr. Menendez, if we can get to them, they may be able to get us to whoever is doing this. And then we can stop all the killing!"

He looked up at her. "Can you lock me up?" he asked her. "I—I have to look as if I was silent, ready to risk incarceration, please."

Jeannette was silent again. And Daniel knew she was thinking about Claude Chirac.

"How much do you really want to live?" she asked him.

He let out a breath. "I... I desperately want to live. And I don't want to... Have you heard about the way some of the people have died?"

"Tell me," Jeannette said quietly.

"Knives, cut after cut, little cuts, salt put in them. Bigger cuts. Blood all over a body, and then honey, and some left out then, bleeding and covered with the stuff, with insects consuming them until they die at last after a long slow torture!"

"The last victims were found just drained—"

"I don't know what the blood is for." He winced. "I do know that there are no real vampires, just someone who has a lust for blood, copious amounts of it. And sometimes... I heard that there had been a man in custody. It was on the news. He killed himself while he was being held for questioning. Don't you see? It was easier for him to kill himself. We all know those who have been involved and who were stopped, who messed up, who offended the main person behind this in any way.

We know those people wind up not just giving blood—but being slowly tortured to death."

"Are you telling me we can't leave you alone for a minute, that you're intending on suicide if we hold you?"

He shook his head. "I don't want to die. But I have heard what has been done and I... I don't want to be tortured to death!"

"Of course not, I understand. But what you don't understand is we can really keep you safe. Obviously, we can put you in protective custody."

Menendez stared at Jeannette, his expression hopeful—and doubtful.

"I told you. I don't know who is really running things, but..."

"Look. Word can go out that you were completely uncooperative, and we can put out a good story about you being charged for...for assaulting someone. You're being held pending charges, and a judge has decreed that you must be held. Please. If you help us, we can give you back your life. If we can stop the monster who is truly behind the crimes, you'll be free to lead a normal life again, one without fear. And," she added, leaning earnestly toward him, "you can save the lives of others!"

He nodded. "You will hold me and protect me?"

"Yes, I promise."

"But you're not even part of the French law enforcement."

"Ah, but I can bring in Gervais LaBlanc, who is one of the highest-ranking officers in the country," she assured him.

"All right. But even if I talk, I don't know if what I give you can help solve anything. I haven't seen the man now in…days? Weeks?" Menendez said, frowning and perplexed.

"I may know who you are talking about. He worked for both the Houses of Montague and Deauville—"

"Yes. A man named Aristide Broussard," Menendez told her earnestly. "I thought he left the House of Montague because…"

"Because?"

Menendez looked around, as if assuring himself no one else was in the room. As if in that moment, he had no understanding that the mirror in the interrogation room was a two-way one and that he was, of course, being observed by others.

"Leticia Montague is…a shrew! She thinks we're back in the dark ages where rich people had servants, and it was legal to beat them! She's a true horror. That's why he left, I mean, at least that's what he told me."

"Is he a friend of yours?"

"Many of us know each other. The wine region here is expansive, but many of the workers from the different houses are friends or at least know one another. Anyway, yes, I thought of Aristide as a friend. I knew he left one winery for another because of Leticia. He told me she struck him right across the face. But then… I saw him one night at the restaurant in Reims, the one we all go to all the time," Menendez told her.

"La Maison de Rivière?" Jeannette asked.

"Yes, there. He was upset. Naturally. He went on and on about the things he'd been asked to do, that he was miserable…but I don't think he was as miserable as he was frightened. I think he'd been told that he had to do…"

"Terrible things? Like kidnap women for someone to torture and kill?" Jeannette asked.

Menendez nodded and told her, "He never said that in so many words. But he was… I think he was scared. And then I never saw him again after that. I'm afraid that…"

"That?"

"That his is one of the bodies you're going to find in the fields," Menendez told her. "But if not… Well, if you can find him alive, he's the one who can tell you who is doing what!"

Jeannette nodded solemnly to him. "Mr. Menendez, we are truly grateful for that information and—"

"And it may do you no good. Aristide might well be dead already."

"And he may not be. And knowing that we need to increase our efforts to find the man might save his life and others. I'm going to have Gervais LaBlanc come in now. He can see to it that you are protected. And I promise, the story that will go out there is that you have been locked up—for being entirely uncooperative."

Menendez nodded and tried to smile as he looked at her.

"You know, you scratched up my knees pretty good."

"I'm sorry. You were running. I had to stop you."

He did smile. "You are very good at what you do."

"We try very hard as investigators," she told him.

He laughed. "I meant you were very good at running."

"Okay. Well, I will take that. Thank you. LaBlanc will be right in."

Jeannette left the interrogation room at last. Gervais LaBlanc walked in.

A second later, Jeannette joined Daniel and Della in the observation room. She shook her head. "I was so hoping we really had something."

"Well, we do. You were great in there," Della told her. "He gave you what he had. And the man is truly terrified of whoever is doing this suspecting that he might know something."

LaBlanc returned to the observation room as well.

"You can really keep the man safe?" Daniel asked him.

"That I can—and will—do," Gervais told them. "We must find this man—Aristide Broussard."

"Police are already searching for him around the country, right?" Daniel asked.

Gervais nodded. "But now…"

"You know, it's gotten quite late, and we could use a meal," Jeannette said. "I think we should head back to La Maison de Rivière."

"There's an idea," Daniel said, looking at Gervais.

"You go. I must arrange for this man's safety. Perhaps there is more to be discovered there. Your friend Alphonse might know something more than he's given so far," Gervais said, looking at Jeannette.

"We need to eat, anyway," Della said. "I'll call Mason and the others. Let them know what we're doing."

"And I'll call our friend the magician. I believe he went back to the B&B when we brought Menendez to the station," Daniel said.

He put through his call to Jules while Della called Mason.

"Gervais, we'll be at the restaurant—and then at the B&B," Daniel told him.

"And Mason and the others had little luck with Giselle and Tomas Deauville," Della said. "Apparently, Tomas was very angry, exploded, said he couldn't possibly know what his people did twenty-four hours a day—and foreigners should get out of his country."

"Do you think that suggests they might be complicit in this?" Gervais asked.

"We haven't any hard evidence in any direction," Daniel reminded him. "They could be guilty, they could be innocent. But—"

"We'll go back together," Gervais said. "I'm not a foreigner—they will pay heed to me. I need to arrange for Menendez to get to a safe house and get the word out he's been arrested. That could get something stirred up, so…"

"Everyone needs to be vigilant. Hypervigilant," Daniel warned.

"I will make sure my officers around the country are aware," Gervais told them.

He looked weary, Daniel thought. Gervais was worn down by the number of corpses that were stacking up in the morgue.

Daniel, Jeannette and Della left the precinct. They were ready to meet up with the others—and Jules—at the restaurant where Menendez had last seen Aristide Broussard.

Mason, Luke and Carly along with Jules were already at a table when they arrived. Alphonse was working and appeared to be happy they had come back. They sat, read the menu and ordered before the discussion turned to the day.

Since Jules remained a character who might be a suspect or the son of a chief suspect, they were careful about what was said. Naturally, he wanted to know all about Gabriel Menendez.

"He's under arrest," Daniel told the man.

"And he didn't want counsel?" Jules asked. "I'm not sure what he can be charged with—he just ran from police and I'm not sure what—"

"I'm not an expert on French law," Daniel told him, "but no one had to worry about anything that might be iffy about holding him. He walked in and assaulted the desk clerk. There's no problem with him being held and charged."

"Oh!" Jules said. He sounded surprised. "But did he know—"

Jeannette interrupted him. "So far, we have nothing. But you never know. When someone runs, it usually means something."

"I guess that's true," Jules said.

"It is," Mason assured him.

"I'm afraid, though, that all of this is slow going," Daniel said. "And of course, Jules, we are so grateful to have all the help you and your mother are giving us."

Daniel smiled.

But he couldn't help thinking about the book they'd found in the closet. Had Delphine Matisse purchased it—or had it been left by a guest? The latter would be quite a coincidence. He didn't believe in coincidence often—then again, it did exist!

Their food came. They chatted casually with Alphonse as he served them. And when he moved on to serve other customers, Daniel asked Mason, "What was your vibe from the Deauville couple? Simple anger or they were hiding something?"

"The attitude is so fierce that I'm not sure," Mason said.

"If you could be locked up for being rude and obnoxious, they'd be in for life," Carly noted.

"I wish they would be locked up for life!" Jules said. They all looked at him. "Sorry! I just… I can't tell you how awful they've been regarding me. In their minds, I'm an ungrateful rat. A vineyard is the pinnacle of existence, and I want to throw it all away to be no better than someone homeless on the streets of Paris. Then again, the Montague couple have been just as wretched."

"We need to get by there again," Mason said.

"But I think any time we're paying a visit to one of the houses, we need to have Gervais with us. They want nothing to do with any of us. They think we have no authority at all in France, and they don't seem to care that people are dying," Carly said.

"Excuse me," Jeannette murmured. "I see Alphonse is taking a bit of a breather. He's looking out the window. I think I'll have a little chat with him."

She rose, heading toward the young waiter. He gave her a smile as she joined him, greeting her and pointing out something in the street.

"You'll be staying at my mother's house a little longer?" Jules asked. "I must return to her now, and quickly, I'm afraid."

"Of course! Forgive us," Daniel said.

"No, it's fine, but I do need to leave and we haven't received—"

"Oh, Jules, please!" Daniel told him. "After all the help you have given us? A meal is the very least we can do for you."

"Well, thank you. I shall accept. You have my number, you know where to find me. Please, keep in touch. And if there is ever anything—I mean anything—that I can do to help, please, please, don't hesitate to ask!"

"Trust me, we won't!" Mason assured him.

"Can he be real?" Luke wondered aloud.

"I wish I knew," Daniel said. "He could be. I believe he truly detests the other families, and I'm sure they have made life very hard for him when they've had the chance. He never lied about knowing the girls. We haven't caught him in any kind of a lie. He arranged for the questioning today. But then again…" He paused, realizing he hadn't had a chance to tell the others about the book in the closet.

He did so.

"I find it so curious. From the beginning of this, Jeannette has compared what is going on to the truth/ legend of Elizabeth Báthory. These people seem to live by a code that was popular and legal hundreds of years ago. Nobility and gentry were allowed to discipline their servants. Beat them. If a servant died, they were fined so the money could be given to the servant's family. Jeannette is very open about the legend—many things became rumor long after the fact of the matter. Scholars can't find any real indication that the woman bathed in blood. There are many trains of thought. Her husband was a brutal warrior, and what he did to his prisoners was barbaric. There are those who believe the couple started torture and murder together, but the real accusations against her didn't begin until after his death. And no one cared when servants disappeared or suddenly died in large numbers because of *cholera*. One of Báthory's accusers was a Lutheran minister—that came about when she refused to let others see the bodies of the deceased. It wasn't until girls of high families, seeking the prestige of the Báthory name, became part of her gynaeceum and then disappeared that anyone cared."

"I think Jeannette has been right," Mason said. "Being here—working in Paris and in France for a while now—we've met many nice, fine people, wonderful law enforcement. Well, except for the house where we worked long and hard to find the members of the H. H. Holmes Society. But people are usually polite and cordial, not all, but most. In all the time we've been here, I haven't come across anyone else like Leticia and George Montague and Giselle and Tomas Deauville."

"The elitism," Della murmured. "But…again. We're back to the fact that being an elitist doesn't make you a…sadist! Whoever is doing this apparently enjoys torture. That's not just being heedless of human life, that's being a psychopath!"

"And we all know a psychopath can appear as normal—even charming—as anyone else," Daniel said.

"And we're sure it is someone involved in the vineyards," Carly said thoughtfully.

Jeannette returned to the table. Daniel looked at her and arched a brow.

"Alphonse knew Aristide, of course, he told me. He thought he had mentioned that to us before. He told me he thought Aristide was a good guy. But the last time he saw him, he thought that he was upset. And yes, he was here with Gabriel Menendez that night," she said.

"So," Mason murmured, "thus far, it seems our man Menendez is telling the truth."

They were all startled when a man at a table near theirs suddenly let out a scream, throwing his wine glass down.

The contents splashed on the snowy-white tablecloth and across the table.

The woman who had been sitting opposite him let out a scream and rose.

Shouts and panic seemed to abound.

Daniel was glad then he had a decent mastery of French as did Mason and Della. They stood. Della headed quickly for the woman as he and Mason hurried over to the man.

As it turned out, their hysterical French turned to English as they realized they were being assisted by Americans and a Scottish man.

"Blood! They served me blood!" the man cried.

"Sir—" Daniel began.

"Monsters! The monsters are here, the killers are here, and now they're trying to make everyone drink blood!" the man cried.

Mason was already on the phone with Gervais, commanding everyone there to stay. The police were on the way along with a forensic team.

The substance in the glass and on the table did, indeed, appear to be blood.

And...

First, they needed to know where it had come from.

Alphonse had served the table. He looked sick, terrified. "I—I got it from the sommelier," he told them. "The wine comes from the basement where the temperature is controlled. We receive our bottles directly from the wineries."

The sommelier, a man of forty-five or so, lean and dignified, gave way to only a bit of panic as he told them that the bottle had come from the basement.

It was supposed to have been a Matisse burgundy. Daniel took the bottle from him and noted that the bottle was in fact labeled Matisse.

The police arrived and took the names of everyone who was dining at the restaurant when the man found the strange red substance that certainly appeared to be blood in his glass.

He looked sick, of course. He believed he had sipped human blood. Daniel didn't think he was worried about illnesses that might have been transmitted. He was simply horrified by the fact his glass had been filled with human blood, and he had brought it to his lips.

One by one, those who had been at other tables were allowed to leave.

A forensic team quickly arrived, ready to take the bloodlike substance that remained in the glass and had spilled on the table. The woman who had the substance splattered onto her clothing was taken with her husband—the man who had received the glass—to the station. There, her clothing could be taken as well, and she could be given something else to wear while it was tested.

Daniel's French was good enough for him to understand she didn't care what they did with her dress—she would never ever wear it again.

Gervais arrived, determined to get to the bottom of the situation. The Blackbird team quickly brought him up to speed on what was happening, and Gervais first demanded to see the bottle from which the wine had been poured. Daniel, with gloved hands, turned it over to Gervais.

He appeared to be soundly puzzled.

"The bottle says *Matisse*...and Jules was here with you, right?" he asked.

"Jules was with us," Mason said. "He was here with us the entire time."

"He never left the table until it was time for him to get back to his mother tonight," Daniel told him.

"We're going to need to verify that it is blood," Gervais said, "which, of course, is something that will happen immediately. This case is a priority above all others."

"It is blood," Jeannette said. "Sadly, we get to know the look, feel and scent of it."

"But, of course," Daniel said, "it could be animal blood."

"And quite frankly, I can't begin to imagine Jules wanting to come here with us if he'd known anything about this. One of us could have ordered a burgundy," Della murmured.

"The thing is..." Gervais murmured.

"What?" Mason asked him.

Gervais shook his head. "This label—it isn't real. I know all of the labels used by the House of Matisse. This one isn't real."

"It was put here by someone wanting the blame to fall on the House of Matisse," Daniel said quietly.

"Or…" Jeannette murmured.

"Or?" Daniel asked her.

She winced. "The label was put here by someone with the House of Matisse. Someone wanting to make it look like they, the House of Matisse, were being set up."

"That's possible," Mason said. "We can't let ourselves be blinded—we must continue to pursue all possible suspects in this."

"And then, of course, there's something else we need to be worried about," Daniel said.

They all looked at him.

"Assuming it is human blood that was in the bottle and in the glass, then whose blood is it?"

Sixteen

The day had stretched on endlessly. When they returned to the B&B at last, they decided to switch guard duty so each couple would take a three-hour shift. Jeannette and Daniel would be on from eleven until two in the morning. Carly and Luke would take over from two until five. Then Mason and Della would end the shifts from five until eight. This would allow everyone company and assurance in the house that had already been almost broken into once. It would give a solid six hours or so of sleep, with a gathering time of eight.

It was almost eleven by the time they finished speaking with everyone involved with the blood wine incident and discovering all that could be discovered.

The restaurant didn't have cameras. So there was no help there.

The blood was real—and human.

And it hadn't taken the scientists at the lab long at all to tell them it had belonged to Patricia Gutterman of Berlin, one of the first discovered victims of the killer.

The manager, Damon Barnier, had been taking his

break when the incident occurred; he had returned to the restaurant dismayed and beside himself. He swore he and the owners were the only ones with keys. They were absentee owners, Leo and Ava Grandville, who lived the majority of the year in Cannes—where they had been for the last three months.

They were, of course, going to be horrified.

Difficulties did exist—the only prints on the bottle belonged to the sommelier, who swore that he had gotten it from the stock brought in from the House of Matisse.

The label that didn't belong to the House of Matisse had been printed on an ordinary printer—one owned by thousands of individuals and businesses in the area and beyond.

Naturally, Delphine Matisse herself had arrived, horrified and furious and, of course, pointing out the differences between her real labels and the one that had been stuck on the bottle.

Gervais attempted to calm her down.

And Jeannette was certain that guilty or not, Gervais's handling of the woman had been top-notch. She needed to believe that Delphine was above suspicion. They needed someone ready to help them—and give them access to places they might need to go.

Jules didn't mind voicing his contempt for Giselle, Tomas, Leticia and George, but Delphine, thinking what she might about their treatment of her son, kept up a decent relationship with her neighbors. There were occasions when cordial cooperation might be needed, for example for certain events, festivals… Who knew what might happen when?

Including torture and murder! Jeannette thought.

But finally, the day came to an end. While Daniel remained in the parlor area of the bed-and-breakfast, Jeannette headed in to find the book on Elizabeth Báthory. On guard duty, she sat next to Daniel on the couch and read, aware that he, with an arm around her, was reading over her shoulder.

"Bloody hell!" he murmured.

She turned to look at him. He frowned, looking at her. "Elizabeth herself never went to trial! A trial and an execution would have made the gentry look bad."

"And her cousin conducted all the interviews between 1610 and 1611," Jeannette said. "György Thurzó, count palatine of Hungary, was the one ordered by King Matthias to investigate and bring the guilty to trial. But you wouldn't want the gentry to look bad, right? He supposedly interviewed people in all the surrounding areas and came up with a number of six hundred victims. My question is if that many people knew she was torturing and killing people, how come no one said anything?" she asked.

"Fear?" he suggested.

"And yet they were all so willing to talk!"

"Well, here's the thing. If she wasn't guilty, what happened to all the victims?"

"I don't know!" Jeannette told him. "Where there's smoke, but…was her family trying to get her property and was it a debt that needed to be canceled?"

"According to what you're reading, it was after the murder of a noble girl in 1609 that the authorities staged a night raid. What they found was horrible—bodies, one still in the fireplace, half burned. Servants testified she burned young women, charring their entire bodies until they died. Her son-in-law brought dogs who discovered bodies buried everywhere around the grounds. What's true and what isn't is lost to history. Oh, look…according to one witness, Elizabeth Báthory kept a book in which she recorded her victims, and there were hundreds. What is true will never be known because records are scant," Daniel said, still staring down at the book.

"Yeah. You wouldn't want to make the nobility look bad," Jeannette said dryly.

"Or the vineyard owners," Daniel murmured. He frowned. "What do you think about the blood showing up in that bottle in the basement of the restaurant?"

"It would have helped if they'd had any kind of security cameras. And, of course…"

"The case of the missing Aristide Broussard?"

She nodded. "And on that, from what we learned from Menendez and it seemed Alphonse verified, he was extremely distraught. Frightened. I think he's purposely disappeared, hoping he won't be a victim himself."

"Or he is a victim, and we haven't discovered his remains yet."

Jeannette closed her eyes and leaned back against his shoulder. "I wonder if Elizabeth Báthory really kept a book of her victims, a journal or whatever to keep count herself. Another thought. If it's true that whoever is doing this is…in awe of—in love with?—the life of Elizabeth Báthory, maybe they're keeping a journal, too."

"And how do you think you're going to find it? We

didn't even get far at the Matisse estate—as nice and helpful as Delphine claims she is."

"We need to get back into the house. And someone needs to keep them occupied while one of us gets into her private quarters."

"I'm not so sure that's legal."

"What?" Jeannette told him innocently. "I wandered, admiring the beauty of the place and found I got myself lost!"

"Let's sleep on it, huh?" Daniel asked her.

She laughed. "When it's our turn."

"Right, of course. We'll run it by the others in the morning."

"Of course, I'm sure Gervais has had a crew checking for traffic or other cameras in the area. We will see dozens of people going into the restaurant—"

"More like hundreds," Jeannette said.

"Okay, but still, we'll see what was happening around the place, and see if we recognize any of our possible suspects—"

"We will. They all go to the restaurant."

"But recently?" he asked.

She grimaced. "You're right. We'll see what we can see. I still think that if we can just get a warrant, get something…"

"And maybe we can," Daniel said. "We'll talk to Gervais. But…"

"But?"

"Just like in the past. Is a judge going to want to cast aspersions on people who are so wealthy, influential and important to the community? Because, of course, it's a wild shot," Daniel reminded her. "And I hate to say it, but that's pretty much the way it is all over the world. When you're going after someone with prestige, you must do it very carefully."

"Ah, but such prestigious people should want to help in the investigation!"

"One would think," Daniel agreed. He straightened, looking toward the hallway from the back bedrooms to the parlor. Luke was already heading their way.

Daniel rose, arching a brow at him.

Luke shrugged. "We're not that early. It's past one thirty. Couldn't sleep. You guys can go and try to get some yourselves."

"I'm not going to fight you," Daniel told him. "Thanks!"

Carly came out from the back to join them. "Morning!" she said cheerfully.

"No, no, no, you look far too awake and happy," Daniel told her.

Jeannette smiled. On the one hand, she was a wee bit jealous again. They'd all worked together before and their camaraderie was so easy. On the other, she was simply grateful to be part of their group, where solving horrible puzzles could be attempted in an atmosphere where honesty was so easy and in which you knew beyond a doubt that your back was covered at all times.

"We can't seem to help it. It's just impossible to tell if Delphine is really as wonderful as she seems, if she's being set up, if she's determined to make it look as if she's being set up... And Jules, is he for real? And then, of course, who is nastier? Leticia or Giselle, and does that mean anything? Or are they just spoiled brats who have been given everything all their lives?"

"We're all seeking the answers to that," Daniel told her.

"What do you have there?" Luke asked.

"The book on Elizabeth Báthory we found in the closet," Jeannette told him.

"Hand it over," Carly said.

Jeannette frowned but as she did so, Carly laughed. "You'll take it to bed. You'll make yourself insane. And you're our key player here, friends with Jules...friends with Alphonse. You need your sleep."

Jeannette grinned and handed her the book. "You're right—I'd take it to bed. Enjoy. Great reading on a dark night in a house where anyone may have a key."

"No one is breaking in tonight," Daniel said.

"Whoever is doing this knows there are six of us—armed—staying here," Luke said. "No one is coming tonight."

"But I also feel...we need to watch our backs very carefully. I'm not sure why—whoever is doing this is taunting us, blood in a wine glass, a fake label on the bottle. We were able to stop them from taking Jeannette's new young friends, and I think whoever is the key player behind this might be worried we are getting close. They're seeing it in two ways—one, the joy of making law enforcement run around like dogs trying to catch their tails. Then, two, when they're not busy enjoying the horror and desperation they're causing, they're worried we may be getting close."

"I agree," Luke told him, and he laughed. "Go to sleep! All four of us out here are getting us nowhere. Go!"

"As ordered!" Daniel told him.

He grinned and caught Jeannette's arm, drawing her away.

"Good night, sleep tight! Don't let the bed bugs bite!" Carly called.

Jeannette had to stop. "Bed bugs? In Delphine Matisse's bed-and-breakfast? Good heavens! She'd die on the spot!"

They all grinned as she and Daniel headed to their room.

"And we should get some sleep," he told her.

"Oh, I agree."

"Clear our heads..."

"Appease our bodies?"

He laughed, and she knew that laughter was good and necessary. Just as it was necessary to curl together, to feel the soaring heat of one another, to know that despite their chosen field or because of it, the wonders of the good in human emotion could remain.

And, of course...

Sensuality could be pretty amazing, too.

And...

Yeah. It was easier to sleep when they lay together. Easier to drift in sweet aftermath, and let sleep claim them slowly, sweetly, completely.

It was good...

Then, of course, the alarm rang. It was time to face what could be horrendously evil once again.

Daniel was the first into the kitchen the next morning, glad they'd set the coffeepot to brew the night before. Coffee.

Good stuff. And, of course, he loved tea as well. But first thing in the morning...

Coffee.

He'd barely poured a cup before there was a knock at the door. Answering it, he discovered that Gervais had arrived bright and early.

"There's been a minor break," Gervais told him. "I'm headed back into Paris. The van has been discovered abandoned. We believe it's the vehicle that Jeannette was being led to with her friends, the young women you met on the wine tour, because the description fits perfectly. It was abandoned in a parking garage near Notre Dame. We may find something. Forensics will be searching for fingerprints, anything. And I—"

"I'll come with you," Mason, who had been in the parlor, announced as he entered the kitchen. "We'll see what's going on with the van, and I'd like to stop and talk to Shelley and the others. They might remember something…anything else that might help us at all. Daniel—"

"We'll follow up with the restaurant," Daniel said. "I take it the techs have been collecting traffic cams and other footage."

Gervais nodded. "We know many people working the vineyards—the big ones along with the family ones—come into that restaurant. The other thing…"

"Is that we know others are working for the Báthory we're seeking," Daniel murmured.

"Pardon?" Gervais said.

Daniel told him more about Jeannette's theory—and how they had found the book.

"Báthory!" Gervais muttered, wincing. "How many bodies are out there? And when and where did this start? Sad to say, Paris has a huge homeless population. Being homeless still allows for hope. Being brutally murdered…"

"No one deserves such a fate. But, Gervais, we were all feeling last night that we are getting closer. This isn't on you—it's on the monster doing it all."

"And there will always be another monster," Mason reminded him.

"I try to tell myself that," Gervais told him. "But as the Americans say, the buck stops with me."

"And with us. But we're heading for the finish line, Gervais. I believe it," Daniel said.

"Let's all have hope in your instincts, *mon ami*!"

Jeannette made her way into the kitchen as well. She greeted Gervais and looked at Daniel and him, saying, "I'd like to get back out to the fields today. We found Jules's card there—maybe a setup just as the wine with the false label might have been a setup. I know police have been through the fields, but I was thinking about going farther west."

Daniel knew she was hoping they'd find their World War II spirit, Jake Clayton. Once again, Jake might have made a few discoveries that they hadn't.

"That's fine," Mason said. "I'll accompany Gervais along with Della, and we'll work at things from the Paris angle. Luke and Carly can work with the video we've gotten from the street. They can run a lot of facial recognition and find out if we've workers entering from all the houses—or if we see any of the elites themselves."

"When you've had your coffee, we'll get going," Gervais told Mason.

"Coffee travels," Mason said. "I'll get Della."

"Della is right here," she assured him, walking over to the coffeepot as well. "Right here and ready to roll," she added.

Luke and Carly arrived in the kitchen and Mason muttered, "Hey, hey, the gang's all here, and as we said, Gervais, Della and I will roll. Luke, you and Carly are getting to the restaurant to collect whatever video tech has managed to accumulate. Daniel and Jeannette are prowling the fields again. Jeannette, keep in touch with Jules during the day."

"Will do," Jeannette promised.

"And...at some point, we'll be back. I intend to talk to our legal people and find out about getting warrants. Delphine says we may explore anywhere, but... she hasn't really put the offer out there. I believe if she's holding with all innocence, I may just need to press it with her. As for the others...we will need legal assistance. I don't want anything thrown out of court if we find the people we're looking for. All right. Hit one on your phones to communicate with all," Mason reminded them.

Nods went around, then Mason and Della left with Gervais.

"Gervais still has officers at the restaurant," Luke told them. "Carly and I will get over there, get the footage we need to inspect and be back here. Obviously, we'll be close if you need us."

"Perfect," Daniel assured him. "Jeannette?"

She looked from him to Luke and Carly. "I may be... well, on another goose chase—"

"Ah, but you're looking for the American fighter ace Jake, right?"

Jeannette nodded. "He must have been an incredibly smart and giving man, loyal and honorable to the core. And he wants this…ended."

"When it is over, I want to get to the American Cemetery and Memorial," Daniel said. "Time goes by. We forget what the fighting forces of World War II went through and… Well, I'd like to honor our new friend, and so many others—Americans, Brits, all those who fought."

"A good plan," Carly assured him. "Luke?"

"Right, we're out, too," Luke said.

"And us," Daniel agreed. "Oh, wait! Remember, whoever comes back here first…take care. I would say that whoever our monster is, he or she knows we're staying here. We need to be careful coming in."

"Got it," Luke assured him. "And leave things—"

"So that we know if anyone touched them, of course," Carly said.

Daniel smiled and looked at Jeannette, and she nodded.

They'd been through this routine before.

Out the door, they started for the fields again, heading for the same place where they'd found the bodies before.

"The police have trampled and trampled these fields when they searched," Daniel reminded Jeannette.

"I know. But we'll go even farther back," she said.

"Right. Long walk."

She grinned at him. "Good thing you have long legs."

"And," he added, "that a ghost might see us coming."

She lowered her head, smiling.

They continued to walk. The sun was up, and it was

a beautiful day with a blue sky and tiny puffs of snow-white clouds. No rain was forecast, and luckily it didn't appear that it had rained in many days.

For at least thirty minutes, they walked over land where the grass and brush had been flattened by the many, many officers walking over the land and searching.

But the land here stretched forever, going from that which was owned, that which was for sale, that which had been forgotten—and that owned by the family vine-yards.

"Just ahead, finally," Daniel noted.

Jeannette paused, reaching into her bag for the map of the fields she carried.

"Ahead—property that belongs to Delphine Matisse," she said.

"That's why the police stopped there."

"But she—and Jules—have said over and over again we're welcome to tear apart anything that they have," Jeannette reminded him.

"But do they mean it? Because, thanks to the faulty label on that bottle, no matter what we find, Delphine can say she's being set up. And maybe she is and maybe she isn't. But she has said that we can look anywhere."

"Oh, I wasn't planning on stopping!" Jeannette told him.

As she spoke, she frowned, seeing someone emerge from a stretch of recently harvested land.

"And we found him!" Jeannette said, turning to Daniel with a satisfied smile.

He nodded and wondered that she could be so unusually prescient, such an amazing thing. Her instincts were right on.

And they were combined with her "gift" for seeing and speaking with the dead.

"Have I told you that you are amazing?" he asked her.

"You have and thank you."

"Am I improving any from just okay?" he teased.

She turned to look at him. "You are the best partner I have ever had," she said lightly, "in each and every way."

They both fell silent. The spirit of Jake Clayton was nearly with them. He appeared to be upset.

"There's another one," he told them.

"A victim...recent?" Daniel asked.

Jake shook his head. "I've made a point of staying here but the fields... I can't be everywhere. This body... It just showed up in the fields, the grapes were just harvested... Someone would have seen a body before, but this... Come. I'll show you."

They followed him through one long, long field and then into a small circle of trees. And there, at the base of one of the tall trees, sat a skeleton.

Almost a skeleton. Enough sinew and flesh remained to allow the skeleton to sit up. The scene had most obviously been planned and set up with a certain delight.

The skull was all but bare, the eye sockets empty. Slim branches had been set here and there as support to keep the barely connected head and spinal cord from falling.

Remnants of denim remained on the body, suggesting that at time of death the person had been wearing jeans and a jean jacket.

The arms were curled downward. The hands were folded in what remained of a lap.

"This is...a taunt!" Jake announced angrily. "And I didn't see anything. I didn't see it when this body was brought here, when it was displayed like this! The killer has to know that this body will be found. It was placed here so it would be found."

"I agree with that," Daniel told him. "But it is so obvious Delphine Matisse would never display it on her own property in this manner."

"Unless..." Jeannette said.

"Unless," Daniel agreed, "it's part of the plan to make it appear like someone is trying hard to make it look like she's obviously guilty."

Daniel looked at their ghost. "Jake, thank you."

"You would have found it without me," Jake told him.

"After hours of searching," Jeannette said. "We're going to let our team know what is going on," she said, drawing out her phone.

"And an ME and a forensic crew will be out," Daniel warned Jake.

Jake grimaced. "I'll make myself invisible. Oh, wait, I am invisible to most people!"

Daniel grimaced in turn. It was difficult to find real humor when the grotesque skeleton seemed to be staring at them from its seat beneath the tree.

"Got them all," Jeannette said. "Gervais and Mason are on their way back. They hadn't quite reached Paris. They turned right around, and Gervais doesn't want anything touched until he gets out here."

"That will be a bit," Daniel said.

"Right. But he's going to tell his people to give him

time. They'll head out here—but they won't touch anything until he's arrived," Jeannette said.

"We'll have a wee bit of time to ourselves," Daniel murmured. "Jake—"

"I never saw whoever came and went. I don't know which way they came in… Matisse property borders Deauville property about half a mile in that direction. And, of course, there are trails for work vehicles through the whole of the fields at various places," Jake told them.

"Carefully in three directions?" Jeannette suggested. "I'll head toward Deauville land," she added.

"What about Montague land?" Daniel asked.

Jake pointed while Jeannette drew out her map.

"There's a road. Across the road, those fields are Montague," Jake pointed out.

"So, we're on Matisse property," Daniel said. "But someone could have come through the fields from either Deauville or Montague property to set this up. Or Delphine arranged it, and we're supposed to be looking at the others for trying to pin everything on her."

"I'm off in my direction," Jeannette told them.

"Likewise," Jake agreed.

Daniel nodded and moved straight forward, examining the ground every step of the way.

Dirt.

Grass.

Tangled vines.

More dirt, grass and tangled vines.

But then he stopped suddenly, looking downward. A tiny sliver of something white was glistening in the sun. Something…uprooted when the field had been worked?

He bent down, knowing before he reached for a glove to pick it up that he'd found a human finger bone.

He stared at it, shaking his head, looking at the ground around him.

Somewhere, perhaps far beneath the earth here, there was another victim. Perhaps a victim who had been buried in the field years and years ago...

Buried so deeply that even working the earth wouldn't bring it up.

He hesitated and then stood. Gervais was on his way out to the fields. When he arrived, he'd take the appropriate action.

Maybe there was no corpse beneath the earth. Maybe the disarticulated finger had been cast about by time and weather, and the person to whom it had once belonged was literally scattered here and there and everywhere.

He called Jeannette first.

"Nothing," she murmured to him. "Anything? An answer?"

"No answer, I'm afraid. Another piece of the puzzle."

"What did you find?"

"A finger bone."

"Just—"

"Just one finger bone. When Gervais gets here, I'll show him. I'm going to stay where I am right now. I don't know if he's going to want to dig up this ground, or if..."

"We'll let him get here. I'm going to come to you. Oh, wait, Gervais is calling through on the main line. Switch over."

They both did and Gervais's voice came through to them.

"Almost there with Mason and Della. But while it's still a little early… Jeannette, will you try to reach your friend Jules the magician?"

"Of course. But what do you want me to tell him?"

Mason came on the line, then. "I want you and Daniel to get him to take you to his mother's house. The estate. Now. One of you keep her busy. The other look around," Mason said. "See if there is anything—anything at all— that would suggest she's the real killer or that she is being set up. It's one thing to offer the house and know we'll take her up on it—when she has time—maybe with Jules— to create a disappearing act on anything that might be on display."

"I will try to reach him. Of course, I can't guarantee he'll be willing to take the time to come here when I believe he does have a performance tonight," Jeannette said. "But…"

Mason laughed softly on the phone. "Jeannette! I know you, and I've seen you in action. You just need to make sure he knows how upset you are about his mother being dragged into all this and being made to look like a monster. Then, that will keep you in good standing if someone does catch you snooping around. You're just in love with the beauty of the place and obviously you want to prove that a nice, lovely woman like Delphine is innocent. Frankly, you can do much more there than Gervais or any French officer who would truly put her on guard."

"No problem, then," Jeannette said. "But there's something else."

"Besides an old skeleton grotesquely set up in front of a tree?" Mason asked.

"A finger bone," Daniel said.

He heard Gervais groan.

"A bone—just one bone?"

"Aye, Gervais. I believe a body has been buried very, very deeply, or that time and the elements have shifted it. But these fields have been worked. If there's a body here, it's down deep. I don't know what action you want to take—"

"A dig," Gervais said. "But I'll see to that. *Mon dieu!* How many bodies are there?"

"We probably don't want to know," Jeannette said softly. "No, families deserve to know… Victims deserve to be buried where they choose, or at least…"

"Accorded a decent resting place," Daniel finished for her.

"Exactly," Gervais said. "Nearly there. Jeannette, please—"

"I will call Jules immediately," she promised.

Daniel waited where he was as Jeannette stepped away. In a few minutes, Jake Clayton came back as well, shaking his head and frowning as he studied Daniel.

Daniel explained his discovery.

"How many…just how many!" Jake said unhappily. "Though, of course…"

"Of course?"

"Back in my day, the enemy might have been any-where. People were shot in the streets. War is hell, let no man ever doubt that. And still…"

He studied the bone Daniel held.

"The skeleton has completely disarticulated but looking at the bone… I don't believe that it's been around over seventy-five years."

As they spoke, Jeannette returned to him. She, too, looked at the bone and shook her head.

"I spoke with Jules," she told him.

"And?"

"He has a show tonight, but he says he has the drive down pat. He can be in here in—" she paused, looking at her watch "—in about an hour and a half from now. He'll meet us at his mother's B&B and drive us out to the estate, the mansion. He says he called her, and we are seeking her help again, and she's happy to have us in for *café au lait*. So we'll head back toward the road—"

"Can't leave this area. I need Gervais to see where I discovered the bone."

"I could wait," Jake said dryly. "But then, if he's with your friends, they're going to need to explain how they know this was where you were."

Jeannette smiled. "Aha, you see. I've solved that problem." She produced a roll of French crime scene tape.

"Where did you steal that?" Daniel asked.

"It was the only thing I did find besides dirt and grass. Hey, I haven't even come across a grape yet!"

"This is good. Help me. Let's create a marker here. We'll tie it to the empty vines."

She helped him as Jake watched, then frowned. "Excuse me. I'm heading for the house," he told them.

"The house?" Daniel asked.

"If you two are going to be there investigating, you may need some warning at times."

"You can just come with us—" Jeannette began.

"I might do a bit of investigating myself first!" he told them. He didn't leave room for argument. As Daniel and Jeannette looked at one another, he knew they were both thinking the same thing.

They didn't need to worry about his insistence that he go ahead, go alone.

There was no way anyone was going to hurt him.

Jake moved on and Daniel looked unhappily at Jeannette.

"What?" she asked him.

"I was thinking about the book we were reading last night. On Elizabeth Báthory. The part about investigators coming in and finding bodies here, there and everywhere. We must discover what is going on— and *where* it's going on. Our modern-day killer—or killers—might have once used much better methods of disposal for their victims, but..."

"But with the way they're now taunting the investigation..."

"There might be bodies *hidden* just as they were *hidden* hundreds of years ago. And there's only one way to find out."

Seventeen

"We found one book," Jeannette said thoughtfully, "but not the other."

She and Daniel had returned to the Matisse bed-and-breakfast to wait for Jules. After they arrived, they weren't worried about going in.

The car Luke and Carly had for the case was in the drive. If they were there, they could be assured no one had infiltrated their mini headquarters.

Luke and Carly were at the dining room table with their computers out to study the video footage.

"You two are like bloodhounds," Luke said, looking up as they came in.

Daniel groaned. "That skeleton was set up because someone wanted it found."

"But then a finger bone—a single finger bone?" Carly asked.

"That was it. The sun just happened to catch it," Daniel explained. "I didn't go any farther nor start digging. Like the skeleton setup at the tree—whoever that bone belonged to has been in the ground a long time. I don't believe even a medical examiner will be able to do anything other than give us an estimation on how long the bone—or the skeleton—has been there."

"And...did you find your friend?" Carly asked Jeannette.

Jeannette nodded. "He showed us the skeleton."

"It's nice when we have help," Carly said lightly. "And now..."

"Now, Jules is on his way here. We're going to go and visit with his mama," Daniel said.

"Well, she was in the restaurant," Luke said, leaning back. "Come around and look," he told them.

They did. Luke hit keys on the computer and footage rolled back.

"This was taken from a traffic light down the street. It shows you the entire block. There's the entrance to the restaurant. And there...walking and chatting with people as she passes..." Luke pointed out.

"Delphine Matisse," Daniel said.

"Ah, but that's not all," Luke told him, hitting computer keys to roll the film back again. "Those workers...they go to the Deauville winery. And right behind them..."

"Monsieur Deauville himself," Carly murmured, "without his wife."

"Ah, but not to leave out the Montague duo," Luke said, once again rolling the footage. "There is Leticia Montague herself with a man who I believe manages the fermenting section of her operation."

"Ah, with a man who is not her husband," Daniel murmured.

"No, but he shows up later. As does Giselle. So,

every one of our vintners came in earlier on the day we were at the restaurant when blood showed up in the chalice," Carly said.

"That's the problem. Everything we do leads us back to all three houses. If we could eliminate just one of them, it would help," Daniel said.

"Ah, but you're off to try to accomplish such a feat," Luke said.

Jeannette sat across from Carly and nodded. "Did you two look at that book we found in the closet last night?"

"We did," Carly told her.

"It's something of a tome," Jeannette said. "But did you notice the part where one of her servants—brought to trial—testified that Elizabeth Báthory kept a book? A journal. And in it, she listed all those she tortured and killed. Now, the book was never found—"

"Perhaps because it was a lie? She might have been guilty of a lot—but not everything?" Luke suggested.

"Possibly. But—"

"This book does rather give credence to the concept that Delphine—or someone—is fascinated by the idea of the Báthory killings. Everything about her became legendary—truth and fiction," Luke said. "Bram Stoker based his book on Vlad Dracul of Transylvania. During Elizabeth's lifetime, her uncles and cousins were rulers of Transylvania, now Romania and not part of Hungary. Though it's in none of his notes, many people believe Elizabeth Báthory was the true inspiration for Stoker's book. And I guess," Luke murmured, "with what we've seen and now this book being found here, in a place owned by a Matisse, the suggestion that someone is in love with the worst depravity of the legend might be very true. What I don't get is this—why were the last bodies just drained of blood and left out so that some-one would definitely find them?"

"Maybe the game itself wasn't fun enough anymore," Daniel suggested.

"We will never really understand the workings of the mind of a psychopath," Jeannette said. "And though I'm no psychiatrist or even a profiler, I think we are looking at a truly twisted mind, someone who has ab-solutely no empathy for others, no regret for any deed, no matter how cruel or heinous. But here is what I'm hoping to find today. I think that our modern Báthory, be they a *he* or a *she* or both, kept a journal. It's some-thing Delphine might have in her private quarters. If we are looking at her and the sweeter-than-sugar thing is all an act, then if not a journal, maybe I'll find some-thing and if not…"

"We're just back to being certain one of them is in-volved. No one else would have the ability to blackmail, coerce, bribe or frighten others into creating this opera-tion where young women are kidnapped for someone else to torture or murder," Daniel said.

"Reading that book…it was so interesting," Carly said. "I was ready to believe she was framed, but ap-parently, it's true that bodies were found and the kill-ings had been going on for a very long time. But many things regarding all that went on seemed to have dis-appeared, and that's too bad because the truth can't be known. The best we can do is dissect the legend."

"And a huge debt was canceled, and her relatives benefitted from her confinement," Daniel commented.

"There you go—a puzzle we never will solve. But this one, we must."

"Amen to that," Luke murmured.

There was a tap at the door. Jeannette knew Jules had a key. And with a household of guests, it was unlikely any of them would be running around undressed. Still, his mother owned the place, but it was polite to knock and he did.

Good magician, bad magician?

"Let's head straight out," Daniel said. "He may need to get back to Paris soon."

The two of them nodded a goodbye to Luke and Carly, then walked to the door, ready to go straight out. As they had expected, it was Jules who stood there.

"I saw them again," he said, looking distraught. "I know you mentioned there was more going on. Police... Medical examiners. And there's been another murder," he said sickly.

"Someone is playing games," Daniel said. "There was a murder, but it happened long ago. Someone thought it would be funny to put skeletal remains in a bizarre display. Whoever it is, they've been dead for ages. But..." He paused, shaking his head.

"What do you think my mother can tell you that she hasn't already?" Jules asked. "I don't mind, I'm sorry. No, I'm horrified, and then last night...blood from a bottle with a fake label from our house. You do realize someone is trying to frame my mother?"

"We think that's highly possible," Daniel told him. "Highly possible. And we're so sorry. We know you need to get back—"

"No, no, it's all right. I have a friend appearing for

me. And if anyone gets upset, they'll get a refund. My money," he said a little defensively. "I am good, and I do well at the box office."

"Jules! We've seen your show a few times. You're great!" Jeannette assured him.

"Maybe not great," he said, his tone a little lighter at last, "but good!"

"Is the lovely young assistant Marni getting her chance tonight?" Daniel asked him.

Jules let out a soft sigh. "No, she's not ready to take the stage herself. She wants to be, but she needs to have many more practice sessions before she's ready. There's nothing that can ruin a career faster than a magician doing a bunch of tricks that don't work," he said. "I have a friend who does events all over France, and he happened to be available tonight so it worked out fine."

"We're really glad to hear that, Jules," Jeannette said sweetly. "We don't want to do anything that will jeopardize your livelihood—your dream."

He smiled at that. "Thank you. Sincerely. Thank you."

They were still standing at the door.

"Oh!" he said. "*Pardonnez-moi!* We need to go, right?"

Jeannette laughed. "Well, we should go, yes. I am glad we're not going to spend the afternoon worrying about your schedule!"

"Shall I drive?" Daniel suggested. "We can bring you back for your car."

"Sure, that would be fine," Jules agreed.

Jeannette insisted he take the front seat, and she crawled behind Daniel, saying that her legs were shorter.

And they drove out.

Soon, they passed the point in the road where the police cars, Gervais's car and other official vehicles were parked on one side. She watched as Jules stared out the window, obviously dismayed.

"The news," he said mournfully. "The news media. In English, in French…in every language, people latch onto anything—say anything. There was a post this morning that warned against Matisse wines—that they might contain blood."

"That will pass. The House of Matisse will be vindicated," Jeannette said.

"But what is going on?" he demanded. "How and why would anyone want to do this to my mother?"

"A very sick mind," Daniel told him.

"But whoever is doing this, it's likely they are walking around acting normal!" Jules exclaimed.

Daniel shrugged. "Sadly, history is filled with killers who were quite charming and walked around normally. In the States alone, you had Ted Bundy, a very charming man who easily lured his victims, often by pretending he needed help. We were on a recent case involving a killer with the H. H. Holmes Society, who idolized a man whose real name was Herman Mudgett, one who was apparently cordial and even charming throughout countless schemes."

"Not that Leticia or Giselle could ever be considered charming," Jules said, making a face.

"I'm sure they're charming to someone," Daniel said.

Jules started to laugh. "Those two? No, I don't think so. They don't need to be charming to anyone. They say what they want and they get it."

"Well, now, come on. They're good when they're

giving their little speeches about their houses and their wines for the tour groups," Jeannette reminded him.

"Okay. True," Jules agreed. "But charming..." He stopped speaking, frowning intensely. "Now, my mother is charming. Everyone likes her. She is as polite to a waiter as she is to her richest friend! I hope that—"

"No, Jules, no. We can see what is being done to your mother. And," Jeannette added, "I'm so glad Gervais LaBlanc immediately knew the label of the so-called bottle from the Matisse vineyards was fake!"

"Gervais spends most of his time in Paris, but he does come out here," Jules said. "He has been here—in Reims and the wine region—for various social events, fundraisers for disasters around the world as well as in France. He's a good man. And I'm grateful."

"Just as we are for help," Daniel assured him.

"The drive is just ahead," Jules pointed out.

"I see it. Thank you," Daniel told him.

They entered the elegant and expansive drive. Getting out of the car, Jeannette again admired the historic beauty of the house and grounds.

Jules saw her staring. He grinned. "Don't worry. I love the house. I have assured my mother I will never let it go. One day I will have children, and they just might want to be the rulers of a wine dynasty!"

Jeannette laughed. "It really is magnificent," she told him.

"I am aware of that. And I am not in the least ungrateful!" He pointed toward the entry. "I see that my mother has been waiting for us."

Delphine was at the open door. She appeared distraught and anxious for them to come in.

"Please, please, come in, and of course, you are welcome here! I…am still so upset over the events of last night! I can only swear…here! On the life of my only child that I had nothing to do with blood in a wine bottle!"

"Thanks," Jules murmured.

"Jules, darling—" Delphine began, growing more anxious.

"I understand!" he assured her. "It's all right!"

"Well, come in. Please. Please."

They came in and went back to the massive dining room. Naturally, she'd seen to it that the table was set with *café au lait* and different pastries.

"You didn't need to go through all this trouble," Jeannette told her. "But thank you."

"Have you dined recently?" she asked.

"Madame, we have not, and this is truly kind," Daniel told her.

"Sit, please," Delphine said.

That day, Jeannette and Daniel went to one side of the end of the table, and Delphine and Jules went to the other. Delphine immediately set them up with plates and *café au lait*.

Daniel had told the truth; they hadn't eaten recently.

And it would be so rude, Jeannette determined, if she didn't have one of the delicacies before taking her phone call and walking out to explore what she could of the house.

Daniel was hungry; he was quick to thank Delphine for a petite sandwich and applaud its deliciousness.

"Have they discovered anything, anything at all? Who could have done that? Well, whoever did is the one who murdered that poor girl," Delphine said. "Obviously, I believe. How else could they have a wine bottle filled with her blood? I know that police techniques are quite incredible these days. Have they discovered who created that awful label, who brought the wine to the cellar?"

"Delphine, the only prints on the bottle belonged to the sommelier," Daniel told her regretfully. "They are still examining the label and hopefully they might discover more through that."

"What do you think is happening?" Daniel asked Jules. "You know these people way better than we do."

"Maman," Jules said, looking over at his mother and asking, "you know me. May I have a bit more sugar?"

Jeannette was a bit surprised at her smile. Of course, she was also surprised Delphine didn't have a housekeeper, someone in the kitchen ready to respond to her every whim. She obviously had to have a cleaning staff—no one could handle such a large place on their own even if they lived alone.

"Jules," she said, shaking her head but smiling. "He has such a sweet tooth! I will be right back."

She rose, smiled and headed to the kitchen.

Jules shook his head, leaning forward. "I'd rather she not hear what I have to say on this. For my mother's sake, I am a cordial and decent human being to the Deauvilles and Montagues. They don't always return the favor. My mother asked them to come to my show once. At first, they didn't want to come. Then, a few years back, they decided that they would. I remember that it was a great night; every move was perfect. I worked with a rabbit and a raven that night and both animals were amazing at their cues." He glanced back at Jeannette. "They work for treats, obviously, but there is never a guarantee with an animal. Anyway…after, they were annoyed that if people chose, they could get tickets that included a backstage or meet-the-magician pass. They were horrified that I met with the crowd, and my mother was going to wait for me so that we could get a bite to eat together after the show. Yes, it's a long drive back for them but I can't tell you the amount of times my mother has gone out of her way for them. Anyway, she had ridden in with Giselle and her husband, and they just couldn't be out that late. They didn't know I felt so desperate, I had to try to entertain the audience afterward." He smiled suddenly and shrugged. "To her credit, my mother didn't hit anyone. After that, relations with them were a bit strained. They all think that even as a successful magician, I'm just playing tricks like a schoolboy. The childish antics should have been out of my system a long, long time ago."

"I think your mother is probably more annoyed they're so ignorant really, as to how important entertainment is in our world," Jeannette told him. "And what matters is your relationship with her. It sounds to me as if she sees them when it's necessary but that…"

"Oh, she has friends! Most of them are in Paris. One of her best friends is an artist who loves my show, so that's very nice," Jules assured her. He straightened, smiling, as his mother returned with a sugar container. "*Merci*, Maman, *merci*!" he told her.

She shrugged, grinning, and sat down. But then, looking at Jeannette and Daniel, she grew somber again. She looked over at Jules and shook her head. "I don't know. I just don't know. It is very difficult to believe this of any of them, but…I did not do this! I did not kill anyone. I did not create a bottle of Matisse wine with blood in it!"

"But have you ever seen your fellow vintners be violent in any way?" Daniel asked her.

"Well, I have seen both Giselle and Leticia scream horribly at their workers," Delphine told them.

"We've seen that, too," Jeannette assured her.

"Did one of them ever scream at you?" Delphine asked, taken aback.

"No," Jeannette assured her. "We heard Leticia when we were on the wine tour. Before our group came in, she was angry with someone. And Giselle Deauville… Our server spilled a drop or two of wine, and Giselle was extremely angry. It wasn't perfect, and of course, they always strive for perfection."

"And the world just isn't perfect," Delphine murmured. She looked at her son and then at Jeannette and Daniel again. "Unless they're disparaging my son—which I don't tolerate—I don't say or do anything mean-spirited. I just immediately let it be known it's not a topic they may discuss. I don't have any issues with them. I have seen all of them yell and treat those who work for them badly. Oh, we don't discuss the house I own and rent out in Reims—the place where you're staying. Renting property is not something that should be done by a woman of my position. But… I love the house!" she told them. "And I love when someone new to the area comes and then tells me about a visit to the cathedral or how they were blown away by the beauty of the architecture. And those who rent the house almost always come on the wine tour, and it is a nice thing to know just a little about the many travelers from around the world who come here."

Daniel leaned forward. "Delphine, think. At any point in your life, did you ever see any of them strike out at someone, get into a physical fight or even—"

"The dog!" she said suddenly.

"The dog," Jeannette said. "What about the dog?"

"A stray… I was leaving a party at the Deauville home," Delphine said. "And there was a little white puppy, obviously lost from somewhere—"

"Or perhaps even tossed out of a car," Jules put in. "People who don't consider themselves evil wind up with animals they can't keep and just let them go wherever."

Delphine waved a hand in the air. "We don't know where the dog came from. But he was…relieving himself on Tomas's Maserati. He went after the poor creature with one of his golf clubs and—"

She paused, looking at Jules.

Jeannette stared at Jules, hoping against hope Tomas hadn't bashed the creature's head in.

They were dealing with possibly dozens of murders involving human beings…

She couldn't help it. She didn't want to hear a horror story about a dog.

But Delphine was looking at her son so that Jules could finish the story. "I was only about thirteen at the time," he said. "And I loved dogs. Still do. I saw him, and I went running out and put myself between him and the dog. I took a good whack to the arm—I'm so happy I didn't break it. A friend of mine from school

had come with us to the party, and he went after the terrified puppy while I screamed and cried. My mother had
a fit. Tomas told my mother it was my fault—I shouldn't
have interfered. If I hadn't, I'd have never gotten hurt."

"What happened to the dog?" Jeannette couldn't help
but ask.

"We named him Chiot, *puppy* in English, and kept
him. He lived on another thirteen years, all through my
college days," Jules said.

"Thank you!" Jeannette said.

Jules grinned at her. "I figured you were worried."

"What about Leticia and George?" Daniel asked.
"Any violence at any time in any way?"

Delphine was thoughtful. "I've seen Leticia grab
a maid by the hair and yank it," she murmured. "And
years ago…"

"Years ago?" Daniel asked.

"George was huge into sports."

"What kind of sports?" Jeannette asked.

"Football—oh, I'm sorry. Soccer to you. And…he
was on the wrestling team at his school, but he never
competed professionally. His father died when he was
about eighteen. He had to leave the school he had
been attending and return here to take over. He'd been
groomed for it all his life, and he even knew that he'd
marry Leticia from the time he was a teenager."

"It was an arranged marriage?" Jeannette said, surprised. "In this day and age?"

"Her father owns a vineyard in the south of France,
and she came with the right pedigree and the right
money," Delphine said. She lifted her hands. "I'll be
honest with you, I'm afraid my story is much the same.

My father was a vintner. I have a brother who is now managing my family's vineyard in Marseille."

"You were in an arranged marriage?" Jeannette asked her.

"Not quite so simple as that," she said, smiling. "My husband and I knew each other for many years. I wasn't forced into the marriage. It was considered a proper one, and I cared for my late husband, Jules's father, deeply."

"My father was a good man, a good father," Jules said.

"That's wonderful," Jeannette told him.

Daniel looked at Jeannette, smiling, but she knew what he was thinking.

This is more messed up than what we expected in the twenty-first century!

And the stories they were hearing might well point to those who had been witnessed being violent to others—including dogs.

But more than that...

It had been the Deauville couple who had employed a man they knew to have been involved. And it was Giselle who had been so inviting to their young friends at the wine tasting, the young friends who had come so close to being forced into the van.

But there was still no solid evidence.

And Jeannette's job here wasn't to engage in conversation, although, of course, that's exactly what Delphine and Jules assumed she was here to do.

She needed to find a time soon to excuse herself.

And to begin a search that couldn't completely exonerate Delphine, but might help them in clearing her if there was nothing...

And yet only a fool would keep something that would implicate them right where they lived. The only thing that just might be "personal" and stuffed into a drawer was a journal...

Even one that was coded, a memory for a killer, nothing to someone who didn't know to look between the lines.

She was reaching, of course. She could look and find no book, and it would mean nothing. But then again, her strange instincts on this case had been right so far, or so it seemed.

Jeannette feigned a jump and pulled out her phone, pretending to study the screen. "Oh! May I, um, excuse myself and wander into the parlor?" she asked. "My family. My brother's wife was expecting when I left, and I have an update coming in here... He wants to talk to me and he's going to be a new dad, and he's so anxious!"

"Of course!" Delphine told her.

"I'm here, it's okay!" Daniel assured her. "Delphine, Jules, you don't mind talking to me, do you? I'm learning so much from you both that could prove to be helpful to us."

"No, no, it's fine," Jules assured him.

"Enjoy the art as you talk!" Delphine told her. "My husband collected many beautiful pieces, paintings and sculptures!"

"Take your time. Calm him down," Daniel said.

Jeannette hurried out to the parlor.

There she discovered that Delphine was right. She recognized a Dalí and a few other paintings just by walking through, looking for the stairway—and hoping the ghost of Jake Clayton was there, and he might direct her to Delphine's private spaces—boudoir and dressing room.

She did find Jake. As she strode across the parlor, seeking a staircase, he came hurrying down the steps.

"Jake!" she said. "I can't take forever. Did you discover where Delphine's bedroom is?" she asked him.

"I know where it isn't, but that's not why I hurried to find you," he told her.

"Why?" she asked him.

"There are other people here. Out back. I saw a man. He was looking into one of the windows!"

"There's no security on this house? There must be!" Jeannette said.

"There is, but I don't believe the alarm is set now. I don't believe the woman hires a full-time or live-in housekeeper. But someone has been wandering around out back."

"And they are there now?"

Jake shook his head. "I don't see them. But…"

"Right. They could still be out there somewhere. All right. Let me do what I'm trying to do quickly, get back to Daniel and then find out what's going on. You said you know where her bedroom isn't—"

"The others are immaculate guest rooms, a library… Her room must be at the end of the right wing of the hallway up there. It's the only place I didn't get to," he told her.

"Thank you!"

Jeannette started for the stairway but he didn't follow her. She paused, looking back. He was walking by the front, searching through the windows, trying to see if anyone was still out there.

He managed to move a drape. She smiled. If there was someone out there...

He would see them.

They would not see him.

Jeannette hurried on up the stairs. And he was right. The room she entered at the far end of the right wing was obviously Delphine's. It was elegant. It offered embroidered draperies that were open now, exposing a balcony that looked out far over the vineyards.

The bed was covered with embroidered satin. But Jeannette was interested in the drawers of the dressing table that offered a large mirror and a chair. Perfumes and other personal accessories sat atop it. There were six drawers and she opened them one by one.

Nothing. Lingerie, lingerie, nightgowns...a drawer of hairbrushes.

She moved quickly, glancing at the closet and the open door to the en suite bathroom. She thought that she saw a stain on the white-painted wood of the door and she hurried toward it. She didn't touch it, but it appeared to be...

A smudge. In blood.

She pushed the door to the bathroom and opened it. She saw a large bathtub and...

For a moment, she just stared. Stunned.

The tub was filled to the brim with a red liquid...

She walked closer.

Yes, a ruby red liquid, and it was...

Blood.

She pulled out her phone. Daniel had to be warned. Now.

But even as she tried to hold the phone and call him,

her fingers suddenly felt like lead and she realized that there was a strange scent in the room.

She tried to hit a number...

Too late.

She didn't know if her fingers had hit it or not.

She sank to the floor, the world turning from red to stygian black, and she keeled over, swept into that complete and total darkness.

Eighteen

"I don't know," Jules said, looking from his mother to Daniel and shaking his head. "I'm afraid to say too much. I mean, I am obviously biased against these people. I may be exaggerating the way they behave because they have not been nice to me. Oh, they were okay until they realized I really intended to hire a manager if...when... I mean—" He broke off, wincing, "Sorry, Maman. If and when—"

"There's no if about it, son," Delphine said. "I will die. And that's the natural order of things—it's horrible when a parent outlives a child. What I never understood was why they were so disapproving." She turned to Daniel. "Jules never intended to sell the vineyard. He just intended to hire a manager and...the vineyard wouldn't have gone out of the family."

"Curious," Daniel said. "Neither the Deauville couple or the Montague pair have children. Do you think that's why they're so bitter about a child who exists and isn't willing to take over?"

"Oh, they have the future of their vineyards secured—

the children of their siblings are due to come and take over here. They want family in charge forever," Delphine said. "In a way, what they want is good. They want the small and unique wineries to go on. They don't want everything to be owned by giant corporations. That is one thing about being family-owned—our dedication to the quality of our product means everything to us."

Daniel felt a buzz and looked down. Jeannette's number popped up on his phone—but there was no message.

He gazed at the phone and looked at Delphine, trying to keep his conversation going while determining if Jeannette needed help.

"We've tasted your wines," he told Delphine and Jules. "And they are wonderful."

"Excuse me," Delphine said, looking at her own phone. "It's one of my managers. I'll handle whatever is happening and be right back."

She left the dining room.

"My mother is good," Jules said. "She is involved every step of the way, and she means what she says. She wants to produce quality."

"Well, now it's my turn," Daniel said. "I'm sorry, Jules, I need to find out what is going on with this phone call!"

He stood and quickly headed out of the room.

He had thought he'd see Delphine speaking on her phone in the elegant parlor.

She wasn't there.

It was then that he saw the spirit of Jake Clayton hurrying down the stairs to the dining room, appearing more than distraught.

"What's happened?" Daniel asked. "Where did Delphine go? Were you with Jeannette? There's a call from her on my phone, but—"

"Come, come, hurry, get your whole team out here!" Jake told him. "She—she's gone now! She came up to Delphine's room while I was trying to see who the hell it was sneaking around the house. And then I went into the room and there's something… She's out, she's on the floor."

Daniel raced up the stairs.

"Far room, right wing!" Jake Clayton called, hurrying after him.

Daniel reached the bathroom. The first thing that drew his attention was the bathtub, filled with a sticky red substance. From the look of it…

Bloodred blood.

But Jeannette was nowhere to be seen. And as he stood there, he noticed a scent and realized that someone had released a filtered gas into the room, a knockout gas of some kind.

Jake said that Jeannette was on the floor. Knocked out, not dead. Now, she's been taken and…

He turned back into the bedroom and saw the open French doors to the balcony.

Racing to it, he looked out.

The balcony featured steps that led down to a garden. And beyond that…

The fields, some planted, some harvested, some wild. Fields led to woods where high trees grew and extended deeper and deeper into overgrown green darkness.

But how much of a head start could the attackers have?

He pulled out his phone, quickly letting Gervais and the Blackbird team know what had happened.

Jeannette was gone.

And so, he realized, was Delphine Matisse.

"Daniel!"

It was Jules calling to him, and he paused to look back and glared at the man.

"What in God's name... That tub... My mother didn't do that!"

"She's gone, too, Jules, and so help me, if you're involved—"

"But she didn't do this! She would never do this!" Jules protested.

Daniel started down the stairs, aware that the ghost of Jake Clayton was behind him. "Take the back entrance from the house. If Delphine Matisse has gone that way, she might lead us to the others."

"They took my mother, too!" Jules cried. "I'm telling you... Oh, my God. She's gone, too. It's not my mother! There's no way my mother could have lifted Jeannette, forced her to do anything. It's not my mother!"

And that was true. But their modern-day Báthory kept "servants" as well—those paid, threatened or bribed to acquire victims...

"Please, you must find her, too. It's not my mother!" Jules cried again, running behind Daniel.

At that moment, Daniel didn't care who the hell it was.

They just had to be stopped.

The gas had been strong. Coming to, Jeannette opened her eyes once and then determined quickly that she had to keep them closed. Because someone else could show up and her current situation could change at any time.

Her first emotion was anger—at herself.

How the hell did I let this happen?

But anger now wouldn't help her. No matter how stupid she had been. She was a trained agent! One who had not thought out every possible detail…

Not helpful now.

Dealing with her current situation did. Staying alive, surviving, was now the main issue.

She was slung over the shoulder of a man, a big man. She felt herself bouncing along as they walked.

Walked.

Walking was good. It meant that even if his footsteps were long and he was walking quickly, Daniel's footsteps were probably longer; and he could move like a bullet when he wanted. Also, he'd have every police officer and the rest of the team after her in a matter of minutes.

I need to play this carefully, very carefully, weigh every moment and wait until my best opportunity to escape or fight.

But…

Delphine Matisse had been down in the dining room, talking to Daniel, when she had found the bathroom and the blood and the…

Gas that had wiped her out.

Then again, they knew many people might be involved; and when they were involved and failed their master, they were killed in return.

So…

This was one of the workers. One of Delphine's workers? Was Jules in on it?

They bounded along. She knew she wasn't at her full strength yet. She didn't have the power to simply bang on this man's back and free herself. But she could play it out. She felt herself becoming more clearheaded by the minute.

Now she felt the slap of leaves and branches that they passed through. Now she could reason. And again…

She had to wait. Find her moment.

Jeannette quickly peeked to see where they might be. They were heading through more overgrown fields and into a forested area. And then…

He shifted, swinging around, and she opened her eyes again to determine where they were going now.

They had come to a structure. Something that resembled a charming little cabin in the woods, like a place in the Blue Ridge Mountains back home.

The man carrying her shoved against the door, heedless of her across his shoulder. She forced herself not to flinch or react and closed her eyes to just a sliver, allowing her some sight.

A second later, she was tossed down on something soft. A bed, a cot…

Yes. A cabin. Possibly the home for a long-ago worker? Maybe a little getaway for the master of the fields if he or she needed a break from work.

There was a cot near the one she lay on, just across from her. And a second later, a body was tossed down on the cot. She couldn't see who was there…

The slit in her eyes allowed her only to know that someone was there…

And there were now two people in the room, two men who had brought them there.

Then…

There was a third person. Someone smaller…a woman.

She desperately wished her understanding of French was better, but she began to get the gist of the conversation. She recognized the woman's voice, but she couldn't determine from where or when. She was asking them questions, demanding to know if they'd really gotten away without being seen.

The men told her they had—but reminded her that the other agent was still with Jules at the house.

So, this has been orchestrated by Delphine Matisse! Does Jules know? Was his job to keep Daniel busy while all this went on?

But then as she lay there, the situation changed. The small woman switched her language to English after telling the men the gas in the bathroom had been too strong.

"Ah, still out, Special Agent Jeannette LaFarge! That's all right. The master isn't here yet, and as much as I would like to begin, I must wait. But rest assured, I will rejoice, clap, applaud every agonizing hurt that comes your way. One would think, well… I didn't think I'd be free when you slipped in to check on the home of our, oh, so sickeningly sweet Delphine! But that bastard who doesn't know that he's every bit as bad as those he disdains doesn't realize he's hiding his greatest talent, holding back when… well, when I could outdo him on any stage!"

The voice.

Of course, she knew the voice.

Managing things as they awaited the "master" was

none other than the lovely assistant Marni, Jules's helper who had, in retrospect, been suspicious from the beginning. So easy to look back and see the minor things they had missed.

Minor things that turned out to be so major.

"Ah, well, my beautiful but dignified and, oh, so professional agent! It will be soon, so soon. And I can't wait. And then…then so much fun when the rest are taken to manage this wonderful fantasy. I want to see you pay, oh, yes, I do! You have no right to be here in France! But at the end, I will really have my revenge because it will be my turn to swallow my tears and take over!" She started to laugh softly with delight. "I do hope you can hear me. No help will come, you know, because your brilliant detectives will be certain we've headed for the roads!"

She straightened and moved away, heading to the front of the cabin to await whoever was coming.

Delphine Matisse? Jules? Leticia and George, or Giselle and Tomas?

But carefully shifting ever so slightly and daring to open her eyes, Jeannette looked over to the other cot to see who had been taken as well, praying that it wasn't Daniel.

It was not.

And it also told her that she now knew at least one person who would not be coming.

Because they were already here.

Gervais was the first to arrive, quickly followed by Carly and Luke within minutes, and then Mason and Della.

Daniel didn't see them; he was already moving far

from the house, certain that time might mean everything. If they made it to a road, God alone knew where they might go and how hard it would be to find them.

He described his location to Mason, who told him Gervais already had a forensic team in and, yes, the substance in the tub was blood. Pints and pints of it... gallons. More than could come from one human body.

"We've got everyone fanning out, heading back," Mason told him. "You might want to wait for backup—"

"Can't, Mason, you know that," Daniel told him. "And I have backup. A friend from World War II is with me."

"Ah, make sure that..."

"He will go ahead if we find anything," Daniel promised, glancing over to the ghost who was keeping pace with him. "Are you holding Jules?" he asked Mason.

"Jules isn't here. We found no one in the house or on the immediate environs," Mason told him.

"Jules kept screaming that his mother didn't do any of this, but there's blood in that tub, and the bathroom was filled with gas. Maybe he's involved. Maybe he isn't," Daniel said and paused. "Then again, Jake said there were people outside the house looking in. He was trying to see who they were and what they were up to, but...then I discovered that Jeannette was gone."

"Keep going and know that a small army is following. We're leaving Gervais here to deal with the house, and the teams are heading out after you. Be careful— Gervais suspects they're heading for the road. He's sent patrol cars out to block traffic, but..."

"But there are work roads that weave in and out of the fields," Daniel said. He heard a sudden shriek and swirled around, looking through the brush that had grown denser as he had walked farther into the forested area from the fields.

He could see patches of fabric and people perhaps fifty yards from him, and he glanced at the ghost of Jake Clayton. Together, they began to hurry through the thick brush and trees. As he moved, he could hear Jules speaking hurriedly, choking now and then, his French barely comprehensible.

But as he listened...

He knew Jules was the one being attacked. He was warning his attackers they needed to let him go, to come to the police with him and turn in whoever was making them do what they were doing. And while under attack himself, he was swearing he would kill them if they harmed a hair on his mother's head.

The man in turn laughed, telling him he should be worrying about himself more than his mother.

There was someone who really wanted Jules to pay and...

He would pay. And dearly.

"I'll go ahead!" Jake Clayton whispered to Daniel, although, of course, he didn't need to whisper. Only Daniel could hear him. "I'll give you a count and weapons check," he added.

Daniel nodded, keeping pace, glad that Jules seemed to be putting up a good fight and keeping them where they might be quickly reached.

Jake moved on past the last trees and called back to Daniel.

"Two men, swearing at Jules, trying to drag him with

them. They're both occupied with him. If you could come up behind... One has a knife, so be careful."

Daniel was careful. He went into stealth mode, escaping the trees for the little trail, drawing out the Glock that Gervais had returned to him after the shooting incident was cleared.

He didn't want to shoot. Rather, he flipped his weapon around, moving swiftly and silently forward once he reached the narrow dirt trail, and headed for the man with the knife. The one man started to turn, but a minute too late.

Daniel slammed the butt of the gun down on the head of the man with the knife, and he went down.

The knife fell to the ground.

Jules took the opportunity to break free from the second man's hold and give him a right hook that would have done any fighter proud.

He stared at Daniel. "I told you, I told you, I told you! Don't you understand? They have my mother, too. Oh, yeah, thank you! Good timing."

On the ground, the first man was groaning. Daniel dropped down and wrenched him up to a sitting position. He was barely conscious.

"Where were you taking him?" he demanded.

"I'm a dead man!" he said in English. "It doesn't matter!"

"You're not dead if you help! That will matter," Daniel told him.

But the man shook his head. "No, no... I have children, I have...a wife. I can't!"

Daniel rose swiftly with his Glock as he heard a rustle in the trees behind them.

"It's me, Mason!" a voice called out, and Daniel knew that it was, indeed, the Blackbird agent.

"The police will protect you!" Daniel quickly told the man before calling out to Mason. "Here! We've just stopped a few fellows trying to drag Jules to wherever they're heading.

"There it is," Daniel told the man. "An army of cops are coming. If anyone dies because we can't get there in time, I promise I will testify when you are sentenced and you can forget about your children!"

Mason came through the trees with Della right behind.

Daniel rose. "Deal with them. Jake and I will move forward."

"Who, uh, who is Jake?" Jules muttered, shaking his head. "You mean me, Jules? I'm coming with you. They have my mother!"

"You'll hold me back. Stay with Della and Mason, and they'll send others on forward while these two are arrested."

"But you're Americans—" sputtered one of the men who grabbed Jules.

"I'm not an American. I'm a Scot," Daniel told him. "But no matter. We will turn you over to the French, and there will be no mercy. Did they head for the road?"

The man groaned and the one Jules had punched suddenly spoke.

"Eventually, but…no time yet. They were waiting."

And the man Daniel had knocked down with his Glock suddenly decided that he was going to be more giving, too.

"A cabin...deep in the forest. There's a cabin. They were waiting..."

"For?" Mason demanded sharply.

"The Countess," the man said.

"Countess?" Daniel snapped. "Who the hell is a countess?"

And the man sounded as if he were laughing and crying at the same time. "The Countess, the Blood Countess!" he told them. "Reincarnated to carry out all that has been left undone!"

Jeannette believed she had her full faculties about her, but as Delphine Matisse was still crumpled up on the cot across from her and hadn't begun to move, she determined she could feign her unconsciousness a while longer. The two large male vineyard workers had stepped out to the porch along with Jules's assistant, Marni.

Jeannette dared to shift; to her astonishment, they hadn't realized she had her Glock in its little holster in the waistband at her back.

She started to move to reach for it, but there was a commotion at the door. Marni turned, staring straight at her.

Had she caught her going for the gun, or was she worried about the sounds coming from the door?

And then, apparently, someone arrived.

And everyone moved back as if the Queen of the World had arrived.

Her eyes were barely open a slit. It took her a minute to make out who it was.

And then she knew.

But she lay very still, and the woman came first to perch on the end of the cot where Delphine lay, just coming to.

The vineyard owner began to mumble in French.

"Réveillez-vous!" the newcomer demanded.

Wake up! Jeannette thought.

"What happened? What's going on?" Delphine cried out, confused and still half out of it. "Where am I?"

The other woman laughed and switched to English, too.

"You are at the end, Delphine. But don't worry! You will go down in history. You will be here with your last victim, the American law girl who thought you were the good one. Alas! Poor Delphine. You knew you were about to be caught, and rather than be arrested, you took your own life!"

"What?" Delphine said incredulously. "Leticia Montague! You have been rude to me, cruel to my son, and each time, I forgave you and moved onward for the sake of...of our product! Of our holding on to precious pieces of land. Are you mad? My son—"

"Your son!" Leticia spat out. "He will pay! I could not bear a son and yet you had one and still! You let him become a grown child, playing endless games instead of loving the vineyards as he should, becoming nothing more than dirt! But... Oh, alas! He is going to be your last murder, Delphine. I do love all this working out so very well. Gervais LaBlanc! Our great French inspector! He knows about the roads; he will be searching high and low—in the wrong place. But, alas..."

She paused, leaning closer to Delphine. "You see, there is someone who hates Jules almost as much as I hate you! He has kept her down, just as you have kept us all down, making a mockery of the wonder of what we own, of what we do! Marni! You do know precious Marni, a magician far superior to your son, and yet he keeps her down, claiming that she needs more practice when she could leave him in the dirt. Well, she is a wonderful student, and I have taught her well! Ah, well, not all can be perfect! She wanted to recreate the ant torture, you know…putting honey all over his naked body and leaving him to be consumed by insects and beasts! No time for such fun play! I have taught her about burning and cutting and spikes beneath the fingernails…"

"You will be caught! The foreign agents are at my house—"

"Oh, and that silly woman is going to save you? I might point out she's right there, and I am speaking English just in case she can hear me! I will deal with her and let you watch as Marni takes care of Jules. She's so good at what she does because of me! Then, Delphine, your remorse! Your horror at what you have done… No, no, no, that's not it. Your determination to end it all because you know that you are going to be stopped, that too many of the peasant class are onto you. They don't want their worthless lives mercilessly ended quickly anymore. So, you see, you will be spared torture—you wouldn't torture yourself. I haven't decided yet if you will hang yourself or stab yourself in the heart!"

"*Mais non!* None will believe it, they will not—"

"Oh, not true at all, Delphine! I'm certain that by now they found the book on Elizabeth Báthory in your closet. And they have suspected all of us… Now they'll know it's you!" Leticia said happily. She stood and Delphine tried to reach out, tried to stop her, to hurt her.

But Leticia merely moved away, laughing as Delphine fell weakly back on the cot.

"No, no…no…no…"

Jeannette knew she would need to make a move soon. Now there were the two large, strong men, those who worked the earth, Marni and Leticia. And if she was here…

"Mon amour!" George said from the doorway. *"Il ne faut pas attendre!"*

Of course. George was here as well.

Warning his wife they didn't have to wait. Because, of course, if Leticia's plan to finish off her kills and leave a dead Delphine to take the blame for everything was going to work, it had to be accomplished before the police did come upon them.

Leticia snapped back at him. Her men had Jules. They needed just seconds more.

When they arrived…

Jeannette knew she would have to make her move. She couldn't allow these people to kill Jules or Delphine and…

She sure as hell didn't want to be tortured to death herself.

Jake Clayton and Daniel found the cabin easily enough. But even as they arrived, carefully watching from the trees, they saw another man, an older man, arrive at the cabin.

Daniel frowned.

George. George Montague. His arrival probably meant that Leticia was in the cabin.

Had she thought of herself as someone high above what she saw as the unwashed crowd of humanity? Or had he been filled with violence, teaching her his ways?

"I need a count, and what's happening," Daniel told Jake.

"And I am on it," Jake said.

Daniel watched as Jake strode toward the cabin, heading right past the one man who appeared to be standing guard or watch at the door. The man gave a little shiver as Jake passed by, causing Daniel to smile.

There were many people who got a little chill when the dead passed them. But that's as far as they were able to sense anything, that strange chill that might have been a breeze on a calm day.

Daniel knew, of course, that backup would be coming through the woods. But he was very afraid he couldn't wait. Soon, someone would realize Jules was not coming, and that something had gone wrong. They would need to act—and probably do so quickly.

But if he went in just shooting, he could endanger Jeannette's life and that of Delphine Matisse, if she was being held as well.

Jake Clayton returned, causing the guard again to shiver a little before he slipped into the trees, ready to report to Daniel.

"Time to move. George is in there telling Leticia they must give up on killing Jules. Marni is arguing, but she's being told she'd best remember her place lest she be left in the cabin herself. Leticia is ready to start… what Leticia does!" he said.

Yes, it was time to move.

Beyond time!

A shot suddenly sounded from within.

When George won the argument, and Leticia smiled and started to move toward her, Jeannette knew she had run out of time and had to do something.

She turned over quickly, secured her Glock and aimed it at the woman.

Leticia stopped dead, stunned.

Then she gathered herself, producing a knife and falling by Delphine Matisse, quickly bringing the blade to her throat.

"Drop your gun."

"I don't think so."

"I will slit her throat."

"That's what you intend to do, anyway."

Leticia started to laugh at that. "You shoot me... these fellows go for you. Two men, Marni and my husband? Just how good are you, Special Agent LaFarge? Maybe we can talk!"

"I've got a gun—" one of her men began.

And there was no choice. Jeannette shot him in the shoulder before he could go for his weapon. Screaming, he staggered back while the other drew a weapon as well and aimed it at Jeannette.

A bullet whizzed through the air.

But not at her.

Daniel had burst into the cabin. The second man fell. When he did, George Montague started to scream as he fell on his knees, putting his hands up and crying out, "It's her! It's all Leticia! She started to think she was

a reincarnation of that woman, that Blood Countess...
and... I didn't do it. I didn't do any of it!"

"You weakling, you coward!" Leticia roared. "You
fool—"

"You were the one who had to wait for Jules!" George
thundered. "We could have driven out, left them all
dead—"

"You hired idiots!"

"You hired the idiots, but with a catch. You threaten
their families, and you let them see the corpses, so they
know what can happen to them, but they're fools! It's
all your fault!" He seemed to realize he was speaking
English and began to swear at her in French.

Leticia swore back. Daniel stood at the doorway, his
Glock trained on her.

One of the wounded guards started to move, as if he
might reach for his fallen weapon. Daniel kicked it far
from him, his own gun now aimed at the man.

"I will still kill Delphine!" Leticia crowed, her teeth
bared like those of a rabid animal as she looked down
at the woman on the cot.

She started to move the knife, to pull it back to strike.
This time, the knife wasn't against Delphine's throat.

She meant to plunge down with it, and plunge down
hard.

Again, no choice.

Jeannette fired. Leticia screamed as her arm seemed
to burst apart, and the knife flew across the room,
nearly hitting Marni.

The young woman screamed and then stared at them
all, and she suddenly bolted for the door.

But Daniel was standing there, and she couldn't get by.

To Jeannette's surprise, he smiled and stepped aside.

Of course, Jeannette thought with a smile, he did so because Gervais LaBlanc was outside with the rest of their team. From inside the cabin, she heard Gervais tell Marni that she was under arrest.

Delphine pushed the wounded Leticia aside and fell to the floor. She crawled over to Jeannette's position and, heedless of the Glock she was holding, threw herself into the agent's arms.

Jeannette holstered the Glock, set an arm around Delphine's shoulder and looked over her head at Daniel. He gave her a grim smile and a nod and stepped aside as police suddenly seemed to swarm the place. EMTs arrived, and it was time for Jeannette to help the weak and sobbing Delphine Matisse out of the cabin.

But just outside, Daniel took Delphine gently from Jeannette's hold, lifted her chin and told her, "He's fine, Delphine. Jules is fine. He's with a police guard, back at the house."

"Merci, merci!" Delphine cried, and she started to collapse.

Mason hurried over to them and collected Delphine in his arms. "I was not much help earlier, but I think they've got this!" he told them, motioning to the French law enforcement.

They were in a crowd, and yet Jeannette and Daniel were left together, facing one another, knowing that it hadn't gone the way they had expected, but...

She had thought they might find some kind of proof in the house.

And they had.

"You scared me half to death!" Daniel told her.

She smiled. "Well, you know. I had to wait for my moment. And I had hoped you'd get here by then... and you did!"

He didn't seem to give a damn about others being around them. He pulled her into his arms and held her close for a moment, pulling apart only when they heard a soft voice.

"Ah, that's beautiful!"

Jeannette turned. Jake Clayton was there.

"Thank you, thank you!" she whispered, with Daniel echoing the words.

"My pleasure and my honor, Special Agent LaFarge! My fight was for the human right to live with peace and justice. You have just allowed me to fight again!"

She smiled and nodded and they all turned to the cabin.

It was going to be the longest day yet. And still...

It was just as Mason said as he walked over to join them. Delphine had been taken by an officer back to her house where she could see her beloved son.

"So!" he announced, nodding his acknowledgment of a job well done to them.

"Blackbird," he said, "has soared once again!"

Epilogue

Some people loved mountains.

Jeannette loved them, too.

But there was nothing like an amazing beach. And as she heard the waiter approach their lounge chairs, she smiled because she'd been practicing. *"Vorrei una Coca-Cola con una cannuccia, per piacere,"* she said, which caused Daniel at her side to smile.

"Me, too, Coke with a straw, please," he said.

"Gotcha," the young Italian waiter said. He started to walk away but he paused and turned back, "Oh, great accent in the right places!" he told Jeannette.

"You can't assume people speak English when you're in their country," she told Daniel.

He grinned. "No, I agree. But I spoke to him when you were in the water. His dad is Italian and his mother is American. He spent most of his years growing up in Kansas."

"Oh."

"But your Italian is coming along nicely."

"Thanks. And yours—"

"My French is still better. And, you know... I've been told that we Scots speak English—kind of!"

She grinned at that. "You don't have that much of an accent."

"Too many years working in too many places," he said dryly. "Oh, wait. You're lying! But...hang on!"

He answered his phone. She felt hers vibrating—somewhere. It was in the bag she had brought down from their room at the hotel on the Italian Riviera. She started to rise, but he shook his head. Whatever he was learning, they weren't being summoned for anything.

They had remained in France for several days following the strange showdown at the cabin. Before leaving, Jeannette had decided that if she was able to do anything at all on her own time, she wanted to go to the American Cemetery and Memorial in Normandy.

And they went, all six members of Blackbird—along with the ghost of Jake Clayton.

She knew that sometimes when human souls believed they had accomplished what they had stayed to do, they felt it was time to move on. And light seemed to burst from nowhere, warm and beautiful and glittering, enveloping the soul and moving it onward to a higher plane.

And she had thought that maybe Jake...

But he had shown them his grave; they had prayed for soldiers lost. And when she looked at Jake, he had just grinned at her.

"Not sure what else, but I'm not ready yet!"

"Then maybe I'll return to see you!" she told him. But then she got it into her head to introduce him to Henriette and returning to Paris, she did so.

She thought Jake might be taking up a new residence in Paris because he didn't want to "hitchhike" anywhere else.

Then Mason had told Jeannette that Adam had made reservations for them. He and the others could tie things up in France and perhaps join them.

Daniel ended his call in just a few minutes and smiled at her.

"That was Mason."

"I got that. And what—"

"He just called to tell us the wrap is over for all of us. Gervais is still dealing with the French legal system on how many people are going to be charged and what the charges are going to be." He winced. "He told me he sometimes wishes they hadn't abolished the death penalty. He thinks it would be truly fitting for Leticia and George. As it is…"

"They'll get life?"

"We can hope. And for a woman like her…maybe that kind of existence will be worse than death. Oh! And a couple more things."

"Oh?"

"The missing Aristide Broussard has been found. He'd been hiding in Norway. When he heard that Leticia has finally been stopped, he came home. He's going to testify against them."

"That's great! He is alive! Wonderful. And?"

"And Delphine Matisse says we have an open invitation anytime we want to come. We're welcome to the house or to stay with her at the mansion. And…"

"And?"

"Jules needs a new assistant. He thinks you'd be great."

She laughed. "Well, if I fail at Blackbird—"

Daniel laughed. "Mason said you're an amazing addition, so… I don't think you should give up the day job for the magic show."

She smiled at that.

"I think I'm happy right where I am," she told him.

She meant those words in so many ways.

And, of course, he knew her smile.

"Think we could take those Cokes we ordered up to the room?"

"Oooh, yeah. Shower off the sand…"

"Aye, showers are good…and…it is still early but…"

"We may just order in."

She grinned.

"I like that idea," she told him.

They did order in.

And later, much later that night, she curled into his arms.

"What are you thinking about?" he asked her.

She grinned and shrugged her shoulders, then looked into his eyes before leaning down against his chest.

"Blackbird soaring!" she told him.

And so, it was.

* * * * *